Two Natures

Oct. 2016

For Ben -

Best wishes for
your writing!

Southern boy Julian Selkirk brings an outsider's wry and engaging sense of humor to his quest to make it in the New York City fashion world. His romp through gay men's urban culture also holds suffering, grief, pathos, and an ongoing struggle with the God of his childhood, as he comes of age during the height of the AIDS crisis. Though he gets distracted along the way — with politicians, preachers, drag queens, activists, Ironman gym buddies and sex, lots of sex — he never stops looking for real love to redeem him. An entertaining novel and a pleasure to read.

—Toby Johnson, author of *Gay Spirituality* and the novels *Secret Matter* and *The Fourth Quill*

This is a must-read for anyone struggling to mend the fracture left by a faith which at times both heals and harms. Christians of all orientations will benefit from a fresh view on the integration of spirituality and sexuality.

—A.M. Leibowitz, author of *Passing on Faith* and *Anthem*

For Julian Selkirk, the dry-witted hero of this complex, wide-reaching, and unfailingly touching *Bildungsroman*, photography is a way of shaping the world while trying to shield himself from it. But "the boy with the camera on the sidelines of the homecoming dance" soon discovers that life and love are too sprawling, unpredictable and flawed to be contained in a viewfinder. To see what is real — we learn along with him — we must hold two natures, beauty and truth, within our vision.

—Tracy Koretsky, author of the novel *Ropeless*, winner of 15 awards, and *Even Before My Own Name*, a memoir in poems

Readers of every sexual orientation and gender identity will be enlightened by a gay man's struggle to balance sexuality and spirituality in *Two Natures*. This eloquent debut novel from gifted poet Jendi Reiter is a rare combination of erotic romance and intelligent reflection on Christian faith. Julian's search for identity leads him to embrace (literally) every false god he can lay his hands on, before finding that Love demands integrity and a life without shame.

—Kittredge Cherry, publisher of *Jesus in Love Newsletter* and author of *The Passion of Christ: A Gay Vision*

If you want to know what life is like in Nineties New York, when Style has become God, sex has become a contact sport, and jobs, money, and survival are always around the corner someplace else, then this late coming-of-age novel is a good place to start.

—Perry Brass, author of the Amazon bestseller *The Manly Art of Seduction*; *The Manly Pursuit of Desire and Love*; and the Ferro-Grumley finalist novel *King of Angels*

Two Natures

Jendi Reiter

Saddle Road Press

Dedicated to the memory of Jimmy Schiavone

CONTENTS

PART I: CROSS

(January-February 1991)

1

I WOKE FROM ANOTHER NIGHTMARE about photographing a wedding. The bride was very loud and everyone's red lipstick was smeared across their teeth like vampires, except vampires would never wear lavender taffeta prom dresses. It's always the wrong people who can't see themselves in mirrors.

The clock buzzed softly next to my pillow and I opened my eyes into the thinning darkness of six a.m. White light edged the windowshade like a square eclipse. The mound of blankets on Dmitri's bed looked uninhabited. My roommate at the Fashion Institute of Technology lived in a different time zone. Long after I'd fallen into an envious slumber over the new issue of *Vogue*, he would be out at a party with his clique of fine arts students, smoking black cigarettes and talking about post-narrative structural iconography, or something else that would earn you a punch in the face in Georgia. As an ambassador from that fair state, I sometimes felt inclined to deliver it myself, but that would be wrong.

I dressed quickly, in the half-dark, as usual running late for my work-study job at the FIT dining hall, wanting also to be gone before the poster on Dmitri's side of the room became visible again in the light that filtered through the shade. New York light, sodium orange and cloudy purple at night, cinderblock white and flame blue by day. I loved being inside it, a part of the machine. Cindy Crawford, photographed by the great Patrick Demarchelier, smiled down from my wall, waiting for me to invoke her benevolent protection. *Hail Cindy, full of grace.*

My pants were all wrong for scrubbing pots. They were equally wrong for everything else, but in a different way. Four months earlier

Mama had packed me off to college with a suitcase of khakis and button-downs like an unpaired Mormon missionary, dependent on the kindness of strangers. Daddy might be resigned to his younger son's face disappearing behind a camera but he'd be god-damned if he'd spend his hard-earned money (what was left after tithing to the liquor store) to send me to New York City to play with girls' clothes all day. I don't know what manly career he envisioned for someone with my skills — crime-scene photographer, perhaps, or war correspondent? I couldn't shoot a duck if it was going for my wallet. Not that it would discover much in there, besides a fake ID and a couple of hopeful condoms.

Finding myself the only boy in class with nothing black to wear, day after day, sitting between a dark-eyed, greasy-haired Romeo with a spike through his ear and a baby queen who flicked a new Liberty scarf around his neck every morning, I'd finally cracked. The proceeds from taking half of my new rags to the consignment shop nearly covered one shirt and two pairs of jeans from Armani Exchange. Since the style called for distress in the knees — the more expensive the label, the bigger the holes — I did my praying standing up.

2

On an icy January night in 1991, this scholarship student's grades were slipping down faster than a cheerleader's tube top. But here I was anyway, making a long day longer at my regular table at the Chelsea nightclub New Eden with Ariana, my regular drinking buddy and source of last-minute term papers.

Our friend Tomas kept us supplied with watered-down Cosmos and didn't check IDs, but wouldn't socialize while he was on the clock. He was touchy about waiting tables. It wasn't so bad among strangers, but with people he knew, he felt "objectified." This was a new word Ariana and I had learned in our Critical Media Studies class and we were getting our money's worth out of it. Tomas stalked around the tables like a flamenco dancer in his white uniform shirt and tight black pants. He was studying to become a chef, starting with the attitude. Around about my second Cosmo I remember the music getting loud enough to hurt my eyes, as if the blue and green sparks flashing off the mirror-balls had joined forces with the electronica soundtrack. Ariana wanted to dance. "You go ahead," I said.

"No one else here is going to dance with me."

"Way to make a guy feel special." I poked her plump white arm, where it peeped out from the shiny black folds of the self-designed dress she was field-testing that night. I thought it looked like a barber's smock.

"Don't blame me for your high self-esteem." She poked me back.

The music choked mid-pulse. A suave male voice reverberated over the sound system. "Ladies and gentlemen — and those of you still undecided — please welcome Miss Anna —"

"Julian, open your eyes," Ariana nudged me. I raised my head, which somehow had dropped below sea level. A statuesque black-haired figure stood in the rose-tinted spotlight of the club's main stage. Miss Anna's silvery gown reflected it back like sunset on sparkling snow. Cardinal-red lips parted for a throaty ballad. "Send in the clowns…"

"Oy," said Ariana.

"I know, I told Frank to listen to the Top 40 for a change."

The chanteuse's voice was mesmerizing, nonetheless, like the kind of drink that goes down mild and hits you in the back of the head like a brick afterwards. That might not sound like a good feeling, but here we were, committing sundry misdemeanors in order to have it again.

"The morning ends…I think about you," Miss Anna warmed to the saddest ballad from Sondheim's *Follies*. "And do they *know*…it's like I'm losing my mind…"

A break; applause, coughing. Waiters, including the sulky Tomas, darted among the tables with their pencils and apron pockets of receipts, snaring drink orders before the next number. Ariana put her hand over my glass.

"Yes, dear," I said sarcastically.

Ariana sighed. Her green eyes were serious behind her cat's-eye glasses.

"What is it? Are you mad because we didn't dance?" In the blue-black shadows, a few couples were clinching, swaying occasionally in time to the mood music they piped in between sets.

"Have you ever felt that way?" Ariana asked. "Like the song?"

"Thank God, no. You?"

She shook her head. "I don't fall in love."

"That's right, you just bite their heads off after you mate."

"I don't mate." She sipped her fresh Cosmo. "I don't see the point."

I stole a sip from her glass. "Does everything have to have a point?"

"Life is short."

"Exactly."

A husky blond guy pulled up a chair to our table. "Hey, mind if I wait here?" His smile was big and loose, like the muscles he flexed as he sat down.

16

"Why wait?" I leaned closer to connect with his light blue eyes. His smile broadened.

"You're the friends of our resident diva, right?" He indicated Miss Anna, who had re-mounted the stage in a Barbra state of mind.

"Julian, the nice man is talking about you."

"Meow," I said. From his eyes I moved to his pecs. The flaking red letters on his tight gray tee read "Wolf Paper & Packaging Co."

"What's wolf paper?" I asked.

"It's like fly paper, only bigger," he said. I must have looked like I believed him, because he guffawed and pointed his finger at me like an imaginary pistol. "Naw, it's where my pop works, back home in Pittsburgh."

"Selkirk Builders, Atlanta," I said. "You know, back where I come from, that was the first thing you asked a new fellow: what does your Daddy do, and where do you go to church?"

"Or synagogue," Ariana cut in.

"Sorry, Golda Meir. Where are my manners." I shook the big guy's hand. "I'm Julian Selkirk, and this credit to her race is Ariana Ziegler."

"Phil Shanahan." His grip was strong, as I'd known it would be.

"I thought your name was Wolf," Ariana said.

"Pop drives a truck, he's not a friggin' CEO," Phil scoffed. I liked his honesty, liked him even more when his blush contradicted the defensive pride in his voice.

"Well, now that we've exchanged business cards," I said quickly, "you can't say you don't know me well enough to dance with me."

"Sure, okay." He seemed relieved to stop talking. We got up from the table. I shouldn't have, but I put my hand on his thick golden-fuzzed forearm. He pulled me into a bear hug, onto the dance floor, where neither of us quite knew the steps. Miss Anna's repertoire was end-of-wedding music, dated ballads for old couples who hadn't been to a nightclub in years.

"Why'd you leave Pittsburgh?" I asked, to distract from my awkward moves.

"You ever been to Pittsburgh?"

"Nope."

"Didn't think so." His chest was touching mine. I stopped pretending to follow the music. "So what's your story?"

I liked hearing him talk, the way he dropped his R's, a change from the nasal over-articulated accent that college students of all races seemed eager to acquire.

"I'm in school. Fashion photography."

"Cool. I bet you meet some awesome celebrities."

"I wish — it'd be a nice change from those late nights alone with my International Male catalog." Oh, stupid. Just because I was gay and presumably so was he, did I have to be such a monkey in heat?

"Seriously, it's more hard work than glamour," I went on. "Making everything perfect till it's boring. They've got me taking a hundred pictures of a glass of water."

"Like the Karate Kid." He grinned. "'Wax on, wax off.'" He moved in close enough for me to smell his sweat, and pinched my upper arm, which seemed scrawny next to his. "You wanna know hard work? Ever put up a roof?"

Just then I wished I could tell a normal father-son story about summer jobs, tough love and the good ache of exhaustion. My big brother, Carter, and I had both served our time swinging clumsy hammers at Selkirk work sites. I remembered the warm, calloused grip of Daddy's hand over mine on the truck's gear shift, the rare touch meaning more to me than the illegal thrill of driving at fourteen, though saying so would have ended the day in shame. But this would also be a story about looking up for praise and hearing Daddy joke with his crew that his sons walked like daughters. Maybe that *is* the normal story, but I'd come to New York to leave that pathetic little boy behind.

So I turned the question back on Phil. "Is that what you do now — construction?"

"Naw, just got a job at the Ironman," he said, referring to a well-known Chelsea gym. "Personal trainer."

A line sprang to mind, but did I dare make a move and risk his laughter? I'd begun to figure out the unspoken code that beckoned a man for a back-room grope, and (after one or two slightly painful and death-defying episodes) how to negotiate what happened when the door closed, but not how to talk to someone who got under my intoxicated skin from the first minute, the way Phil did.

"Maybe, later, you could show me some, uh, exercises?" I fumbled.

Still grinning, Phil was about to respond when the emcee's voice blasted over the loudspeaker. "New Eden, please give it up for Miss Anna Bollocks!"

Applause, applause. The spotlight switched off and the waves of electronica closed seamlessly over our heads.

Phil let his hand drop from my waist. "I guess we ought to go wait for Frank."

We reclaimed our table, where Ariana was dispensing advice to a chubby dude in a pink feather boa.

"Olive green is going to be *the* color this decade," she opined confidently. "Remember, the 80s are over."

"But the 50s, darlings, are still alive and well!" Miss Anna descended on us in a cloud of endorphins and Jean Naté. Kisses all around.

"Great show, Frank," I said.

"I've never seen anything like it," Phil marveled.

"Well, he *is* from Pittsburgh," I commented to the table at large.

Phil planted a kiss on those lacquered lips. One thing I like about kissing boys is you don't have to worry about wiping their face off. But Frank was on his way to becoming a professional makeup artist and knew how to keep himself unsmudged through most adventures — including those that, in my opinion, he didn't deserve.

"I see you've met my boyfriend," Frank beamed. He perched on Phil's lap, posing like those USO girls who entertained the troops in World War II. Phil leaned his square strawberry-blond head on a bosom I'd stuffed with rolled-up pantyhose in the men's room a couple of hours ago. Ariana would say this was no time for me to be having a problem with illusions. Making my excuses, I left her and boa boy discussing body piercings as class signifiers.

Phil and Frank's love-fest had soured me on spending the rest of the evening at the club. Never mind being happy for my new friends. For myself, at least, I should have been grateful to find a place in the world where two men, one of them wearing frilly panties, could sincerely kiss in public. But not enough had changed for me. I was the boy with the camera on the sidelines of the homecoming dance.

Don't get me wrong, the handjobs in New York were much better, and didn't finish off with a punch in the gut to ensure my discretion, a favorite defense from the jocks' playbook back home. I'd been amazed the first time a man went down on me, a few weeks after I arrived in the city. A stranger, with no reason to care, kneeling at my feet, pressing his warm mouth between my legs, to taste me and open to me. The liquid joy of that release had brought tears to my eyes, which I covered with the pretense of an allergy to the pungent disinfectant in the bus station bathroom. I wasn't sure how great I was at returning the favor. They didn't usually stick around afterwards for a performance review. I had to savor those moments when the hard thighs I locked my arms around shook and went weak, as I strained to swallow the proof that I'd met his secret need.

One way or another, I reflected, those nights ended just the same as this one, with me heading home alone in the cold. Dmitri was probably tucked into bed with one of the gypsy-skirted girls he picked up at poetry readings in Soho. Tucking my hands in my pockets for warmth, I walked along Tenth Avenue, between the dark slabs of office buildings and the blinding fluorescents of gas stations and car dealerships. The working girls were out in their bolero ski jackets and fishnet stockings. In the shadow of a doorway I stopped to watch them saunter up to passing cars, headlights sweeping momentarily over their hard painted faces. One of them spotted the flash of my ever-present camera and, fearing I was a cop, hid behind her friend, a towering black girl who offered to do a variety of illegal things to me in exchange for the film. I paid her fifty bucks and let her pat me down for weapons, which hopefully she enjoyed more than I did.

"You want to get inside someplace warm?" she suggested. She had a complex face, wide eyes ringed with mascara, bruised-plum lips above a mannish jawline.

"We could go back to my room," I ventured. I must not have been as sober as I thought. I figured I didn't have anything worth stealing except my cameras, and in the unlikely event that she knifed me, my family would probably be relieved that I'd found such a straight-acting way to die.

The few dark, windy blocks back to the dorm had never seemed so long. Could you get arrested for walking with a girl whose skirt barely covered her butt cheeks? There was no way to make this look like anything but what it wasn't. Fortunately, city style was a shifty thing, unlike the strict seasonal palette and respectable hemlines of Mama's cocktail-party set. The New York look was out of the corner of the eye, pretending not to see, not to want to be seen.

Her stride was brisk and long, making direct conversation difficult. "What's your name?" I spoke up when we paused at a don't-walk sign.

"What do you want it to be?" The husky tenor of her voice sounded worn, like an old cello rehearsing a much-requested song.

"Uh...whatever it is?"

"Yeah, okay," she said wearily. "Desirée." I heard the invisible quotes around the name, clearly not hers, or not all the time. And we were on the move again, through the wind tunnel of high buildings flanking the narrow street.

"Look," I said, when we'd reached the warmth of the dormitory lobby, "I'm not like those other guys. I don't even, uh, have sex with girls."

She stared at the elevator panel. "Greek style, cost you fifty bucks extra."

"No, no," I said, peering nervously down the brightly lit hallway for fear that someone would hear us. "What I meant was, I only want to take some pictures of you for my class. With your clothes on. Well, not your clothes, but *clothes*. Okay?"

"Uh-huh." The numbers could have been television, she watched them that intently, counting down till the doors opened for us on the lobby level.

I thought the costumes would cheer her up, bright props I was always gathering in anticipation of a suitable wearer. She had a Mardi Gras face, regal and sensual, meant to be softened by purple and gold plumes. I draped the fake feathers around her shoulders, stiff in a yellow brocade jacket whose frayed underarms only showed if she moved the wrong way. Despite our conversation in the lobby, she kept rubbing her leg up against mine when I got too close.

"You sure you don't like girls?" she purred. "Maybe you just need a nice girl to show you how to have a good time."

"No, thank you," I said, because my Mama raised me to be polite, even to the type of woman she pretended didn't exist outside of the Bible. I could smell Desirée's musky skin and floral hairspray. How was I made, that I was unmoved by her scent — repulsed, even, to imagine the overlay of touch upon touch that had gone into it, like fingerprints on a greasy doorknob?

I stepped back. The colors were festive and rich, perfect against her dark skin, as I'd imagined. She stood like a bright bird unaware that it could fly. She needed to see herself, I thought, then she would be proud. I positioned her by the mirror on the closet door. "Okay, pose," I encouraged her. Like a kitten stalking its reflection, she leaned toward it, tipping out her cleavage, pouted her puffed violet lips and mimed French-kissing herself.

"No, not a sex pose…like a model," I tried to explain. "You like fashion magazines? You know, *Elle, Vogue, Glamour?*"

"Do you work for a magazine?" I thought I heard a little excitement there.

"Well, not yet. But maybe someday."

"Oh, okay. Okay. How about this?" She propped one stiletto boot heel on our sagging armchair, angled her hands on her hips, and flashed me her idea of a Hollywood smile. I snapped some pictures to please her, but her expressions remained exaggerated and false, a drugstore version of a luxury perfume. *If you like Cindy, you'll love Desirée.*

"Let's try something different," I suggested. I helped her into a drop-waisted cocktail dress in a sugary pink. Like my other thrift-shop finds, this one had been cast off for showing signs of wear: the constellation of seed pearls at the neckline showed some gaps, and one or two of the skirt's fluttery overlapping petals were frayed at the bottom, as if snagged by an exuberant dancing heel. Actually, I supposed the only thing it had going for it was the color, defiantly feminine and optimistic in a city of grays, designed to awaken a hidden nostalgia for Easter bonnets and Princess phones. It wouldn't zip all the way up Desirée's broad back, but you couldn't really tell when she was reclining on Dmitri's bed. I asked her to rest her head on the pillow.

"Talk to me," I said.

"You're such a naughty boy," she said. "I bet you have a big, hard…"

"Please, stop." I put down my camera. "Talk to me about something you like. Not sex," I quickly added.

Her eyes searched the room for answers. I resumed clicking away, hoping to catch that moment when the mahogany angles of her face softened into dreaming. But there's the wonder and stupidity of my profession, the promise that a dress as pink as a birthday cake can roll back the clock to girlhood, simple as that.

"I like bubble baths," she droned on, "French restaurants, dancing at the club…" Her wristwatch beeped and she sat up. "You want another half hour? Twenty dollars."

Since I'd already spent both of the fifties Mama had smuggled into this month's letter from home — on booze and cheap women, no less — I had to decline.

Getting out of bed, she noticed for the first time the poster on Dmitri's side of the room. "That's a nice picture of Jesus. Did you do that?"

I shook my head vehemently. "It's my roommate's. I mean, it's not by him. Andres Serrano took it. A famous guy." I gathered up the clothes she'd come in with. "Here's your stuff."

She didn't take the bundle I thrust at her. "Can I use the toilet?"

"Sure, go to town." I dropped her skirt and ski jacket back on the floor.

Our bathroom door was warped and didn't latch properly. This wasn't usually a problem for me and Dmitri, as we were rarely home at the same time and equally uninterested in seeing each other naked. Despite myself, I caught a glimpse of pink gauze over brown thigh and was compelled to linger. Had I ever actually seen a vagina, outside of health-class videos and my brother's stolen magazines? Casually, I edged toward the door and brushed my shoulder against it, nudging it open a bit wider than I'd intended. The pink dress was rucked up over her round hips. The curve of her belly descended into a patch of dark fur that did not make it into the picture I submitted as that week's homework assignment in Intro to Fashion Photography for a much-needed B-plus, a picture of that moment before the shocked modesty of her wide brown eyes became cool and unreadable as a doll's gaze. I tipped her another five singles and she left.

Alone at last, I switched off the light and lay down in bed, but an oppressive presence filled the room. It was thick as the red-gold billows surrounding the crucifix on the poster, that she hadn't known was urine. Even in the dark I couldn't forget it was there, and every night that I coexisted with it, it confirmed my buried fears about the choices that had led me here, making my guts knot up with a pang of shame.

What harm had Jesus ever done, that anyone should want to piss on him? In our family's Baptist church we'd learned to sing "I Dreamed I Drove the Nails". The preacher groaned about the spitting soldiers and the crown of thorns while I studied Daddy's confident face at the altar call. The bruises on his knuckles weren't from work. And the painted Jesus smiled over us from his hill of clouds, victorious and clean, tender shepherd of other people's children. Kneeling in silent anger on the carpeted steps, I'd wanted to give Jesus a broken arm like mine, Carter's black eye, our little sister Laura Sue's fingernails nervously bitten down to blood. But that only proved I was my father's son.

I'd parted ways with that Jesus years ago, or tried to. Serrano's soiled crucifix forced me to recall the one my French-Catholic Uncle Jimmy, Mama's brother, had given me from his curio shop in Savannah. We'd moved in with him and Memère for a month when I was ten, till Daddy wooed Mama back with roses and a remodeled kitchen. On the worst nights, that scrawny, dented carving in my hand had allowed me to pretend there was a different Jesus, one who had no super-powers and couldn't help anyone, but would keep me company. I imagined feeling his presence like a warm breath, a feather-weight on my pillow. Sometimes I let him say to me, *I love you, Julian, I've always loved you.* But later I felt ashamed that this was childish, and then that it was something worse. Something too close to the half-seen men who embraced me in dreams that left my sheets sticky. So I had to lose that Jesus as well.

The degraded image on Dmitri's wall seemed to mock my boyish wish to protect Jesus from my unclean thoughts. If what the preachers said about Christ's two natures was true, I didn't know how he could stand his life anyhow, being split down the middle between the part of him that remembered heaven and the human part that would have touched me back.

This drunken soul-searching, however, had to be weighed against the more immediate problem of ridicule from my roommate whenever I hinted that I didn't appreciate the decor. Last time, he'd pretended to ignore me, blowing cigarette smoke out of his nostrils, his eyes half-closed behind his thick black-framed rectangular glasses, and then later he and his friends made sure I overheard them calling me "Jesse Helms" in a fake Southern yokel voice. So I tossed and turned on my bed, and dreamed about processing drywall invoices for Daddy's company.

3

THE FOLLOWING WEEK, I was nursing a hangover and a B-minus, both of which were becoming rather too regular occurrences, when Ariana found me taking a break in the cafeteria.

"Hey, are you Louis Vuitton? Because you've got bags under your eyes."

I groaned, but tried to smile too. "Not tonight, dear, I have a headache."

She slid her tray over to me. "Here, have a donut."

"That'll really be the end."

"Yeah, you're welcome."

I took my hand away from my eyes, wincing at the fluorescent glare. Ariana was patiently eating her donut. Today she was wearing a denim jumper over a black turtleneck and leggings, finished off with skull-patterned Converse high-tops. At the far end of the table, two girls in low-rise jeans shared a diet soda. Bright hoops dangled from their ears.

"Ariana — are you ever scared that you don't have what it takes?"

She chased a crumb around her plate with her fingertip. "Isn't everybody?"

"I guess…but how do you know if you're right?"

"You don't ever really *know*. Whatever you came here to do, whatever you're willing to try a hundred times to get a little closer to the picture in your mind — just do it and stop waiting for someone to give you a gold star that says 'Good'."

I rubbed my itchy eyes as if that could blur and change my marked-up portfolio into a vision of success. "I'd like to believe that, but if I don't pick up a few gold stars soon, I'll lose my scholarship, and then it's back to the polyester wasteland for me."

"Says the man who drinks Cosmos on a school night."

I sighed, not really able to argue the point. "I guess so…but when I go out, it's like, I finally found my tribe. Not my fault they don't meet in a church basement. Besides, the entire Salvation Army brass band couldn't make Mr. Koble want to see what I see. 'Beauty is cheap,' what the fuck does he mean?"

Ari picked up the manila folder that I'd been shielding with my arm. She took her time leafing through my photos of our classmate Jessica, a tall blonde with a porcelain princess face, modeling sportswear on a sun-drenched morning at the dog park. Too romantic, my teacher had said. Too perfect, too clean. (He hadn't seen what I stepped in when I pulled back for the wide-angle.)

My friend didn't bother reading his comments. "It is what it is, Julian. You can't be so sensitive. Fashion is just fads. People get tired of nice pretty things, they want the opposite, then they go back again."

"Anyone who gets tired of beauty, their life has been too god-damn easy." I thought about the high school portfolio that had won me this spot at FIT. Had Mr. Koble seen it? Or was it buried in an admissions office drawer like the photo morgue at the newspaper — the picture of Mama brushing graceful strokes of makeup over lips, eyes, cheeks, till the bruise on her face disappeared? I'd slipped that one in after she proofread my application, not sure if it was the best or the worst thing I'd ever done with my camera.

Ariana dabbed her mouth with a paper napkin. "Come on, I want to show you something I'm working on."

I stood up too quickly, feeling my brains slide around like boxes in a badly packed U-Haul. "You've got frosting on your chin."

"It's my new look." But she wiped it off.

In the students' workroom, a row of dummies in unfinished dresses lined the wall behind the sewing machines that were bolted to the floor. Some wore only a patchwork of paper pattern sections with swatches pinned to them for future reference, while on others the architecture of the dress was becoming visible in layers of velvet, cotton and lace. Waiting for that mythical last piece, the dollmaker's wind-up key or the enchanted shoes, that turns a confection of cloth and paint into a real girl. For Frank, the transition to Miss Anna couldn't take place until someone (lately, me) placed her sable-haired beehive wig on his head and said "Come out, come out, wherever you are." Cliché, I know, but we'd tried several alternate catchphrases including "Hocus-pocus" and "You make me feel like a natural woman," and what can I say, Miss Anna knew what she liked.

Ariana unwound a sheet of dry-cleaners' plastic wrap from her dress form. She stood back and waited for my reaction. I saw a starched white floor-length sheath with long tight sleeves and a cowl neck, which, as Ariana demonstrated, ought to be pulled up into a hood except that the dummy had no head. That part creeped me out.

"Here, this is the last piece I have to sew on," she said, pulling out a small bundle of bead-encrusted white cloth from the foot locker beside her sewing machine.

"Isn't that — no, not the Chanel!" I'd found this vintage evening bag for her in a plastic bin of accessories at Goodwill on one of our frequent shopping adventures. On that particular occasion we were celebrating, or possibly commiserating over, her eighteenth birthday, which she said only meant three more years before it was legal to be as drunk as she was right then.

Now the bag's fabric shell lay unfolded on the table, its satin insides pried open like an oyster, snipped away from the metal clasp and frame. Ariana plucked a couple of pins from the dummy's neck and used them to fasten the beaded strip across the bodice. The effect was transformative. She was at once naked and cloaked, she, the invisible wearer of the dress, a hooded vestal and Madonna sporting her brassiere outside her clothes.

"It's for you," she said.

"For me? No…"

"To use, for one of your assignments. You said you were worried about finding a theme for your midterm project. Maybe this will give you some ideas?"

"It's amazing."

"I know."

"Of course you do." Ariana wasn't the hugging kind, so I simply said, "Thank you. Thank you so much...Now all I have to do is find the right girl."

Ariana busied herself with rewrapping the dummy in its protective plastic. "Sorry, it's too small for Frank."

"Hey, Ariana..." I gently tucked the plastic around where the dummy's feet would have been. "Why don't you ever make clothes like this —" I nearly said, *in your size.* "For yourself?"

"Why don't you take pictures of yourself?"

"That's not quite —"

"That's right, you'd grow hair on your palms. Now...don't you have a paper on *Madame Bovary* due this afternoon?"

"For my sins."

In my opinion, a book on the perils of too much shopping didn't seem like appropriate reading for aspiring fashion professionals, unless it was some sort of equal time policy, like the ads with Joe Camel telling kids they were too young to smoke. It was hard to concentrate because I was daydreaming about my next shoot. I hadn't wanted to hurt Ari's feelings but I already knew the perfect girl for her perfect dress: Dmitri's latest improbable conquest, Cady Beauclair, a fashion marketing major and former homecoming queen from Jackson, Mississippi. Cady had a high-boned face framed by waves of champagne-colored hair, strikingly married with dark-fringed eyes of blue deepening to violet. Beyond her physical appeal, her candid friendliness reminded me of the girls I'd photographed for the high school yearbook — stars of their small world, generously sharing heat with any eager boy, believing their charms would protect them forever. If Cady looked that good in the top half of Dmitri's red flannel pajamas, accented with Dorito dust from their post-marijuana munchies, imagine how much more brightly she'd shine when she became my muse.

4

THE THRILL OF ARTISTIC INSPIRATION was almost, but not quite, enough to distract me from Frank dancing with his hands on Phil's ass, the next time we all went out together. There are so many kinds of being in love, and most of them have nothing to do with the heart. The cock, the eyes, the flattered ear — it all lives in the mind, like the best photographs, the ones you'll never take.

For a change of pace, we were at a warehouse party down in Tribeca, in a shuttered printing press that the owner had been converting into artists' lofts before the recession hit. Huge empty spindles that had once held rolls of newspaper loomed in the shadows behind the hastily constructed cash bar.

Tomas knew the DJ and got us in, and that was the last we saw of him. The other member of our party was a sandy-haired guy named Stan, whom Frank had met at Phil's gym. He was unusually muscular for a short guy, which only accentuated his compactness. So far, I liked Stan, who was studying to be a pharmacist and had an unshakeably placid temperament, two facts that might or might not be related. My somewhat wishful belief was that he was interested in Frank but lacked the initiative to snatch him out of another man's (larger) arms.

Thinking him the easiest one to approach, I edged up to him and fell into dancing to the rhythm of the group. Phil, looking solid in jeans and workmen's boots, moved with that loose-limbed confidence that I loved, spreading the unfocused warmth of his smile around the room. He pressed in closer to Stan, sandwiching the little guy between his bulky form and Frank's stork-like height. I found myself paired off with Frank. As Miss Anna, he could execute a fine Argentine tango, but as himself he mainly bobbed up and down.

Now, I considered myself a pretty smooth dancer; I knew Madonna's "Vogue" video backwards and forwards. So it took me some time to realize, as I went through my moves, that Phil was aping my every gesture, for laughs. When I thrust out my pelvis, he sashayed his hips with a mincing expression; I raised my hands in the air, he fluttered his. I was wearing these leather pants that I'd saved up for by eating peanut butter crackers and instant soup for three weeks. Unfortunately they tended to slide down, like cheap pantyhose, from the sweat and agitation of dancing. When I hitched them up, discreetly as I thought, Phil mimed groping frantically for his crotch and finding nothing there. A straight couple near us noticed and laughed, which finally got Frank's attention.

"Dude, that's not cool," he told Phil.

"Whaddya mean? It's a joke. Look, they all think it's funny," Phil insisted.

I felt the chill of embarrassment, the familiar sickness. From the locker rooms of my suburban high school to the bars of New York, that echo would never die, the baying of the pack.

"Of course they do. Sissies are always funny if you aren't one," Frank snapped.

"I wasn't making fun of *you*."

"Frank, it's okay," I said. My heart pulsed in my throat. This new Phil, with his sulky mouth and half-clenched fists, inspired even more yearning than the smiling blond giant. I could almost hold him in my lap, like a toddler on the verge of tears.

"I'm sick of this place. It's full of posers. You wanna go?" Phil asked Frank.

Both Frank and I converged our gaze on Stan — Frank awkwardly, seeking to share blame for his choice, me silently urging the little guy to step up.

"I...I think we're going to dance some more," Stan said. He gathered the nerve to put one hand on Frank's arm. Frank looked relieved.

"Fuck that. I need some air. I'm going out for a smoke," declared Phil.

The back of the warehouse had a fire escape that you reached by crawling through one of the windows that was propped open with a stick. Refugees from the dance floor came and went, seeking brief hits of sobriety from the sting of cold air on their flushed faces, or trading smokes and other items in hand-to-hand transactions with a studied casualness. I followed Phil out there. He was hunched over the rusty railing, flicking ash down to the street two stories below. I leaned on the railing next to him, saying nothing. He wasn't able to ignore me for long.

"What're *you* doing here?"

I shrugged. He didn't know what to make of my silence. Next to us, two guys in knit stocking caps shook hands a little too long and then ducked inside through separate windows. I wished I'd brought my own hat and coat, like Phil who'd had the sense to retrieve his parka before braving the elements.

"You think you're too good to fight with me?" he needled me again. "You gonna call your rich daddy to teach me a lesson?"

"My daddy would kick your faggot ass into next week," I said, "just like he did to me."

Phil took a long drag on his cigarette and tossed it over the edge. "Sucks to be us, huh."

"Guess so." I almost caught him smiling, but then he turned away, pretending to watch this boy and girl at the far end of the terrace who were sucking each other's faces hard enough to create a vacuum seal.

"So what's the problem here?" I asked. "I thought we sort of connected that first night at New Eden, but now you're being a jerk."

"Don't play dumb."

"I'm not playing." I dared to touch the back of his hand lightly. What if we were wrong and he wasn't one of us, just slumming in fairyland? The pavement was a long way down.

He flinched but didn't shake off my touch. "Frank told me you were talking shit about me," he muttered. "How you didn't think I was good enough for him because my pop drives a truck for the paper company."

"Oh, shit. First of all, that's not what I said, and second —"

"I'm proud of my pop, okay? He might be an asshole, but he works hard for every damn thing in his life, and so do I."

"Phil — " I grabbed his shoulders. He loomed over me like a prizefighter awaiting the bell. Why couldn't I fall for a pretty boy like Tomas, who would never risk damaging his hands in a fistfight? "Phil, listen. I like where you come from. I like everything about you. I only talked trash to Frank because I wanted to put him off you."

He blinked, confused, breathing hard. "So now you have...are you happy?"

"No...I'm sorry. It was a stupid thing to do. But, I mean, I'm happy you're here with me...alone, right now."

He stepped back, out of reach. "Why should I believe anything you say?"

In response, I sneezed, twice. Yankee weather wasn't kind to me. Phil made for the window, to continue our conversation inside, I hoped. But the tonsil-hockey couple had already had the same idea and, with the obliviousness of lovers, had pulled the stick in after them. Phil rattled the unyielding window frame. I added my useless efforts to his.

"Must've latched itself from the inside," he said. "I know how these places are built."

"Did you work at the paper factory too?"

"What is this, a job interview?"

"Just making conversation." I sneezed again. Phil kicked the window. "You think you can break in?" I asked.

"The panes are too small, dumb-ass. We couldn't get through."

"No, but you could break the one near the latch and reach in and open it, like a burglar."

"Why me?"

"Because I'm just a poser." I flicked my wrist at him.

"Yeah, sorry about that. I was really pissed off."

"Try taking your aggressions out on that glass."

"And then what? My hand'll get cut to shreds."

"In the movies, the burglar usually wraps his jacket around his arm or something."

"I see you've appointed yourself the brains of this operation."

"You said it, Bugsy."

Phil scoped out the window, looking for the best spot, but the panes closest to where he thought the latch might be were boarded up. So much for our caper. I shifted from foot to foot, trying to warm up.

"Here, put your arms through my sleeves." Phil arranged his parka over us so that he covered my back like a cape. I tucked myself into the curve of his body, feeling his growing hardness through his jeans.

"I never thought you would like me," he said after awhile. His breath was hot against my neck.

"Why not?"

"Because you're one of those, what are they called, the beautiful people?"

"You look pretty fine yourself," I said. One side of my face was warm where his stubbly cheek was pressed against mine; the other side was whipped by the wind.

He heated up my whole body by kissing me right then. I opened my mouth to his tongue. Just then, under the cold black sky, we were the two luckiest boys in the world, to have found this corner where nobody would notice us falling into each other's arms.

Of course, we couldn't go further than that without risking frostbite in some very inconvenient places. Disengaging from my embrace, Phil suddenly hoisted himself up to sit on the railing. "Let's get out of here."

"Brilliant idea. Why didn't I think of that."

"We'll climb down. It's no big deal." To prove his point, Phil lifted his hands off the railing, with the crazy grin of a kid on a rollercoaster, balancing only on that beautiful rear that I worried would never be mine if he took a tumble onto the cement.

"Am I scaring you?" he teased.

"Don't be an idiot."

"Trust me, I know what I'm doing." He took hold of the railing again, and I went back to breathing. "I've done roof repairs since I was sixteen and my pop kicked me out of the house. My balance can't be beat." He nudged me with the toe of his boot. "Come on, just do what I do and you'll be fine."

Slowly, following his lead, I gripped the icy metal and swung myself over the edge, inching my hands down the bars until my feet were dangling just shy of the railing one story below. There were stairs between the levels, but they were gated off with a barrier that was too high and sharp to climb over.

"Phil — " I called out, my voice sounding thin as a thread blowing in the wind. What I really wanted was to ask him to catch me, but I wouldn't give him the satisfaction. "Is it true what they say, that you shouldn't look down?"

"I dunno, try it and let me know how it goes." He swung his legs in toward the lower level, letting go of his handhold once his feet were secure. Sparing me further humiliation, since my pants were sliding down, he pulled me in. The ladder attached to the bottom of this level ended eight or nine feet above the street, child's play compared to what we'd just done. He stole a couple more kisses while I got my second wind.

"Why'd your father kick you out?"

"Found my magazines."

"Reading or posing?"

"Hey, I never thought of that — would've beat freezing my ass off on old man Henderson's shingles." He gave mine a love tap. "Up you go."

Swinging over the railing was no more fun the second time around, but the squeaky ladder managed to hold our weight, and at last we smacked down on hard ground.

We flashed our hand stamps at the bored bouncer to get back in the club, ostensibly to retrieve my coat, but really because I felt guilty about not making an effort to find Frank before I ran off with his so-called boyfriend. I squinted into the darkness, scanning faces by the intermittent bursts of white light that flared up like an electrical fire, but didn't see anyone I recognized. When I re-emerged, Phil was savoring another cigarette near the entrance.

"Did you get lucky in there or what?" he said impatiently.

"I was wondering about Frank...don't you think we should... shouldn't we...?"

Phil tossed down his cigarette and stamped it out. "Eh. It's not like we're exclusive."

Him and Frank, or him and me? With his arm around my waist, I didn't ask questions. He must have sensed my unease, because as we walked down to the subway, he asked, "Do you have a problem with that? Being open?"

"I don't know, it's not something I've ever had to think about before."

He rubbed the small of my back. It felt good, like everything we'd done so far, but I moved out of range, honestly not to play games but because we were on the subway platform now and I didn't want these people, these tired hotel maids and hopped-up young lawyers, to stare at two boys with their hands in each other's pants. I studied the hollow darkness of the tunnel as if willpower could make the train rattle into view.

"There was this guy," Phil said, and paused, glancing at me to check that I was in the mood to listen. "I crashed with him for awhile after I left home, after my cousin's place with her goddamn noisy kids. At first it was cool, we would go to the bar, the video store or whatever, and if one of us found someone good, okay, we didn't check up on each other. But when I began saving money to come to New York, he got all weird and clingy, started waiting up for me when I worked nights, leaving these little notes in my lunch bag like he was my freakin' mom."

"Ever tempted to stay?"

"He was a sweet guy, but..." Phil shook the thought from his head. "Look, I couldn't see myself becoming one of those old queens who works in the post office and walks his little dog, and everyone knows he's 'very close friends' with the choir director but it's okay as long as they're never together in public." He grabbed me roughly around the waist and pulled me toward him.

"As long as we're baring our souls," I said, "I should tell you that

I'm only out of the closet in two neighborhoods and this isn't one of them."

"It is now." He squeezed me harder.

On the tunnel wall behind us was a parade of ripped and written-on posters advertising Big Macs, accident lawyers, and Whitney Houston's concert tour. Someone had slapped a couple of wrinkled black and pink *Silence=Death* stickers over a promo for Caribbean vacations. The swimsuited girl's eyes and teeth were blacked out with magic marker. I quickly turned away.

After I explained the roommate situation, Phil reluctantly took me back to his place, which turned out to be a two-room basement apartment on West 18th Street, underneath a consignment shop with a shabby fur coat in the window. A formica countertop with a hot plate and a microwave served as his kitchen. Besides that and the usual bathroom fixtures, the only furniture was a TV, a mattress heaped with blankets on the floor, and a desk cobbled together from a plank and cinder blocks, bearing up a stack of books. I picked up the topmost one, on sports medicine.

"Nice," I said.

"Eh, fuck off," Phil replied, but he was grinning again, with no trace of the dark mood that had come over him when he talked about Pittsburgh.

"You ever bring Frank here?" I asked before I could stop myself.

"Why, you jealous?"

"No."

"You want to hear about where Frank and I did it?"

"No, forget it. I just felt weird for a second."

"I told you, he's not my wife." Phil pulled me toward him. His kisses tasted like cigarettes and whiskey. We sank into his low mattress, squatting side by side on the edge.

"What am I?" I hated myself for asking, having already learned the language of our bars and back rooms, where "fuck me" meant "nice to meet you" and "call me" meant "goodbye." Meanwhile my hands explored the taut muscles under his T-shirt while he worked on peeling off those damned leather pants.

"You know how I found out I was into guys?" Phil mused, rubbing between my legs with the palm of his big hand, with firm, sure strokes that left me speechless. "Mom and Pop took us to the circus one time. My sisters were going nuts over the dumb ballerinas on white ponies. Then all of a sudden this man in tights flew down from the sky. I'll never forget, he had a high forehead and dark red hair — like yours — " With his other hand, he brushed my hair out of my eyes and smoothed it back. "And these fine lips — like yours — " Phil's tongue traced my mouth. "And when he grabbed the trapeze with his long legs, I wanted him so much I didn't even know what I wanted him for."

"I think I can show you."

Naked, we burrowed under his flannel blankets. The cement-walled room was clean and dry but chilly, with a draft creeping in from the street-level casement window. He made little low noises in his throat as I tongued the salty tip of his thick shaft. Unlike the guys I'd tried before, he didn't mind my hesitation, that pause for fear I didn't know how to do this right because it shouldn't be done. Combing his fingers through my hair, he guided my head. I relaxed my throat and drew him in deeper, inhaling the earthy scent, different from mine yet familiar, like a dusty room that held good secrets. I thought of all the boys like us, touching ourselves in the darkness of bunk beds, replaying a precious glimpse of a stranger's face, learning to be quiet. I carefully slid one finger between his cheeks and his noises got louder.

"Now," he groaned. I lifted myself off him. He surprised me by rolling the condom over my erect cock instead of his own. I had to will myself not to come as soon as he gripped me. He rolled over onto his stomach, offering me his flat, well-muscled ass.

"Wow, you want me to fuck you?"

"Something wrong with that?" Another flash of that stone-cold angry expression I'd seen on the fire escape. As before, something childish in Phil's mood swings tugged at my heart. I answered honestly.

"I didn't think you could be any more perfect, but you are."

Holding my breath, I eased inside his tight puckered opening.

"Harder," he grunted. He rubbed himself against the mattress, clenching my cock inside him. He was so strong, I couldn't hurt him, so at last I dug my knees into his sides and rode him hard, the way we both wanted. He reared up against me, again and again, till I cried out and collapsed on top of him. I lay there, nuzzling the blond fuzz at the nape of his neck, feeling the rise and fall of his breathing as it slowed and I thought he was asleep.

He pulled the blanket over us. "If you wanna wash up before breakfast, don't use the tub, it's clogged. I've been showering at the gym."

The problems of morning, of which that was one, seemed comfortably far away. Wrapping my legs around his, I drifted off to sleep, to the occasional sounds of footsteps criss-crossing the sidewalk outside our window. For the first time since moving to New York, I felt completely at home.

5

You KNOW what mornings-after are like, if you're lucky, so I'll pass over the expected montage: how you wake up first and hesitate before stroking his sleep-tousled hair, waiting for that lazy smile to spread across his face when he sees it's you; the awkward moments in the bathroom when you're both wondering whether it's too intimate to brush your teeth in front of someone who had your cock in his mouth the night before; then coffee is swallowed, vague words exchanged, doors closed. All I'll say is that if you're not a morning person, don't date someone who works at a gym.

Dating being an overly optimistic assessment of the situation, perhaps, since the week went by and Phil didn't return my calls. Okay, one call; I have my pride. I was in that awful mood where returning to the manhunt seemed nearly as empty and exhausting as waiting by the phone like a teenage girl. When you're eighteen, you think you have all the time in the world to do your work. Sex is being alive right now. It's finding out that you can look forward to more than hurried, shame-faced relief while faking diarrhea in your parents' upstairs bathroom, the double fiction that you're not jacking off and that if you are, you're not thinking about David Hasselhoff. It might not be such a bad thing for Phil and me to remain open, but I wished I knew the ground rules, like the ones that help Southern wives maintain whatever sanity they started with. Simple things like not bringing your mistress to the company barbecue or introducing her to your children.

So I wasn't in a very tolerant mood that week, feeling like everywhere I stood was shaky ground, and suddenly one afternoon I walked into our dorm and decided I couldn't look at that damn poster one more minute.

"What do you think you're doing?" Dmitri's nasal voice rang out.

"What does it look like I'm doing?" For those of you listening at home, I was standing on his bed, peeling off the Blu-Tac that affixed "Piss Christ" to the wall. I considered it a sufficient nod to courtesy that I had taken my shoes off.

"That's my side of the room. That's *my* stuff."

"Oh, we believe in private property now?" The poster sagged, unattached at its top corners. I rolled it down carefully. There ought to be a respectful protocol for disposing of these things, like a torn American flag: were you supposed to burn it, or bury it?

"I believe in free speech," he proclaimed. True to his word, he didn't push me off the bed, but let me continue rolling the poster into a chaste, anonymous tube. But that was the Yankee way, they'd rather talk you to death than have a good clean fistfight. I made the mistake of answering him back.

"How is it speech to pee on Jesus?"

"That's not Jesus. It's just an image."

"Yeah, but it's an image that a real person peed on. That's the whole point, right?" I was standing on the bed but it no longer felt like the moral high ground, so I hopped down. Eye to eye, I was a bit taller than Dmitri, whose slouching, bony frame was dwarfed by layers of sweaters and one of his long striped mufflers.

"Give me that back," he said. He was probably the kid in his class who always got his hat stolen on the playground for keep-away. I waved the poster tube out of his reach.

"I'm sick of people like you," Dmitri burst out. "You don't care about the kind of world we live in. But they'll be coming for you next."

Bo-ring. I'd heard speeches like this before in my Critical Media Studies class. Everyone was up in arms about the government's decision to deny funding to artists whose work didn't meet "general standards of decency"; there was even a pending Supreme Court case about it. I made what seemed to me the quite reasonable argument that my family wouldn't pay for me to photograph a guy with a bullwhip up his ass, so why should the American taxpayer? That was the last time I spoke up in that class. Now here was Dmitri playing the gay Holocaust card again.

"You're not gay — why don't you let me take care of myself?"

"Because you're selling us out."

"Us?"

"Us real artists." He reached for the poster again but I held on to my end so it would tear if he pulled too hard. He fell back. "You're all like, don't mind me, I'm just a silly old hairdresser, I'll stay in my little ghetto and not bother anyone."

My hand shot out and grabbed his wrist. "Is that a swish? 'Cause if you swish that wrist it's gonna be limp for a lot longer than you reckoned."

He squirmed. "Ow, Julian, come on, man."

I stared him down. "All I ask," I said slowly, "is for one *fucking* place...where I don't have to walk on fucking *eggshells*...for once in my fucking *life*." I let him think that over. My heart was racing. I felt far away from my body, like I was seeing myself through a fog. I released him and the poster, both. How did Jesus feel when he threw the money-changers out of the temple? Did part of him, maybe the part that dropped meteorites on the dinosaurs to hear them go boom, enjoy the snap of table legs and the trembling expectancy of faces waiting to be struck?

Dmitri rubbed his wrist. "That's exactly what I meant."

I handed him back the poster. "What?" I forced out. My throat closed on further apologies.

"Religious oppression. You know."

"So it's *not* just an image."

"That's what they think. But we know it is. So they get mad."

Was I part of the "we" or the "they"? My brother Carter was a second-string quarterback at UGA. I'd seen photos of his team, padded out in the Bulldogs' colors, all over my parents' house when I went back for Christmas. My sister Laura Sue was taking child-development classes at the community college while finishing her junior year of high school. Uncle Curtis was still selling Cadillacs, and his vending machine with the Stars & Bars decals was probably still the first thing you saw when you walked into the dealership. Mama was proofing the galleys for her book on party platters, which would duly find a place on all her children's bookshelves even though the only meals I could cook were hot dogs and cheese grits. And Daddy, like the Pope, admitted no mistakes. It was the rest of us who feared how every dropped ball, bad grade or burnt casserole might be repaid with backhanded bruises in private, or in public with the noisy ridicule that his business buddies considered a great sense of humor. Were I to take my place in the family albums, it would be at the side of some cropped picture, my single arm around a sibling, or in time, one of their children. The birds of the air have nests, and the foxes have holes, and Julian Selkirk needs a place to bring his boyfriend if he should ever find one who returns his phone calls.

"Okay, but Dmitri, I really have a hard time getting laid when Jesus is staring at me." He laughed, and I figured I'd join in. "Doesn't it bother your girlfriends?"

"Oh, I don't find it hard to distract them." He leered.

"Well, when we're stuck being roommates again in hell, don't say I didn't warn y'all." Dmitri, naturally, didn't think hell was any more real than Ronald McDonald, and perhaps if I pretended to agree with him long enough, I would start believing it too.

Besides, I had to stay on his good side at least until the photo session with Cady, who was going to be dressed in the purest white, floating on the turquoise shimmer of the Ironman Gym's swimming pool with a scarlet shoe dangling from her hand. Frank had arranged for Phil to let us in for free if we showed up before the gym opened on Sunday morning, and I didn't let on that I was anything less than grateful.

6

WE FORMED A STRANGE PARADE, lined up by the back door of the gym shortly after daybreak: me with my cameras in a waterproof tote, Frank with his case of makeup, and Ariana carrying the white dress over her shoulder in a cocoon of plastic wrap. She herself was wearing something that looked like Chinese red silk pajama pants under a black sweater-poncho fastened with a ceramic clown-faced pin. Frank had a key card for the door, which meant he'd spent the night with Phil, which distracted me so much that I nearly let the door slam in Ariana's face. A thin pink dawn was spreading upwards into the gray sky, quietly lingering over the brief hours before the city would rise for its Sunday bustle of newspapers, dog-walking, and standing in line for brunch.

We trudged past rows of unmanned exercycles and weight machines, dodging the short dark men who were mopping the floor while nodding to Spanish music on their headsets, and made our way to the pool. A big man was unfolding an inflatable pool raft from a stack of equipment. He turned around when he heard us come in, and I found myself looking into Phil's blue eyes.

"I didn't know you'd be here."

"I had to unlock the equipment closet." He matched me stare for stare. "This is what you wanted, right?"

I checked the size of the raft. "I don't know. Try blowing it up."

"Why don't you?"

"I have to set up my camera."

"Your model's not even here yet."

"I talked to her last night, she said she would be here and she will." I let the unspoken contrast hang in the air. How I'd waited for his call — yes, though he said we wouldn't be exclusive, yes, though I did some of that waiting with my pants down around my ankles, I'd been thinking of him constantly, and he ought to know that.

"Go ahead then, do what you gotta do." He bent down to pick up the bicycle pump they used for the rafts and inner tubes.

"Phil — " I swallowed hard. He looked up at me. His bare skin was close enough to touch. Didn't he remember me sleeping on his pillow, his broad forehead tucked into the hollow of my neck, his open-mouthed breathing warming my chest?

"Yeah?" His voice dropped. He waited for me to speak. I didn't understand him at all. He had made fun of someone who loved him back in Pittsburgh, who gave him a roof over his head, and he expected me to pursue him? The worst part was, I still wanted to.

"I'm going to see you again," I said. It came out like a question, grammar notwithstanding.

"When?" He pretended to concentrate on blowing up the raft, but I could hear his breath quicken, the way it had that night on the fire escape, when he first admitted liking me. Liking, or wanting? Which lasted longer?

"Tonight."

"Can't. I'll call you, okay?"

"Julian?" Ariana's voice echoed off the damp tiles of the empty room. "How do I set up the tripod?"

"Just a minute!" To Phil, I said, "Oh, *please*. I know what that means. You could at least be honest, after...everything we talked about."

The raft rippled and swelled with air, flopping like a giant tongue. Finished, Phil stood up. "I don't know why you want to be with me, if I'm a liar."

I didn't have a good answer for that. The most important things come to me as pictures, not words, more like a burst of sunlight than a little train of logic chugging from station to station. A guy I knew in high school could skim a whole novel in three hours; he said he somehow flashed on an overall impression of the page and didn't have to read every line. Falling for Phil was kind of like that, only I wasn't so sure the words were there to follow if I had to retrace my steps.

A clatter and a crash, as Ariana tipped over the tripod. She wasn't usually a klutz, so I figured she was nervous about The Dress. I dropped my end of the raft and started in the direction of the noise.

"I lost your number, okay?" Phil spoke up. "And I couldn't ask anyone for it."

"So Frank doesn't know?"

"What don't I know?" Frank came up beside us. Phil's face reddened. No, he probably wasn't lying before, because he sucked at it now.

"Um, where the model is," he covered.

Frank looked puzzled. "Why would I know that?"

Oh, right, the model. Prioritize, Julian. "I should go wait by the door, to let her in," I said.

The gym's rear door had no window, so I had to keep propping it open to peer down the street, then closing it again when the gusts of wind became too much for me. At last I spotted her at the end of the alley. In her plain black down jacket and sweatpants, with her hair tied back in a ponytail, she was glamorous without even trying. To be that beautiful must be like having only hundred-dollar bills in your wallet. I was suddenly embarrassed by my crew — sullen Phil, gawky unshaven Frank, Ariana in her circus-tent clothing — as if I were asking Cinderella to step into a coach that was still pulpy with pumpkin seeds.

When we came up to the pool, Ariana seemed to be winning her battle with the tripod. The guys had abandoned the raft close to the pool's edge and were having an intense, muttered conversation while Frank set out his makeup kit along the locker room sink.

"Um, Phil, maybe you want to go now? We can take it from here," I suggested.

"Why are you telling him what to do?" Frank retorted. I laid my hand on his shoulder.

"Forget it. Look at this face." I beckoned to Cady, who showed no self-consciousness about sauntering into the men's locker room. "This is, like, the Sistine Chapel of faces. So get to work, Michelangelo."

Work calmed Frank down. I caught him humming "People Who Need People" as he brushed soft shadows on Cady's cheekbones and accentuated the fine arches of her eyebrows. She wanted to talk every moment that he wasn't working on her mouth, mostly asking me questions about what I was studying, my pictures, my vision for the shoot. I began to relax for the first time in days. The sound of a splash broke my reverie.

"Phil's going for a swim," Frank said, drawing a sharp black line along the curve of Cady's eyelid.

"Hey, Ariana, could you bring the dress?" I thought she might want to be part of the action. Besides, why should she get to watch Phil swim when I couldn't?

Cady barely glanced at the newcomer. Ariana hung back by the doorway, crossing one skull-patterned sneaker over her other ankle. She took some time to rub a spot off her eyeglasses. "Would you like to tell Cady about the inspiration for your design?" I asked, with forced cheer.

Cady smiled sweetly at the other girl. "Actually, I like to form my own impressions of the clothes, to let them speak to me without preconceptions," she said. "But hey, could you get me a diet Coke? With a straw, you know, because of the lipstick?"

Ariana bit her lip and said nothing. Well, if she was going to play photographer's assistant, she needed to hang up her pride along with that awful poncho. I would jump to take out Patrick Demarchelier's garbage.

"There's a vending machine down the hall, to the left of the yoga mats," Frank said to me. I went off on Cady's errand, leaving him draping a towel around her neck to avoid makeup smudges while Ariana zipped her into the long, slender column of fabric.

Once she was laid out on the raft, for a little while everything came together the way I'd dreamed: gold, scarlet, turquoise, pearl. Cady preened as though she were really soaking up the warm tropical sun, flowing into poses more lively than the passive tableau I'd planned. I found myself murmuring nonsense to her, like a rider coaxing a horse: "Come on, darling, that's right, that's beautiful, yes…"

Water darkened the sleeves of the dress. Losing air, the raft had begun to tilt, and to drift out of position, its motion threatening to blur my photos. "Someone needs to swim under there and hold it steady," I said. No one volunteered. "Well, *I* can't do it, I'm taking the picture!"

"Oh, all right," Phil said, unwrapping the towel from his shoulders in preparation for going back in the pool. "I think I can hold my breath for awhile." He winked at me, and my body grew hot with the memory of his mouth.

"No," Frank said curtly.

"Whaddya mean, *no?*"

"I don't want you to help him anymore, Phil."

"I can do it if I want to."

"I *said*, I'll do it," Frank raised his voice. He stripped down to his undershirt and boxers, and jumped into the water, sending up a splash that dangerously rocked the raft.

Cady gripped the edges. "Julian, don't be mad — I forgot to tell you, I can't swim."

"Frank, hold that thing steady," I shouted. Softening my tone, I told Cady, "Don't worry, sweetheart, the shallow end is only four feet deep."

"Five," Phil corrected.

"Right, but she's more than five feet tall. Aren't you, *sweetheart?*" Ariana sang out.

"You people are so totally unprofessional I can't even believe it," I exclaimed. "This is a fashion shoot. This is our *job*. Behave yourselves!"

Frank burst up to the surface, sputtering for air. Cady smiled bravely at the lens. "Move your head," I motioned to him.

"Kiss my ass."

"Come on, Frank, chill," Phil urged. "Julian and I were just having a little fun that night, keeping warm, that's all."

"That's all? That's *all*?" I stepped away from the camera. "So, what, were you bullshitting me, all that heavy stuff you said about your dad, and…and the trapeze artist?" I was yelling now.

Phil balled up his fists. "Shut up. That's nobody's business."

"Y'all want to hear what he told me about his childhood?"

"I said, shut *up*!" Phil lunged for me, but his bare feet slipped on the wet tiles. I could have stopped him, I guess, but the shot of his startled face as he disappeared over the side was too good to miss. The next instant all hell broke loose. Phil's behind hit the corner of the raft, tipping Cady into the water. Frank reached out to help her but the raft's recoil smacked him in the chest. Cady, thrashing around in four, okay five, feet of water when anyone with a bit of sense would lie still and float, bumped her nose on the pool ladder. A blossom of blood unfurled in the water. Flinging off her sneakers and poncho, Ariana climbed down the ladder and managed to catch hold of Cady's shoulders. My model's wet hair curtained her face like fronds of seaweed. A red splash now decorated the pearled bodice. Ariana helped her into the women's room, holding a towel to her nose.

"Get out, everybody, get out!" Phil yelled. "The gym opens in fifteen minutes. You're going to get me fired!"

Frank cursed and wrung out his undershirt. He had to put his jeans back on over wet shorts, which didn't improve his mood. I had my hands full packing up my camera and accessories, so obviously I couldn't help anyone. I went to look for the girls afterward but they were gone. Ariana's clown brooch lay in a puddle on the tiles, its pin backing bent. It seemed like the perfect commentary on our disastrous morning, so I snapped one last picture before pocketing the sad little thing.

7

No one spoke to me for the whole next week. Like it was *my* fault that Phil was a slut and Frank belonged on "The Young and the Restless". I had no time to drown my sorrows on the dance floor, since I was cramming for midterms (thank you, CliffsNotes) and no money, either. Mama's latest note contained one wrinkly twenty-dollar bill. She wrote that Daddy was seeking a loan extension for the subdivision he was building in Marietta, and that my sister might be going steady with our old pastor's son, who was a chemistry honors student.

The mention of Laura Sue's name brought a twinge of guilt. Though I wasn't the most effective protector, my departure for college left them with no man in the house except Daddy. I fantasized that he might calm down, the alpha dog now in undisputed control of his turf. My fear of the answer dovetailed perfectly with Mama's relentless avoidance of unpleasant topics. "I am working hard and learning a lot," I wrote back. "New York is full of pretty girls." That was all true as far as it went, but I despaired of finding another one to pose for me before my project was due. I nearly had a date lined up with Jessica, despite Mr. Koble's disdain for her all-American charms, but I came down with a dreadful head cold and spent the next 48 hours shivering in my blankets, obsessively checking my throat glands for lumps and having nightmares about broken condoms.

Thus I had no choice but to sweat it out while Mr. Koble judged my parody of a portfolio. On the day we were to present our midterm projects, our teacher was joined at the front of the classroom by a tanned, elegant, bald man in his late forties, in a perfectly fitted charcoal gray suit over a collarless shirt. His eyes were a lighter gray, his nose not quite large enough to be called Roman. "Today we have a special guest," our teacher said. His next words sent an excited whisper around the room. "Richard Molineux, the creative director of *Femme NY*, has kindly agreed to give you feedback on your portfolios."

You might not find *Femme NY* in the checkout lane of your average supermarket, but serious fashion people revered the magazine's unpredictable fusion of celebrity and street culture. *Femme NY* had discovered supermodel Ludmila Gorchakova when she was still a magician's assistant in Atlantic City, before she became Millie Gordon the Christian pop singer. Their pages might feature the pregnant Duchess of Sarracena next to a story on Japanese Goth bands. Most recently, *Femme NY* had scored post-op photos of former child star Charlie Donnegan, beloved as Dickie Baker on the 1970s family sitcom "Baker's Dozen"; as Charlene, Donnegan dazzled in the spring collection from up-and-coming designer Michael Kors. There were all sorts of rumors about Richard Molineux, the magazine's founder, but I wasn't enough of an insider to know any of them. If you believed Page Six, *everyone* in the fashion business was secretly gay (or straight, if they were gay), addicted to prescription drugs, recovering from liposuction, or laundering money as the silent partner in a nightclub. Apparently we all did our work in our spare time.

I held my breath as Richard Molineux paced back and forth before the wall where our photos were mounted. Darryl, Mr. Koble's prize student, had come up with another example of his crime-scene aesthetic: prone figures in doorways and beneath car fenders, high heels dangling off windowsills, their heads cropped out. I hated it, but we'd been told it was the future — another reason to dislike science fiction, along with those cold metal suits and food replicator pills. Feminist-theory maven Suzanne, another of our teacher's pets, continued her fixation on extreme close-ups of faces, backs and feet; you couldn't hardly see the clothes at all. Another possible future, I supposed; bodies without clothes, books without words, paintings without mountains or bowls of oranges or fat ladies, every idea purified to a bar code. No one's feelings would be hurt because no one would know what the hell was going on.

Richard Molineux kept returning to the spot where my work appeared. I willed him to be looking at something else, to be finding profound meaning in Josiah's tribute to his girlfriend's D-cups. His terse comments on the other students' pictures didn't register with me. Oh, no, there went his hand, taking down my image of a bloody-nosed Cady tilting her head back against Ariana's black woolly shoulder.

"Whose work is this?" I couldn't read anything from his tone.

I exhaled slowly. "Mine, sir." Muffled snickering from the back of the room. Well, excuse me for knowing how to address my elders.

"And you are?" The steel-gray eyes seemed amused.

"Oh, uh, Julian Selkirk. Sorry."

"*Eh bien*, what were you thinking, Mr. Selkirk, when you composed this story?"

It was a *story*? "I, uh, I thought the first scene was beautiful, and then things kind of got out of hand, so I decided to go with it." Well, buy me a corncob pipe and a tractor, because I sure sounded like a hick.

Mr. Koble frowned. Richard Molineux smiled. "Exactly! Theory, it is nothing. If the eye says no, the mind says — who cares?" He pulled a silver pen from his breast pocket and pointed to the first image, the only one that I thought had come out right. "You see, we begin with beauty, and then there is disaster." His pointer moved to the image of Cady's white face stained with a moustache of blood. "There is romance — " he gestured toward Frank's head in the water — " and then we become fools. This is life." He addressed the class. "This is not a trick to be imitated. The only trick is knowing what you are looking at."

With that, he sat down in Mr. Koble's swivel chair, crossed one slim leg over the other, and said no more. His distant expression suggested that his mind had already moved on to other projects, perhaps other continents, leaving our teacher to complete the lowly task of commenting on the other ten students' work. This he did, finally, setting them all to scribbling his pronouncements about composition, lighting, and (his favorite phrase) the importance of keeping one's finger on the pulse of the political situation. Personally, there were a lot of other places I'd sooner put my finger. Ariana said being apolitical was a privilege of white men, but her parents were happily married psychologists in Teaneck, so I wasn't taking any sob stories from her.

I tried without success to catch Richard Molineux's eye. I still wasn't sure whether he'd thought my work was good. Or maybe he was trying to tell me that that wasn't the point — that, in fact, it wasn't even mine. Which is all very well when you're writing *War and Peace*, but clients don't want to hear about you channeling the divine spark, they want you to sell the lipstick. I wondered if beauty itself would become boring, after the hundredth perfect girl, the twentieth first-class flight to Paris. Champagne and caviar, coffee and donuts. Perhaps it had become boring to the icy-calm eyes of Richard Molineux, who felt young again when he saw perfection bleed and boyish strength take a dive.

The bell rang, we scraped our chairs back from our desks and hoisted our bookbags, chattering, griping, somehow let down. When I walked past the front desk, Richard Molineux suddenly addressed me. "Whose is the dress?"

"Oh, that was by Ariana Ziegler," I said. "A friend of mine who's studying design here." I decided to spare him the knowledge that she was the other girl in the photo; not her finest hour.

He nodded approvingly. "But it is ruined, I suppose."

"I'm sure she could make another one. But maybe not exactly like it, because that front bit, with the pearls…" I hated to admit it. "Well, it was kind of…a Chanel purse, in a past life."

"A Chanel!" For the first time, I heard how Richard Molineux laughed: a short, dry cough. "You are two of a kind." He handed me a business card from a silver case in his jacket pocket. "Send me these pictures, and how you spell your friend's name." He walked away to speak with Mr. Koble, and I understood that I was dismissed — the clearest thing about our entire conversation.

Its import became clearer, if not more believable, a few days later when his assistant (a treble-voiced man who spoke as if he had beans stuffed up his nose) phoned to tell me that *Femme NY* wanted to run three of my photos — *my photos!* — as a front-of-the-book item in April. Stammering, I agreed to accept the princely sum of $250, which I'd mentally spent before I laid the phone down. I knew a shoestore in the West 30s that specialized in hard-to-find sizes; there was a pair of size-12 gold slingbacks in Miss Anna's future. A gift certificate to NYC Fabric House might get Ariana talking to me again; right now she was even ignoring the free cookies I saved her from my cafeteria shift. Another fifty to bribe Stan to take Frank out to dinner, and that left me with negative twenty-five dollars for Cosmos and dry-cleaning. But, like Uncle Curtis said when he pawned Aunt Louella's wedding china, if you don't invest in yourself, no one else will.

As it turned out, Ariana couldn't stay mad at me, even before the check cleared, because she needed moral support for a trip to the Junior Misses section of Macy's to buy an actual dress — one that she couldn't cut up or decorate with fabric-marker hieroglyphics — for her brother's bar mitzvah. Worse yet, I was invited.

"Do they know I'm not your date?" I asked for the third or fourth time, as Ariana scowled at the price tag on a size-fourteen navy blue dress with polka dots.

"Oh, sure. They're totally cool. We have a gay uncle."

"Is he cute?"

"*Julian.*" She punched my arm. "If I can't be myself at this party, neither can you."

I pretended to be downcast, but was inwardly relieved that we were back to normal. Besides, at a party of two hundred people, there would have to be at least five who might swing my way; it was in the Kinsey Report.

All thoughts of becoming Mrs. Dr. Grossman fled my mind, however, when the phone rang in my dorm room that night. "Selkirk Studios, how may I direct your call?"

"You got that magazine we were in yet?"`

"Hello to you too," I told Phil. Silence. Breathing, or static? I didn't hear the click of a hung-up phone, so I relented and said, "It's not coming out till April."

"Haven't seen the pictures, even," he grumbled.

"Frank didn't show them to you?"

"Shut up."

"Hey, I'm just asking," I said brightly, "since we're all being so open with each other."

"I'm not with Frank anymore. Obviously."

"Not even part-time?"

"Nah, he turned out to be a girl, even when he took off the makeup."

"You think only girls fall in love?"

Another pause. "Who said anything about love?" His voice was husky.

"I did."

The silence stretched out like a tightrope. Finally, he asked, "You doing anything tonight?"

"Just sitting here studying my Torah portion."

"Maybe...I could come over and see how the photos came out? If your crazy roommate won't be in the way."

"Yeah, I guess you could do that," I said. Dmitri had actually become much more cooperative since I had gotten his girlfriend into a real live magazine, though he still refused to compromise on his excremental choice of wall art. As for Cady, once the blood had dried, she'd taken the whole episode as an enormous joke. That girl had style.

But, Dmitri wouldn't have to find out if I just temporarily took the Serrano down, so that Phil and I could renew our acquaintance. Fucking a lapsed altar boy under a picture of Jesus was the kind of thing that could bring on the apocalypse.

I stopped in front of the poster, for once looking straight-on at the image I'd grown used to avoiding, the familiar cruciform plunging through a red-gold cloud — of liquid, light or air? — really the only lush spot of color amid our whitewashed walls and fibreboard furniture. Cindy Crawford on the beach was all coolness next to its blurry heat. Disgusting thing, silly gesture, unearned rebellion. I wished I could see it through the eyes of Richard Molineux. I guess it could be beautiful, if you looked at it a certain way, but whether that was the way I was supposed to look at it, I still couldn't say.

Part II: Home Away From Home

(Spring 1992)

8

"No repeats," I told Phil. Again.

"What if there's no one new around?"

Phil's sulky tone, and the tickling of his fingers up my bare leg, distracted me in opposite ways from fixing us the sole breakfast dish in my repertoire, green tea and cheese grits, with a little something extra to chase away his hangover. "Try a different club. This is New York. They have more than one."

"I don't tell you what to do at your fancy-ass parties."

"There are no parties. The only time I get down on my knees is to fix the wind machine." Fourteen-hour days in the studio didn't leave me much time to enjoy the no-strings-attached side of our relationship. Sure, I'd squeezed in a few gropes and groans in the back room of New Eden, jolts of furtive pleasure that left me dizzy with the momentary assurance that catching a boy like Phil hadn't been just a fluke. Until I remembered that he could have the same adventures, and more, all day at the Ironman, training athletes who bench-pressed more than I weighed, while I was hauling tripods on the subway.

"So...no repeats, right?" I breathed out in a rush, before his hand between my legs could sidetrack the conversation. My arm jostled the pot on the stove, spattering the dingy wall.

"Okay, okay," he murmured into my neck. His breath was hot, like cigarette embers. Phil was like that, rough words at cross-purposes with his body language. I was happier when I only believed half of it.

"And no bringing them back here." I pressed my advantage, and my hip into his groin.

"You paying rent?"

"I will be, next month, I promise. But that's not the point. I thought maybe, out of the goodness of your heart, you would spare me the sight of somebody else's pubes on my soap when I shower in the morning."

"Come on, maybe you'd like one of them. Probably take him away from me 'cause you're so gorgeous."

You're all I want, I nearly said, but smiled and settled for the compliment, rather than admit something I wasn't sure was true. Two months into living with Phil, and more than a year since our first hookup, I was working up the nerve to clarify our open relationship, and gaining a begrudging appreciation for its opposite. Marriage has the advantage of simplicity, like government forfeiture of your assets. Over here: you get the last name, the bankbook, the steering wheel, the 60-hour workweek, and the drunken tumble with your wife's best friend. And you: here's the kids, the white dress, the dinner table, the paid-up mortgage, and the moral high ground. As for me, right now the good life looked like a mattress in the basement with only two pairs of sneakers by the door, but this was proving more complicated than ordering a McDonald's Happy Meal without the fries.

I was in my final semester at the Fashion Institute of Technology, and interning as an unpaid assistant to the photographer Dane Langley. More like assistant to the assistants; while Pierre accompanied Dane to Paris and Vince lunched with ad agency reps, I fixed lighting equipment and shopped for organic baby food. Everyone at school said I was lucky to have landed a spot with Langley, who had done album covers for Paula Abdul and Gloria Estefan, and had an ad contract with Revlon. Last week his girlfriend had dropped by with their new baby, which they left with me, sans backup diaper, while they went to lunch at Lutèce. The baby's name was Taylor, which didn't give me a clue to its gender. I figured, since the girlfriend was Swedish, it might respond to Abba, and indeed, it fell asleep for a full twenty-five minutes after I sang "Dancing Queen" four-and-a-half times.

Between these glamorous assignments and my job pouring three-dollar coffees at The Big Cup, I was barely at school anymore except to pick up my mail. Phil had resisted my switching my address to his apartment, claiming that his sublet wasn't, technically speaking, totally legal. On the bright side, this spared me from telling my parents that I was living with him.

Having a male roommate wasn't suspicious in itself, but combined with a career in fashion, and the fact that Phil and I could quote long stretches of dialogue from "The Prince of Tides," my mother might be forced to recognize that her sensitive boy was experimenting with the homosexual lifestyle. Then would come the weekly letters, suddenly seeded with references to girls I hadn't thought about since junior high, who had all grown up to be God-fearing, bosomy A-students and were miraculously still single. Last week in Dane's studio I had seen *Allure* cover model Cheryl Kingston's rose-tipped breasts, pale and translucent as porcelain teacups. I was replacing the roll of seamless paper for the backdrop, and she ignored me, as was her right. Dane was all honey to her, a come-to-Papa smile on his swarthy bearded face. She didn't have to worry about being touched, not like your average Tatiana or Mary Lou, as Dane guided them into poses for some designer's spring catalog, his hand steering this one's waist, unbuttoning that one's sweater. The Swedish girlfriend was half his age. They seemed very happy, but that was probably because her mother knew where to send her mail.

I was sorting through the latest stack of bills and credit card offers on our bed one morning while Phil fed me strawberries. He could be very sweet. Just when I'd gotten used to his blue-collar tough-guy routine, he'd surprise me with little things like washing my back in the shower, or reading to me from one of the books he read to make up for not going to college. As pillow talk, I ranked the *I Ching* above *Atlas Shrugged* but below *Arnold: The Education of a Bodybuilder*. But it's the thought that counts. Without Phil, I might have forgotten that there were publications without pictures in them.

Leaning back against Phil's warm bare stomach, I tossed my junk mail on the floor without looking through it. He ran juice-stained fingers through my hair. Sometimes I was so happy that a place like this existed, where I could be with a guy, naked and alone. He understood what it meant, too, a privilege that was all ours, no matter how many hours we spent running other people's errands.

"Wait, that looks like a real letter," he said, picking an envelope out of the discard pile.

I recognized my mother's square ivory-tinted stationery. "See, I told you I'd be able to pay the rent."

After depositing two fifties in the coffee tin on the windowsill (I never worried about our communal accounting; Phil had too much pride to be a sponger), I skimmed the closely written pages. "Huh, my sister's looking at colleges in — whoa!" I caught my breath and my vision blurred for a moment. My jerky hands hunted around for the envelope. "What's the postmark on this letter?"

Phil found the cast-off envelope under our rumpled blanket. "Last Monday. Why?"

"You see, this is what happens because I don't get my mail here," I snapped at him.

"Man, we've been *through* this. What is your problem?"

I reread the paragraph that had raised my heart rate faster than a triple espresso. "They're coming."

"Who? Where? Careful, your elbow's in the bowl." Phil rescued the strawberries in time to spare me from washing the sheets twice this month.

"My family. Here. Next week."

Unreal, an invasion from another world. I could handle them, barely, if they stayed put in Marietta, in a past that I could revisit on holidays. As for Laura Sue, I was glad she was moving away for college, but didn't want her trailing me around New York, looking primly over my shoulder.

Phil didn't see cause for alarm. "They won't come *here*," he said confidently, gesturing at our meager space.

"Well, I've got to do *something* with them."

"Take them on a Circle Line cruise and push them overboard when everyone's doing the electric slide."

Ignoring him, I read further down the page. "Laura Sue's interviewing at NYU. She's decided she wants to be a social worker."

"Oh, great." Phil chewed a strawberry with his mouth open.

"Taking kids away from their parents 'cause they've got holes in their shoes."

"You know, for once, this isn't about you and your class resentment."

"Who said it was?"

"Just be nice."

"Eh. Nice is for people who believe in Santa." He ran his hands down my chest, and then lower. "But you're all grown up, aren't you?"

I hastened to assure him on this point, which naturally led to the sheets getting dirty again.

9

BECAUSE MY LIFE WASN'T INSANE ENOUGH, I decided we had to throw a dinner party for my parents. Sure, this was New York, city of eight million restaurants, but did any of them serve Daddy's favorite chicken-fried steak with marshmallow sweet potatoes? Did Mario Batali know how to skin a squirrel?

As kids, we'd frightened each other by reading aloud from the less well-thumbed pages of my mother's copy of *The Joy of Cooking*. "Skin, clean and soak overnight: 1 raccoon." "Beaver tail: Hold over open flame." Mama, by contrast, had made her reputation in the pages of *Southern Living* with more highbrow cuisine, the kind that involved putting little paper frills on the meat after you'd killed and roasted it.

Of my family, she alone looked forward to bragging about my future *Vogue* byline. Daddy had put my brother, fresh out of the University of Georgia with a C average, in charge of a townhouse building job in Smyrna. Carter was tooling around Cobb County in a brand-new silver Buick and cultivating a taste for single-malt scotch, hopefully not at the same time. As for my shy, serious little sister, though Daddy typically thought of women as coffeemakers with tits, he was pretty puffed-up that one of his offspring had a shot at a top-tier college. Falling below Lulu in the pecking order was too much for me to bear. Daddy didn't know how to praise one person without putting down another. Hence my vision of showing them the life of a successful fashion photographer, with wine and good food, an apartment overlooking Times Square, and maybe a lingerie model or two to feign attraction to me for the price of a meal.

If I'd said any of this to Phil, he would have talked me out of it, so I went to our friend Tomas. He wasn't making much money as a line cook at a French restaurant near Carnegie Hall, but he'd hooked up with an older guy, a violinist, who was letting him live rent-free in his apartment while the guy toured with the Romanian Philharmonic. "What do I have to do for you to let me use your place for one night?" I asked Tomas.

"You could do *me*." He slid closer to me on the white leather couch.

"Thanks for making me feel like a whore." I didn't move away, though. "What is it with fags, why does everything have to be about fucking? It's so predictable."

"Fine, I want sex *and* a pair of Bruno Magli shoes." Tomas pouted, half-seriously, knowing I wouldn't deliver the one and couldn't afford the other. We'd had fun together a couple of times, but sleeping with two people I saw on a regular basis would get weird in a hurry. Phil acted like there could never be too much sex. He would scope out a nightclub like a football player honing in on the strategic spot in a scrimmage. A few hard knocks and you were all pals afterwards. Tomas, I surmised, would be more of a champagne-and-roses guy, which I suppose I am too, but two of us in the same household would fight like cats in a handbag.

"Look, Tomas, this is your opportunity to show your creativity. You're always saying how bored you are, chopping vegetables all day. Imagine the possibilities — *coq au vin en croute! Parfum de volailles printanière!*"

Tomas snickered. "That's not even a real dish."

"Ah — but it *could* be."

"Spring chicken perfume?"

"Whatever. You're the detail man. Just give us the list, Phil and I will buy the groceries and take care of the washing-up. It'll be great."

10

THE DAY BEFORE my family was due to arrive, Tomas played master chef and Phil and I hauled groceries up to his apartment. He had planned an elegant menu: Cornish hens, scalloped potatoes, a fine Bordeaux, and a dessert that he was keeping secret. I hoped it didn't involve open flames.

Unable to take me for a spin in the violinist's Jacuzzi with Tomas watching, Phil had to wait for his consolation in our modest bathtub. We dimmed the yellowish ceiling globe to a flicker, the poor man's candlelight. He dug his heels into my back and shoved my face down into the foamy water between his legs. I stuck my soap-slick fingers inside him, grazing his balls with my nails. We splashed and bumped around, ignoring our bruised knees as we rubbed our hard, impatient flesh together.

Afterward, in the cooling water, he washed my hair so gently that I almost said I loved him. Words were hard for us, our own words. Schwarzenegger's memoir didn't quite provide the relevant *bon mot*.

"Failure is not an option," I read aloud from a page Phil had bookmarked. "Everyone has to succeed."

In response, he rolled onto his side of the mattress and stubbed out his cigarette in the ashtray on the floor by his pillow. "If everyone succeeds, what's success? You got an answer for that, Ah-nuld?"

"Maybe everyone succeeds at different things. Like, right now, you're succeeding at being an asshole."

"Yeah, but I'm *your* asshole." He laughed, sunshine after rain, and pulled the blanket over us. I expected more, but he lay still, his head tucked under my chin, the way he liked to sleep. I reached up for the switch that shut off the overhead light. One thing I could say for this apartment, everything was in easy reach. I could have cooked breakfast while sitting on the toilet.

Awhile later, in the dark, he said, "You wouldn't lie to me, Julian, right?"

"What would I lie about?"

"Nothing."

"Phil, you know, if you really wanted to be exclusive, I'd give it a shot. Otherwise, please let's not dish the details."

"You're lying to them." His voice sounded mad, but his thick fingers were entwined with mine, warm and strong, squeezing my hand.

"Lying is my family's preferred form of communication. It's traditional and cultural, like chopsticks."

"But you're different."

"When I'm with you, I am." I kissed his blond hair. He liked that, but the questions weren't over yet.

"Who are you going to say I am?"

"You're my roommate," I said firmly. I've always tried to avoid pointless arguments, and since it seems to me there's scarcely any other kind, I consider myself a fairly easy person to live with.

"And my bed-mate." Phil climbed on top of me and tickled me unmercifully. "And my soul-mate, and my...mating mate."

We tussled a bit before settling down to sleep. Could I have bargained with him then, traded my coming-out for his fidelity? How terribly serious that would have been, all of a sudden, how much like buying the ring and booking the chapel. Like the readers of *Woman's Day*, I wanted to have it all: "Five Delicious Cake Recipes!" *and* "Thin Thighs in Thirty Days."

11

MY FAMILY had booked a room at a hotel across from Madison Square Garden. I sat in the lobby for nearly an hour, waiting for their taxi to arrive from the airport. Groups of Japanese airline stewardesses and Russian beauticians traversed the russet-colored marble lobby, dressed in uniforms and towing identical black suitcases on wheels. I took a few pictures, from sheer boredom, and ate the honey-roasted peanuts I'd bought from a street vendor for lunch.

There, I saw Daddy's broad-shouldered figure in the crowd, wrestling his suitcase through the hotel's revolving door. A stranger would have thought him handsome in a fleshy way, with his strong jaw and combed-back fair hair going gray, a casting director's pick for senator or tough-but-beloved football coach. My chest tightened at the sight, an instinct from years of waiting for him to come through the door after work, preparing to read his mood. Then I told myself to snap out of it. He was on my turf now.

Mama was behind him, hoisting her paisley carry-on bag in one hand, patting down her henna curls with the other. I avoided eye contact with them while I scanned the sea of heads for Laura Sue's auburn pixie cut. My sister appeared through a side door, and I ran to her first. Her hair had grown out, and was pulled back in a headband, accentuating the old-fashioned look of her pale blue shirtwaist dress. Her face lit up when she spotted me. I felt an unexpected twinge of joy in my chest, driving out the anxiety and resentment that were always close companions *chez* Selkirk. What the hell, I was home, or home had come to me.

"Lulu! Welcome to the big city!" I hugged her tightly.

She squeezed me back. "It's so good to see you, Jule. It feels like it's been forever." The light in her eyes was sincere, but her face looked paler and thinner than I remembered.

"Are you feeling okay?"

"Just a rough flight." She kept smiling, hanging onto my arm. "After they're settled, maybe we could — "

But then our parents were upon us, and I duly kissed Mama's powdered cheek (feeling another pang at the familiar whiff of Estée Lauder "White Linen") and surprised Daddy with the strength of my handshake (one benefit of dating a personal trainer, even one who dried his sweatsocks in the oven to save money at the laundromat). Daddy was in a jovial mood and freely shared his impressions of the airport ("why did they put in those murals of Mexicans?"), the Pakistani cab driver, and his first sight of Manhattan in a decade ("best damn skyline in the world, and that's my professional opinion"). I laughed in all the right places and carried the ladies' bags to the elevator. Upstairs, the hotel was decidedly less impressive, a warren of identical hallways with gray walls and well-trodden forest green carpeting.

"So, this is what you folks call a suite?" Daddy propped the door open with his suitcase and scanned the room: two double beds, a desk, a swivel chair and an armchair, all freely sharing one another's personal space. The bathroom was about the size of the elevator, with checkerboard tiles and a claw-footed bathtub.

"Yeah, Sweet 'n Low," I said.

Daddy laughed and slapped me on the back. "Hell yeah. Bitsy, looks like you're gonna sleep in the bathtub." To me, he said, "What kind of place do you live in?"

"My...friend and I share a studio." I set the bags on the luggage stand. Mama darted into the bathroom to touch up her face, while my sister lowered herself into the armchair that was wedged between the bed and the radiator, and looked out the window at the lit marquee of the Garden. Daddy let the door slam.

"Must be doing well, taking pictures of ladies' panties."

"Daddy, in New York, 'studio' means 'closet with indoor plumbing'."

"Hey, don't go getting all het-up. I'd like a cushy job like that myself. Beats pouring concrete into a hole in the ground."

I shrugged, as always thinking it best to let him have the last word, and sat down on the footstool beside Laura Sue. "Looks exciting out there, huh?" I teased her. "Daddy, if you and Mama want to relax before dinner, I can take Lulu on a tour of Herald Square."

"Yes, let's," my sister said, suddenly animated.

"What are you talking about, we just got here, we're gonna see the damn sights!" Daddy boomed. "Life is short and so's your mother. Right, Bitsy?"

"I wouldn't mind lying down for just a little bit," Mama wavered, but she still had her coat on, so it was a lost cause.

"Come on, you can rest on the bus."

Resistance being futile, Daddy hustled us all onto the upper deck of one of those red tour buses that clog the arteries of Times Square, their sides plastered with advertisements for "Cats". As we crawled along, the driver announced over his loudspeaker that we were "now passing the NBC Studios, home of 'Cheers' and 'The Tonight Show'." My mother shared a moment of enthusiasm with the German lady beside her. I pulled my hat down lower.

"Are we passing a mattress factory? Because I might need to jump," Lulu whispered.

"Just lie back and think of the Empire State Building."

"Jule…tonight…we've got to get away. Just you and me."

"On your left, the world-famous Harley-Davidson Cafe!" the loudspeaker blared. The German lady's son made "vroom-vroom" sounds. Daddy grunted. He believed motorcycles were for Democrats having a midlife crisis.

Daddy made us get off the bus before it reached the Plaza Hotel, saying the exhaust fumes were ruining his trip. "Great city, New York, but do they know how to build a road? Takes a damn hour to go half a mile."

"You know what the bumper stickers say, it's the journey, not the destination," I said.

"Right now I want to take a journey to the bottom of a cup of coffee. You got any good places to eat around here?" He nudged me. "Someplace where the models hang out?"

They were suitably impressed by the Bryant Park Cafe, a hushed, wood-paneled establishment tucked up against the imposing marble backside of the 42nd Street Library. We didn't see any models, because they don't feed in the daytime, but the thin, haughty girlfriends of the young lawyers around us were glamorous enough to make Daddy feel he was getting his money's worth. His money, because when I tried to pick up the check, he slapped my wallet away.

"I guess you can take this one," I said, "because tomorrow night you're getting your own private chef."

"Ooh, le French chef," Daddy jested.

"Spanish, actually."

"Oh, honey, you know Mexican food gives me…difficulties," Mama said.

"No, real Spanish. From Spain," I said, to avoid any misunderstanding. "And it's going to be great, we've got excellent wine, and a surprise dessert, and Phil and I helped make the stuffing for the Cornish hens — "

"Who's Phil?" Laura Sue asked.

"My roommate."

"Is he handsome?" Mama winked at my sister, who didn't respond.

"Very," I said without thinking. My face grew hot with anxiety that they'd figure out the truth. Real guys don't notice how other guys look. Laura Sue understood, because she was careful not to meet my eyes. She was the only one who knew about me, officially; my brother had probably guessed by now, but didn't care.

I remembered that late spring afternoon, right before I left for college, the scents of lilacs and laundry detergent wafting on the warm breeze through the windows of the den. The TV newscaster was talking about us the way they did back then, as boys dying or pretending to die, lying down on the street outside the White House in black *Silence=Death* T-shirts, six-foot-tall bald creatures in feather boas bursting into St. Patrick's Cathedral. I'd thought I was alone in the room. *Don't be like that,* my sister had murmured. I faced her quietly, undefended. Laura Sue, who still kept a diary with pink sticker hearts on the cover. *I'm worried about you,* she'd said, as solemnly as the little girl who had made me take her doll's temperature by sticking a cocktail stirrer in its mouth. And so we'd sat on the couch and watched the rest of the news together, holding hands.

"Hey, you know who lives in New York?" Daddy exclaimed. The pretty Asian waitress interrupted to drop off his credit card, beaming at his generous tip. "Andy Crosby! You remember my old business partner Andy Crosby? I should call him up, see if he wants to knock back a few beers. How about it, son — you want to come along, learn how to drink with the big boys?"

I could fantasize about matching Daddy glass for glass like Indiana Jones, but I'd promised Lulu some private time. "Thanks, but you'll have to school me later. I've got an end-of-term project to finish. As someone once told me, 'You've got to work hard before you play hard.'"

Daddy was pleased to hear one of his maxims quoted back to him. I thanked him for dinner and excused myself to take a walk with my sister while he escorted Mama back to the hotel. My mood was bright as a Macy's Christmas window. Daddy was talking to me like a man, if only for want of competition.

Laura Sue asked to go someplace quiet. I had to think for a minute. "Carriage ride through Central Park?" She shook her head with an indulgent smile. "You're right, you didn't come all this way just to look at another horse's ass." She let out a small laugh that sounded more like a cough, or a sob.

"Hey, hey," I said, holding her, patting her back. "It'll get better. You'll be in college before you know it. Then all you'll have to worry about is keg parties and all-nighters."

"You got out," she said, her voice low and intense, unlike her usual girlish tones. "I've got to get out."

"I'll be here." I meant it, without believing it completely. She might need a hand to hold, before she found new girlfriends, but after a couple of months the phone calls would grow more infrequent. Which was fine, because what could I tell her about my life — that Dane did coke with Cheryl Kingston in the bathroom between takes; that I got a five-cent tip for putting too much milk in some guy's grande mocha skim latte?

We walked up Fifth Avenue, past Tiffany's and toward the lower edge of Central Park. Finding the Plaza's red carpets and chandeliers too overstimulating, we came to rest on a bench not far into the park, on that winding path of hexagonal cobblestones where the caricature artists would line up in daylight. Under a dark row of trees, our privacy was broken only by the occasional carriage horse plodding through his circuit.

Laura Sue and I peered upward at the one or two stars we could spot through the city's atmosphere. The canopy of leaves flickered above us, lit from beneath by dim greenish light globes on poles. "Jule...when do you think...a person gets a soul?"

"Are we talking about anyone in particular?"

"Just...anyone." She picked at the peeling polish on one fingernail, an old habit of hers.

"I don't know, isn't the soul the same as the person? In the stories, when you sell your soul, you're the one who goes to...New Jersey." I broke off. "This isn't helping, is it?"

Lulu was quiet for a bit. "Do you still attend church?"

"Sometimes." I prayed, anyhow. Silently, so Phil wouldn't crack a joke about altar boys on their knees. When I was growing up, I used to look forward to Sunday mornings: crisp clothes, French cocoa for breakfast, Mama and Daddy bookending us in the red-cushioned pews of our Baptist church, straight-backed and smiling and so wonderfully silent as the praise band struck up its first reverent yet gentle melody. Those times when Daddy slept in with a sore head, it was an extra twenty minutes of heaven for the four of us, in the car with the radio burbling doo-wop oldies, till the inevitable right turn into the church parking lot cut off my guilty fantasy that we could keep on going. *Some glad morning, when this life is over.* Now Sundays were the only day

Phil and I both had off, so the closest I generally came to a house of worship was driving Dane to important funerals. The back pages of the *Times* were full of them, those discreet half-columns for designers dead at 38, 40, 46: lived, loved, invented the T-shirt dress, died, details of last illness not disclosed.

"Can you keep a secret?" My sister seized my hand.

"I grew up in this family, you have to ask?"

"No, a real secret. Not the kind nobody talks about — the kind nobody knows." Her voice was high and tight with nerves.

"Yes, for you, yes."

She bowed her head and took a deep breath. "I — I'm pregnant."

"Oh fuck."

"You've got to help me." She gripped my fingers painfully. I tried to put my arms around her but she shrank away.

"What about...the guy?" I said stupidly. I couldn't bring myself to say "father".

"We broke up. It doesn't matter now."

"But does he know?"

"You don't understand." She dug her nails into my hand. "I'm getting *out*."

My mind raced. Like me, Laura Sue took after the Dupuis side of the family, thin and fine-boned. There was no way she could disguise her pregnancy weight till college started this fall. "Okay. Jesus. Okay. I'll find you a place to stay, up here, a place for both of us. You'll need some excuse to quit high school early — I don't know, a religious thing? Remember when Uncle Curtis cheated on Aunt Louella and she made him go on that prayer retreat?"

"Jule," she said bitterly, "this isn't *The Three Musketeers*. You can't stick me in a convent." She stared at the cobblestone walkway curving into the darkness of the trees. "I can't do this alone. I need you to go with me to the clinic."

"No — not — " I bit back words that would only make her feel worse. *My niece, my nephew.* Why did I have to be the only person who knew about this? Unfair, to make their lives depend on my belief in their little Tinkerbell souls.

"I already made the appointment for Thursday. I called from a pay phone at the airport while Mama and Daddy were in baggage claim."

When had my sister learned how to arrange a secret abortion? Cigarettes, drugs, sex, any kid could score on a street corner, but this — she might as well have told me that she'd dismembered a body in her bathtub, which on a micro scale wasn't far from the truth. Surely she remembered our youth group piling into buses headed for Washington every January, with our Precious Feet pins on our ski jackets and our cardboard-mounted photos of tiny severed heads.

"Please, Lulu." I blinked away tears. "You should get out, of course you should, but isn't there another way? One where you don't have to hurt...yourself, or...anyone else, you know what I mean?"

"Sure, you want to send another child to be raised by Mama and Daddy? Talk about hurt."

"So what does that mean? We should never have been born?"

"This isn't *about* you." Her voice broke. "I really hoped you, out of everyone, would care about me for a change. But no, you've got yours, showing off your big success. Whether I go to college is an afterthought."

"That's not fair! Yes, I'm doing well, that's why I could help you take care of the — the baby, somehow — " I promised wildly.

"You and your boyfriend?"

"I told you, he's my roommate, nothing more."

"But you're still — " My sister left the word "gay" unspoken in the air, that word with its cheap sparkles of fairy dust. Queer, fag, homo: these were names for boys to call each other, names she'd never say. Perverted, sinful, abomination: words for the doctors and the preachers, sharp instruments from their bag of tricks. Fruit, queen, nancy, light in the loafers: jokes for our parents' comedians, those fat men in their wives' dresses.

"I've changed a lot since I came to New York," I said. "I'm thinking that might have been just a phase."

The sarcasm was there if she'd been willing to hear it. Which of us was the hypocrite? Which one had actually changed? Though her judgments hurt me, I'd tried to sympathize with her need for faith's absolutes, the rock she clung to and I stumbled over. But it seemed she had one standard for me and another for herself.

Too wrapped up in her dilemma to celebrate this narrow escape for my immortal soul, my sister scrubbed the tears from her eyes and straightened her headband. "If I go through with it Thursday, you will come with me?"

"Promise me you'll think it over again tomorrow?"

Her shoulders sagged. "All right. I promise." And because we were both Selkirks, it was easy for us to believe that the other person was telling the truth, despite what we knew of our own duplicity.

I took a cab back to the hotel with Laura Sue, who was skittish about the subway, and from there walked downtown to Phil's place. Letting myself into our basement apartment, I saw — and smelled — it from a newly sober perspective. The funk of cigarettes, wet clothes, old newspapers, and suspiciously recent sex disgusted me. The only kind of family I could raise here would have whiskers and a tail. In the darkness I made out Phil's white unclothed body on the mattress. I decided against waking him to fill him in on our family drama. In the morning, maybe I would do the laundry. I opened the bathroom door, anticipating a hot shower to blast my tension away.

"Whoa!" A bronzed, trim young man, naked except for his socks and a Tom Selleck mustache, hopped backward as I stepped inside. Now, I am a flexible person, and believe in seizing every opportunity, and under normal circumstances I might even appreciate that my boyfriend had left me this reasonably well-hung surprise. However, Magnum P.I. here was not meeting me at my best. I shut the door in his face, and reflected with irritation that I couldn't even freeze Phil out by sleeping on the couch, that eternal refuge of jilted husbands, because we didn't have a couch.

But Tomas did.

12

My morning shift at The Big Cup passed excruciatingly slowly at first. As I went through the motions of grinding coffee and steaming milk, I pictured Laura Sue in her navy blue interview suit, speaking with modest assurance about how rewarding it was to clean up inner-city playgrounds with her Baptist youth group. And me, what tidy story could I make of my life? My goals were three or four times removed from what I was doing with my actual time, like those cartoon devices where the cat knocks the marble out of the birdcage into the scales that flip on the switch that sets the time bomb ticking to blow up the bank. Coffee was my income; Dane's errands left me hardly any time to build up my portfolio. I needed a fresh, edgy idea to present to *Femme NY* before they forgot who I was.

"Excuse me, is that decaf? I asked for decaf," a sweet, tentative voice asked.

"Oh, I'm sorry, I was distracted." My customer was an Indian girl about my age with lively brown eyes. "Here, you can have this one on me, if you tell me where you got that purse. Isn't that from Nina Ricci's new collection?"

She gave a shy little laugh. "How did you know?"

"I'm studying to be a fashion photographer, but it doesn't pay much at first, that's why I work here." I presented her with two cups of coffee, one decaf, the other regular. The man behind her in line shuffled his feet impatiently, but didn't interrupt us, maybe remembering his own desperate pickup strategies from the past. "Hang on, let me help this guy, but I'd like to ask you something."

While I stirred and foamed and poured, I said to the girl, "Do you mind if I take a picture of you, for my portfolio? You've got such a great look, really cute and up-to-date. I promise to send you a copy."

She was hesitant, but still smiling, torn between flattery and self-preservation, as girls always are.

"Don't worry," I added, "I have a boyfriend."

At that she relaxed, and agreed. I gave her one of Dane's cards, explaining that he was my boss, so she'd know I was honest. Taking an unscheduled five-minute break, I snapped a couple of pictures of her, with the sunlight from the window picking up the golden flecks in her eyes and firing the colors of her orange silk scarf. That morning I tried my new technique on five other girls and got two sets of pictures, one of a very tall girl with deep black skin and size-zero jeans, and the other a pair of Spanish-speaking teens in leather caps and fluffy jackets. The free coffee came out of my paycheck, but at last I felt like I was working, planning for a future that might include someone besides myself.

We had decided to tell my family that Tomas was house-sitting for the violinist, who was not around to disclose what else my friend had been sitting on. One of the oldest tricks in the real-estate business is to bake cookies in a house you're trying to sell. The agent who moved a lot of Daddy's properties had once given him, as a joke, a spray-can of cookie aroma, designed for busy people to simulate the home-baked scent. As I recall, it was something like cinnamon mixed with artificial butter-flavored popcorn. If you could compress the air of family stability into a can, would it smell of roasting Cornish hens, candle smoke, stacks of yellowing sheet music, and fresh lilacs in a glass vase? I certainly hoped so.

Phil and I arrived separately, me from school, him from work. At the gym, he'd showered and changed into khaki slacks and a plaid sport coat that no self-respecting gay person would wear. Even so, it didn't disguise the splendid muscles of his back and biceps. I wanted to run my hands over the cheap wool weave. I knew his vibes too well, though, the crackling of static when he was in an untouchable mood. Fine, we would be Method actors tonight, getting into character as roommates, forgoing that last supportive kiss. We helped Tomas set the table, folding the violinist's maroon linen napkins on top of gold-edged china plates. Tomas hummed the bullfight song from "Carmen" as he tossed the salad. Ariana, who had agreed against her better judgment to be my date, arrived looking elegant in a black cardigan with metallic threads over a belted gray dress, both of her own design. She'd never be beautiful, but twenty years from now, all the beautiful people would clamor to attend her parties.

"You look like someone who could hit me up for a million bucks," I said. "What's your favorite charity?"

"You are." She winked at me and made a beeline for Phil, greeting him with atypical enthusiasm, as if to console him for the deception.

Just as Tomas was beginning to fret that the birds were drying out in the oven, my family arrived. Introductions were made all around. I hugged my sister. She was pale but more relaxed than the day before. I'd meant to seat her between Ariana and me, but when we approached the table, I found that someone (who else but Phil?) had reshuffled the place cards so that she was next to Tomas while I was stuck between Phil and Daddy.

Tomas had thrown every possible flourish into the salad, an assortment of greens with more exotic shapes than a Thierry Mugler runway show, plus baby shrimp and some pickled things that could have been Japanese radishes. Older women love Tomas; he's the guy their husbands haven't been since prom night. All he had to do was ask Mama her opinion about trends in regional cuisine and they were off like a house afire. I noticed that he promoted himself to sous-chef when describing his job. Daddy praised the white wine. He and Phil both tossed off a full glass while the rest of us were maneuvering the slippery greens onto our forks. Laura Sue quietly picked the shrimp out of her salad and tucked it under a lettuce leaf. Ariana asked my sister about her college plans. Leaning across me, Daddy and Phil started a friendly argument about whether the Mets could beat the Braves this year. My sister said she'd liked NYU better than Emory, and was hoping to become a social worker for abused children. Mama broke off a discussion of sauce-thickening methods to say that she really didn't think such heavy subjects belonged at the dinner table, dear. Ariana told a funny story about the time the bathtub fell through the ceiling in our dorm. She implied that I spent a lot of time in her room. I swallowed a shrimp tail. Daddy called Mets pitcher Dwight Gooden a faggot. Phil poured another glass of wine.

Tomas and I brought out the Cornish hens on plates sprinkled with parsley flakes. Red wine followed white. The sauce that pooled around the meat was dark red and smelled like stewed fruit. Ariana adjusted her eyeglasses on her snub nose and asked Daddy whether he'd seen our photos in *Femme NY*. My sister didn't know what to do with her Cornish hen. Daddy asked me why I hadn't brought the model as my date. I said she was spending the semester in Russia. Phil ate a drumstick with his hands. Mama asked about my internship with Dane Langley and whether I had met a lot of celebrities. All eyes were temporarily on me, except for Tomas who was showing my sister how to cut the bird apart neatly. Speaking too quickly, like an amateur comedian racing through his material before he forgets it, I told them about setting up a shoot for Dane and Cheryl Kingston on a windy day at Pier 17, and how my job was keeping the seagulls from flying into the lighting umbrellas. Mama said she had read an interview with Cheryl in *Good Housekeeping* and wasn't it a shame about her and that racecar driver. Phil made a joke about my carrying Cheryl's bags, cupping his hands at his chest. Daddy laughed. Tomas sliced Laura Sue's hen down the middle. She covered her mouth with her napkin and raced for the bathroom, but found the linen closet instead. Ariana followed her before I had the chance to stand up. Tomas' face looked like someone had thrown his favorite toy on the ground and stomped on it.

"P-M-S," I mouthed the words to him across the table, but not quietly enough to escape Daddy's notice.

"Now there's a great subject for the dinner table, right, Bitsy?" he winked. "Remember the time you lost it at the Hansons' garden party?" The tell-tale flush, the shine of alcohol, had spread over his wide round face. I nudged Phil to stop refilling our glasses, but he pretended not to understand.

My mother's treble voice climbed even higher up the register. "Yes, we all thought it was the heat, but it turned out I was pregnant with you, dear!" she exclaimed to me.

"She took one look at that egg salad, and — whoops!" Daddy continued his story as if my birth were not the point. Lacking a cigar to re-enact the momentous occasion, Phil lit a cigarette and dropped the match onto the remains of his dinner.

"Lazlo doesn't let people smoke in the house," Tomas fussed.

"Who's Lazlo?" Mama asked.

"He's Julian's imaginary friend," Phil said.

"He's the violinist," I corrected, getting up to clear the plates.

"Well, Lazlo's not here, is he, now?" was Phil's reply.

Daddy chuckled. "You know, that reminds me of what Carter said — Carter's my eldest, you'd like him — one time when Pastor Ed told him he couldn't wear his peewee football uniform to church..."

I escaped to the kitchen. "Tomas," I moaned, as we scraped the salvageable leftovers into Tupperwares, "why did you let me do this? I mean, in what alternate universe would this have been a good idea?"

"Relax. Just wait till I bring out the triple-layer mocha marzipan cheesecake."

Tomas telling me to relax was the living end. "I hope so. It's like the Charge of the fucking Light Brigade out there."

Ariana, solo, stopped by the kitchen to tell us sternly that my sister was allergic to shellfish.

"You didn't warn me," Tomas reproached me.

"She's very self-conscious about it," I fibbed madly, "since my mother's people are from Louisiana." Was it the taste that upset her pregnant stomach, or the resemblance to the tiny pink creature curled inside her?

Ariana came over to take a closer look at me. "*How* much have you had to drink?"

"Not enough."

When we returned to the table, with Tomas bearing the cheesecake on a silver stand, Laura Sue was sitting in my seat. She and Daddy were turned toward Phil while he cheerfully answered Daddy's questions about his background. "Right now I'm a personal trainer, but someday soon I'd like to go back to school to study sports medicine."

"How about that, Laura Sue — a doctor!" Daddy actually sounded impressed.

"Not exactly," Phil demurred, "more like a physical therapist, you know, rehab for injured athletes."

"Yeah, you figure, some of those guys must get paid a bundle to shoot steroids into Deion Sanders's knee."

I listened to their love-fest with half an ear while complying with Mama's request for a photo of herself and Tomas with the cake. It was a grand specimen, decorated with a pattern of light and dark brown ripples that made me think of a ballroom floor. Tomas bragged that he had soaked the espresso beans overnight in Frangelico, and I understood why he had let me walk into this death-trap. He was a mad scientist, caring only for the elegance of his nuclear bomb.

Daddy was still attempting to find common interests for Phil and my sister. It was slow going at first, since Laura Sue was unmoved by sumo wrestling and Phil had scarcely anything to say about theories of early-childhood education, but it turned out they both favored tighter immigration controls and thought Princess Di had been treated shamefully by the Royal Family.

Ariana tucked into a large slice of cake. I ate a few bites off her plate.

"Does she like you?" I whispered.

"Your sister? Yeah, I guess. She's a nice kid."

"Good. Hold my hand."

"Someday you will pay for toying with my girlish affections."

"Please, Ari."

Fresh from her college interviews, Laura Sue was rattling off a list of her extracurriculars. Tomas passed around coffee with brandy. The guys skipped the coffee part. Ariana prepared to feed me a bite of cake. Daddy said something about going bass-fishing with Andy Crosby and asked Phil about his hobbies.

"Not much time for that," Phil said. "Basically, I get off work, I like to go home, take a hot shower, watch 'Entertainment Tonight', and get fucked up the ass by your son."

Ariana dropped the cake on my white shirt. Mama put her hand up to her mouth, that old useless gesture for keeping words in or fists out. I went around the table to my sister but she pushed her chair back and walked stiffly to the bathroom. My stomach churned, as when in dreams you approach that deadly room you always return to, where the black dog leaps out of the shadows and your mother's body is lying on the ground. That place whose furniture you recognize instantly — the crooked picture, the curtains drawn shut — which never stops you from walking back inside, makes it seem more inevitable, in fact, than waking in your own bed.

"The hell you think you are, talkin' like that to me?" Daddy bellowed. He propped himself halfway upright, his big hands spread on the table, and loomed over Phil, who squared his shoulders and jutted out his jaw. Daddy was bigger and meaner, but Phil was in better condition. Either way it wouldn't be pretty.

"Daddy — " Unsteady on my feet, I wedged myself in between them.

"You think I'm the kind of man, you can say that to my face?" Daddy continued to harangue Phil, both of them standing now. Phil said nothing; he was a noble statue, the kind the Greeks prayed to when they still thought beauty could save them from the volcano.

"Phil didn't mean anything, he was making a joke, about me," I pleaded.

"A joke? I'll tell you what's the joke." Daddy turned on me. "You and your fruity friends, inviting us to this dolls' tea party." The sweep of his arm knocked his wine glass to the floor. At the other end of the table, Ariana and Tomas were clearing Lazlo's precious dishes as fast as humanly possible. Mama cried softly into a wadded-up napkin.

"I thought you were doing so *well*," she wailed at me. "I thought everything was just fine."

"'Everythin' was jes' fi-ine,'" Daddy mimicked Mama's soprano drawl. "Only you would think that, Bitsy. Hell, I've known Julie was a fag ever since he cried at the Fourth of July picnic."

"I was scared of the fireworks," I said stupidly, a kid again in sweaty T-shirt and bare feet, listening for the gunshot echo after each burst of gold and silver light.

"That's not what you said," Daddy taunted. "You said you were crying because they were so *byoo-tee-ful.*"

Phil threw the contents of his glass in Daddy's face. My sister chose this moment to return from the bathroom. Daddy's red face grew redder from the wine dripping down into his shirt collar.

"Get out, Phil! Get *out!*" I shoved him backward, my palm against his chest. The hurt in his eyes gave me only a moment's pause.

"Why do you have to be like them? They're never going to want you. Why do you keep doing this?"

"Just go, now!"

Daddy kicked Phil's chair over, but Phil was already at the door, out of range of his fists. Good food and drink, and twenty-five years behind the desk of Selkirk Builders, had robbed my father of the agility to pursue bigger game than women and children.

Laura Sue clung to my shoulder. She dabbed at the cake stain on my shirtfront with a wet napkin, spreading a watery brown smudge all across the breast pocket. "We'd better go," she said.

"Lulu, I'm so sorry, I don't know how this happened."

"It's always like this," she said, sounding much older than her eighteen years. "There's nothing you can do."

"Please don't let this change...your plans."

"Nothing's changed."

When Mama returned from retrieving the family's coats, I bent to kiss her cheek, but she turned aside with a tragic expression. Southern women love no-account men; every smashed glass and squandered dollar is another stitch in their martyrs' robes. In her mind she was probably already toting up the love she had wasted on her second son, starting with her fourteen hours in labor.

So at last it was only me and Tomas and Ariana with the remains of the cheesecake, like seagulls picking through a shipwreck. I washed the dishes in steaming hot water, refusing conversation. Without being asked, Tomas made up my bed on the couch. Ariana dried the dishes with a towel patterned with musical notes, which is not the sort of thing you expect a real musician to have. Maybe they were a gift from Lazlo's mother; maybe she visited once a year from Romania, dropping in unannounced with a box of honey cakes and the phone number of a nice Jewish girl he should call.

"You don't have to do that," I said to Ariana.

"I know." Putting a wineglass down perilously close to the edge of the sink, she came over and kissed me.

"You don't have to do that, either. No one's here."

"Asshole." She held me tight and I pressed my face into her warm hair, letting my tears fall, tears that had nothing to do with beauty, however much I might wish it otherwise, for both of us.

13

THE LENS OF SOBRIETY is a cold one for looking at your life; the morning-after lens, even more so. It's an electron microscope that turns every pore into a crater and magnifies the beastly hairs on the stem of the flower. The plastic baby in my hand was the size of a peach pit, and fit just as neatly into the scuffed red plastic socket of the cross-sectioned womb on the countertop in the examining room. The clinic had to show these fetal models to my sister, some kind of second-chances law passed by Republicans.

I had expected picket signs and nuns lying down in traffic, but had underestimated the anonymity and lack of parking space that defined the Manhattan way of doing business. Our local Planned Parenthood franchise was a discreet suite of rooms on the ninth floor of a high-rise near Columbus Circle. We could have been in a dentist's office, with the same smell of disinfectant, the same Phil Collins songs piped through speakers in the drop ceiling. Only the posters were different, not cartoons of decaying teeth but photos of smiling teen girls, who clearly respected themselves enough to stay in school and use protection. Fashion is aspirational, meaning, not for you. But who you might be, ten years forward or back, with those breasts or without those hips — that's what you see through the lens of the night before, always the best-case scenario. Make the right choices and these girls could be your friends. They could be you.

The nurse let me have a few minutes alone with Laura Sue, while she sat on the examining table in her paper gown and took some painkillers with a cup of juice. I had nothing useful to say. The plastic baby, that low-tech Cracker Jack prize, couldn't compete with the posters promising her her life back.

"What if you're sick afterward? What'll you tell our parents?" The three of them were flying back to Atlanta that night.

"Mama knows I get bad periods. And you know Daddy, the less he hears about 'female troubles', the better."

"I can't believe you're talking about this so...rationally. Step one, step two, step three." I dropped the plastic baby in the garbage. "Okay, there's step one."

My sister didn't cry. This worried me. When we were kids, all I had to do was hold the scissors over Barbie's hair and the waterworks would start. "You're supposed to be here to support me."

"I was ready to support you, but no, you decided your baby was better off dead than raised by two fags."

Her mouth was set in a thin line, and her face was hard, but her hands trembled. She breathed heavily. The music of Kenny G spiraled out of the ceiling speakers, a nasal, directionless melody.

"Oh, Lulu. Oh, Lulu," I repeated, my voice breaking. I rubbed between her thin shoulderblades. She crushed the paper cup in her hands. The nurse came in with another woman in scrubs, and told me to wait outside. She noticed the missing component of her federally-mandated womb display.

"Julian threw it away," I heard my sister say. I closed the door and returned to the waiting room. All the old magazines irritated me, those profligate stacks of faces, their loud opinions about strangers, spread freely as yesterday's newspaper on the floor of a puppy's cage. Goodbye, little Harvey Milk Selkirk or Coco Chanel Selkirk. Jefferson Davis Selkirk will never sit on his uncle's knee. Linda Evangelista Selkirk will not be having tea at the Plaza. Forgive me, Cindy Crawford Selkirk, for I have sinned.

A burly man in jeans walked through the waiting room, swinging a toolbox in his hand, and conferred with the receptionist about her broken fax machine. The heavy tread of his Doc Martens reminded me of Phil. I could no longer avoid asking myself why I hadn't told him what was at stake, before he could sabotage our evening. Because — and surely I had always known this, even as I promised my sister the moon — there was no conversation I could invent that ended in Phil welcoming baby Harvey with open arms, and just as surely I was also relieved to avoid the choice that conversation would have forced upon me.

My sister leaving the clinic looked the same as when she'd gone in: her polite goodbyes to the nurses, her careful steps, the neat fall of her corduroy skirt over her flat belly. In the cab back to the hotel, she promised to call me, I told her I didn't know where I'd be living, promised to call her first. When we reached our destination, she gathered her coat around her, and a twinge made her put her hand to her stomach, but her expression scarcely changed. "You're very brave," I said, too late and not entirely sincere.

"Don't ever talk about this again. Not to anyone," was all she said.

I had a lot of practice in that department. For the hollow-cheeked boys on the evening news, silence might equal death, but really death came whether you talked about it or not. Silence equaled a picture that was worth a thousand words, a meal where no one cried, a warm bed without an argument. Silence was also what Phil heard when he phoned Lazlo's apartment, looking for me, the third night in a row that I didn't come home. "Did he apologize?" I asked Tomas, who shook his head. I turned over on the couch and pulled the blankets over my face. Home is the place where, when you go there, you don't have to put out.

I worked as late as I could every night, retouching images, taking inventory of props, scheduling appointments across time zones. Dane offered me a paying job when I graduated, though in typical Dane fashion, he did it through his second assistant, Vince. If my boss said more than seven words a day to me, my lack of importance might rub off on him. So when Richard Molineux's assistant called the studio and asked for me, Dane almost said it was a wrong number, before he remembered that Julian Selkirk was that guy who was over there unscrewing the radiator grille to find out where that smell was coming from. I had dropped off my coffee-shop pictures at *Femme NY* earlier in the week, not expecting much. It turned out they were launching a new back-of-the-book feature called "Street Style" and wanted me to cover their New York beat, spotting emerging trends and taking candids of the best-dressed girls, with an emphasis on "diversity". There would also be pages for Paris, London and L.A.

A real job, a paying job, doing my real work. If I'd had a home, I would have been able to pay rent. I accepted envy-tinged congratulations (the best kind) from the other assistants. Three times during the day I picked up the phone, wishing to celebrate with someone, and replaced the receiver without dialing. Family is a movie you know so well that the syndicated images flickering across the TV screen are unnecessary to the dialogue in your head. My father would make an off-color joke and my mother would worry about something implausible, and then Laura Sue would come on and we would have a painfully meaningless conversation to avoid asking ourselves, or one another, whether it would have changed anything if this good fortune had come my way before her last day in New York.

After a solitary dinner of sushi and beer, I bought a new white dress shirt at Armani Exchange and loitered in front of the shop window on Fifth Avenue for a while, waiting for someone to spot the halo of success around my head. Some young guys in pencil-thin jeans were gossiping in the doorway. One made eye contact with me and I looked him over, giving the tiniest nod of approval to his taut abs and sleek black hair. Then he lit a cigarette and I thought of Phil. I rounded the corner before the stranger could look my way again.

The caption makes all the difference to the picture. Call it "the last time" and you forget how the trash barrels outside your window stank on a sunny day, or your upstairs neighbor's dog yapped all night when you were studying for a test. The geraniums Phil had brought home were clinging to life in their stone planter despite the cigarette butts embedded in the soil. I still had the key, which one had to turn exactly 90 degrees in the lock while simultaneously pulling down on the door handle, so it was only because I was in an observant frame of mind that I noticed the new strip of plastic tape beside the door buzzer. I ran my finger over the embossed letters: *Shanahan/Selkirk*.

Reaching for the light switch, my hand brushed against a rough piece of wood projecting from the wall of our narrow foyer. The overhead bulb flickered on and I saw two mail holders, the kind they sold in arts-and-crafts stores, nailed one above the other. The bottom one was painted blue and read "Phil" in yellow block capitals; the top one, with the colors reversed, read "Julian".

I must have stood in the foyer for a long time, thinking I was thinking, imagining that I was weighing the pros and cons of this homecoming, as carefully as one should always weigh the consequences of dropping one's trousers. In truth I was dozing with my eyes open, my head against the fingerprint-smudged wall — Phil's fingerprints, some of them, where he must have pressed his hand against the wall to measure the space and steady the wood beneath the hammer. Or had groped for the switch, coming home to a dark and empty apartment, sometimes alone.

I laid my camera bag and jacket on the end table where I had been accustomed to keep my things — the one touch of decor I had added to the place, a round glass top supported by three white plastic mannequin legs, which we'd found in a secondhand shop on the Lower East Side. The odd number of legs, radiating tarantula-like from the center, turned a piece of 70s kitsch into a work of disturbed genius.

After my shower, it was time for the familiar ritual of shoving the handle end of the toilet plunger down the bathtub drain so the water would go down. With my regular paycheck from *Femme NY*, maybe now we could get it fixed. *We*. I had fleeting visions of a Miami vacation, new sunglasses, a ring light for my Nikon. I could get a full-body massage and wax my chest hair. Or we could move someplace with 20th-century plumbing.

I wasn't asleep for long before I felt Phil's warm body on top of me. He covered the back of my head with kisses. I let out a deep sigh. He massaged my neck. I was putting off the moment of looking at his face again, that square stubbly face with the blue eyes that could be mocking and angry one minute, then just as suddenly tender again.

"How'd you know I'd come back?" I murmured into the pillow.

"Because you love me."

His impish grin lit a tiny warmth inside me, spreading like an ache in my chest, a slow thaw after frostbite. "I never said that," I replied, pulling him nearer, closing my mouth over his. Phil's hands roamed below my waist. All at once I found I couldn't breathe. The blanket wound around us was stifling me. I began to shiver uncontrollably. Phil wiped my wet face with the corner of the blanket. I hadn't realized I was crying.

"Are you sick?" He touched my forehead.

My breaths came fast and loud. Phil put his ear against my chest. I pictured him someday rushing to athletes injured on the field, laying a calming hand on three hundred pounds of groaning muscle.

"I let something terrible happen," I said, in such a low voice he could scarcely hear me.

Phil gathered me into his arms. He waited for me to explain but I couldn't speak. "To you?"

"To everyone."

"It's not your fault."

"You don't know that."

Phil frowned. Perhaps he'd been expecting me to reciprocate, with an absolution I couldn't give. He propped himself partway up against the pillows and lit a cigarette. I settled my head on his shoulder. He drew the blanket over us again. Gradually my heart rate slowed. The orange tip of his cigarette traced a mesmerizing path through the darkness as he took a drag, tapped the embers into the ashtray, and brought it back to his mouth. I watched it every time I opened my eyes, at intervals that came farther and farther apart.

"I love you too," Phil muttered in my ear. I could have let him go on thinking I was asleep, but I smiled, eyes closed and unmoving, hoping that he would see, that it would be enough.

PART III: WHAT GOES AROUND

(Fall-Winter 1993)

14

THE CHANDELIER above the stage of the Amato Opera House ascended on a cable over our heads. The little theater on the Bowery looked like someplace the stagecoaches would stop in a spaghetti Western, and indoors, their special effects were just as creaky. Sitting in the tattered red velvet seat next to mine, Richard Molineux hummed a melody I didn't recognize. No one who watches TV can avoid learning a few arias, at the risk of forming indelible associations between "La donna è mobile" and spaghetti sauce, or the "Ride of the Valkyries" and Bugs Bunny. Richard's tune was in a minor key, a meandering sequence that never resolved on the expected notes. He noticed me listening and his steel-gray eyes brightened.

"Do you know it?" he asked, in an amused voice. I shook my head. His thin lips upturned slightly.

"That is Britten."

Though Richard's English could betray him at times with an odd turn of phrase, I concluded that he was talking about a composer I'd never heard of, rather than a country I had, and I nodded as if he'd told me something useful. His arm, in his crisp gray suit jacket, pressed against mine on the narrow armrest. Some would call opera a queen's cliché, but if this were true of Richard, it was only in the way that two dozen long-stemmed roses and a diamond ring are cliché. In other words, sign me up.

The house went dark. On my other side, Cheryl Kingston continued retouching her face powder with a compact mirror that included a tiny flashlight bulb, one of the promotional items from her Revlon gift bag. I do believe in being versatile, but this object struck me as particularly silly, unless one needed to do a line of coke during a power outage.

White spotlights bathed the stage. A full-throated soprano voice was amplified through the theater, keening an Italian aria over a pounding techno soundtrack. Richard's nose flared as if he had smelled something unpleasant. He muttered a comment to Marcia, his wife, who sat between him and my boss, the photographer Dane Langley, with her pencil poised over her notebook. I heard little of her response, in her tobacco-husky Long Island voice, except the words "with the times," but it made him chuckle.

Marcia Molineux — fortyish, flat-chested, tall as a man, with close-cropped chestnut hair and a fondness for olive green pants suits — was the publisher of *Femme NY*, the dollars-and-francs foundation of Richard's castle in the clouds. People with a romantic imagination claimed that he had named the magazine for her. It couldn't be an accident, though, that his long slim fingers kept brushing the back of my hand. My mind spun through a series of calculations with too many variables: self-interest times pleasure divided by risk.

Cheryl offered me a piece of her chewing gum, which I accepted only to be polite. It was thanks to her, after all, that Dane had brought me along. Since my promotion to second assistant — my predecessor, Vince, having launched an illustrious career photographing silicone-injected blondes for *For Him Magazine* — Dane had gone from slighting me because I was unimportant to slighting me as a potential competitor. We worked well enough together, but for invitations to New York Fashion Week and other places where my presence wasn't strictly necessary, I had to lean pretty heavily on the fact that I'd kept Cheryl from falling into the Central Park duck pond during a feature shoot for *Mademoiselle*.

I chewed for a few seconds before the unpleasant taste alerted me that it was Nicorette — a complete waste, smoking being one vice that had never tempted me. I thought of asking Cheryl if she had any gum that tasted like married men, but decided that this was inappropriate to say at the opera, even if there wasn't any opera going on.

What there was, on stage, was a parade of runway models showcasing the designs of Anton Fische, whose suddenly-trendy logo (a jagged F resembling a lightning bolt) was displayed in black against the silver backdrop. The theme of the show, according to our programs, was "Les Pêcheurs de Perles". That might explain why one of the girls wore a wetsuit with a ballerina skirt, while another sported a fin-like hairdo spiked with gel above a turtleneck dress made of chain mail. Over the synthesized backbeat, the diva sang a sequence of inhumanly high notes, sharp as icicles dropping off a roof.

"Controlled excess," Richard said, apropos of nothing, or everything.

"That makes no sense, honey," Marcia said, scribbling in her notebook.

"Exactly," Richard replied, and they both laughed lightly. Dane laughed too, though they hadn't been talking to him. The *Femme NY* editors threw a fair amount of work our way, but I got the sense that they didn't personally care for my boss. The womanizing, the drug rumors, the chest hair — it was all very 1980s, too many shots of beauty queens on beaches. It's hard to be ironic in Florida. He knew that I knew the score, so we both edged our way in on either side of the Molineux' conversation, while Cheryl, miffed at not sitting next to Dane, chewed her gum loudly, and hardly anyone remembered to look at the clothes.

A woman with silver bands across her chest walked downstage, her collar frill rising above her head like a clamshell. I thought Fische had outsmarted himself with the setting. Next to the theater's gilded plaster curlicues and red velvet, the models looked like Martians who had crash-landed in a Wild West bordello. I ventured to say as much to Richard, who replied, "It is to be memorable, that is the new beauty."

"So's a bus accident," Marcia quipped. One might think she was putting him down, except for the fact that Dane's latest feature for them had had an earthquake theme. Models clinging to collapsed windowsills with their lacquered fingernails, swinging their high-heeled boots over a chasm of rubble. We had staged it on the site of an elementary school in the Bronx that was being demolished. Smells of chalk and bubble gum, and probably asbestos, were set free by the wrecking ball, undetectable in the picture. I found an unbroken red crayon in a pile of sand and Dane turned it into a moment of pathos, the girl holding it up to her smudged face like a child playing with her mother's lipstick. That was our favorite shot, but Richard took it out.

"But yes, the shock of what you do not understand, the wrong thing in the wrong place, that is what takes you — beyond," Richard went on.

"Like the music?" I asked.

"No, the music is merely terrible."

The show came to a close, much to the relief of Richard's eardrums, and the models all returned to the stage with Fische to share in the applause.

"You know I used to model swimsuits for him in Miami when he was still Tony Fusco," Cheryl said to the group at large.

"So you've said," Marcia responded, at the same time as I said "No." Lately I wasn't sure how much to believe Cheryl's stories. The one about the Italian underwear model in the hot-air balloon was somewhat plausible, but that business with the polo team sounded anatomically impossible. A cry for help, my sister would have called it, but she was a sophomore psychology student at NYU and thought it was a cry for help when I ate a foot-long hot dog at Gray's Papaya.

Fische, or Fusco, was a deeply tanned man with close-set eyes above a long sharp nose. He had probably once been skinny, but success was filling out the torso inside that shiny black jacket, the same color and sheen as his hair. His designs, popular with rich young Europeans, were just now starting to penetrate the American market. Rumor had it that he was looking for a photographer for the ad campaign for his new ready-to-wear line; an even more unrepeatable rumor was that Dane had been considered and rejected. Still, Dane was invited to the after-show party and I wasn't, notwithstanding how hard I had tried to appreciate Richard's latest fancies, which included raw oysters, gladiator sandals, and the music of Alban Berg. I always worried that he would grow tired of playing Henry Higgins to my Eliza Doolittle. There were, after all, a lot of ignorant boys in New York — I had one myself at home — and I still couldn't tell whether he cared about my good looks. Even if he swung that way (another mystery), perhaps he would prefer a lover with a third eye or a hump.

As for me, I had certain rules. I had sipped cocktails with the photo editor of *Details* in Marcia Molineux's living room, under the Roy Lichtenstein painting of the cartoon six-shooter that said "Bang!" in yellow letters. I had sat on her sofa across from the view of Central Park and looked through pictures of her father's button factory on the Lower East Side, the warehouse that became *Femme NY*'s first editorial offices when they were married in 1977. And of course they were publishing my regular "Street Style" feature, which I was hoping to expand to Miami as well as New York, since Dane and I stopped there so often on the way to Caribbean shoots. If I had conceived an unlikely fondness for Richard's bald head and aquiline nose, if his soft precise voice could convince me that the sky was green and birds flew backwards, well, I could put that on my Christmas wish list next to the Ferrari, but I'd better learn to enjoy my lump of coal.

15

LEST ANYONE IMAGINE that Julian Selkirk was lacking male companionship, Phil and I were still officially a couple, as officially as we'd ever been, anyhow. I didn't mind the occasional breakups as much as the fights over stupid things, like the time this past spring when we were drinking in this punk dive in Alphabet City with some of his gym buddies and he demanded that we get tattoos of each other's names. Now, there's a reason why tattoo parlors are located next to bars, but when I suggested quite logically that we were in no condition to make life-altering fashion choices, he knocked his beer bottle to the floor and the bartender asked us to step outside. "If we break up, you could change it to 'Philly'," he'd argued.

"I don't like Philly. It's too cold and their football team sucks."

"You afraid *Ree-shard* won't like it?"

"Richard has no settled opinions." Except that if he could see me standing in the rain, arguing with my drunk boyfriend, outside a club populated by teenagers with thumbtacks through their eyebrows, he would probably share my opinion that I was an idiot.

Things had improved over the summer when Phil and I moved into a bigger apartment in Chelsea. It was no palace but it had a bedroom with a door you could close, and a window that looked out on something besides feet. Gradually the space sorted itself out into his and mine: the kitchen/living room a jumble of Phil's books, ashtrays, clothes and bodybuilding magazines, the bedroom a neater space for my cameras and growing portfolio. Sometimes I missed the closeness of the old place, where we'd always been on top of each other, like two gerbils in a nest of paper shavings. Then I would turn on the clean, steady stream of water from the shower and decide it was all for the best.

Phil had been spending more time at the Ironman Gym since he'd been offered the chance to teach a powerlifting class in addition to his one-on-one training. I had recently joined Ironman myself, feeling the need to keep up with his new heavily-muscled pals. So I retreated to the weight room, after Fische's show ended, for a quick upper-body workout and the chance to stare at the type of beauty you didn't need a Ph.D to appreciate. Girls were getting smaller as guys were getting bigger. The TV superheroes of my childhood were nerds in pajamas, compared to the defined bulk sported by every waiter and shoe salesman in our neighborhood.

Afterwards I joined Phil and his friends in the sauna. He was in an affectionate mood and rubbed lotion into my sore shoulders while I stretched out on the wooden plank seating. Stan was there, sitting a little ways apart from the others, with his towel wound tightly around his narrow waist, as if any of us could forget that he was off-limits to the friendly groping that occurred all the time in the steam room. We often teased him that this was the only place he could get away from Frank, his better half (height-wise, his better two-thirds), who wilted in the heat like the cheap corsages his drag-queen alter ego Miss Anna wore. Stan played along with being the object of our pity, but with a certain smugness underneath, like he'd bought a house while the rest of us kids were still renting.

"Steroids," he was saying. "It's so unfair, it's ridiculous."

Since it was unusual for Stan to get upset about anything, I assumed he must have lost big on a sports bet. "Which baseball player is it this time?"

"I mean, come on, it's not like we're doing crack in here," he went on, too incensed to slow down and clue me in.

"Two of the trainers got busted," Phil told me. "There was an exposé in *Gay Downtown*. Some columnist, calls himself 'Spartacus'."

"Using?" My heart sank. I would never be able to keep up with these people. Sure, I wanted six-pack abs, but not enough to risk shrinking my dick to the size of a peanut.

"Dealing, too."

"Not you, though."

"I'm still here, aren't I?" Which was all the reassurance Phil could give me in public, now that no one knew whom to trust.

"I mean, have a heart, do you know what it's like to see some poz guy come in here looking like death? Do we all have to know his business?" Stan continued to make the case for drug use, not altogether unexpectedly, since he was a pharmacist.

"Seems to me this dumb-ass 'Spartacus' thinks we all deserve AIDS for fucking around," another guy said, provoking a murmur of outraged agreement around the room. Phil defiantly planted a wet kiss on my mouth. I stirred beneath my towel. It wouldn't take much to persuade all of us to get naked and fight the power. Poor Stan, sidelined by the revolution.

"It's not about what we deserve, it's about being smart," another voice cut through the clouds of steam. Oh no, it was that guy, Phil's new buddy, the yoga instructor. Peter. I'd noticed his name slipping into conversations at our house, more and more. *Peter loaned me this video about labor unions. Peter says the government could cure AIDS if they wanted to.* It would be one thing if they would just fuck and get it over with, but Phil said it wasn't like that. Peter didn't hook up with anyone at the Ironman.

Yet here he was, easing his big half-naked body onto a creaking plank across from us. Unlike a lot of the boys here, he didn't bother waxing or shaving anything below the chin. The damp fur on his chest was black and curly as the unruly hair crowning his broad, flat face. He slouched, hiding those worked-over pecs. It was the same way he walked, like he'd grown up in a house where the ceilings were too low. His hazel eyes met mine sharply and I looked away, pretending I hadn't been staring. There was nothing to stare at. We were having a conversation and he'd butted in. What was it about? Oh yes, the health and safety of the American faggot.

"You know what they say — men don't make passes at boys who are smart asses," I goaded him.

"That doesn't even *scan.*" Everybody laughed at that. What, he was going to teach us poetry, as well as yoga? Peter's pale sweaty face colored. But he surprised me by continuing to argue his point. "And what *I'm* saying is, it had better be one hell of a fuck, to be worth dying for."

"Whoa, whoa, nobody's dying here," Phil tried to calm the waters. "We were talking about whether it was unfair to fire Rick and Ted."

Peter snorted. "Tell 'em to phone my dad, he'll have a jury believing it's our constitutional right to swallow pills till our biceps explode."

"Better than wasting away," Stan said. We couldn't fling this topic from us fast enough; like a deadly boomerang, it only rebounded with greater momentum.

"You bitches are depressing me," snapped the guy next to Stan, the one who'd provoked Peter's first comment. He stood up, letting his towel slip past his hips. His bronzed body was smooth and hard as a plastic doll's. "We're all goin' the same way, so this girl says, why not live hard and die gorgeous?"

"Go ahead Leo, we'll see how good you look when you're crapping your bed at St. Vincent's." Peter let out a deep, ragged breath. He lay back on the sauna bench and rubbed his eyes. "God, I'm sorry, you guys. I just had a really shitty day at Housing Works. One of my clients is going to get evicted for smoking pot. The city doesn't care that it's the only way he can eat without puking. So forgive me if six-pack abs aren't my highest priority."

"Beauty cheers people up," I said. "When Mama's arm got broken, she didn't want to leave the house, till her girlfriends came and did her hair and makeup for her."

I expected Peter to object, but he turned his head toward me and slowly smiled. It warmed me inside, then made me nervous, as if he'd heard things I hadn't meant to disclose.

"I know what would cheer us up. Let's go to Trapdoor. You coming, babe?" Phil flicked his towel at me.

"That place again?"

"I like it. It's hardcore," Phil insisted. "You in, Peter?"

Peter stretched lazily. "I dunno. I could use a break, but saving the world pays *bupkes*, even with two jobs. There's a reason Batman is independently wealthy."

"Come on, I'll stand you a drink," I offered. I must have felt guilty about picking on him earlier.

Trapdoor was a rougher place than New Eden, the campy little hangout from our student days. The club was so named because of a cage in the middle of the dance floor, surrounding a raised stage where dancers in leather thongs would periodically pop out of a hole in the floor. For the right price, you could go downstairs and join them.

Phil bought our first round of drinks — three martinis, a Cosmo for me, and a beer for Stan, who feared hard liquor would have a solvent effect on the bonds of monogamy. "You're pretty flush," I said, noticing the wad of twenties in my boyfriend's wallet. "Did you take on another class at the gym?"

His face reddened. "I'm, uh, I'm making a workout video."

"That's awesome! Why didn't you tell me? Who's filming it? Maybe I could help."

"It's nothing, we're still just messing around, we're not ready yet." Phil looked bashful. I squeezed his hand, sorry to have embarrassed him.

"But you got paid already?" Peter asked.

"That was for the rights," Phil said vaguely.

"You want to dance?" I asked Peter, to get him off Phil's case, or maybe to get on his nerves, because I was sure he'd come up with some long-winded explanation about how dancing was a waste of energy that could be spent marching on Washington. The boy had cross-examination in his genes. Peter's father was Nathan Edelman, a notorious civil-rights lawyer and talk-radio host, wrapping the First Amendment's mantle around everything from panhandling to pornography. I could tolerate it for about five minutes at a time, but Phil liked to argue with the radio, though he rarely worked up the nerve to phone in. I wondered what the elder Edelman thought of his son's career path. Peter was obviously the smartest one in the steam room, but Phil said he'd dropped out of Columbia in his senior year.

Fathers want sons but are never happy with them, from God and Adam on down.

After glancing at Phil for permission, Peter did follow me into the swaying crowd on the dance floor. The sounds were harder here too, a lot of German house music with lyrics spoken in an eerie monotone over repetitive blips. The shadows were shades of blue and black, cut by white lights. In the dance cage, an Adonis wearing studded straps pretended (at least I hoped he was pretending) to hump a lithe black man in glittery body paint.

Too literal, Richard often said about designs that failed to inspire him: a skirt that looked like a skirt instead of a lampshade or a mushroom cloud, a photo (maybe mine) or a pretty girl doing what pretty girls do, sipping lemonade in the park while the birds flew overhead, not picking up dogshit with a spatula or whatever cockamamie thing I'd have to do to get the attention of a designer like Fische. Those boys in the cage would have made Richard yawn.

Peter danced with great concentration, eyes closed, body jerking with a suppressed energy that I hadn't seen in him before. The darkness of his chest hair showed where he'd sweated through his T-shirt. I couldn't help myself, I tickled his belly.

His eyes shot open, and in the moment he was caught off-guard and saw me laughing, a simple sweetness lit up his face. Then, once again, the curtain dropped and he was the Peter we all knew, polite and watchful, too decent to be honest.

"What are you doing here?" I shouted over the music.

"Same thing you are," he shouted back, but he looked away. What was he afraid I'd read in his eyes?

"Wasting time, you mean." We were almost touching, pressed together by the crowd. The air was stifling. A fog hazed the multicolored lights.

"Why don't you take Phil home?"

"He'll go when he's ready to go." I wanted to reach out to Peter again, to take hold of his large, strong hands, just to see what he'd do. This would have been an ordinary person's cue to ask me to leave with him, or to come downstairs and hump along with the grunting, groaning boys packed into the dark room like cattle on a feedlot. But I wasn't ready to find out that Peter was just an ordinary person, so I took a step back, as far as the environment would allow, and bumped into a bulked-up soldier boy in cutoff camos who grabbed my waist and spun me around so I was dancing with him, if you could call it dancing to be bounced up and down like a jackhammer.

Phil rescued me, throwing his arms around my shoulders in a sloppy hug. He rubbed his face against my neck, and his warmth began to dissolve the tension I'd been carrying around unawares, a feeling of pins and needles under my skin making me critical and contrary. Perhaps I'd been working too hard. I held him close.

"Here, Julian, this is for you." With an affectionate, sleepy smile, he held out a small white pill.

I evaded the fingers reaching for my mouth. "What is it?"

"It's the good stuff. Come on." He teased my lips apart. "Take your happy pill."

Ecstasy, again. Nights at Trapdoor rarely ended in the same reality where we'd begun. I knew how the next few hours could go. The lights would soften to a lavender cloud, the steam of the dancers' bodies would enfold me like an ocean, all stupid jokes would seem pathetically sweet as a child's crayon drawing, and pretty soon I'd be telling my life story to the Caterpillar and the Red Queen while the Rabbit stuck a teapot up my ass.

"Don't you wanna be happy?" Phil asked, in a sing-song voice, waving the pill under my nose.

"That is actually a very profound question," I said, "which it might be more productive to discuss when you're not stoned out of your fucking head."

"Huh?" Phil smiled indulgently at me. His eyes were dreamy, like a sky suffused with sunlight, shining for me alone. How tempting to meet him on the other side of consciousness, where my heart would no longer be hardened, where I would feel that way about him too.

In the center of the dance floor, the glitter-painted performer was reaching for Peter's hand to coax him up onto the stage. My mind recoiled from the thought of meeting up with Peter in the trapdoor room.

"I'm not into it tonight," I told Phil, pushing his hand away. "Can't we go home? We never do anything by ourselves anymore."

"But I want to be with *people!*" he gushed.

"I don't know if you noticed, but I'm a person."

Because of the drug, my sarcasm made Phil laugh, whereas otherwise he might have sulked. I steered us out the door and into a cab, an expensive indulgence since we lived within walking distance, but better than letting him walk down the street in full political baby-kissing mode. On Ecstasy, everyone's your friend, the cops and the Latin Kings and the little old ladies who send their nickels to Jerry Falwell — a quick, nonviolent shortcut to Peter's socialist utopia.

I had to admit, Phil was a more attentive lover when high. Not stopping to shower, because we liked the smell of our bodies together, we sank into our new bed, with the mattress that he always complained was too soft for optimal spine alignment. He got lost in foreplay, grazing my nipples with his teeth, flicking his tongue-tip along my shaft. I held myself still, my muscles aching with desire and tension. Sometimes he liked me to pretend to be helpless while he worked away on top of me. He licked the drops from the head of my cock. When I eased myself into him, and he wrapped his legs around my waist, he sighed and told me I was beautiful. Though I couldn't be sure what he was seeing, I yielded to his closeness.

Love and murder are just brain chemistry, Stan had argued one night when we were over at his and Frank's place, watching the classic movies channel. The late-night film was some black-and-white screamer about an evil hypnotist, and in the interest of us all getting a good night's sleep, Stan had explained that it was bogus science. Hypnosis only removed some inhibitions from doing what you'd naturally do anyhow, he said; it couldn't turn a good person into a bad one. Not having been raised Christian, he didn't see a contradiction there. Was Ecstasy fake love, or did it unblock the love that was already there? The bookmark in Phil's current bedside volume, Napoleon

Hill's *Think and Grow Rich*, had been stuck in the same page for a month. Rather than wake him to discuss philosophy, I kissed Phil's damp blond hair and promised myself to pay more attention to him. As soon as I nailed down my first editorial feature assignment — and it would be any day now, if I read Richard's signals right — I would take my boy out to celebrate.

16

"WHAT IS LOVE?" the girl's ripped pink T-shirt asked. Gravity drew her uneven black bangs over her eyes, dipped her silver pendant into the bony hollow between her breasts, as she squatted on the edge of the red and yellow metal roundabout in the Sheridan Square playground. Her skin mirrored the colors of the sandbox, pale beige buffed to glittery whiteness by the sun. Tamiko was shy, when I approached her in the park with my camera, shy but resigned, somehow, to being interpreted by others, keeping her distance from her own experience of being looked at. Even when our picture ran on the back page of *Femme NY*, and I suggested to her that modeling might be a more rewarding career than delivering takeout lunches by bicycle, she hesitated, maybe still believing that her life wouldn't change if she did nothing about it. On the other hand, the age (eighteen) she put down on the release form was at least two years older than the truth, and Marcia suspected she'd forged her father's signature on the form as well.

A full-page photo was a step up for me, and I was sure that a feature story couldn't be far behind. Dane commended my eye for new talent and talked about bringing Tamiko into the studio for test shots. No doubt about it, he wanted to steal my model. Then we got a weekend job in L.A., and the exhaustion of two transcontinental flights in 48 hours pushed all minor projects, such as ruining my career, from my boss's mind.

"Hollywood, Phil," I'd cajoled my boyfriend, urging him to come with me. "Surfer boys as far as the eye can see. You can touch the cement where Streisand put her feet." I wasn't completely sure that La Barbra was one of the celebs so honored, but all peddlers of holy relics had been known to stretch the truth for a good cause.

"Nah, you're just gonna be working the whole time," he objected. "What I really want is to go to the White Party in Miami."

I nearly objected that circuit parties were expensive, but then Phil's pride would have been wounded and he would have made a point of splitting our trip expenses fifty-fifty, down to the last pack of condoms and bottle of suntan lotion. Since I did want to treat him to a nice vacation, I followed the example of the U.S. government and borrowed the money on my credit card.

What I wasn't expecting was that my portfolio with the latest "Street Style" pictures would be returned to me by Richard's assistant, with a note (at least it was in his handwriting) that there was no room for my work in this month's feature. I called his office but the story was that he was in Milan. Marcia took pity on me and agreed to have lunch with me instead.

I held my breath anxiously as we walked past several West Village restaurants where a salad would cost me half a day's wages. Marcia chose a luncheonette with overstuffed blue vinyl booths. She scanned the laminated menu cheerfully.

"Richard never wants to eat in places like this," she said. "Order the fries, honey."

I didn't have much appetite, but Marcia subscribed to the universal female belief that food eaten off a male companion's plate has no calories. I picked at my grilled cheese sandwich.

"Don't frown, Julian. Boys get wrinkles too," she advised, pointing a French fry at me for emphasis. "It's true," she went on, when I didn't react. "One day your forehead just *goes*. And then you have to make a choice."

"Botox or charm school?"

"Kid catches on quick."

"So have I not been charming enough?"

"You're asking me?" Marcia wiped ketchup and lipstick from her mouth with her napkin. I studied the pile of French fries, which reminded me of the sculpture in the front hallway of her apartment, a crosswise jumble of metal tubes that sat on a marble pedestal like a beer can on a throne, daring the uninitiated to laugh. Assuming she knew what I was talking about — and I really wasn't that hard to understand; in the art gallery of life, I was "Praying Hands" — I had just asked her whether I had made a mistake in not sleeping with her husband.

"What I don't get," I said, retreating from the precipice that was never far away in conversations with either Molineux, "is that I thought Tamiko was my best picture yet."

"Yes, it was."

"Then…?"

Maddeningly, Marcia simply continued eating my fries, along with the cup of clam chowder she'd ordered. Her appetite was hard to reconcile with her tall, wiry figure and size-two wardrobe. Plausible explanations — smoking, Dexatrim, bulimia — were too Lifetime TV-movie for her. Perhaps she only ate one meal a week, and the rest of the time Richard kept her on a diet of ortolans and *eau minérale*.

"Are you saying I've peaked at age twenty-one?" I squeaked out.

"Have you?"

"Of course not," I bluffed.

Marcia looked disappointed. Would she have found creative anguish more stimulating? "Listen, honey," she said, deciding to throw me a bone of enlightenment, "beauty doesn't cut it. That extra thing, for Richard, it's like the Tabasco sauce on the ice cream, the lobster on the Easter bonnet. And even then…"

"But what do you think?"

She glided over this transparent attempt to play off mommy's rules against daddy's. "It's the choice he loves. Seeing what happens next."

From this I chose to conclude that he hadn't simply lost interest in me, that I'd been given some sort of a test, to see how I'd perform under pressure. The conversation eased into hard-luck stories not involving yours truly. Marcia told me about her grandfather who'd sold clothes out of a pushcart on the Lower East Side. I told her about the time Uncle Curtis had started a mail-order business selling homemade shampoo, which folded when the Gwinnett County Regional High

School cheerleading squad began shedding clumps of blonde hair during a particularly vigorous halftime show.

In the end, I had nothing to sell but myself, the point of most jobs being to stave off such an end. Back in the day, Mama used to read us a picture book called *The Giving Tree*. This tree, who's of course female, loves a little boy so much, she gives him her one red apple. As he grows older, he takes her branches, her leaves, her bark, her wood, cuts her down to build a house and moves away. The tree is always happy and the boy never is. In the end, the broken-down old dude comes back to sit on the stump of the tree. Moral: grow more apples.

17

SO DESPERATE WAS I for artistic inspiration that I asked Phil if I could tag along on his next movie night with Peter. They were meeting at the Angelika Film Center, an art-house theater near Soho. "What are we seeing, anyway?" I asked, as we hurried down Houston, past lanes of stalled, honking traffic.

"'Battle for the Trees'. I think it's some kinda foreign sci-fi cartoon."

"Perfect." Richard loved ironic use of children's media, at least this month. The current issue of *Femme NY* included a photo of a six-foot Jamaican woman with scarlet dreads and a Raggedy Ann dress, hustling on Sunset Boulevard. Such a thing would never have occurred to me, which was better news for my soul than for my career.

However, "Battle" turned out to be a Canadian documentary about the conflict between loggers and conservationists. I should have known. They'd gone to some film about migrant fruit-pickers while Dane and I were in the Caribbean. I'm sure it was all very sad in an important way, but what was I going to do, stop eating fruit? Man does not live by Muscle Milk bars alone.

Peter was waiting outside the theater with a short but handsome young black man in a plaid flannel coat. At last, I thought, we meet the boyfriend. He introduced Kevin as his co-worker at Housing Works, where they were both case management technicians. "A fancy name for the guy who shows up at your house and nags you to take your AZT," Kevin said modestly. He had large, sad-looking brown eyes that lit up when he laughed. I wrapped my arm tighter around Phil's waist.

Just as we neared the front of the ticket line, another guy raced up to us, alighting at Kevin's side in a flurry of elbows and knees, like a crane roosting. Kevin kissed him on the lips, which were painted an artificial strawberry color, and introduced him as his boyfriend, DeWayne. I immediately liked the two of them a lot better.

DeWayne taught high school science and had the corduroy wardrobe to prove it. The lipstick, I surmised, was not part of his daytime look. During the preview for a film about depressed French teenagers, he sighed that one of his students was skipping school because the other kids called her a dyke, and he wished he could do more but he was afraid of losing his job. Phil munched popcorn and said school wasn't all it was cracked up to be. I tuned out the talking heads on screen and the ones around me, leaned back and watched the soaring redwoods topple, slicing through the air like a giant's sword.

The night was warm for October in New York ("Destruction of the ozone layer," DeWayne said darkly) so we camped out on the benches in Washington Square Park, with a bag of cookies from a nearby Italian pastry shop, and talked about the movie. I tried to avoid giving an opinion, since I was only there to get ideas for fashion magazine articles which, if successful, would entail the destruction of more trees.

"Eh, I liked 'The Lorax' better," Phil cracked. No reaction. "Y'know? Dr. Seuss?" My boyfriend's loud voice tried to breathe life into the joke. I got it now, what he was doing with them. He was hoping their smarts would rub off on him, but just as much, he resented the effort.

"Too much talk," Peter said. "That's why people think good causes are boring. Just show the damn trees, make us fall in love with the trees, and then pow! Chop 'em down."

I was surprised, because that was my reaction too. He was looking at me but I turned away. Kevin unearthed a leather pouch from his jacket pocket and rolled a joint. "For entertainment purposes only, as they say on Miss Cleo's psychic hotline," he assured us. In other words, he didn't want us assuming he was poz, just because he worked for an AIDS services organization. DeWayne talked about showing the film to his class, and fretted some more about his lesbian dropout.

"You're going back to finish your degree next term, right, Peter?"

Peter took a long drag of sweet smoke from the joint that was making the rounds. "I guess. Depends on if Prue — if everybody's coping okay at home." He flicked a wary glance at me, apparently remembering I wasn't in on this story that the others knew. His hesitation irritated me. Why would he trust big-mouth Phil over me?

"I thought your dad got the charges dropped," my boyfriend blurted out, true to form.

"Uh-oh, did you hook up with some underage girl whose daddy has a shotgun? You just slumming with us queers?" I needled Peter. He coughed.

Phil ignored his discomfort and DeWayne's bitchy looks, so eager was he to prove he was in the know. Weed always made him a chatterbox. "Prue's his half-sister, she's like a teenage math genius, she hacked into the computer where she was working at McDonald's and gave their money away to PETA —"

"Farm Sanctuary, actually," corrected Peter. "She likes cows." A touch of pride and affection leavened his embarrassment. His friends seemed to share the feeling. As for me, the most political thing I did as a teenager was mow "REAGAN 88" into our front lawn, and then mainly as an excuse not to cut the rest of the grass.

"That's charming, but why is it your problem?" I pushed back. Maybe he thought the judgment in my voice was directed at him, or his red-diaper kid sister, but for a moment I was lost in memories of school plays missed and Little League games forfeited because "Daddy has a headache" or "Mama sprained her ankle again".

"Because I'm the only one in that house who can fry a fucking egg," Peter growled.

Kevin put a hand on his shoulder, easing us back onto safer ground. "You can do a lot more than that. Just consider, you've only got four credits standing between you and a promotion. Don't you want to be my boss someday?"

Peter's anger had come and gone in an instant, leaving no trace. He was his usual unassuming self when he replied, "Don't worry about me, Kev. I'm glad I took a break from all that stress, you know, exams every week, and that guy I was seeing…" He exhaled. "There's only so many times I want to get fisted while watching 'Battlestar Galactica' reruns."

The others cracked up, as if it was obvious that plain-vanilla Peter could only be kidding. Faces are my business, though, and I saw something else. He knew it, too. After a moment, he smiled sheepishly, going along with the group's ragging, and passed me the joint. Marijuana's not my favorite escape, but my Mama did raise me to eat what was put on my plate. The damp end of the joint was still warm from his mouth, and everyone's, the taste of him indistinguishable from the others.

18

NOVEMBER'S APPROACH intensified Phil's determination to get us in shape for the White Party. To ensure that my wallet was also bulked-up, I went back to my old barista job at The Big Cup for two mornings a week on the 7 AM shift. Sometimes my arms were almost too sore to lift the coffee urn.

"Ab-so-lute-ly not," I puffed, hoisting the 90-pound barbell for what felt like the thousandth bench-press, while he spotted me. "I am not waxing my chest hair."

"That's the circuit party *look*. It's in all the magazines."

"But I don't — hardly — *have* any chest hair." I clanged the barbell back into its metal holder and lay exhausted on the vinyl bench.

Phil pulled up my tank top and groped around. "Hmm. I don't know, what do you guys think?"

More bodies came to stand around us. At the touch of another hand on my skin, I opened my eyes. When I saw it was Peter, I sat up so fast that I bumped my forehead on the bar.

"Screw this, I want y'all to love me for my mind."

"Yeah, we can do that later. Now drop and give me fifty."

Though Phil found it hard to quit the drill-sergeant role when we were between the sheets, the results of his program were impressive. Even Dane had noticed, in his inimitable way, ordering me to "stop looking at yourself in the mirror and set up the cameras." So I obediently hit the mat.

I had the locker room to myself until Peter walked in. Expecting him to strip down, I averted my eyes, annoyed by my own discomfort, unsure of the reason. Couldn't I have him, if I wanted him? He was only friends with Phil, and we were far from monogamous. And if he was the rare one who told me no, my reputation wouldn't suffer. If anything, it would make Peter seem even weirder, more out of step with the Ironman crowd. I felt a terrible twinge of pleasure at that thought, followed hard by a rush of protective feeling toward the stoop-shouldered giant in the locker room doorway, in his gray sweatpants and purple T-shirt reading "ABA Legal Malpractice Conference 1989".

"Sorry about before," Peter said.

I stood behind my locker door to undress. "Before what?"

"When I, uh, felt up your chest." He laughed self-consciously.

"I don't mind if you don't." I kept my tone friendly rather than seductive, but meanwhile, I rolled down my gym shorts. At the critical moment, I turned my back to him to deploy a concealing towel.

"But you *are* upset." He wouldn't leave me alone.

"Not about you. I...well, I recently lost my regular freelance job, and this trip to Miami is making me worry about money."

"I thought maybe it was about Phil's video...have you seen it?"

"What? Oh, no, he's kept that under wraps. Guess he's nervous what I'd think about its artistic qualities."

I sensed Peter was disappointed in me, or Phil, or the human race. If it were up to him, we'd be making a documentary about the endangered marmoset.

"But otherwise...you're not jealous?"

I would not, could not show that his disrespect mattered to me at all. "I love Phil. I want him to be a success. He's hot, he's good at what he does, let him work it." I adjusted my towel to allow him an accidental peek at what he'd be missing. Then I carried my shampoo bottles into the shower stall and drew the mildew-spotted curtain, hoping he'd get the message.

"Julian...wait up."

Oh, now he was going to play sorry, after the damage was done, Ferdinand the flower-sniffing bull in the china shop.

"Hey." He tapped on the shower curtain. I backed up against it so the plastic showed the outline of my ass. "One of my yoga clients is an editor at *Gay Downtown*. I bet I could interest him in buying your pictures from the White Party."

"Like I'm the only photographer going there."

"Well, you've got to be the best." He drew a breath, and mumbled, "I — I went and looked at your magazine, *Femme NY*, in the library."

I rinsed my hair, taking my time to react. "Okay. Thanks. I'll be in touch when we get back."

Silence. He must have gone already. Then I felt a gentle pat on my rear end before his footsteps retreated across the puddled floor. That warmth spreading inside me was just my muscles diligently burning away whatever stood between me and circuit-queen perfection.

Have you ever wanted to step into a picture so you could taste blue water, hear the music of the wind-swept clouds, feel diamond-flecked sand against your soles? Most of the time the picture is better, your added senses dulling one another like too many conversations in a room. It's the reason so many myths connect sight and punishment. Beauty lies about where it comes from.

So I was unprepared for the scene at the Hotel Tropicana. There we were, Phil and I, with our rolled-up winter parkas under our arms, towing our black wheeled suitcases, as we welcomed the moist warmth of the Florida air, and everywhere, everywhere, the men. Men like us, flapping their hands while they chatted on the lobby sofas, rubbing each other's backs in plain sight beside the swimming pool, air-kissing in the elevator. We laughed each time we heard laughter, we listened in on gossip about people we didn't know, just to hear the whispers and exclamations echoed again and again with that intonation that could only be ours. *Did you really...? Would he ever? Oh, girl!* Dancing broke out in hallways, rhythms glimpsed through half-open doors, bodies pumping and preening, a few with an intensity that most reserved for nightfall, when the pulse would quicken and we would turn to each other and confess what we ached for, secret no more.

To begin with, though, I only stood in the lobby with my mouth hanging open, dumb as the lost sheep must have been when he discovered his ninety-nine brothers. "Are you happy?" Phil asked, putting his arm around my waist.

"It's amazing."

Phil beamed at me. "I'm so glad we're here."

I tucked a strand of his blond hair behind his ear. His severe summer crew-cut was growing out into the scruffy look I preferred. "I have a surprise for you."

I'd booked us a session in the hotel spa, to loosen the last grip of a New York November on our tense muscles. Phil bravely endured the green mud facial and the pedicure, which he was too macho to admit he enjoyed, and then we both savored a massage from a huge man who was definitely one of the tribe. It was like a B-movie scenario: we'd crash-landed on a planet occupied by a superior race that wanted to mate with us. When Phil rolled onto his back, I could see the aroused lump beneath his towel, which made me smirk till I realized I had the same problem.

The first afternoon passed in a golden haze. Phil nursed an expensive drink that was like every artificial fruit flavor you could imagine, blended with a pinch of dynamite. I thought about all the cocktail umbrellas in the world and how quickly they were discarded, then laughed at myself for such a sentimentally faggy thought. Why not mourn toothpaste caps, old tires, worn-out underwear? Humans compulsively create and shed objects, it's what we do, like frogs laying thousands of eggs. I swam laps in the heated pool till I grew tired, then snuggled up to Phil's sun-warmed body on the lounge chair. His skin was tacky with coconut-scented suntan lotion.

"You're so lucky you're naturally tan. I'm a pale Irish potato," he said, applying a touch-up to his nose and forehead.

"If you're the potato, I'm the gravy." I searched for a spot on his body that would taste normal, and settled on his big toe.

"Mmm, let's go upstairs."

After showering together, we ate fried clams on the rear balcony of the hotel overlooking the beach, and watched the sun sink into pale bands of lavender and lemon-yellow on the horizon. Phil was sticking close to me. I had expected him to be on the prowl by now. His eyes were sleepy, heavy-lidded.

Back home he'd been keeping strange hours. He trained clients before their workday began, came home to sleep in the middle of the day, then back to the gym to work on his body and go clubbing with his pals. His irregular schedule took the pressure off me because I was also working around the clock. When I wasn't assisting Dane, I was traipsing around to modeling agencies in search of girls who needed head shots. When Phil and I managed to have dinner together, settling into the couch to watch the evening news with our cartons of shrimp lo mein, it had the feeling of a fortunate chance encounter. I told myself that it kept our relationship fresh. But now, as we ate in companionable silence, I thought perhaps a little routine wouldn't be so bad. As if reading my mind, Phil took my hand. "We don't get to be alone enough," he said, and yawned.

I kissed his fingers. "Yeah, I know."

Down below our balcony, on the sand, some boys were dancing to a portable radio while others ran through the surf. Barely dressed, but dressed in white, each and every one, white Speedos or tight cut-off pants, white feathers and streamers, even one white tennis skirt that showed hairy naked buttocks underneath when its wearer leapt into the air.

"What do you think Peter would say about this scene?" I asked.

"End of the world, probably," he said in a bored voice.

"Or the start of a new one." My camera and I took in the diners on the balcony, these fit and graceful men who sat hand in hand, three or four of them together, and greeted strangers with ecstatic kisses. "There could be, like, ten thousand people here. What if we all did something together? Why can't the rest of the world be like this?"

"Eh, let's not get into that political shit now."

"You used to care," I said, impatiently. "You used to read stuff."

Phil only shrugged.

"What's going on with you?" I nudged him.

"Just trying to be happy with what I got. Like you." He squeezed my hand. I returned the pressure with a warmth I didn't feel. What had happened to us, to me, that there was nothing inside? We could even now be appearing in someone else's tourist photos, two golden boys holding hands on the terrace, the perfect face of the White Party. I recalled the abstinence lectures that were forced on us in Sunday school: the two cardboard hearts pasted together and peeled apart and pasted together again, over and over, until they were tattered and smudged, as unattractive as we couldn't bear to be. But wasn't the heart made of muscle, didn't muscles get stronger with use?

Phil yawned again and leaned his head on his arms, smiling drowsily. I kissed his cheek, which was flushed, maybe from the beer we'd been drinking with the clams. The softness of his skin moved me. He'd become such a hardbody this year, purging himself of the little-boy awkwardness that I used to love. "Hey, babe, if you don't want to go to Vizcaya tonight, it's okay. We can walk along the beach and talk about our feelings," I said.

His hand on my knee showed me just what he was feeling. "Yeah? Okay, let's go downstairs."

I was making a sacrifice because Vizcaya was party central, a weird-sounding Italianate villa that some robber baron had built out of coral, right before World War I made wastefulness go out of style. No photo spread for *Gay Downtown* would be complete without it.

Phil and I passed a group of young guys who were stoking a driftwood fire at the water's edge. The breeze off the ocean had grown cooler now that it was dark. Firelight streaked their naked bodies.

"Always with the pictures," Phil complained.

"It's my job." I clicked the shutter again.

"Take a picture of me."

"Okay, stand over there." I motioned toward the fire.

"No, right here."

"The light's not good."

"I don't care." He dug his bare feet into the sand. Two guys raced past us, one chasing the other into the brown water that foamed along the shoreline.

"Hey, Randy! Randy O'Tool!" a voice called excitedly. I didn't think anything of it until one of the bonfire guys, the one who'd been chased into the surf, ran up to Phil and me. Closer up, he looked familiar. The black hair, pale skin and jade-colored eyes were a memorable combination, but I couldn't place him. The lapse made me oddly sad, as if I'd been in heaven too long and started taking it for granted that angels would sit next to me on the subway.

"Wow, Randy O'Tool," Mr. Green Eyes panted, shaking Phil's hand. "Man, I loved you in 'Pump Me Hard 3'."

"Pump me hard?" I sputtered. "*Three?*"

Phil glanced from his admirer to me, sheepishly. "My, uh, workout video," he said, knowing the game was up, but opening his blue eyes all round and innocent, just as he must have looked (I was sure) offering up his sweet pink ass to the camera, to be pumped one, two, three.

So many things I hadn't seen, like unfamiliar lipstick on a cheating husband's collar, clues to a vanished body, waiting to be assembled. Of course I'd watched porn but I wasn't a hardcore fan like a lot of fags. Working all day with images, I found there was no substitute for touch, while I could still get it. Not like Stan and Frank, whose definition of monogamy was elastic enough to include a gang-bang as long as it was on-screen. They had to know. *Everybody* knew but me. Spartacus, whoever the fuck he was, had heard the little cries Phil made when he came. He probably rewound and replayed them so he could find just the right words for how much he disapproved of us. I remembered Stan reading out one of his dumb-ass columns in the locker room, a few days before we left for Miami. It was the 15th anniversary of Harvey Milk's assassination, and our boy Sparky was lamenting how gay men today knew more about porn stars than about our civil-rights martyrs.

I needed to talk to Phil, but his biggest fan wouldn't leave us alone. I caught the tail end of their conversation: "...fashion photographer?" Green Eyes was saying. "Wow, small world. I did some modeling for Calvin Klein."

"I thought I recognized you from that billboard on Houston

Street," I said. No wonder I'd spaced on the memory; his face hadn't been the most stimulating part of that picture.

"You guys want to come to Vizcaya with us?" Green Eyes asked. "We're just waiting for Roger."

"Sure," I answered, forestalling Phil's refusal. "Who's Roger?"

He laughed, with impervious, perhaps chemically assisted, high spirits. "You don't know Roger? Everybody knows Roger."

"I don't know nearly as much as some people think I do."

Phil tugged my hand. "Aw, Jule...maybe we better go."

"Nonsense. This is what we came here for. Food, folks and fun. Fashionable fucking. And photos." To our new friend I said, "You want to take a picture together, for *Gay Downtown?*"

"Awesome," he said, moving into position, with his arms draped gracefully around Phil's burly shoulders, while the flickering bonfire striped their bodies with patterns of light and shadow. Phil looked about to cry. His face got redder and he bit his lower lip, the way he always did when Shirley MacLaine got left at the altar at the end of "Sweet Charity".

A tall, willowy, bald black man chose that moment to greet Green Eyes with cool air-kisses to both cheeks. He was pushing the outer age range for the circuit, definitely on the far side of thirty-five, but sleek as a jaguar, not a single bulge anywhere it shouldn't be. Green Eyes introduced him as Roger Banta.

"It's great to meet you," I said earnestly. "I'm Julian Selkirk, I'm a photographer for *Femme NY*. Street Style," I added when he showed no reaction.

"Oh, yes. I liked that Japanese girl in the playground. Great emotion."

I beamed. Up until I saw Roger, I'd been almost willing to relent towards Phil, to the extent of taking him back to our room and putting him through a long conversation about our relationship instead of the makeup sex he was no doubt hoping for. But Banta was the booker for Manhattan Model Management, one of the city's top agencies, and the one responsible for casting Fische's runway show. Suddenly it seemed like a good idea, a positively delightful idea, to go wherever Roger wanted us to go.

The four of us drove to Vizcaya in Roger's Mercedes. Phil got in the back and was expecting me to join him, but I let go of his hand and slid into the passenger seat beside Roger. He had the radio on too loud for us to talk shop, which would have been gauche of me anyhow, so I concentrated on looking available. He drove with one hand on the steering wheel and the other squeezing my bare knee. I thought of Richard, and wondered whether Roger was married, and if so, what difference it would make. The vast majority of people will buy a bloody steak in plastic wrap but would shrink from bringing the mallet down between the cow's stupid brown eyes. And I have never pretended to be better than the vast majority of people.

Vizcaya was aglow with pink and gold spotlights that lent a warm tinge to the white-costumed bodies in the courtyard. Most everyone was shirtless, some in tight white shorts or sailor pants, others in swimsuits, or silly carnival costumes of sashes, wings and glitter. It was like a wedding where everyone was the bride. Then I saw a couple of guys sipping drinks through Day-Glo straws shaped like the male anatomy, and thought no, this was the bachelorette party.

Green moss was reclaiming Vizcaya's coral terraces even faster than we were. The tiles of the piazza by the water were cracked and furred with lichen. A short distance from the shore, a stone barge heavily ornamented with worn-down statuary rose out of the black water. Boys were going back and forth from the barge in a small boat. It was too crowded and narrow to dance on the stone surface so they lay across one another, laughing and waving their arms, like so many pink undersea polyps, as the music from the loudspeakers carried across to them. It was that opera-trance stuff that had so offended Richard's cultural purism. But it suited this imitation haunt of Medicis and pirates in the midst of Miami's neon and concrete sprawl.

Roger and Green Eyes ditched us to go across to the barge for "something fun" but promised to meet up with us in the Venus grotto, wherever that was. I fell into the rhythm of dancing with some guys

129

on the terrace. Phil hung back at the edge of the group with a glum expression. "Go, have fun," I waved him away, keeping my tone light. It was difficult to look at his face and not imagine someone coming on it. There was a pain in my chest that I chalked up to the effort of keeping up with the dancers.

"Please, babe, please," Phil said when I paused for breath. I looked away from him, toward the house and its gardens.

"Roger should be back by now. Let's find that stupid grotto. Did he say Venus or Venice?"

"Same thing, no? Wet and smells like fish."

Used to be, I loved Phil's dopey jokes. Loved *him*. The word hurt me, because it was as fake as angel feathers, its rules as flimsy as our clothing.

I pushed ahead, down crumbling coral steps and through scrolled archways streaked black from sooty rains. Lanterns replaced spotlights once we reached the gardens, where grass, moss and ferns crept up the pedestals of the classical statues. The air was moist and heavy, as if a midnight rainstorm were about to break over us. The soft moans we heard could have been wind in the trees, but more likely came from the dark figures entwined beneath them. Despite my anger and the uncanniness of the place, or maybe because of them, I felt aroused. Sensing this, Phil pulled me into a deep kiss. His skin, his taste, were so familiar, so easy to get lost in, like a chemical high, and about as long-lasting. I shoved him away.

Tears blurred his eyes. "I wanted to be with you. Just with you," he said in a small voice.

This was so absurd I almost burst out laughing, except I was afraid it would turn into crying. "Since when?"

"Since now." He lowered his head. "I was going to tell you tonight."

Beneath the pulse of righteous indignation was another feeling I didn't want to face, a weariness that was all mine, whispering in my ear that it was too late for forever. "I don't believe you anymore."

"Because of the video?" He seemed genuinely surprised.

"*Videos*. Or were you not in 'Pump Me Hard' 1 and 2?"

"Well..." Phil shuffled his feet. "I dunno, does it have to be such a big deal? It was just something I did for a little fun, a little cash. 'Cause we weren't being exclusive, before."

"But we didn't lie to each other. At least I had that."

"We didn't tell each other every damn thing, either. You can go off to the ballet and eat snails with *Ree-shard*, I can do what I want."

"Phil, this is different, I don't know why, it's like..." I squeezed my eyes shut against the unwelcome scenes my imagination forced on me. "It's like you cheated on me with everybody in the fucking *world*. Like, even if we stayed together, it would still be out there, all these guys I don't know, watching you, beating off to...you."

"Even if...?" His defiant expression crumpled. He slumped against a moss-pocked statue, then recoiled. "Ugh, this shit is gross. Why did we come here?"

"It's got to be the wrong place. I'm going to look for Roger."

"That's not what I meant."

"Look, this was your idea, okay?"

"Everything's my idea because you're never around."

"I do have a career."

"Yeah, well, you're not the only celebrity on earth. Most guys would be psyched to be dating Randy O'Tool."

"You didn't have to do this to get my attention." I touched his bare chest. It had been easier when I could blame him for everything. Now I was back to being torn in too many directions.

"Maybe it's not all about you," he pouted, unconvincingly.

"Who — Peter?" My heart turned leaden again, though I couldn't have said why.

"Naw, don't be a dope, you know he'd never break up a couple, he's too uptight."

"Why are you friends with a prig like him?"

"I dunno, he's cool. He thinks about serious shit."

Phil looked wistful all of a sudden. If I let my heart soften, it might never harden again. Then I'd be a true Southern wife, a fallen fruit, turning sweeter and more bruised, day by day.

Searchlights swept the sky, emanating from the main house, where the live music was beginning. The dancers' cheers mingled with the throbbing beat. A female-sounding voice swooped and trilled through a Whitney Houston remix. I headed out of the darkened garden, Phil trailing behind me. As it turned out, the Venus grotto wasn't hard to identify, since it was where the transvestites were clustered. Why a reasonably handsome man would want to look like a middle-aged librarian in size-ten heels is a concept that has so far eluded me, though Frank says it's because I prefer beauty to truth. At Vizcaya, however, at least some of the female impersonators were a cut above. I recognized a swimsuit from Fische's collection, a complicated maillot with cut-outs and metal rings, as well as several Norma Kamali designs.

Roger had a drink in one hand and was lavishly stroking Green Eyes' rippling abs with the other, but he lost interest in the model when we appeared, coming over to kiss me noisily on both cheeks. He had a heavy sweet smell, like alcohol and cologne. His dark eyes were warm but vacant, like the deep black water beyond the stone barge, where no doubt he'd scored a very enjoyable substance or two. I was relieved when he moved on to Phil, leaving Green Eyes to play with me in a contemptuous way that perversely suited my mood.

Indoors, the marble-arched ballroom was more gently lit with chandeliers and honey-colored lights behind banks of ferns. This scene was dominated by the romantic couples and the older men who were keeping their shirts on. A genuinely pretty figure in a Barbie wig sat on the white spiral staircase, the folds of her prom dress billowing at her feet. I remembered to take a picture while I still had the ability. Dane liked to tell the story of how he'd spent spring break in Fort Lauderdale, as a horny college student, and gotten so drunk that he turned his camera backward by accident and wound up with 27 pictures of his eyeball instead of the tits and ass he was hoping for.

I danced with Green Eyes, who finally bothered to tell me his name was Misha, while Roger and his friends sized up Phil's muscles like breeders admiring a racehorse. The older man's shadowy eyes met mine for an instant, flicking back and forth from Phil to me with a calculating gaze, making the question clear. The smallest nod of agreement, barely a smile, because I didn't feel like smiling, ingratiating myself with anyone, for one more minute. We were all men here. When the music spun me and Misha around again, Roger and Phil were gone.

I can't entirely say what happened after that. Some guys Misha knew were having a private party at their hotel, which was about half a mile down the beach from the Tropicana, so we drove there in their car. I was feeling irritable and I told myself it was because I hadn't gotten any action yet, except with Phil, which didn't count. The boy next to me was waving out the window and laughing hysterically. He handed me some pills and I took them. Then the other one bent his head down to my lap but he was so wasted that he could only rub his face against me like a kitten. The highway lights streamed past, waving orange tails through the foggy black sky.

The hotel suite's chilly silver and black decor was a relief from Vizcaya's swamp. I imagined I was walking into a freezer to sleep till a cure could be found for everything that ailed me. Around that point the scene began to split into flashes of light. There were at least three of us in the Jacuzzi, and we must have messed around some, but that could've been all in our heads, because I remember once or a dozen times getting the idea to move my hand up someone's thigh and then sinking back into the hot slick stupor of our bodies piled atop one another like sleeping puppies. One of the guys panicked about something — I guess you never get too old for the phobia about falling down the bathtub drain — and eventually we unstuck ourselves and flopped around the bedroom. It seemed like there were more people coming and going throughout the night. I remember bending someone over the back of a chair, working away on top of him with the terrible urgency we bring in dreams to some all-important, incomprehensible task. His slender back was white as moonlight.

I always wind up crying when I'm on E, but I've been known to cry at dog-food commercials. Around dawn I found myself wrapped in blankets on the floor, sweating. Intertwined shadows slowly rocked on the bed. I cried thinking of my photographs, how they would never capture how I felt at this moment. Colors pooled behind my eyelids, poison green and angel white, the burning blue of tropical horizons, the lighter blue of Phil's eyes. A heavy body mounted me. I heard the rustle of stiff fabric. Thick fingers moved down my arms, my naked back. I thought of the gowned man at Roger's side in the grotto, the stout Kabuki-painted diva draped with swags of white feathers. Could it be her waxed and pushed-up bosom now crushed against my shoulders, her white skirt settling like a tent over my shivering body, as those tree-trunk thighs enfolded me?

I dared a glance over my shoulder, or thought I did, in my dream, for it was the kind of dream where you wake up again and again without being awake, and you glimpse what death could be like. That rough, powder-streaked double chin, so clearly a man's, those red lips slightly smeared, like a little boy caught with the jam jar, like Phil's face the one time our tussling got out of hand and suddenly he had a bloody nose and neither of us quite knew what to say. The stranger's hands parted my cheeks and he thrust into me, so thick it ached. "Oh, Julian," he murmured into my hair, "I love you, Julian, I've always loved you." My heart banged in my throat. Gasping for air, with my face pressed into the shag carpet, I fought against the conviction that Phil was there, behind this stranger's white face-paint and black curled eyelashes, Phil who would no more be caught in drag than an elephant in Prada slingbacks. "I'm sorry, I'm sorry," I sobbed. He whispered again, "I've always loved you, Julian, always," and laid his full weight on me. Then my body broke apart into the darkness.

19

I woke up on a blazing-hot slab of concrete with my ass cheeks glued together. Everywhere my burning eyes looked was white, above, below. My face was dry and flushed, but down below I felt dirty and wet, like a child who soils the bed in his sleep. After a hundred panicked blinks the whiteness resolved itself into the overcast Miami sky, a cloud cover that scarcely cooled the sun's rays. Beneath me was a crumpled bath towel that someone must have wrapped around me before I passed out on the terrace of the hotel suite. I rolled over, and winced as red stars exploded inside my forehead when I tried sitting up. I tugged the glass door that led back into the suite and was desperately relieved to find it unlocked.

When I staggered into the room, one of the fresh-faced boys sitting on the bed turned to his companion and said, "I'll have what *he's* having." They laughed. I couldn't recall if they'd been there the night before.

"I've got news for you, honey, you already did," I drawled. Not waiting for permission, I hastened to the bathroom for a hot shower. As I scrubbed myself with the rind of soap, the words rang over and over in my brain: *Too late, too late.* Soap couldn't wash it out of my body, my blood. Only blood washed blood. What was I saying? Hocus-pocus, Bible verse bingo, these fragments of faith that stayed in me like broken needles, infection without cure.

There were no clean towels, so I dried myself with a bedsheet and went to look for my pants. I had a dim memory of wrapping my camera in them last night, before things heated up with Misha and company. Yes, thankfully, the bundle was still there under the bed. By some miracle I hadn't lost my room key, but I had no money for a taxi, and I was too mortified to ask anyone for a ride. The Tropicana was only a half-mile walk down the beach. Underestimating the strength of my hangover, I decided the exercise would do me good.

In the hallway I spotted Misha. He gave me a friendly wave. How nice, I thought, we might both be dead before we're thirty. send me a thank-you note, why don't you. But nothing was his fault any more or less than it was mine, so I smiled back and then had the impulse to ask him a question: "Hey, do you know who that guy was in here last night, the big drag queen with the white face paint?"

"Sorry, man, I don't remember anyone like that."

I tried not to take this as a sign that I was losing my mind. Considering that in the past 24 hours I had pimped out my boyfriend, taken unidentified drugs from a stranger, and apparently done a lot of other things without benefit of a condom, maybe I hadn't had much of a mind to start with. And my body could soon follow. Trudging down the beach under the hot white sky, I shivered despite the concealed sun beating down on my bare shoulders. Apart from one or two slip-ups, Phil and I had always played safely together. I'd been tested once, two years ago, when I was nineteen and paranoid, new to the city's pleasures and convinced that the hand of God was waiting to strike me down for my first mistake. After the results came back negative, that fear lost its teeth, until now. Now it sucked the air out of my lungs and turned my tongue to sandpaper.

Permanent wounds are for other people, you think; you don't believe you could be the one whose story goes *He never...* Never walked again, saw the ocean, left the neighborhood, blew out 25 candles on his birthday cake. Even when you live with death, as queers do, he's the DJ, not your lover — up there on stage, sweetening the music of your swiftly passing night. He's a name you drop, like JFK or Judy Garland, someone you're all supposed to know, but not too well. *Where were you when you heard...?* The question means, tell me about the time you remembered you were still alive.

Such was the delirious drama in my head by the time I dragged myself up the steps of the Hotel Tropicana. The bright-blue water of the pool looked so cool and inviting, giving off its sharp sterilizing vapors of chlorine. The few boys lounging alongside it were as golden and contented as they'd been yesterday. This picture-postcard sameness was the thing that finally made the ache in my head unbearable. I retreated to the air-conditioned dimness of my room, took another shower, threw up (barely managing not to do both at the same time), pulled the curtains closed, and buried myself under the blankets. Hours passed. My dreams were intense, incoherent, and so brief that part of me was always aware of trying to sleep, and failing. Phil didn't come. How many hours was it? I was burning up, so thirsty but I couldn't make it to the bathroom for a drink. I wanted him there, to bring it to me, my heart was breaking, but not for him really. Someone else, no one real.

I opened my eyes again and the room was cooler, darker. Night, maybe. There was a party going on, I'd seen the signs in the lobby, they were having a costume contest and exotic dancers. What if I went blind? Would I be sorry I'd missed it? Unless I was going to throw myself off a balcony, like one of Richard's hefty operatic heroines, I needed that freelance income from *Gay Downtown*. I cleaned myself some more, unnecessarily, gulped a few aspirin and went downstairs to blend into the scene.

The costume contest was something of an oxymoron because the hopefuls had barely a yard of fabric between them. First prize went to a fellow in a white thong and a foot-high headdress hung with chandelier crystals. The music cheered me, a bubbly disco mix. Between photos I looked for Phil everywhere. He wasn't by the bar, or in the toilet stalls, or in the cluster of men who pushed up to the stage to stuff dollar bills into the dancers' thongs. I was, though. The curly-haired stripper's friendly brown eyes met mine as I tucked a fifty between his cheeks, and we smiled at each other. Money I would need for pills, maybe, for rent and bedpans and a funeral at St. Patrick's Cathedral with a hundred fucking white doves with black crepe streamers around their little necks. That would probably impress my mother.

After the show, the stripper and I wound up in a corner of the patio, behind some potted palms. Silver moonlight made tracks on the smooth black ocean. He was a sweet kisser, not hasty, without the stagey hunger that often goes along with these encounters. His body felt good and normal, the ordinary muscles and soft belly of a guy who should be playing Frisbee on the front page of a college catalog. I gently pushed his fingers away from my fly.

"Greg..." I whispered hoarsely.

"It's Craig, actually." His lopsided grin showed no resentment.

"I'm sorry, I must've heard you wrong in there."

"No biggie."

"Let's not do this. I think..." My voice stuck in my throat like gravel. "I think I could be poz."

Craig continued to hold me, patiently. "That's okay," he murmured in my ear, "I probably am too."

"Probably? You didn't go for the test?"

He shook his head, not speaking right away, maybe wondering how much to tell me, how much I cared. I tightened my arm around his waist. The waves sighed rhythmically against the shore.

"My lover, Ken, tested positive last year. He's the one who's sick." Craig's soft voice quavered on that word. "After that...we just couldn't handle any more bad news, you know? Even though we both know...I just couldn't lay that on him."

"What...happened to Ken?"

"He's here. Down by the pool. He likes to swim a lot. It helps with the pain in his feet." Craig broke off, reluctant to scare me further. He brought his freckled hand to my cheek, to draw me in for another kiss, but I could see the tenderness in his eyes wasn't for me.

"I wish I'd gotten to you first, sweetheart," I said, pressing my last two twenties into his hand. "Buy Ken a drink for me, okay?"

Then I went upstairs and fell into a black hole of sleep until daylight and the smell of cigarette smoke brought me back. The doors to our tiny balcony were open, with the parrot-printed curtains snapping in the breeze, and Phil was leaning over the railing, blowing smoke and coughing. It was a non-smoking room so he had to do this to avoid setting the sprinklers off. His suitcase was open on the floor with his dirty clothes rolled into bundles. Our flight was leaving mid-day. I pulled on last night's pants and joined him.

"You okay?" I asked after a long silence. I was afraid to touch him, as if I'd never done it before.

"Yeah, it was awesome." He blew out a long stream of smoke. I couldn't tell if he was being sarcastic.

"No, really." His arm was so close to mine. All it would take was a little shift, a move I didn't dare make.

"Roger is cool. His friends had a yacht. You shoulda stuck around." He waited for my reaction, coughing again.

"You want water?"

Phil tossed his cigarette over the edge. "Nah, I gotta give this shit up. Bad for my teeth. Now that I'm a movie star." He showed off his grin and I smiled back, tentatively.

"I bet *you* had a good time," he said, his tone revealing nothing. "I stopped in yesterday and you were totally wasted. What were you on?"

"Damned if I know," I said, and we both laughed as if it were funny.

The rest of the trip home was just like that, distant small talk, shallow jokes. The airport was full of guys coming home from the party, all sunburned and mellow, air-kisses toned down to goodbye handshakes now that we were back in the straight world. I thought I saw Craig, with his arm around a stooped, skinny guy who must have been Ken, but I didn't try to make eye contact.

At home I threw myself into busywork: doing our laundry, dropping off my party photos, visiting nine antique shops in one day to find the right kind of gilded rotary telephone for Dane and Cheryl's new editorial — a glamorized, color-saturated homage to the 1950s housewife that *Vogue* would run with the headline "The Feminine Mystique". As I watched my clothes bleach whiter than white, wishing for a bottle or two of Valium, I tried to raise my consciousness enough to think about what to say to Phil. That other test, the life-and-death one, was too scary for me still. I furtively scanned books in the

Health section of Barnes & Noble, grabbing a George Foreman diet manual for cover when anyone walked past. Everyone had a different opinion. Take the test as soon as you're exposed (how I hated that word, like losing your shorts in gym class, like sunlight burning the pictures out of your film). Start your meds right away, you could live another five years instead of one or two. No, stay off the drugs as long as possible, they'll destroy your liver. There was even a book denying the connection between HIV and AIDS, but keeping up with the conventional wisdom was already giving me hives, so I left that alone.

20

IT SO HAPPENED that I was spared the relationship talk. I came home from work one day, about a week after our trip, and Phil had cleaned out all his stuff. Empty hangers jangled in his half of the closet. The copy of Tom Peters' *In Search of Excellence* holding up the short leg of our dinette table had been replaced by a folded-over *Women's Wear Daily*. Though December's first snow was falling, I opened the windows to blow away the stale cigarette smoke. The apartment seemed very quiet. I looked in the fridge but Phil had taken the rest of the energy drinks, so I poured myself a glass of orange juice and considered going home to Atlanta for the holidays, as my sister had asked me that morning. A last Christmas with my family had sort of a sentimental ring to it, that could swell to a full carillon under the influence of Daddy's best bourbon. On the other hand, if next year at this time I might be shitting into a plastic bedpan, shouldn't I do something important with my final days of health, like feed orphans, or sleep with Leonardo DiCaprio? Shouldn't I live the dream?

Meanwhile I kept going to the Ironman, because the worst part of divorce is losing all your friends, or so say the women's magazines. Phil and I saw each other in passing, in the weight room or the showers, even talked with our buddies at the same time, the crowd a buffer between us. He acted casual and carefree, like our breakup had been friendly, which an outsider might say it had been. But it would have been more real, more what we both deserved, if he'd smashed a bottle of red wine on the carpet and put my dress shirt through the paper-shredder, the way Tomas did when he caught a clarinet player practicing his woodwind skills on Lazlo.

My pictures in *Gay Downtown* were all the rage. I signed a couple of copies for the guys at the gym, though Phil signed even more. The one of him and Misha on the beach was captioned, "Randy O'Tool, star of 'Pump Me Hard 4', and a fan." I didn't realize he was up to episode four but that's capitalism for you, billions and billions served, as Ronald McDonald would say.

In the locker room, I leafed through one of my unsigned copies, letting the images take me back to our first bright hours in Miami, like the fading tang of brine on shells brought home from the beach. It was beautiful, but was it true? The truth, the whole truth, and nothing but the truth? Well, for the other side of the story, there was always Spartacus.

I read the column two or three times, my face burning with shame and anger. He was going on about guys who exposed themselves to HIV and didn't get tested. We were living in a fantasy world while our community was dying, he said, we were killing ourselves because we didn't take death seriously. The red ribbon is no yellow star, he said, we don't need a fascist government to exterminate the homosexuals, we're doing it all by ourselves.

Peter had spouted that exact line to Phil, months ago, when we were all at Frank and Stan's place watching the Tony Awards. I'd been coming back from the kitchen with a fresh bowl of popcorn and heard Phil's half-hearted "Yeah, maybe, but —" before Chita Rivera came on-screen and Frank made everybody shut up.

And who should have the grave misfortune to come into the locker room that instant but Clark Kent himself, Peter Edelman, with his stupid yoga pants and a sweat-stained sleeveless tee that stuck to his body in all the right places. Yeah, and Judas had a nice haircut.

"Hey, Julian, nice pictures," he said, in that shy way he had when he wasn't raving about politics. I ignored him. He touched my shoulder lightly, maybe telling himself I hadn't heard. "Julian?"

"You self-righteous son of a bitch." I shoved the newspaper at him. "You happy now, you got Phil all to yourself?"

"It's not my fault — " He checked whatever angry words he was going to say, continuing more quietly, "We're friends. Can't two gay guys just be friends? That's the problem with our community — "

"If you're gay, honey, you're the biggest self-hating faggot I ever did see." I read back a line from his column. "'We're not dying for beauty or love or Jerry Falwell's imaginary god. We're dying of stupidity and self-delusion.' You're Spartacus, aren't you?"

Peter nodded. He didn't seem offended, or anxious about his cover being blown. "I thought you'd figure it out. No one else here did." His eyes sent me an urgent message I couldn't decode, some private understanding he thought we shared. I was too upset to run through his mental maze.

"Where do you get off, calling the rest of us cowards, like we don't all *know* we're going to die, whether we take the fucking test or not? All except you, because you're too scared to have sex, you'd rather stay home and jerk off to videos of my boyfriend." With each word I'd edged in closer to him and was poking him in the chest by the time I was through.

"You don't know anything about...*anything!* I told him not to make those videos. I told him he was worth more than that. Nobody believes me."

"Well, I sure as hell don't. Why would he tell you the truth and not me? You're the most judgmental faggot I've ever met. Here you are, telling a guy that he's sick, and stupid, and dirty, because he forgot to use this little piece of rubber one time, he deserves to die before he's twenty-five?"

"Would you stuff the self-pity and listen? We're not doomed — we don't have to be. I wrote this — " he smacked the newspaper in my hand — " to wake you up, because I *care* — "

"Care?" I sneered. "Like my daddy *cared* enough to beat the devil out of me. Like good Christians *care* enough to remind me I'm an abomination. You want to get in line to save my soul? Fine. But don't — *don't* bullshit yourself that there's any caring going on here." I threw the paper at his feet.

"But...but that hellfire stuff isn't real. AIDS is real."

"You're an idiot."

Peter sighed. "What are we really fighting about?"

143

"Nothing. Fighting with you is a waste of the very limited time I have in this fallen world." I turned away, but his big hands gripped my shoulders, bringing me round.

"Oh my God, Julian, not you, no…" His face went totally white. I felt sad for him, more sorrow than I'd been willing to feel for myself.

"I don't know." I tried to shrug it off, regretting that I'd let him in this far. His pity was stifling me. "Do I have to? I mean, we could all get hit by a bus tomorrow, right?"

"Not you. Oh, God. Oh, shit."

Before I knew quite how it happened, he had enfolded me in his arms. I hung my head. It wound up resting on his chest. I willed the tears not to come. I was struck by what it really meant to die soon — to lose all of this warmth, to lose the chance to matter to someone like him.

"Can I go to the doctor with you? For the…for the test?" he asked softly, after awhile. Stupid reality intruding into the heat of his face against my hair, my arms around his waist. But with Peter, reality would always be part of the package deal. Don't fall for a vegan if you won't eat tofu.

"Depends — who am I getting? You, or Spartacus?"

"I would never write anything personal about you."

I pulled away. "That's not good enough. I'm not winding up as a goddamn sermon illustration. You've got to stop writing this shit if you want us to be friends."

I saw his internal struggle in his gentle hazel eyes. What did those eyes see? Did they see me, or was I merely an example of something larger and less concrete — the misguided queer guy, the sick animal to be rescued and quarantined?

"You're right. I crossed a line this time, and I'm sorry. But I can't stop writing. I see all this suffering and nobody cares and it drives me crazy."

"Just tell me, then — how can you be so sweet in person and such a bitch in print?"

"I don't know, maybe I'm not all that nice in person, either," he mumbled. "Can I please go with you for the test?"

"The test is nothing, sweetheart. Julian Selkirk has never been afraid of a little prick. Unless you need it too...?"

He shook his head, a bit too vehemently, and I felt annoyed with him again. Annoyed was easier than terrified. Peter belonged to the safe world, the healthy world, and I would say I was mad because he felt just a little bit entitled to his good fortune, except that in truth I would have been mad at an earthworm if it was going to outlive me. I would have struggled not to crush it underfoot.

"I would...*really*...like it if you'd go with me for the results, though," I said quietly.

He beamed, and his broad shoulders relaxed. "Of course. Call me."

I was hoping he would hold me again but the moment had passed. "You'll be waiting by the phone?" I teased him.

For a second I saw longing in his eyes, something passionate and unthinking, and I wondered again why he kept himself so buttoned-up. The only reason I knew was religion, but he'd said once that his family were the kind of Jews who worshipped at Zabar's on Sunday morning.

"Yeah, I'll wait," he said. Some guys barged into the locker room and he ducked out without another glance my way.

21

THE TEST was a bit more than nothing but I wouldn't have told him that. No matter how many times you've gritted your teeth against the sting of a belt-lashing or spread your body beneath a stranger's hands, submission to the needle can make the bravest man light-headed. It says as clearly as the click of handcuffs around your wrists: you're just meat.

After that, I was the one waiting by the phone. They said results would be ready in two weeks, which was creeping up on Christmas. New York was heavy with snow and tourists, its shop windows twinkling with golden lights and glitter-dusted red velvet bows, and here and there the orange glow of a cheap electric menorah. The maintenance workers in Dane's building were on strike and stood all day on the sidewalk below our window, playing "Jingle Bell Rock" on a boom box at migraine-inducing volume.

I was a week behind on my rent because I couldn't decide if I wanted to live there anymore. I thought of apartments as bad places to die. What would Richard Molineux do? They'd invited me to their New Year's Eve party, the first I'd heard from them since September. Richard might put on a fur coat and drink a bottle of champagne and lie down in the woods and freeze to death. At least, he would probably advise me to do that, if I asked him, but there was no proof that he would follow through on it himself.

"What are you thinking?" Laura Sue asked me, as we hesitated on the sidewalk outside Macy's, scanning for an opening in the crowd that shuffled past the famous window display of *Miracle on 34th Street*. I had agreed to fly down with her for Christmas at our parents' house, so there we were, with several thousand other wayward sons and daughters, praying that a Brooks Brothers necktie or a bottle of Chanel No. 5 would be sufficient repayment for the gift of life.

"That's not a miracle," I said, waving dismissively at the sequence of windows where an animatronic bailiff spilled a sack of letters in front of Kris Kringle, who nodded with infinite patience in the witness box. "The guy just got a lot of fan mail, he didn't raise the dead."

"No, but I don't think Jesus would work for Macy's." My sister was very serious these days. She waited for me to assume my usual role as the jester to her straight man, but I didn't have the energy for G-rated howlers at the moment. "That's not what you were really thinking," she probed.

"Whatever I said, it wouldn't be true," I observed mildly.

"That's what our clinical psych teacher told us," she sighed.

"He told your class 'Julian Selkirk is a liar'? Wait, he must be that guy I picked up at Trapdoor last week, who wanted my phone number."

"*She* said people only believe things because it makes them feel better, or because of their parents, or something." Laura Sue's mittened hand tugged my sleeve. "You don't think so, do you?"

"Well, on that theory, my opinion wouldn't count for much."

"But Jule..." she whined, unsatisfied with my dodge. I spotted a break in the wall of gawkers and pulled her along, up close to the window where Santa in full vestments waved from a parade float.

"See that?" I proclaimed. "There's your answer. Reality is consensus. Yes, Virginia, there is a Santa Claus."

Laura Sue blinked back tears. "No — that's what they all say, at school — but not God. Either He is or He isn't."

I had nothing to say. Perhaps, deep down, I had hoped she was wrong, ever since I grew into the wrong kind of man — hoped that God was like a child's night-light, switched on after a bad dream, switched off when I needed to do something private under the sheets.

"You don't know how hard it is, hearing these teachers pick apart everything I grew up believing — that I still believe — as if it was a dead animal in biology class," my sister said. "And I don't have a good answer, half the time, except how can you do this job, work with these terrible broken minds, if you have no eternal hope? And the rest of the time I feel like a coward. I parrot back what they want to hear so I can graduate with good grades, because I tell myself God put me here not to win arguments, but to help kids like…we were." There, she'd almost said it, the thing we never labelled, that was just Daddy being Daddy, nothing that belonged in a textbook.

"Sounds like being in the closet."

My sister turned on me. "It's not like that at all!"

The family behind us nudged me to move along. The whole scene made me suddenly sick with rage: the double-chinned dad and mom with their fidgety daughters, their robot counterparts under the Christmas tree in the window, husband and wife, husband and wife, down to Santa whose court suit was presumably ironed by an offstage Mrs. Claus. Peter and Phil and I didn't exist here. But so be it, soon we wouldn't exist anywhere, while the old story replayed and rewound, fresh as the day it was staged.

22

CHRISTMAS PASSED in a blur, aided by the straight man's drugs of choice, alcohol and football. My brother Carter brought home a leggy California blonde whom he introduced as his fiancée, Stefanie. She laughed heartily and often, showing big teeth, and sassed him right back when he made fun of her maniacal driving. No one mentioned the little bump in her stomach, which might have been my imagination. I'd intended to be more attentive to every moment, now that the well-worn patterns of our lives might be changing, but instead found myself drifting through these scenes like a ghost who'd run out of gas on the road to heaven.

Back in my cold apartment, a letter was waiting, stuffed in among the bills and holiday catalogs in my overflowing mailbox. It was New Year's Eve, the early hours of a dark rainy evening. Phil hadn't sent me a card, and I didn't know where he was living. The holidays are bad that way, stirring up ersatz memories of love with every long-distance phone-service commercial. I held the letter from the clinic in shaking hands. They weren't supposed to do this; the nurse had said they'd call me to come in and get my results from a counselor. Like that would help. I already knew the five stages of grief: denial, cruising, repentance, bed-wetting, and death.

I tried Peter's phone but got voicemail. With the unopened letter in my coat pocket, I went out for an aimless walk through the slushy streets of Chelsea. Many stores were shut, their gated windows interspersed with bright and noisy restaurants. Richard's party wouldn't start until ten, but I had no appetite. I found myself climbing the footworn stone steps of St. Vincent de Paul's. The massive wooden doors remained unlocked for late-night confessors to deduct their fiscal year's worth of sins. Inside I was enveloped in that smell of incense, mildew and candle wax that I used to believe was what adults meant by "the odor of sanctity". A bank of votive candles flickered in red glass jars. I lit one for myself, but that felt stupid, narrow-minded somehow, because what could I do for myself? I prayed for my sister, and Phil, and Peter, and the rest of my family, dropping coins for each candle into the tin box like an old lady feeding a slot machine.

When I exited the church, a light drizzle had begun, and I had no umbrella, so I turned back. As soon as I stepped into my apartment, the phone rang. Peter, calling me back.

"I got my test results. I think."

He breathed in sharply. "Are you...okay?"

"I don't know. I couldn't open the letter."

"You want to come over? I'm at my dad's party but we could go downstairs to my place."

"Your place?"

"Don't laugh, all right? Yes, I live in my parents' basement."

"Part of your charm, darling."

Peter gave me directions to his father's brownstone on Bedford Street, a quaint side street in the West Village. Lucky bastard, growing up in gay Ground Zero while our PTA nearly got my ninth-grade English teacher fired for assigning poems by W.H. Auden. *Lay your sleeping head, my love,/Human on my faithless arm.*

Peter's father opened the door, greeting me with a handshake that was almost a hug. Nathan was a short, boisterous man with a fringe of reddish hair and a dreadful necktie silk-screened with hourglasses and champagne bottles, but his quick brown eyes betrayed the legal mind that had bested so many sputtering talk-show guests. Behind him, Peter towered awkwardly, waiting to rescue me. Jazz music competed with a jumble of opinionated voices holding forth on topics from Hillary Clinton to gallstones.

Nathan offered us caviar but I didn't trust my nervous stomach. He steered us over to the non-working fireplace, where a petite black-haired woman in a red dress (a Diane von Furstenberg, if I wasn't mistaken) was quoting a poem from memory to a young man who was attempting a goatee. She punctuated her recital with fierce drags on her cigarette. I overheard the words "ruby placenta". Well, I supposed Baby New Year had to come from somewhere, but personally I was happier believing in the stork. The woman's striking emerald eyes were her only point in common with the sullen teenage girl who slouched against the mantel, brown hair masking one side of her face, wrinkled plaid shirt and ripped cargo pants contrasting with the others' holiday finery.

"Come meet my wife and daughter," Nathan urged me. Peter put his arm around my shoulders, drawing me away. The girl looked even more depressed, if this was possible, when she saw that her brother wasn't coming over.

"Maybe later, Dad."

Nathan looked frustrated, as if this conflict was routine between them. Then, recovering his sprightly attitude, he winked at us. "All right, play safely, and don't forget to come up before midnight for Dick Clark."

The dim light of the basement stairs was enough to show me Peter blushing furiously. Because the grass is always greener on the other side of the gene pool, I didn't make things worse by saying that I'd liked Nathan. "Your mom's got great fashion sense."

"Ada's not my mom."

"Oh. I see. I'm sorry."

He shrugged it off. The offbeat domesticity, the sweet smallness of his problems, made me momentarily forget why we were here. We were two high school kids in a TV-movie; he would teach me to study and I would teach him to French-kiss.

I put my hand over his as he fumbled for the light switch. "I'd like to dress you up and take you on a cruise," I murmured, "like Bette Davis in 'Now, Voyager'."

"'Oh, Jerry, don't let's ask for the moon, we have the stars,'" he quoted back to me. "Actually, uh, we do."

I couldn't suppress a laugh when I saw the glow-in-the-dark decals on the ceiling. "What, have you lived down here since you were twelve? She really is a wicked stepmother."

"Shut up — I was a total stoner in high school, and then I, uh, couldn't peel them off." But his voice trembled as we stood close together in the dark, our fingers entwined. My other hand encircled the back of his neck. Our lips were so close that I could feel his breath.

"Julian..." I knew that tone. That was Spartacus, the voice of reason, the great gay censor. Or was it the angel in the thicket: *Abraham, Abraham! Don't sacrifice that boy.* I took my hands off him.

"I get it...you need to know first...whether I'm poz."

"You think that would change how I — care about you?" His voice was low and rough.

"Peter, please, don't turn on the light," I gasped. He held me tight. "I don't have to know, do I? What if I didn't know?" His silence answered me beyond all doubt.

We sat down on his futon bed. He switched on the gooseneck reading lamp, which threw a small spotlight across our bodies. "Can I see the letter?" he asked. I drew it out of my pocket. "Do you want me to read it first?" Unable to speak, I nodded.

For what felt like the longest few seconds of my life, he scanned the paper. He let out a huge sigh, then another, while I began to panic. "It's okay...it's okay..." he choked out, his eyes tearing. I snatched up the letter. Oh, the sweetest word, sweeter than love or Jesus. *Negative.*

"Oh, God, thank you, God." I collapsed onto the bed. We lay side by side, holding hands. It seemed like enough, for awhile. I don't know how to explain it except to say that holding Peter's hand was like sex would be with another guy.

That is, until he shut the light. My heartbeat sang through my whole body, *alive, alive.* I kissed his warm mouth.

"Why'd you do that?" he whispered.

"What do you mean? I thought...I'm here, right? In your bed?"

"But what's it about?"

"I don't know," I confessed, with a touch of irritation. Life came rattling back with all its mistakes, a crowded, rushing train that I couldn't steer. Maybe he was no longer interested in me, now that I was safe.

Despite his questions, his body pressed closer into me, hip to hip, belly to belly, heating me up. I slid my hands down his broad back, coming to rest on his firm behind. His pants were too big. We'd have to fix that. Something else big hardened against my thigh. I shifted my leg a little bit, to rub him where he needed it, without seeming too eager. He breathed heavily, rocking into my rhythm, but then disengaged his legs from mine, too soon. Leaning over me, he cradled my face in his large hands. His wide-eyed gaze — searching, needing, seeing all that I was and was not — took the air out of my lungs.

"Just let it be...whatever it's going to be," I murmured, gently redirecting his hand to my waist, guiding his fingers to the top of my zipper. I shivered at that touch, nervous as a virgin in a teen-pregnancy movie. "You think too much, darling."

"I think too much about you." Tentatively, he smoothed down the fabric over my aching cock.

He was a talker, I guessed. I wanted to hear him make other sounds. I wanted to break down his resistance. And then what would I have? What would belong to me, naked in my careless hands?

"What do you think about me?" I dutifully responded, though I covered his mouth with a long wet kiss before I let him speak.

Peter closed his eyes, embarrassed. He stopped teasing my hard-on and encircled me in his arms so that my head was nestled against his chest. "I think about having you here, alone...safe from everything outside, for always." He buried his face in my hair. "That's stupid. I shouldn't have said that."

"No...not stupid." Scary, though. When his thick fingers were stroking me into a frenzy, I'd been ready to promise him forever, but my forever was a lot longer than it had seemed an hour ago. I was so tempted, though, to take his comfort, to bathe in his clean warmth. Was I drunk on his sweetness, or merely dizzy with relief at my reprieve, my payment deferred?

Only one way to find out. I rolled on top of him and started undoing his shirt buttons, planting a kiss on his breastbone each step of the way. I wasn't done with three when he sat up, taking me with him, squeezing me tight.

"All right, sweetcakes, I get the hint." I patted his curly head.

"No — I want it," he argued, but his eyes were round with anxiety, and his body felt rigid in my arms. He put his hand back in my lap, kneading my thigh mechanically. It was weird. Suddenly I wanted out of this dingy hideaway, to stand under real stars, breathing the real smells of winter rain and the exhaust of a hundred taxicabs carrying happy people to their New Year's parties.

"The party!" The memory struck me. His clock radio read 10:35. "Hey, I have to go to the *Femme NY* New Year's party, why don't you come?" I tongued his ear softly. "We can pick this up later…whenever you're ready."

He made some lame excuses about his dad expecting him upstairs, but I prodded (and tickled) him till he admitted the real reason. "I have to say, fashion people scare me."

"I'm a fashion person."

"And your point is…?"

Not taking no for an answer, I made him change out of his button-down shirt and chinos, with more than one regretful peek at his big furry chest. It was a challenge to find anything suitable in his closet, but I cobbled together an outfit out of a pair of black jeans, a Buddha T-shirt and the tuxedo jacket from his senior prom.

"Are you sure this looks good?"

"Let me tell you a big secret," I said, smoothing the jacket down over his rear. "First rule of fashion: Ugly becomes pretty if you believe in it."

I had high hopes for Peter when he recognized the geometric wooden totem pole in the Molineux' foyer as a Brancusi sculpture. I'd almost hung my coat on it the first time I visited. High, I was high as the stars over Central Park, extravagantly high as diamonds tossed from a balcony, even before I gulped the glass of champagne that the caterer's waiter waved under my nose. Since I'd last been here, they'd repainted the living room in pale green and ivory. Throwing off winter's depression for a night, bare shoulders gleamed white above black silk, earrings winked in candlelight, voices trilled over one another in manic conversation. Peter looked stunned. I handed him off to Marcia, figuring they'd have something in common since they'd both started out Jewish. "Tell him about your grandfather and the tailors' union," I hinted. Trotskyism wouldn't be the first thing I'd talk about to a woman wearing thousand-dollar earrings, but you work with what you've got.

Negative. I was weightless, immortal. When that clock struck midnight, my life would go on. I would photograph more beautiful faces, bodies, skies, seas…on and on and on. What, to me, was an unpaid electric bill, or a date who was standing alone by the bookcase, absent-mindedly dripping cocktail sauce onto his pants? I felt like calling my sister to tell her not to worry about me, only I'd never told her what there was to worry about in the first place, and now (with an incredible naiveté that I can only blame on the Puccini aria on the stereo) I wished I'd been honest with her.

Marcia's allotted hostess time with Peter was up, and she'd moved on to greet a regal white-haired couple with matching silver-handled canes. Peter studied the painting over his head with too much interest, an abstract field of muddy brown and brick-red stripes. He could probably explain what it meant, but no one cared. I was cut off from him by a swell of dressed-up revelers, their golden cuffs and diamond chokers flinging out flashes of light like the sun on choppy waters. A boy of uncanny beauty, pale with ebony hair and blushing lips like Snow White, caught me around the waist. It was Gio, a model from one of Dane's shoots. He invited me to feel the silkiness of his companion's shirt, shiny black with a subtle leopard print. I touched it as introduction, as reverence, before learning his name, Stefan. Not that it mattered. They were a magazine come to life, a magic page inviting me to enter the story that others only read. I motioned for Peter to join us. "This is — " I started, but Stefan, mistaking him for the waiter, plopped his dirty wineglass into Peter's outstretched hand. The young gods sashayed off.

Peter was momentarily speechless. I relieved him of the glass, in which a balled-up napkin was soaking up the dregs of Richard's best merlot, but then I didn't know where to set it down, either.

"So nothing's changed," Peter said.

"What should change?" I rubbed the bulge of his bicep through his jacket, claiming him publicly, but he wasn't satisfied.

"*You* should. I thought, after your scare — maybe you'd see through all this — "

"God, do you have to be such a death's head?" I dropped his arm. "What's so great about *seeing through*, anyway? Seeing through is for atheists and X-ray machines. I just want to *see*. While I still can."

I was spared more untimely scolding because Tamiko ran up to us. Like a glass of bubbly, she sparkled in a body-hugging gold lamé dress daringly paired with green stilettos. Hard to believe that a few months ago she'd been cutting her own hair with kitchen scissors and wearing a restaurant worker's uniform. Only her nasal, unsure voice exposed the teenage girl who was common to both incarnations, and someone — maybe Richard, maybe me — would soon train that out of her.

She congratulated me on booking Fische's job. I tried to pretend that my agent had already conveyed this unbelievable news, which explained why I was back in Richard and Marcia's good graces. "When Roger suggested me as the new face of the brand —" she giggled at her own quick fall into fashion-speak — "they wanted, like, someone famous, like that guy Dane, but I was like, no, I'm working with Julian, because none of this would've happened without him!"

Her grateful little face, eager for praise, made me break into a sweat as I remembered that hazy weekend in Miami. File it away now, let it sink into the ocean, seal it off from your life because you see, it didn't affect you at all. Before I could question her story, Tamiko was on to Peter.

"Is this your boyfriend? He's so cute," she said, patting the dreadful fake velvet I now noticed on his lapels.

"We're just friends," he said stiffly, then added "for now," with a sheepish grin.

After Tamiko had fluttered off to another knot of admirers, Peter muttered to me, "Did I say the wrong thing?"

"Second rule of fashion, darling: No one remembers anything you say five minutes after you say it." I walked away in search of more alcohol.

Peter could fend for himself, I thought. He could bench-press 200 pounds and he was raised by lawyers. If I hurt his feelings, he wouldn't get drunk on margaritas and come home at 3 a.m. wearing someone else's underwear. He would never slash his wrists or lose his driver's license. He was going to be absolutely fucking A-okay for the rest of his life and I wished we were still on that bed in his basement even though he would rather talk about the racial politics of Star Trek than have sex with me.

Richard found me by the picture window, shielded by the cream-colored drapes, as I nursed my drink. "Ah, the blush of youth," he said, tender yet ironic, by which I understood that I should be less obvious about my insobriety.

"Richard," I said, "I'm not going to die."

His eyes crinkled at the corners. "Of course you are. But you are not going to die right now." He held out a small plate with some fishy-smelling ochre jelly on it. "*Konawata?*"

Some would say I'm not fastidious about what I put in my mouth, but that was the most disgusting thing I'd ever tasted. Richard was waiting for my reaction, but not (I finally understood) because my opinion mattered.

"Unforgettable," I said truthfully. "At least until next year."

Richard favored me with one of his rare smiles. He moved in closer till his hand touched my thigh. For once there was nothing obscure about the emotion behind his gray eyes: an ordinary need, an openness, wide as the polar seas.

The chatter behind us in the living room grew more excited as someone switched on the TV for the inevitable countdown. Glasses clinked, liquids were poured. I sensed that Richard wanted me to stand still while his finger caressed my bottom lip. There was just time enough, if he had his way, he could kiss me in the last minutes of the old year rather than the promise of the new. I turned my face to the crowd. I make my living from my eyes, so I have to believe them, but sometimes, when I think about everything that followed, I wonder whether I really saw Marcia Molineux nod to me (with encouragement? with resignation?) before her husband's briny kiss welcomed me into 1994.

PART IV: EXPOSURES

(1994-95)

23

BEFORE ME, the figure of a man eating his sons. His sated, shocked, weary face forever immobilized in that moment by the unforgiving marble.

Paris in winter. My first big job. Jet-lag made haloes around the too-bright museum lights that prickled my fatigued eyes. A wanderer when I should have been sleeping, I paced before these monumental bodies that I'd only seen in flat textbook copies, avid for the ancient ones to speak.

Avant-garde designer Anton Fische had chosen me, out of all the other young nobodies in Manhattan, to shoot his new high-concept ad campaign. The Musée d'Orsay, where my new friend the marble cannibal resided, was the setting for this week's pictures. The collection was housed in a converted 19th-century railway station, a lofty latticework of steel permeated by wintery light. However, our models' flowing gestures were intended to have an underwater feel, and they were also wearing a series of feathery helmet-crest hats that suited neither the aquatic nor the railway storyline. And they say Germans are supposed to be logical.

The placard informed me that I was staring at Rodin's rendition of Count Ugolino from Dante's Inferno, who'd been locked up with his sons to starve to death in a tower. The legend went that the devoted boys offered their flesh as food to the man who'd given them life. A likely story, with no witnesses. I rubbed my eyes and retraced my steps through the galleries toward the main hall to see if Tamiko was done with hair and makeup. Turn left at "The Hanged Man's House", right at "The Annunciation"...

The majestic room rang with the click and clatter of shifting tripods and spotlights and the din of several languages. The photo assistants were local Frenchmen whose slang would have baffled Berlitz, the stylist was Brazilian, and the head makeup artist was a plump Aussie matron with serpentine tattoos. Without saying it in so many words, Dora the Aussie gave me the impression that our boss was a striver who surrounded himself with a United Nations of minions in order to feel like a global celebrity. My theory was that our work would go faster, and turn out weirder, if we were unable to talk to each other.

Be that as it may, the noisy isolation and my upside-down schedule made my trapped thoughts echo strangely inside me, like loud indistinct voices in a dream. February weather in Paris discourages the sensible hours that would have reset my body clock. The days were gray with drizzle, slippery on the cobblestones of the crooked side streets, where toy-like compact cars whizzed madly around corners when I least expected them. People carried the most remarkable loads on their bicycles. I kept waiting for a soft-voiced hunk with wavy hair and a huge baguette to run me down at the crosswalk, apologize with a candlelit dinner, and spend the night making fondue for two. If only my life were an Audrey Hepburn movie. My closest encounter was with a pushcart of sardines.

I succumbed to starting out at night, like the scowling cats that patrolled the courtyards of the little old houses. As the blush of early dusk brought out the city lights that tourists dream about, I would browse the rickety stalls of postcard dealers along the Seine. I flipped through shoeboxes for a picture that would impress Daddy but not intimidate him. You can't go wrong with the Eiffel Tower. At least it was a vintage sketch and not a standard photo, but I imagined the dealer sneering at my predictable American choice. On the back I name-dropped the famous models I'd been working with, and added an insincere complaint about the odd foreign food. Mama's cookbook research had long ago familiarized us kids with blood puddings and cheese that was moldy on purpose. We must have been the only middle-schoolers in Marietta, Georgia to be served escargot for supper, though I wouldn't swear that we all ate it.

Defying logic, as the great myths do, my first round of photos came out so well, I found it hard to believe I'd taken them. My mind remembered arranging the props and selecting the light filters, but my eyes told me these were candids from Poseidon's underworld. I scared myself. Everyone else on the crew seemed blasé about it, or happy in a businesslike way. Keeping my ghosts to myself, I joined the others in packing up the gear for our next location, but stole glances at Tamiko and the other bubbly-voiced young models, wondering how a few streaks of face paint and scraps of cloth had transubstantiated these spindly teenagers into Nereids. My recent reprieve from death might be just another of the gods' tricks, keeping me guessing whether I'd been turned loose in a city of lovers or spared to seek a sign that would bring me to Jesus. Or Apollo, or Marianne the Spirit of the Republic — whoever promised to keep my flesh on my bones, and my fly zipped.

Before leaving the museum, I bought a postcard of a medieval tapestry with sailors fighting a sea-monster, for Peter. The day I arrived, I'd sent him a card with Rodin's "Gates of Hell" and written on it, *Isn't all art really an excuse to show naked people?* His response, arriving a few days later in a sealed letter: *Or the other way around?*

Peter's dad was still letting him live at home, though he didn't pay rent and resisted Nathan's half-hearted pressure to finish his last semester of college. As he'd written to me: *Words and books — feels like the walls closing in. I want to see that I'm helping someone face to face. Or am I bullshitting myself? Lazy?*

Great question to ask a guy who has breakfast at 1 PM, I thought, licking the spoon from my *chocolat chaud.* What was help? The Lord helps those who help themselves, my Daddy often said. If I was dying in his home, he would've expected me to pay for my own bedpans. Well, I wasn't dying there, was I? My T-cells and I were enjoying a view of the Seine, and I had a paycheck in my pocket that would cover two months' rent, three if I skipped meals.

Through his case-manager job at Housing Works, Peter had befriended a young lawyer from Harlem, Shawn Defalque, a union organizer who was running for State Assembly. He wanted to hire Peter to manage his campaign. Judging from his pseudonymous columns that continued to scorch the pages of *Gay Downtown*, Peter had smarts and anger to spare, was responsible to the point of neurosis and good at concealing his true feelings — a natural for politics. On the back of the tapestry postcard, I wrote, *Good times at the soup kitchen — fish sandwiches for everyone! Go get 'em.* Then I sealed it in an air-mail envelope addressed to his dad's house.

So I wrote to him every day, so what? Nine postcards. Maybe a hundred words, hundred-fifty. He'd sent me two letters, the best air-mail could do. I only skipped the day Richard Molineux pulled me out of the office to go look at clowns.

Les Molineux owned a small apartment on the Left Bank where they stayed when business took them to *Femme NY*'s Paris office. They were currently in town for Fashion Week. Whenever I could grab a break for a meal and a few minutes' exercise, I scouted out pictures to submit to the magazine's "Street Style" page. They already had regular freelancers for the Paris beat, but in fashion anything and anyone can be replaced, and usually should be.

That day, I lingered in the magazine's office after dropping off my photos, hoping Richard or Marcia would pass by and invite me to a runway show. Fische didn't pal around with his crew; I had to savor the new confections from Dior and Chanel in the trade papers next day like any amateur. The receptionist, a slim blue-eyed darling my age with lips frozen halfway between a kiss and a sneer, must have been used to striving boys flirting with him. I didn't try. Just as my idling was becoming conspicuous, I heard Marcia's raspy voice through the swinging glass doors: " — afford a *hang-glider?*" Against etiquette, I ran to the closed door and rapped on it, miming an exaggerated "hello" as though I fully expected them to be delighted to see me.

Marcia reciprocated, anyhow, pecking me firmly on both cheeks. Richard nodded over the printout he was studying. Creative differences hung in the air. She asked about my work, and I mentioned the "Street Style" photos, which didn't seem to interest her. "If you're looking for a real job, I need a photographer to cover the Ozwald Boateng runway debut tonight. Do you know who Ozwald Boateng is?"

I knew something almost as important, which was that no one fakes out Marcia. "No."

"Neither does anyone else. That's why I'm interested."

"But no, Julian is coming with me, to the festival — " Richard slipped into excitable French that sounded something like "the elevation of Saint Mustache," but I couldn't swear to it. I looked questioningly from one to the other.

"It's some kind of Catholic street fair Mardi Gras thing," she explained impatiently. "Which has nothing to do with our new magazine launch, honey."

"It is my *inspiration*," Richard insisted.

Marcia talked right over him. "We've finally raised the capital to launch the menswear title that *you* always wanted to publish. Boateng could be the next new thing, you said so last week."

"He is a tailor. From Ghana." Richard sniffed. "Come, Julian, we must go now to catch the procession at sunset. We will have plenty of time for your little runway show." He steered me out the door with the gentle pressure of his manicured hand on my waist. The receptionist's glass-blue stare hurried me forward.

If you asked me afterward what the ritual was about, I'd have said it was about six hours. In reality, at most two. But reality was a whole other time zone from those circling figures robed in black and white, chanting antiphons in Latin and French as the flickering torches crackled. In that light, Richard resembled a holy ancestor of himself, a faded and tranquil effigy. Some tourists on the periphery snapped off a few flash photos. Damn cameras everywhere. Some moments should be exempt, surely, otherwise why would Richard and I be here, reverencing someone who probably never existed, in a language I didn't understand?

The quacking horns of motorbikes on the bridge overhead passed through our ancient music and trailed away. Torches sputtered in the cold drizzle. Acolytes hoisted a crudely painted plaster statue above their heads. Raised and lowered, raised and lowered, it tilted as they grew tired from its weight. I jumped when the clowns leapt into the crowd, spiraling their arms like boys playing airplane. Faces painted like mimes, they wore parodies of priestly styles, mitres with dangling bells, too-short cassocks with codpieces and striped tights. They leered and tumbled while the worshippers carried on regardless.

My knees felt stiff, my feet damp, and I worried about a torch falling over on me. What time was it? Would I be too bedraggled for the runway show by Oz-whatever? By now I knew the tune the priests had chanted about six hundred times, so to re-focus I sang along under my breath, substituting words that childhood ritual had lodged in my mind: "What a friend we have in Jesus, all our sins and griefs to bear..."

The clowns had windmilled their way through the small crowd to the heart of the procession where the acolytes gamely shouldered the saint on his plywood platform. They yielded without surprise when the clowns, with a theatrical sweep of their arms, toppled the statue headfirst to the cobbled pavement, where it smashed like a teacup. With a sigh, the ring of onlookers stepped backward. "It is done," Richard said, pulling me away into the street, though some activity and chanting continued behind us.

I did make it to photograph Boateng, who was a tall, luscious black man wearing an impeccable orchid-hued double-breasted suit that would have looked fantastic on the cover of *Homme NY*. However, Richard got his way about the hang-glider after all, so the Afro-Brit designer was relegated to a feature story, and the cover model was an Austrian banking heir and extreme sports aficionado who would die in a shark attack shortly after our issue hit the newsstands. I couldn't imagine an appropriate postcard for the occasion so I sent Peter a Boateng pocket square to wear at his new job. Violet with gray chevrons. It would go nicely with his black hair.

24

WHITE SUNLIGHT the next morning lit rivers of silver in the gutters. I didn't have to be at work till late afternoon, so it was time to force myself to be a tourist and ascend the Eiffel Tower. Since I'd sent the postcard to Daddy, I was committed. I'd be back in Marietta in April for Carter and Stefanie's shotgun wedding and I wouldn't tolerate any more ribbing about fear of heights. Fifteen years since I'd wet my pants on the Ferris wheel and I hadn't lived it down. I suppose Daddy felt bad that he'd taken a rare day off to show us a good time and I'd spoiled it.

Accustomed to seeing the tower in miniature, on the horizon or in kitschy gift designs, I was awed by the metal buttresses at the base that arched over our heads. *It's a cathedral*, I thought, no longer scared, and wondered why a hundred thousand pictures hadn't told me this.

The elevator ride made my stomach lurch once or twice. I breathed deeply and took photos, shoulder to shoulder with tourists aiming their disposable Kodaks, while the guide reeled off facts and dates in accented English. At the top, I leaned out, no camera to shield my view, letting the moist wind comb my hair. There were the buildings and roads below, the flapping awnings and scooting cars, the filigree church spires. Somewhere down there our models were getting ready for our last day of shooting, submitting to the hot rollers and curling irons, while the makeup artist readied his miniature jars of bronze, ruby, and midnight blue. Girls in horn-rimmed glasses were rushing down corridors with racks of plastic-bagged garments. My assistant was trying to remember how everybody on set liked their coffee and losing his temper at the barista when he got confused. And soon we would all come together and produce a picture that hadn't existed before.

What was my role in this? I felt like so far I'd stumbled into beauty, taking lucky shots of miracles I didn't cause, being praised for effects I couldn't control. Up here, clinging to the railing as the wind's energy streamed over me, I had a sense that it was much simpler than I had believed, that it was not a matter of looking harder (for what?) but of letting some filter fall away.

Beams creaked, like a bridge swaying, and I backed away from the edge. The bell rang for the elevator down.

25

Paris Fashion Week was over, and so was my job for Fische. Peter had sent me a third letter: *Shawn is encouraging me to finish my degree by mail. I can do the coursework while I'm on the road for him. I don't want to sit behind a desk again. Have to quit Housing Works for now, no time. I brought meals yesterday to a client with no teeth. Gave me his lunch while he drank whiskey. Why? With Shawn I can work on the root causes. No point otherwise.*

Whatever happened to "helping face to face," I wanted to ask, but as I wasn't even trying to help anyone's face or any other body part, I didn't have standing to use Peter's own words against him. There were certain lines we didn't cross with each other yet. Talking about Phil was another one. No reason those two shouldn't stay friends, probably co-workers too, since Peter remained on staff at the Ironman as a yoga instructor. To put a stop to the awkwardness, I'd started a trial membership at David Barton Gym — a total meat market, and pricey too. Peter did his part by saying things that I could choose to understand, or not: *Kevin and I and some other guys had a great time at the Mets game…I heard from one of the guys at the gym that Leo was training for Mr. Olympia…* But I was getting tired of these stupid games. Why should I be afraid to look Phil in the eye? He was a whore long before I turned him out.

Richard Molineux distracted me from this Chelsea-boy drama with a train trip to Versailles. He insisted it was an essential part of my education, though the era was not my favorite. I'd seen enough pictures of short white fascists in Cobb County, Georgia. Napoleon changed the world, I suppose, but any fool with a bulldozer can knock things down. Richard actually thought this was an intelligent point of view — like a bar menu, it sounded better in French.

It wasn't a great day for sightseeing, but it was the only one we had. He and Marcia were departing for Milan the next day. The resurgent rain was soaking the geometric hedges, driving all but a few determined visitors indoors to pay their respects to the little emperor. We bought umbrellas in the gift shop and squelched through the manicured gardens, round the oval walkways and down the long allées, where the occasional side path led to small white temples hidden among trees. Born armless, these minor gods and nymphs, to be admired, not implored to save.

"Is Versailles a cliché?" I asked, as Richard peered at the eroded inscription on a fountain.

"Oh, *absolument*."

"Then I shouldn't take pictures of it, I guess."

"Take what you want." His voice was gentle as the rain.

"Perhaps I want the wrong things…?"

The fountain, he deduced, belonged to History, or rather Clio, the marble nude who gazed demurely into its algae-stained basin. I was skeptical about the casting. "She is not responsible for what happens, only the writing about it," he explained.

The wind turned our umbrellas inside-out. We were relieved that the gift shop sold bath towels. Nonetheless, we could only bring ourselves to buy one enormous terrycloth tricolor, which we took turns wrapping around ourselves on the train back to Paris. That would have been enough, to fade out to the music of a harmonica, in one of those black-and-white movies where the Mr. and Mrs. slept in twin beds. But Marcia was delayed in a meeting at *Femme NY*'s Paris office, and the feather bed was warm and dry, and Richard and I knew what we were doing, as much as two people can ever know.

He took me slowly, from behind, both of us sinking beneath the white billows of the down comforter. His lean and leathery body, his slight paunch furred with graying hair, were like the finest old furniture, scarred and polished by use, crafted to survive. He thought using condoms was very American. I felt the same way about coming all over the French flag, even if it was a bath towel. His hands glided up and down my body while he leaned into me. I made more noise than he did. I figured this was true of Marcia as well, but I wasn't jealous. *The young can weep,* Richard had said once, of a novel he hadn't enjoyed. He sighed and I cried out and he let me sleep next to him for hours, until he had to dress for dinner with Marcia, who, if she'd come home at all, had known enough not to open the bedroom door.

I had nothing to do with myself the next day, in the long hours until my red-eye flight back home. I was sated with history, overstuffed with sensation and yet also drained. Wherever I might go, I was in a city, a country, a continent where nobody knew me but Jesus, who would probably cross the street to avoid me after the night I'd had.

Postcards, brochures, ticket stubs, the litter of my week demanded sorting into my suitcase or the trash. There was no point writing to Peter since I would arrive before the mail did. I hesitated over a postcard with a shadowy painting of Pygmalion and Galatea, the statue-girl's white marble body blushing into flesh as she bent toward the sculptor's kiss. If I sent this to Richard, some way without Marcia knowing, would he think I was a fool? Well, wasn't that what I craved from him — to teach me not to be one? To be honest, I was sick, not only at the thought of our cheating (though who knew what that marriage was really like?), but sick of everything I'd idolized before. Gods in heaven, statues on towers, girls in magazines — all cold, second-hand life. Richard's touch had surprised me, so slow and kind. Now he had had me, or I him, and I ought to know nothing would come of it except losing the best contact I had in my newborn career. But life, real life — if a picture was worth a thousand words, what was worth a thousand pictures? For what would I throw it all away?

The Pygmalion postcard was almost one of the throwaways, but at the last minute I fished it out of the wastebasket and wrote to Peter: *What's the most important thing in this picture?* I'd be gone before he could answer.

26

Spring brought work and a wedding. My brother married his six-months-pregnant girlfriend under a pavilion decked with azaleas at our family's country club. He seemed pleased with the arrangement, apart from his predictable discomfort at taking center stage in a rented tux. Daddy gave a coherent toast about being proud of his children, including me. He told several of his friends that I'd been working in Paris, though he said the ads were for Christian Dior, maybe because that's the only designer he could remember. When he sent Mama to find the magazine and he saw Fische's ad, he scolded her that she'd gotten it wrong.

My sister, a bridesmaid of course, hadn't brought a date. I danced respectably with her and a few of the single young women Mama herded in my direction. In her mind, I suppose, my queer tastes were no greater obstacle to marriage than the other flaws that women learned to work around: the big spenders, the boardroom warriors, the silent men. I was touched that she respected me enough, or was at any rate loyal enough, to inflict me on these Junior League versions of herself.

As soon as was proper, I slipped away to watch from outside, through the flowered trellis strung with fairy lights. The dancers circled around the gleaming floorboards, mothers and sons, fathers and daughters, as the soft warm night surrounded the pavilion but did not intrude on its glow. If I'd had a natural place in this scene, would I have given over my life to taking pictures, or would I just have lived?

Richard's marriage was not like this marriage. He would not see enough beauty here to publish. Perhaps beauty was even too moral a word for his ideal. For me, too. It was a little girl's word, and Julian

Selkirk would never be a bridesmaid. For me, the leap into darkness, the flash of impact, bruising myself against the unknown till I learned to locate what was worth knowing.

Back in New York, this meant taking every paying job my agent could finagle me into. It was immature, I decided, to turn up my nose at a *Glamour* editorial on 30 mix-and-match looks for the office, or (I bore it manfully) a K-Mart ad. Amid such banality a moment of unscripted revelation might be hidden, and wouldn't that be a greater coup than the stagey shocks of the avant-garde? Besides, my rent check was one piece of paper I was always proud to sign my name to.

So for a couple of months I was almost too busy to pull my pants down. I field-tested two roommates, neither of whom wanted to sleep with me; it was like an open relationship without the sex. After the second one left cigarette burns on my grandmother's rocking chair, I borrowed against my credit card so I could afford to live solo. I couldn't explain why I got so mad. Like the song says, smoke gets in your eyes. Smoke that reminds you of someone who shouldn't be that different from eight million other guys, but he is. I shot an editorial on bathing suits for a new plus-size fashion magazine called (unimaginatively) *Curves*. Every couple of years some well-meaning person starts one of these, and they put out four or five issues with a size-8 white girl or Queen Latifah on the cover, and then they go broke. I told them about Ariana and they offered to do a feature on her but she didn't want her clothes associated with that market, even though Ari herself is, as they say in the Garment District, *zaftig*. You see what I mean.

Meanwhile I kept struggling to regain a foothold at *Femme NY* while the editors steered me toward its newly launched male counterpart. *Homme NY* certainly offered me enough scope for experimentation, and then some. Their payment schedule, unfortunately, was as unpredictable as Richard's affections. So far there had been no repeat of our Parisian tryst, but he would sometimes toy with me when we ran into each other at industry events. In the midst of conversation about subscription rates and publishers' mergers, he would casually stroke the nape of my neck, or spoon an hors d'oeuvre into my mouth, with the ease of longtime lovers who forget they're out in public. No one remarked on it to our faces. Whether they saw it as one of Richard's affectations, or imagined he cared deeply enough about me to be indiscreet, it wasn't worth losing money over. I was sometimes glad the paycheck was undependable because I dreaded becoming the ultimate cliché, the girl who sleeps her way to the top. As if there was anything pure in fashion. Does Linda Evangelista expect to be loved for her mind?

No matter, there remained the occasional consolations of New Eden's back room. I fell into the old routine with Frank, Stan, and the others. One loud voice, one ruddy face, was always missing. Perhaps I liked it better in my imagination. I reread *The Bridges of Madison County* and told my friends that the perfect romance was a single week of passion with a handsome drifter. They all thought I was full of it except Ari, who said that sounded admirably efficient.

27

ONE RAINY MORNING in early summer, I was face-down on my pillow, waiting for the slot machine in my head to stop spinning. I planned to savor this one day of rest between an unwise night of dancing and my upcoming red-eye to Vegas. Tamiko had given up on couture after several runway bookers rejected her as "too ethnic", and was now the spokesmodel for the Mirage Casino. I was flying out there to shoot the billboard ads.

My phone's shrill ringing interrupted my dream of cheap buffet food. Peter was finally moving into his own apartment, and he'd picked a fine day to do it.

"I can't put it off again. It took me three weeks to reserve the elevator pass from the super. Kevin's already over there waiting for my fridge delivery, and he still has to work today."

"So where do I come in?"

"Umm…somebody…said he would pick up the U-Haul for me yesterday, but he never showed, and he's not answering the phone."

"Oh honey, you don't have to do this anymore, really. You can mention him. My ears won't fall off."

Peter sighed, breathing out tension. "I actually haven't seen Phil in over a month. He's never at the Ironman, doesn't come to the movies with us anymore. I hope I didn't make him mad somehow."

"Don't torture yourself — he's probably sucking cock on a movie set in sunny California right now, only he was too embarrassed to send you tickets to his debut in 'Leather Pervs #5'."

"I can see you're totally over him. Such inner peace you've got." Peter snorted. "Anyway, I guess you wouldn't know anyone who can drive a truck?"

"You can't?"

"I grew up in Manhattan. Enough said."

"Well, as it so happens, I do know a very well-built, sexually available young man who interned at a construction company as a teenager — you might have heard of Selkirk Builders in Atlanta?"

"Wow, Jule, you're — *amazing.* Okay, here's the reservation number. I hope they still have the truck. Come to my dad's place ASAP. But don't go in the main door."

I had no spare attention to wonder about this last directive as I threaded the U-Haul through the needle's eye of crooked West Village streets. I parked someplace that seemed legal. Nathan's front door was open, I noticed with surprise, and a woman in a bathrobe was smoking a cigarette on the stoop, cupping the flame against the driving rain. She wore a red slipper on one foot. Bare of makeup, the face beneath her bob of black hair appeared familiar, but I didn't want to catch her attention by staring. As I went down the other steps to Peter's entryway, I heard through his cracked-open casement a girl's throaty alto singing along to a guitar: *The first time I shot her, I shot her in the side…It was hard to watch her suffer, but with the second shot she died…* Then Peter's slightly flat baritone came in on the chorus: *Delia's gone, one more round, Delia's gone.*

"Sorry I'm late," I said when they let me in. "I shot a man in Reno, just to watch him die."

The girl laid down her guitar on the bed. "Yeah, I always need the Man in Black on a moving day."

"You remember Julian — my sister, Prue," Peter re-introduced us. Her handshake was firm. She was a lanky teenager with a lopsided smile and an unstyled tangle of short brown hair that flopped over her eyes. As on the night of the New Year's Eve party, she wore a slouchy flannel shirt and cargo pants. With a shock, I connected her with the last time I'd seen the woman in the bathrobe upstairs.

"Did something happen today?" I asked cautiously. "Is your mom…okay?"

"What's she doing? Is she drinking wine in the bathtub, or tearing up her books?" Peter quizzed me. I told them what I'd seen.

"Oh, that's all right," Prue said, not in a very convincing tone. "She's almost at the end of the cycle. Soon she'll go up to her room and write a poem for *The Paris Review*, and everything will be fine."

"Until she hits the next manic phase ten weeks from now and tries to buy another parrot from the *Village Voice* classifieds," Peter countered. Prue gave him a ball-shriveling look. "Come on, you know it's true."

"She's had a hard life," Prue said stoutly. It sounded like a debate they'd had many times before, but without anger.

Peter gave a dispirited look around his old room, unfurnished except for the worn-out bed and two stacks of taped-up cardboard boxes. "Maybe I shouldn't leave yet."

"I better check on the truck while you work this out," I broke in. "I swear the meter maid on Barrow Street was packing heat."

"No, let's do this thing." Prue slapped her hands together. "Next time the Bipolar Express rolls through town, I'll be programming computers in the dyke capital of America."

"P-Town?"

"Right state, further west. Hampshire College is letting me double-major in guitar composition and smashing the military-industrial complex."

"Bless your heart," I said.

By the time the three of us had loaded the truck, we were soaked and sore, but our mood had lifted. Ada had gone indoors to practice her Jack Kerouac impression. Prue hugged us both goodbye and we began our crawl through traffic to the Upper West Side.

On the drive, I kept the conversation away from the drama we'd left behind, telling Peter about my latest assignments. "Richard referred me for an editorial in this magazine called *Crash* — very arty, you know, very insider, with the boys in black lipstick and the typefaces that go sideways? Only, what they want me to do is a fashion shoot with amputees, but not, like, inspirational. Is that sick? I mean, what good is a Burberry jacket to a teenage girl with a hook hand? For one thing, she can't even button it."

179

Peter chewed his bottom lip, thinking. "You feel damaged people are ugly?"

So we were back to his embarrassment about Ada. I shouldn't have brought it up, but I had no one else whose opinion I valued. "Fashion should make you feel better. Cover up the damage, not roll it out for shock value."

"But it's the cover-up that feels shitty. The scars are your life. Like Spider-Man, right? It's because he was bitten by a spider that he became — anything."

"Thanks. You just salvaged my next paycheck." I dared to squeeze his big hand, holding it longer than a friend would.

"All in a day's work for Spartacus, the conscience of America." He returned the pressure, his warm fingers kneading mine, till I reluctantly had to grab the steering wheel again. He pushed back the sleeve of his shapeless blue Henley shirt to check his watch — long sleeves in summer, an odd choice, but maybe he'd packed all the other clean ones.

"Speaking of scars...what's that on your arm?" I touched my fingertips to the purplish welt on his wrist.

"Oh — oh that, it's stupid, you know those Velcro straps you use to lift big weights so the barbell doesn't slip? Well, I was working out and, duh, it slipped." He smiled, hunching his shoulders. "I ought to claim workers' comp."

I forced out the question, "But you're being safe, right?"

"Safe?" Peter's laugh was tense. "Yeah, I obey all the rules."

"What more can you do."

"What indeed."

He changed the subject to Defalque's campaign, which had him working on the issue of securing more state funding for city homeless shelters and drug rehab programs. Meanwhile, in Congress, Cobb County's other native son Newt Gingrich was whipping up resentment against welfare mothers and crackheads, a message that probably played well in upstate New York's hollowed-out steel towns. Getting elected was only the beginning of Shawn's problems.

Though I really should have been preparing for my trip that evening, I stayed to help Peter and Kevin unload the truck and supervise the delivery of the futon. He needed moral support, and I needed more time alone with him. I had my chance when Kevin left for his shift at Housing Works. Peter was anxious that his boxes of books, videos, and pictures had gotten wet in the rain and ought to be unpacked before they soaked through.

This was a challenge, as the apartment was smaller than the place we'd left. It was basically one room with an indentation for the kitchen and a small bathroom across from it, the whole place carpeted in a thin wall-to-wall the color of dead mice. Cinderblock and plank shelves were soon creaking under serious piles of books — a photojournalist's tour of Israel, innumerable *Star Wars* novelizations, and *A People's History of the United States*, to name just a few. I picked up *The Poems of W.B. Yeats*, saw "Phil Shanahan" penned on the flyleaf in tipsy block capitals, and quickly stuck it back on the shelf. I returned to tearing open the cartons of videos and arranging them in the plywood wardrobe that substituted for a closet. That was just like Peter, to store his clothes in plastic bins under the bed and save the best spot for his movies. He had an incredible collection of 1940s noir and silent classics, some that were new to me.

"I love this stuff too," I remarked, searching for a spot to shelve "The Cabinet of Dr. Caligari". "It's almost the same challenge as photography, how to tell a story with just visuals."

Peter leaned over my shoulder. "Did anyone ever tell you, you look like a young Conrad Weidt?"

"I never met anyone else who would know who he was." Except maybe Richard, I thought, but Peter made me want to forget that those practiced, curious hands had ever roamed over my body, forget that I'd dragged down our artistic discipleship to the level of dumb hormones.

"You want to take a break and watch something?" Standing behind me, he crossed his arms over my chest. I rested my cheek on his sleeve, with a covert glance at his wristwatch. I'd blown past any chance of a nap before my flight. If the afternoon developed as I hoped it would, I might miss the plane altogether, a very bad career move.

"Sure, if it's short. How about — whoa!" Underneath a Barbara Stanwyck boxed set was a tape headlined "Dungeon Daddies".

"Oops, wrong box." Peter snatched it up with an impish smile.

"Gross," I said. His smile evaporated. Too bad. If this was another masterpiece from my poetry-spouting, ass-peddling ex-boyfriend, I didn't want to know about it. And if it was here for another reason, I *really* didn't want to know. Not that my fantasy reel was all kisses and candlelight, either; I'd jerked off to the galley slaves scene in "Ben-Hur", though I didn't feel good afterward.

We settled onto the futon bed in front of the TV as the afternoon light washed away into a gray dusk. There wasn't any popcorn, so we ate cereal out of the box. We fell under the spell of Joan Crawford in "A Woman's Face", a fevered melodrama about a disfigured master criminal who falls in love with her plastic surgeon. Halfway through the movie we were lying in each other's arms, Peter's head on my chest, our legs casually entangled. On screen, horse-drawn sleighs raced through fake snow. The violins sang of danger.

"I've seen this three times, and I still get scared she's going to kill the little boy," Peter murmured.

"Shh, don't tell me what happens."

Everything worked out for the best, with a well-aimed bullet or two. We were alone with the unpacked boxes and the clock ticking down to Vegas. The first move was his, I decided.

"I saved all your postcards."

"I needed you there to talk to...it was the next best thing." We were whispering, as though we were in a real movie theater.

"So talk." He swung his body over mine, our faces inches apart. His hazel eyes were intent as a cat's in the half-dark.

A dozen questions fought for my first breath. But they all rang false as fortune-cookie wisdom, punchlines to the joke about the mountaintop guru and the climber who wastes his one chance asking the wrong advice.

I opened my lips, but instead of words, I kissed him. He responded at once, hungrily, the pressure of his mouth almost too rough, not at all like our last clinch in his teenage lair. I had the fleeting thought that perhaps I'd made the wrong assumption about his role in the dungeon fantasy. A little more pain wouldn't do me any harm, I supposed.

But nothing like that happened. He rolled my T-shirt over my head with smooth, slow strokes of his hands across my chest, my arms, finally my face which he traced with his tongue. I was rather quicker to tug off his shirt and pull his heavy weight closer. His skin was soft, smelling of good sharp sweat and Ivory soap, his muscles hard underneath except for his furry stomach. He moaned when I grazed his neck with my teeth. I could understand why girls love vampires almost as much as ponies — that vicarious power, that permission to hunger so single-mindedly that nothing is left of you that fears death. What if he really did burn for punishment, what if I could give him enough bruises to please him? I shuddered. His hardness ground against mine, chafed by the confining denim. It would be just too embarrassing if I came in my jeans, my elaborate airmail seduction plan finished off in less time than it took to hang up his Batman poster.

Peter lifted his head. Our eyes met again. My skin cooled beneath his tender fingers, my frenzy giving way to a suspended anxiety as he painstakingly traced a line down past my navel to my zipper. I forgot to breathe. In my mind I could already feel his touch in my most sensitive place, nothing between us at last. Did we have any condoms? Did it matter? I gripped his ass, spreading it as much as his ill-fitting khakis would allow. He relaxed eagerly into the position. If he didn't like it that way before, I'd make sure he did now.

The knocking on the door sounded loud as Joan Crawford's pistol. We sprang away from each other, panting, embarrassed.

"Goddamn landlord better not be after me about the goddamn elevator scratch," Peter growled. "I told those schmucks to use the blankets."

"Quiet, maybe he'll think we're not here." But as I spoke, I was pulling my shirt on, calculating how I could still catch my flight.

The staccato rapping came again. "Peter, it's Prue, are you home? I'm sorry, there's an emergency."

Fumbling into his clothes, Peter opened the door.

"Sorry," she repeated. "Your phone service wasn't switched on yet. I thought you'd want to know."

"Can't this family function without me for one fucking minute? How far do I have to go? I should've moved to Israel with my *real* mother."

If his tirade hurt Prue, she didn't show it. "It's not us, it's your friend Phil. He's in the hospital."

"Where? What's wrong?" I demanded.

"He said St. Vincent's. I think he was in the ER. I don't know what's the matter but he sounded like he couldn't breathe, coughing a lot, and then we got cut off because I guess he ran out of change for the phone."

"We better go." I grabbed Peter's arm.

"Should I come too?" his sister asked.

Prue's kind offer woke Peter from his trance. "No, it's okay, kiddo, you've done enough for today. Sorry I flipped out on you." The girl shrugged, no stranger to emotional storms.

At St. Vincent's, a timid volunteer at the information desk told us Phil had been taken to the ICU, but then her supervisor bustled over and refused to tell us anything more. Visiting was out of the question. "Sir, if you don't calm down, I am gonna have to re-*move* you," she warned, with a bossy lilt to her voice that suggested she made a hobby of kicking men to the curb.

"Can you just tell me, why is he in the ICU? Is he going to be okay?"

Her pen scratched across the form she was filling out. She didn't raise her mountainous head. "Are you his next of kin?" she said skeptically.

"Uh —"

She sighed, speaking with exaggerated slowness. "Are you his brother, his father, or his son?" We both knew I obviously was not.

"I'm, uh, his boyfriend." I could feel the stares of people in the waiting room, avid for a distraction from Junior's sniffles or Grandpa's kidney stones. *Look mommy, faggots.*

"Now that's funny," the nurse sang out, not smiling, "I had some circus act in a lady's dress come in here an hour ago, *claiming* to be his wife. You think he's been cheating?"

Oh God, Frank, you dummy. Life is not a Jack Lemmon film.

"Won't you please..." I said, tears starting in my eyes, but she'd made herself conspicuously busy arranging color-coded files at the other end of the nurses' station.

I was shaking with frustration and fear, and the adrenalin overhang of our interrupted grappling. Peter wrapped his arms around me. I felt a tremor go through him too.

"I should find a phone to call the Mirage, let them know I'm off the job — "

"No." He took deep, slow breaths, the rhythm of his body calming me as well. "Listen, Julian — if it's what we think it is — "

"It is. You know it is!"

"Then he's going to need our help till he can go back to work. If we have the chance to make any extra cash, we should do it. What I've seen at Housing Works — guys we used to dance with, sleeping on the streets — "

"You had no idea he was sick?"

He let go of me. "Really, Julian? You really think I'm that kind of guy? That I'd lie to you, either of you, because I wanted — never mind."

"Forget it. I'll do whatever you say. Just call me as soon as you hear anything, okay?"

"Yeah, don't worry, I'll get in to see him. Shawn negotiated a good contract for the nurses' union. I bet he can call in some favors."

I raced back to my apartment to throw my camera equipment and a change of clothes into an overnight bag. Two messages blinked on my phone. Phil's voice, raspy and faint. "Julian, where are you? I'm sick, I don't know what..." Click. "Julian? Why aren't you there?" Several seconds of coughing. "Gonna try to make it to the ER...hate those places...call me back?" Click.

The downpour was my ally, delaying my flight long enough for me to catch the last call for boarding. I thought I'd never sleep again, but I conked out five minutes into the in-flight movie. I'm lucky that way; a guilty conscience has no effect on my circadian rhythms. I must take after Daddy, who could stay up two days straight to close a deal, then sleep through a ten-piece orchestra's rendition of "How Great Thou Art".

Vegas in July was a Martian red-dust furnace kept at bay by extravagant systems that sucked air and water out of the landscape to feed the Mirage's tropical foliage. Slot machines everywhere, starting with the airport. I half expected the toilet tank to come up three cherries when I flushed the handle. The Mirage's lobby featured two giant fiberglass camels, a koi pond, and a chocolate fountain trapped behind glass. If you couldn't taste it, I thought, it might as well be mud. It was my job to notice such things, and then promptly to forget them, because the Broadway exuberance of my commissioned photos was a fantasy with no resemblance to the serious hush of those rooms where night and day are forgotten and chips on a table weigh more than houses, cars, or wives.

I rushed through the shoot in one nightmarish 16-hour day, pleasing my paymasters and bringing two models to the brink of heat exhaustion. Peter called with the news that Phil was being treated for pneumocystis pneumonia. Shawn had sweet-talked around the visitation policy, and Nathan would help us fill out a health-care proxy form so we wouldn't be frozen out again. Phil didn't want his family in Pittsburgh to know, not yet. Even now, we didn't voice the dreaded acronym, but when a bodybuilder in his twenties gets pneumonia in the middle of the summer — as my Uncle Curtis would say, it's all over but the shouting.

28

OF COURSE you promise the moon to someone who's going to go blind. If he can't breathe, you want to give him oceans, blue dreams where drowning loses its power to scare. "You're going to be all right," I told Phil.

"Eh, fuck that." He grinned weakly. Purple shadows gathered in the hollows under his eyes. I kissed his strawberry-blond hair, still thick and wavy, but limp from a week unwashed.

"Dr. Prasad said you could come home in a few days."

Phil searched my face for reassurance, then quickly looked away. He'd heard me: *come* home, not *go* home. Maybe we could get away with not talking about it.

"I gotta get back to work." He flexed his big hands, swatting away the cord from the monitor clipped to his finger. The damn thing beeped every time he squirmed around too much. It was like sleeping in a garage with trucks backing up all night.

"You still at the Ironman?" I asked cautiously.

"Yeah...and dancing." He winked. "Hey, big spender..."

"When your name is Charity Hope Valentine, what else can you do?"

He sighed with relief that I'd gone along with his Shirley MacLaine act instead of taking offense. His body relaxed too far, setting off another bout of dry coughs.

"Get away," he croaked, when I brought the plastic cup of water to his mouth.

"I won't catch it."

"Yeah, but who knows what the hell else I got. Monkey flu, or some shit." He drained the cup. "Hey...you're still negative, right?"

"Far as I know."

"Don't be a dumb-ass. I should've been tested before. Wasn't fair..." He sucked in his breath and swallowed hard to suppress the cough. His eyes had to speak for him. Now that it was finally on offer, I found his apology too painful to bear.

"It's okay," I said, rubbing his back, too hard.

He shook his head. "Must've been before Miami..."

"I figured."

"They pay more if you don't use a rubber," he said, almost pensively.

"Who?"

"Who do you think? The Motion Picture Association of America?"

"I wish you wouldn't talk about that."

"Who else am I gonna talk to?"

I had nothing to say to that. Phil looked at the overhead TV, which was set on the Tranquility channel, playing scenes of water spilling over rocky cliffs. I kissed him on the lips.

"Now I've got the monkey flu too," I said. "Chee-chee-chee."

He returned my smile. "Ooh-ooh-ooh," he grunted like a gorilla, and tried to scratch his pits, which set off the monitor beeper. "Ugh no like."

The following week we moved Phil into my apartment. He was still pretty weak but the insurance wouldn't cover any more days in the hospital. He made some jokes about how the lime Jell-O was killing him quicker than anything. He'd readily agreed it made no sense for both of us to pay full rent on two separate places. Money, the language of men's feelings.

Tomas brought a stack of casseroles for my freezer "because I know you could burn water, cariño." He'd also smuggled two bottles of wine out of the Soho bistro where he was sous-chef. "Mother's little helper," he said, handing them to me.

I set down my shopping bag of pill bottles in the bathroom. Was it two blue ones in the morning and one yellow one with lunch, or the yellow ones on an empty stomach and the white ones after dinner? Some book had said to make a practice run with jellybeans but we didn't have time for that. What was all this crap in my medicine cabinet? Hair product, moisturizers, condoms, Alka-Seltzer (for those post-party heaves), more hair product, suntan lotion, lube, and a pair of red plastic novelty handcuffs that one of us must have bought for Valentine's Day. Well, I'd probably still need the Alka-Seltzer. I shoved the other junk into the empty bag and spent far too much time rearranging the pill bottles on the shelves. From the bedroom came Peter's voice, explaining some Medicaid paperwork, and Phil's reply, too hushed for me to make out the words. Alphabetical or in order of size, frequency, or time? I could make a Pride rainbow — red pills, yellow pills, blue pills. My sister used to do things like that. She went through a superstitious phase, which maybe a lot of kids do, but hers lasted longer, until she was nine or ten. Eat the red M&Ms first, then green, then brown. Take exactly three sips of juice between each bite of breakfast. And if you don't...?

Tomas couldn't stay long. No one could. The dinnertime rush was beginning. He made Phil smile, pretending to speed-chop a stack of vegetables with a kitchen knife in each hand. If he started juggling, I was going to call the Make-A-Wish Foundation. Frank stopped by long enough to drop off some used movies he'd bought at the video store. "They're all clean," he said, meaning the content, but that gave me a new worry. Should we have anything in the house that other people had touched? Mama used to say that germs died after three days, but that could've been a comforting fiction, like Julia Child's ten-second "oopsie!" rule when she dropped the chicken on the floor.

Peter was the last to go. The dinner hour meant there were voters to call, to interrupt their rice and beans in order to discuss Shawn's positions on rent control and community policing. I'd skimmed some of his campaign literature when I had nothing else to read in the hospital. New York was undergoing a racial backlash after the Crown Heights riots and the ineffectual Mayor Dinkins. Crime, welfare reform, and affirmative action kept the *Post* columnists busy typing exclamation points. I had endured several afternoons of the Rush Limbaugh show in Phil's room. "You know he hates fags," I'd protested once.

"Eh, he hates everybody. It's funny," Phil had said, listening with eyes closed.

Driving steadily down the middle of this mine-filled road was Shawn Defalque, whose materials alluded to all the hot issues while leaving the details to your wishful thinking. Peter said I was being too cynical. Defalque had negotiated hazard pay for hospital janitors. He had personally fixed the locks in the East 4th Street housing project after a girl was assaulted on the roof. Peter stopped short of claiming that he had made the sun shine an extra hour every day, but no doubt it was on his to-do list.

As Peter was leaving the apartment, I apologized for my skepticism. "Politicians just rub me the wrong way," I confessed, but spoiled the effect with my double-entendre.

"Oh, I'm not touching that," Peter played along.

"So *you* say." Oh, it was too easy to make him squirm. That boy was bad for me. Or would have been, in that alternate life where there was no one but the two of us and Joan Crawford.

My place — our place, again — fell into a palpable silence. Time to begin hacking a path through the frozen lasagna. But first, I went back to the bedroom to see if Phil was sleeping all right. His face was pale but restful, his lips slightly parted, one arm flung out atop the cover with his fingers unfurled, palm up. I was responsible for him, I suddenly realized, in that quiet where we were the only two breathing. The weight of him, his body and his hours. Later, he would sleep through dinner and I would open a can of soup, then crawl into bed beside him for some warm half-awake groping that we weren't ready to take further. Later still, he would toss and turn, and I would make up the couch-bed, a space away from his soiled tissues and night sweats. Later and later till morning, and work, and tears, but no, it's not that late, not yet. There's still time for dust motes in the late sunlight, and two heartbeats.

29

We couldn't sleep together right away, another respite from conversation about what, if anything, would follow from that. Phil's body was adjusting to the meds. He was restless at night and, rather than disturb me, he'd migrate to the living room to watch a doze-inducing show on public access TV. I missed that lump in the bed next to me, reaching out to find a cooling mound of blankets where he had been when I drifted off. I could disgust myself if I chose, picturing all the bodies our bodies had lain with, especially his, but there was no substance to that story now. I couldn't afford to indulge in it. Sooner or later each night I'd wind up where he was, letting the late-night programs soothe me with the trivial surprise of what was on next: a pre-recorded city council debate about mass transit, perhaps, followed by a documentary on Byzantine icons.

The latter program gave me a way to handle the *Crash* photo shoot. Seamless paper in warm tan and ochre tones could reference the gilded backgrounds of altar panels without overpowering my couture-clad amputees, posed head-on with no pretense of being caught in a candid inattentive moment. Their only furniture was themselves. For St. Agatha with her breasts on a platter, read Lesley unsheathing her mastectomy scar from a Vera Wang bodice. St. Catherine's wheel, meet Michelle's chair. There's no rule that you can't pair a ventilator with pearls. It's not like white shoes after Labor Day. That was her joke, not mine, but I wouldn't let her smile for the camera. Saints aren't obliged to break the ice.

I sent my two favorite pictures from the job to *Femme NY*, to show them my new direction. No time to wait till the magazine came out.

Phil was tired of eating boiled chicken and rice from God's Love We Deliver. As Peter had predicted, we needed every dollar we could earn.

Richard phoned me soon after that, one weekend in August. The Metropolitan Museum was open late tonight, there was a string quartet playing, did I want to come out for a drink with him? It was unusual for Richard to pursue me, if that's what he was doing. His voice was deep and soporific as cello music, smooth as brandy. Just a taste, I bargained with myself, let me sink into that heat with no future, now more than ever, when morning will be cold and white as a hospital bed.

We met on the second floor of the museum, outside the special exhibit of early 20th-century German art. Richard kissed me on both cheeks. We were alone, except for everyone else there. The string quartet was sawing through a slow movement from one of the Brandenburg Concertos. He bought us plastic cups of white wine and we found seats in the marble gallery that overlooked the lobby. Other visitors walked past us, their attention clicking from Chinese pottery to Bach harmonies to Egon Schiele's nude pen-and-ink whores, with perhaps a ten-second stop to notice two men, the older and the younger, sitting with their knees touching.

"Your young friends, are they reading the men's magazines?" Richard asked.

"As in motorcycle repair, or as in Pamela Anderson's boobs?" I made a face, and not just because the wine was too dry. Tonight I needed a friend, not an editor.

"Exactly. There is the fashion, in these lad books, but there is nothing cultured for a young man, for your lifestyle." His gray eyes met mine on the last word, suggesting later delights — in an hour? a year? — or perhaps by then he would decide, like the couple sitting too close to the viola player, that unheard melodies were sweeter.

"And what exactly is my *lifestyle*, Richard?" I said with sudden irritation. "I mean, I've seen the word on a pack of condoms, but I guess I need somebody to show me the ins and outs."

Richard's brow creased. "Are you bored with the music?" he asked after a pause.

"Yes," I said, though that wasn't the right word. The thrumming of the cello reminded me of cicadas in my parents' backyard, during those childhood summers when I'd doze off in the sun and wake with drums pounding in my sunburned head. I never learned.

"Let us walk, then." As we ambled through the German exhibit, Richard fretted that his publication was losing ground to its vulgar competitors. The early 1990s had launched a new generation of knock-offs of the British lad books that were more youthful and aggressively sexual than your father's *GQ*. "*Homme NY* is not for the young salesman who goes to the strip club," he said, pausing before a painting of a gaudily made-up woman with an unlaced corset and a predatory stare. "Look, Otto Dix. Amazing."

"I thought you didn't like strippers."

"But no, this is real life, not your pumped-up plastic dolls. This is what real life does to a woman."

"How's Marcia?"

Now he was really cross with me. "She is splendid, as always." He swept onward, to a grotesque drawing of a disfigured soldier from World War I. "And this is life for a man. Do you understand, Julian?"

Part of the soldier's face had been shot away, exposing teeth and jawbone through a wound in his unshaven cheek. One eye socket was empty. Yet the other burning eye revealed that still, he lived. Phil might look like this, falling to pieces underground, unless we cremated him. I collapsed onto the bench in the middle of the gallery and sat hunched over with my back to the image.

Presently Richard came to sit beside me. "This is a silly game that you are playing," he scolded me gently. "I am married, you know. Did you think I would take you every night to the disco? There is a time and a place for this."

"There isn't any game."

He lifted his hand from the nape of my neck. "Then what is there?"

"Richard, Phil's dying. He has AIDS."

The change in his gray eyes was as faint as the line between sky and sea on a winter horizon. "Who is Phil?"

"He's — he was my boyfriend, until recently."

"But you have left him?" No judgment in his voice.

"He's moved back in now...but I don't know what we are...I don't know what I should do." Visitors continued to circulate through the gallery, nodding with detached appreciation at the painted horrors from battles eighty years past. One hears of hasty weddings before every war. Forever seems shorter then. I'd been greedy for life beyond Phil, those future decades I took for granted. "Richard...why do you stay with Marcia?"

The personal question took him aback. He pursed his lips. "She is my partner," he said stiffly.

"But do you have sex?"

"You do not need to know this, like a supermarket magazine." He looked irritated and disappointed. "When I am with my wife, I am with her, and you are not there." Just as quickly, he let go of his cross mood, like a stone slipping beneath the glassy surface of a lake. "And now you are here." He rested his fingertips on the back of my hand, which was gripping the edge of the bench.

"You remember Phil," I said impulsively. "He was in the pool photos, that first story of mine you ever saw, when you visited our class at FIT?" Richard's expression was blank. "That crazy scene," I went on, anxious now, "where Cady had a nosebleed, and Ariana was wearing those big red pants? No?"

Richard smiled politely. "I remember I have always admired your work very much."

"Are you okay?" I asked. Richard couldn't be losing his mind. He was too young.

"Of course. Why would I not be?" The familiar glint returned to his eyes. "Time passes, Julian. *Mignonne, allons voir si la rose/Qui ce matin avoit desclose/Sa robe de pourpre au Soleil/A point perdu ceste vesprée...*"

"Well, la-de-fucking-dah."

Incredibly, he chuckled. "Come along. I know you do not need talking now."

Outside the museum, in the blue dusk, we embraced in front of the spotlit fountains that sent up their foamy jets in a neat row. He held me longer than a friend would, close to his firm wiry body scented with sandalwood soap. "Where shall we go?" he murmured. For Richard, forgetfulness was the closest thing to forgiveness.

I really wanted to go to his apartment, to fall asleep in his bed and have breakfast the next morning in the apple-green dining room with him — and Marcia too, bizarre as that sounded. But if he'd wanted me there, he would have said so. "My place?" I asked half-heartedly. Richard hesitated. As far as I was concerned, that exhausted all the available options. I mean, what could he have in mind — a bathroom at the Port Authority? the back of a horse-drawn carriage in Central Park? I would rather not do it at all, I thought, surprised by the anger that welled up in me, like a thunderstorm that could break and cleanse us, flaying our clothes to rags.

"But what could I learn there?" Richard objected.

"How about, how to change a bedpan?"

Had I mined some buried golden vein of empathy in Richard Molineux? Sadness shadowed his face, not his usual detached pity for others' failings, but a pain of his own. "No, you misunderstand. I have taken you here and there, shown you what you should see. Now do you have anything to teach me?"

"But I don't know anything. And despite what you've always said about my work, that isn't enough. This random life, these accidental pictures — ugh. I hate it," I burst out, sounding like a child reduced to tears by what was on his plate. "I'm useless."

Richard touched my arm, once, twice, like an artist retracing a line he's drawn, to get it right. "And to be useful, this is so important? More than to be what you are?" He brushed my sleeve a final time with a brisk slap. "If you do not want this boy in your home, he should not be there."

"I wish it were that simple."

"Simple is not the same as easy." He was losing interest, gazing down the boulevard of Fifth Avenue, where the tangerine haze of sunset spread across the windows of white-fronted embassy mansions. I thought I understood the famine and the fear he would not admit. He needed me, but not as much as he needed the precious minutes he might waste, talking me into something I no longer wanted to do again.

I gave the first excuse that came to mind. "I should go. I promised my friend I'd attend this political meeting tonight. I'm sorry."

I'd been penciling Defalque's campaign events into my calendar whenever Peter stopped by with a care package for Phil, but that had been the extent of my support thus far. From the brochures, I knew that the aspiring assemblyman was a sharp dresser, sporting custom-tailored suits and Hugo Boss neckties. Even Peter had stepped up his personal grooming to match, something I'd never been able to achieve with him.

In a rare moment of negativity about his fearless leader, Peter had once complained to me that Shawn spent a three-figure sum on a plum-striped shirt from Thomas Pink. The poor you have always with you, I'd said, but nobody is going to vote for them. The more you're disrespected, the more it makes sense to fix the outside first. Our housekeeper's church hats cost more than Mama's. This had led to an argument where Peter called me racist for comparing Shawn to a black maid, and I said his ripped jeans were a sign of white privilege, which was one of those conversation-killing catchphrases that Ariana had taught me in college.

So I left Richard hailing a taxi outside the Met, and took the crosstown bus to a public school on West 97th Street for Defalque's first debate against his opponent, a jowly dark man whose posture was as careworn as his suit. I expected mild educational boredom for the next forty minutes. I was mainly there for the clothes, and to inflate Peter's assessment of my intellectual gravitas. There'd been a time when Daddy thought I was the smart one of us three kids, like Carter was athletic and Laura Sue was good. When I made honors list freshman year of high school, he gave me a secondhand briefcase and a summer internship at Selkirk Builders. It was half adding up balance sheets and half digging holes in the ground. I preferred the holes. The next term I got a C-minus in social studies and a belt buckle scar across my backside and the briefcase passed to Carter.

Defalque's opponent reminded me of my old history teacher, tortoise-like, wise in drab details but defeated by our undisciplined impatience for action. Shawn could not have been more different.

The face above the charcoal shirt and ivory necktie had features perfectly formed as a pharaoh's on an Egyptian bas-relief, save for a small scar that puckered the edge of his lower lip. They must have airbrushed that out in the campaign literature, a dumb decision to make him look slick and generic. I could do a better job. It takes an artist to translate the dynamism of voice and presence into a still image. Before he'd said a word, Defalque seemed more awake, more *there* than anyone around him. Of course he was handsome, and I don't mind looking at a handsome man, but he wasn't inviting in that way. His energy was like a shot of espresso after the dreamy liqueur of Richard's aphorisms. Peter would probably tell me that was a racist metaphor, that is if he gave me credit for knowing what a metaphor was.

"Too many times, we think it's too late to turn ourselves around. Too many times, we think, because we've got *less power*, that we're power-*less*. That's a mistake. A mistake that's killing us. But when we remember who we are, we come back to life."

Shawn was responding to some question about crime and whether the answer was more cops on the streets, despite ongoing problems with police brutality. I knew he wasn't addressing us queer boys — or was he? Was this a double meaning that Peter had slipped into his talking points? With respect to the crime question, he was saying people could take care of their own neighborhoods instead of waiting for a big man with a gun to rescue them. I had a memory of Daddy locking the car doors when we drove through downtown Atlanta, staring grimly over the steering wheel at the young black men sharing a pack of Kools on the street corner. He would read us stories of burglaries and carjackings from the *Journal-Constitution*, illustrated with grainy mug shots of dark faces. Out in the suburbs, with our own kind, we were safe. And all of us round the breakfast table had to agree.

"Because one person is never just one person. Break that window, you affect the world. Help your neighbor fix that window, you change the world back how it ought to be, little by little. Everything you do matters. Cast your vote, you're saying, 'I am just one person, but I'm responsible for my community, as much as anyone else.'"

Far as I knew, I was still registered to vote in Cobb County, Georgia, which was like having a choice to kiss a pig or a donkey. I ought to update my residency. Not that Shawn's policies would impact my corner of Chelsea very much, but anything was better than lying around waiting to look pretty at our funerals. I went home to change the world, one bedpan at a time.

30

LIKE BABIES, Phil was easier to love when he was asleep. I'd forgotten his moody days, inability to find the laundry hamper, and talk-radio addiction. Maybe he'd forgotten whatever annoying habits I had, like my constant fretting about work and my bluegrass collection, which he called "that ding-dang redneck music". But now we carefully checked our complaints. The frustration was there, in a dirty look or a drawer slammed too hard, but it was like a TV soap opera with the sound turned off. All except for one thing. "I have had enough — you are going to stop that or — or — " We both knew I couldn't think of a threat I would make good on. In desperation I snatched the cigarette from his smug lips and stubbed it out in his breakfast cereal.

"Hey, I wasn't done with that."

I looked at the butt floating in his Cheerios, blackening the milk with swirls of ash. This was one of the good days, when he was eating. Dr. Prasad had warned us that the drugs would make him nauseous. My face burned. Unable to meet his eyes, I got up to rinse out the bowl. "I'll make you another one," I muttered, standing at the sink.

"It's not like I got time to quit," Phil said. Waving me away from the cereal box, he ate some Cheerios out of his hand.

"Don't say that. We're still trying to get you into that clinical trial. But you've got to stay healthy." I scrubbed the bowl for the third time.

Phil gulped his food. "I don't want to...I mean, I worked so damn hard, all my life, when am I gonna get a break, if not now?" He looked down at the floor. "I don't know if I can do it."

I moved closer to him. "Come on, I'll give up something too." The words caught in my throat. He couldn't know what I'd already given up because of him. I prayed I'd never hate him enough to tell him.

"Like what?"

"Anything. You name it."

Phil's impish grin returned. "Like, even Cosmos, and picking up guys at New Eden?"

"Sure." Like I said to my sister, I don't have a drinking problem; I have problems, and I like drinking.

"Would you give me your leather jacket from Paris?"

Richard had picked that out for me at a sample sale. "It won't fit you, but yeah." We had to believe that Phil's getting thinner was a temporary issue. Red-faced and wheezing, he forced himself to lift weights three times a week, determined to hang onto his job at the Ironman.

Phil's expression grew serious. "Eh, you don't care about that stuff anyway. Gimme something real. What do you care about?"

"You, you idiot." I picked up Phil's pack of cigarettes and shook them out into the trash, and just to make sure, tossed the wet filter from his morning coffee on top of them. He laughed and grabbed me, and we kissed long enough that it would have led to something, except we were running late for his doctor's appointment.

I'd volunteered to spend the rest of the day tailing Peter's boss for a campaign video shoot. The Defalque team could afford the late-night WPIX TV spot or the videographer, but not both. I owed him a favor from when Phil was in the hospital, and I was looking to branch out into different media. Some fashion photographers were making big money filming music videos. If Shawn felt like setting a guitar on fire to protest working conditions at the Fender factory, I'd be on it.

But I told Peter in advance, I wouldn't spoil my portfolio with political clichés. No images of Shawn standing with shirtsleeves rolled up under a waving American flag while he gives a little girl a lollipop. No grateful old ladies or hard-hat handshakes.

I met up with the team outside an office building near City Hall, a towering slab of reflecting window glass and black girders. Shawn had removed his suit jacket, his one concession to the heat. His white button-down was crisp and dry. He was getting miked to address the group on the pavement: ten or so garbagemen in coveralls, about twice that number of women with a few fidgety children in tow, and a seven-foot inflatable rubber rat.

"Can you make the crowd look bigger?" Peter shouted in my ear. The garbagemen drummed on their overturned metal cans. A baby wailed.

"What's this about anyway?"

"Welfare office," was all I caught. I went closer to the building for a shot of the Human Resources Administration logo, and must have crossed some invisible property line that brought out two rent-a-cops to flex their chest muscles at me. The rat swayed on its guy ropes, bloodshot eyes aimed at someone behind those anonymous windows.

Shawn spoke briefly in support of the protest against a new welfare-to-work regulation that was sending the mothers out to pick up trash in the park in exchange for food stamps. The garbagemen were there because they were losing union jobs to what Shawn called slave labor. The kids were there because they couldn't afford to be anywhere else.

Glaring guards, grey rubber skin, a small dark face laughing with bouncing braids, and the clouds like ocean waves sweeping across twenty stories of mirrored glass. A few frames later we were on our way to lunch with Shawn's family. We wouldn't actually have time to eat it, but the camera could feast on the fresh-baked rolls and glazed ham that his aunt Rose set out on her lace tablecloth. He introduced his whole crew to her and uncle Felix, who had raised him, and his girlfriend Serena, a schoolteacher. I zoomed in for a shot of them displaying polite affection over the coffee pot. Serena straightened the pocket square Shawn wore in his dark-gray jacket. Violet with gray chevrons? I interrupted them, touching him like a prop I needed to adjust, my hands repeating her gesture more roughly. His back stiffened. He didn't like my attitude, but he couldn't say anything, not with a microphone stuck under his chin on one side and his aunt passing the green bean casserole on the other.

Peter offered me a ham biscuit on the way to our next location. I pushed it aside. No space for conversation in our crowded van. That was the Ozwald Boateng handkerchief I'd sent him from Paris, I was sure of it. A sample from the runway show, not produced for sale in stores. He'd given my gift away. Save me from people who think they're too good for beauty. Stubborn Peter, resisting any nice thing that was just for himself, just because he was special in my eyes even though he'd never see it.

I looked again at Shawn's near-flawless profile over the edge of the passenger seat. Sure, it fit his style more naturally, but that was why he shouldn't have it. Cinderella was the one who needed the glass slipper. Then Peter, in the back seat, leaned across me to have a word with his boss up front. Heads bent toward each other, they shared a laugh at Shawn's quip about someone whose name I didn't recognize. A knot formed in the pit of my stomach. The handkerchief could mean something else, too. Would Defalque really have the balls to flaunt his lavender love-token on camera? Politicians love risk, and Peter loved secrets.

We pulled up to the back entrance of a big plain brick church in Hell's Kitchen. Behind us was a row of cheese-colored warehouses and half-built apartment complexes overlooking the West Side Highway. A line of stoop-shouldered older men moved slowly up the steps to the parish hall. They were stuffed into layers of sweatshirts and vests despite the summer heat, most likely having no place to store a change of clothes except on their backs. Peter gave the closest man the biscuit I regretted turning down. If the others resented his arbitrary good fortune, they didn't show it. Each was sunk in his own fermented thoughts until reaching the table where the pantry volunteers handed them coffee cups and sandwiches in wax paper. Shawn put on an apron and joined the crew.

"This is his church. He does this for real, twice a month," Peter said to me, under his breath, in case I was having cynical thoughts about the photo op.

"I give free handjobs twice a month at New Eden, but you don't see me taking out a PSA about it."

"Well, they say you shouldn't let your left hand know what your right hand is doing."

As soon as I had my footage, Shawn stepped out of the breadline. He dropped his crumpled apron on a folding chair behind the table with its dwindling pile of sandwiches. The procession continued steadily up the steps. Some women had joined in, mostly weathered old-timers like the men, and a young slender one with long-lashed almond eyes and a hard, beautiful mouth. She wore a tattered hoodie and no makeup, trying not to look as attractive as she was, the way hookers do in the daytime. The walls behind us thrummed with the stop-and-start chords of the organist rehearsing next Sunday's service music. I caught the tune our housekeeper used to sing to herself while laying out supper for us kids in the kitchen. *Sometimes I feel like a motherless chile...a long way from ho-ome.* Mama made us call her "Miss Della" because she was our elder, but the adults referred to her as "our girl". *Sometimes I feel like I'm almost gone...then I git down on my knees an' pray.* I wondered who cleaned Peter's house when he was growing up. They probably made him do it himself while they were busy writing poems and suing people.

Shawn motioned us out the side door so we wouldn't interfere with the hungry people filing in. The organ thundered above us for a few minutes as we crept down the side aisle between lovingly polished wooden pews. Then we doubled back along the street to our van. Shawn squinted into the sun, eyes narrowed, fixated on the doorway where volunteers with an empty tray were now turning the street people away. "Well, Edelman, that was one step up from making absolutely no difference at all."

Peter stood at his side, saying nothing.

"Are we done?" I broke in. This job had taken almost a whole day, for no pay, and I had a backlog of photos to process for *Glamour*.

Shawn put his smooth face back on. "Yes, thank you, you've really helped us out. Where's your studio? We'll give you a ride back with your equipment."

"No need, it's only a few blocks away. I'm from Georgia. I like a walk on a hot day." I sized him up once more, lingering on that pocket square to see if a hidden understanding would make him flinch. He didn't. "Can I ask you something — off the record?"

"Go right ahead."

I took a deep breath. "I overheard what you said to Peter, about making no difference? Seems to me...if I did this kind of work, I'd either get a savior complex or want to jump off a roof. How do you not...lose your grip, I guess?"

The lines of his face softened. He looked down to collect his thoughts. "Guess you caught me at a weak moment. But I'll tell you what Reverend Crowell told me — that's my pastor from the church we were just at. He says I'm better off not thinking of myself at all, as one thing or the other. Do what Jesus told me to do, leave the fruits up to him."

"Oh, like the mustard seed of faith."

His smile was genuine, warm with surprise. "You go to church?"

"No."

After a pause, we shook hands and parted. I shouldered my camera bag for the trudge downtown. The bastard had a firm handshake. But so did I.

When I got home that evening, Phil was in his usual spot, on the couch in front of the TV, wearing an undershirt and sweat pants. I sat down on the floor and leaned my head against his knee. "Hey," he said, pleasantly surprised. Had it been that long since I touched him, as anything more than a caretaker? He rubbed the nape of my neck.

"Let's go out somewhere," I said.

On-screen, a shaggy brown bear waded into a foaming stream to scoop out a fish, while a soothing British voice talked about hibernation. "I want to go camping," Phil said.

"I meant tonight." I tried to laugh off his demand, hoping he'd realize how impossible it was.

"Tonight I want to go to Miss Chin's. But seriously — we gotta do this. Soon."

"Phil..." I struggled to keep the irritation out of my voice, knowing what I had to say would humiliate him enough. "You can't..." Already

I saw his face shut down, the mask of apathy returning. I put my hand over his to stop him reaching for the TV remote. "Sweetheart, I'm sorry. I'm scared for you."

He was my boy again, his blue eyes brightening, welcoming me back. "What are you scared of, babe?"

"You could...you could catch cold, or eat something with dirt on it, and get bitten by a raccoon, and die."

"Yeah, and I could sit here on my ass and die too."

"No, you remember what Dr. Prasad said today, he's pretty sure he can get you into the trials for that new drug combo."

"About that..." Phil switched off the TV, always a bad sign. "I've been reading stuff. It's a study, right? I remember high school science. You got one bunch of rats you feed the vitamins to, and this other bunch that get a plain food pellet. The rats don't know what's what 'cause they're rats, see?"

"So?"

"So, I might get a dummy pill, or some shit that nobody knows what it'll do to me. At least now I'm taking the real thing."

When you let go of the rock you've been pushing uphill, like as not it rolls down and crushes you. I'd been pushing us toward October and the start of the drug trials with this crazy certainty that I could turn off my worries once Phil started the new treatment. Rumor had it that some guys who'd been counting their T-cells on one hand were walking out of the hospital, back to apartments and lovers they'd never expected to see again. But then, these days any fag could tell you a story about some poz guy — a friend of a friend, or maybe he saw it on "Oprah" — who'd knocked down his viral load through acupuncture and eating five pounds of carrots a day.

"But with the current treatment...I mean, realistically, you could...we've only got...no, you know, never mind."

"Say it, Jule." He gripped my wrists. I couldn't speak. "I got maybe a year or two, okay? So I want to hear the fucking tree fall in the forest. You coming or not?"

I sank into his arms, still strong enough for me. "Of course I am."

"It'll be fun. Maybe some of the guys will want to come. We can rent a van," he mused, resting his face on my hair.

"Yeah, good luck. Frank's idea of 'camp' is to put on a pink wig."

Our favorite drag queen had turned us on to Miss Chin's, a new club on Avenue B where the waiters dressed up as Asian courtesans. They always acted happy to be photographed with you, like the guys in the Mickey Mouse rubber heads at Disney World.

Phil and I were served dumplings by a towering black queen in a red silk cheongsam, with white face paint and slanty-eyed mascara. The conflation of racisms was too weird not to capture on film. I had given up Richard's touch but not his eye for the uncanny; I hoped to show him that I could scrape beneath the surface, to find...more surface? We speak as if truth were under the skin, but everyone runs out of skin, muscle, blood and bone, and then the truth is that they don't exist.

We went to see "True Lies" after dinner because Phil was looking for a movie "where nobody cries or learns anything." Schwarzenegger as a cuckolded spy pretty much delivered. "He's not my type," I said afterward, sensing that Phil had become self-conscious about his body. Later I'd develop his picture with the waitress and see it more clearly: the ropy muscles of his neck and forearms, the rash creeping above his collar. I'd thought the picture would capture a playful mood, but the chalk-faced figure in stiff silk — neither black nor white, neither male nor female — brought back a disquieting half-memory of something that had happened to me in Miami's delirium.

"Thanks for being nice again," Phil murmured when we got into bed.

"Oh, I'm not done with you yet." I found his hardness beneath the blanket. He pressed against my thigh. We'd wasted too much time, I thought. The sweat of his neck smelled good to me.

"Wait, let me pull down the shade." He scooted out of bed.

"We're on the 12th floor. No one's looking."

"It's not that..." A full moon was adding its white glow to the ever-present city lights. Sharp shadows carved the outlines of Phil's flat buttocks, half-erect cock, ribcage, up to his somber face.

"You don't want me to look?" I could tell from his silence that I was right. "You're beautiful."

"Not like I used to be."

"But you are, because…this is who you are, where we are, right now."

Though I was spinning any words I could imagine to comfort him, as soon as they left my mouth I knew them to be true. That's the grace you work toward, as an artist, even a petty one like me, when you find the lens to discover what you know.

This relaxed him, but he didn't like it when I reached for my camera. "Hey, I don't do porn anymore. I'm reformed."

"Then put something on." I tossed him a sock, one of several he'd left lying on the floor, as usual. Playfully, he slid it over his cock. "There you go, there's the *Homme NY* cover."

A few frames later, in a scene that only exists on the film of my mind and his, wherever he is now, I was kneeling before him. He leaned on me, I gripped his legs, both of us trembling a little. He pulled out before he came, and sucked on me, lying next to me on the bed. We were careful enough.

31

"ALBANY IS THE ARMPIT OF THE UNIVERSE," Peter said, throwing the last of our camping gear into the back of the rented van. It was a big black Chevy with tinted windows and a serious sound system that was currently broadcasting the "Grease" soundtrack to my entire neighborhood.

"You've never been to Scranton," Phil shot back.

"Does he really need you out there?" I asked.

"I don't know what he needs." Putting on a brighter tone, Peter added, "Probably I'll be here a lot. Constituent service, you know — I'll be the guy you call to complain that a crack house moved in next door to your daycare center."

"Nice to know what it takes to get your attention."

As I'd anticipated, Frank and Tomas shared Oscar Wilde's low opinion of the outdoors, and Stan had to work, so it was just us three heading out to the Catskills on that late-September weekend. I popped the CD out of the stereo and fiddled with the AM dial. "What's that, the third time you've checked the weather this morning? Stop being such a mom," Phil ragged me.

But he got his come-uppance when Peter stole his pack of Marlboros and tossed it out the window. "No smoking in here or Hertz is going to charge me extra."

"Daddy, Peter's littering."

"No I'm not. I'm donating to the homeless."

The Chevy handled like an ocean liner. It reminded me of when Uncle Curtis had let Carter and me take turns driving his truck around the dealership parking lot, when I was a short ten-year-old who had to arch his back and point his toes to reach the gas pedal.

Peter gave directions from the back seat while Phil, sitting beside me, flipped through our CD collection. We swung onto the northbound highway, getting our first glimpse of green hills tinged with the rust color of turning leaves, as John Travolta and Olivia Newton-John giddily sang "You're the One That I Want". We all joined in on the "ooh, ooh, ooh's".

"He was my first celebrity crush," Peter chuckled. "The way he walks down that street at the beginning of 'Saturday Night Fever'...!"

"Yeah, you like the boys who are gonna treat you like shit," I said. "More to choose from."

"Mine was Errol Flynn, 'Robin Hood'," Phil said, looking at me. "I go for the redheads. What about you, Jule?"

"Tom Hanks," I said without thinking.

Phil snorted. "No way! He's not sexy at all."

In the rearview mirror, I saw Peter's plain boyish face, his curly black hair. "Okay, okay, I was just messing with you. Freddie Mercury."

The three of us fell silent. The Queen frontman had died of AIDS nearly three years earlier, having denied his illness till the very end. "I don't care what anybody says, I think 'Barcelona' is a great album," Phil finally said. He slid another CD into the stereo and soon we were singing along, too loudly, to Patti LuPone's confession that she got no kick from champagne.

Peter took over the driving at the rest stop midway through our trip. My shameless boyfriend bummed a cigarette off the gas station attendant, complaining to him that his "brothers" were forcing him to quit. I took pictures and watched the sky for thunderclouds.

"Here, you should eat." I tossed a packet of cheese pretzels at Phil. "Peter...?"

"It's in my pack," he said, sotto voce, though no one could hear us in the car. "I didn't want us to get pulled over."

"What is?"

Phil grinned at me. "My girlfriend, Miss Mary Jane."

"Dude, no one calls it that anymore," Peter said.

"No one says 'dude' either," I piled on.

Phil took his pills with some ginger ale and a few of the pretzels. He stretched out on the back seat with his head on my lap to catch some sleep. His forehead felt warm beneath my palm. At his last appointment, Dr. Prasad had said his CD4 count was rising, which was a good sign. Maybe he'd hang on long enough for them to find better drugs, a cure even. But he hated it when I talked like this.

Meanwhile, the Ironman's management had cut Phil's hours after his hospital stay, and at the end of the summer, they laid him off. They made excuses about the recession, but we could hear them thinking that he might sneeze in the steam room and set off an epidemic of litigation. There's never been a good time to be queer (well, maybe the Roman Empire) but the days of Newt Gingrich's "Contract with America" were, in my limited experience, a low point. Stupid Phil believed in that stuff. He was the angry white guy they played to. Stop the special-interest victim groups, et cetera. Instead of suing, he shut his mouth and got a part-time gig loading UPS trucks. Peter wrote a column about the situation, under his "Spartacus" byline, titled "Real Men Don't Need Civil Rights". *Gay Downtown* twice postponed running it, to make room for a tanning-parlor ad. It was almost enough to make me give a shit.

The storm hit when we were about an hour south of the campgrounds. Sheets of rain covered the Chevy's windshield. We crawled along, following the fuzzy glow of the taillights in front of us. Peter searched the AM band for a local station that could give us traffic and weather. I refrained from saying that we could see both of those by looking out the window. There's the difference between us: he likes to *know* that he can't do anything about a situation, while I just *assume* it.

Up ahead, flashing lights and a row of orange cones marked a lane closed off by a wreck we couldn't make out. Peter was all for pulling off the highway and finding a shortcut via the local roads. Phil's presence made me less adventurous. We had to get this right. If he'd been awake to vote, though, he would have sided with Indiana Jones, so I resigned myself to studying the map for the shortest possible detour. "Hey, did you know there's a city in New York called Sodom?"

"Is it anywhere near Coxsackie?"

We bounced along winding roads through tired towns that blended together in the rain: another white clapboard with a sagging porch, another vintage Pepsi sign over a liquor-store marquee ("happy 21st birthday Amanda!"), more black and white cows grazing around a metal silo. I never went in for that Depression-documentary stuff. People who wear overalls deserve their privacy.

After half an hour we seemed to have outrun the rain, but finding our way back to the highway was another story. We stopped for coffee and pie in a diner with turquoise vinyl siding, where the waitress gave us directions to the campsite. I could have sworn one of the truckers at the lunch counter was cruising me. If I hadn't been with my boys, I might have gone for him, and probably gotten myself murdered. It's not a good idea to die luridly if no one knows you're a celebrity. I doubted whether the local Walgreen's carried *Femme NY*.

We crested the hill leading into the campgrounds as a yellow-gray sunset was filtering through the pines. Peter surveyed the scene and frowned. "Guys, I don't think this is it."

"Nah, I saw the sign, just like the waitress told us — Deer Mountain Nature Preserve," Phil said.

"But it's not how I remember it, from when we used to come here — I thought there was a lake, and this little bunkhouse with showers."

"Maybe we're on the other end."

"Does it really matter?" I asked impatiently. "Nature is nature, right?"

"And why is it called a nature preserve? Maybe we're not even allowed in here," Peter fretted.

"Cool, we'll be, like, anarchist squatters," Phil said. Thus outvoted, Peter pulled the Chevy into a broad clearing with a view of the mountains, where we would pitch our tents. He'd brought two, in case Phil and I wanted some privacy. The ground was damp and spongy under a fragrant carpet of pine needles. I sprayed a mist of bug repellent all around us. In the forest, you think it's quiet, but it really isn't, once you let go of expecting to hear human voices. Phil had brought a battery-operated radio that played staticky doo-wop oldies (the only station we could find out there) while I built a campfire.

The sky slowly turned from purple-gray to black. We drank Cokes because Peter didn't like mixing beer and weed, and cooked hot dogs on sticks over the sputtering fire. Phil tried to get away without eating anything with his evening pills. "I thought you always had an appetite for this," I said, waggling a plump hot dog in front of his face. We ate that one from both ends and met in the middle, and Peter sang the Italian-restaurant song from "Lady and the Tramp", and I laughed so hard the soda came out of my nose.

The radio was off. If we strained our eyes, we could see faint stars that vanished into the cloud cover when we looked directly at them. "I want to try and find the lake," Peter said.

"It's too cold to swim," I said. "We should have come sooner."

"I just want you guys to see it."

A nearly-full moon had risen, cresting and sinking in the swells of clouds that drifted across its light. That and our flashlights helped us find a marked trail. There was no reason to think that it led to any lake, but we were buzzed and lucky to be there, and why not hope our luck would hold?

Phil slapped at the mosquitos that were drawn to our flashlight beams. "So there, suckers — my blood is toxic."

"Must you think about that every minute?" I said.

"I got a right."

Peter slowed down to put his arm around my shoulders as we trudged uphill on the winding trail. My tense breathing eased and I began to enjoy the trek in spite of myself. The spindly pines swayed above us in the wind. Our slow progress through the dark was hypnotic. Peter hummed a tune under his breath and we joined in intermittently to stay focused. I heard Phil cough a couple of times but he didn't stop walking or look back at us, so I couldn't do anything.

The trail ended at the edge of a rocky outcropping overlooking a valley. Silver light flashed below us, a fast-moving stream tumbling over glistening rocks. To our left, a thicker, darker gray cloudbank was building up, edged with moonglow.

I reached out to pull Phil closer to me so we were all holding each other. Maybe it was the whisper of the stream we heard, or maybe it was too far away and we only heard the trees tossing in the wind.

Warm from the climb, I spread my top-layer sweatshirt on the ground for Phil and me to sit on. We leaned against each other and kissed, while Peter sat cross-legged on Phil's other side, holding his hand.

"Got your camera?" Phil whispered. "Like you ever don't."

"Too dark…besides, right now…let's just be here."

"Yeah, I know what you mean."

Oh, those blue eyes. I saw you, Phil, I was inside you, closer than sex, clearer than words. And you in me. I hope, I believe. In the end, you trust it or you don't, the ground under your feet, the air in your lungs, and something surrounding you that's more than particles of heat and scent and skin.

The distant sky rumbled. A small flock of dark birds swooped and scattered into the valley. Phil sneezed. I took off my other sweatshirt and wrapped it around him. He didn't object. Peter stretched out on the ground, propping his chin in his hands, and looked down at the stream with a sigh. "I guess this is as far as we're going to get."

"It's all right," Phil said. "I'm happy here."

"Good, 'cause we're going to leave you here," I deadpanned.

He slugged my arm. "Hey, you promised me an ice floe."

"What's the big deal about the lake?" I asked, since Peter was still acting glum.

"It's where he lost his virginity," Phil teased.

Peter rolled over and swatted at him. "Ah, screw you."

"Is it?" I pressed him.

"For your information, I lost my virginity in the back of a comic-book store in Brooklyn Heights. And I bet I was ahead of either of you guys, too."

I wolf-whistled. Phil said, "I moved in with Ted, that was my first boyfriend, when I was sixteen, but we'd been doing it since the year before. He worked construction, like me, and the first time, we were fixing up this old lady's attic and we all of a sudden got all over each other, and when she complained about the noise we told her she had squirrels." Peter and I laughed. Phil looked expectantly at me.

"Define virginity," I stalled.

"Fucking or being fucked. Messing around doesn't count."

"So how old were you?" I asked Peter.

He hesitated. "Thirteen."

Phil made a face, like he didn't believe this, but I didn't think Peter was kidding. "Who the hell would do you at thirteen?" I blurted out.

Peter looked away. "Hey, I wasn't *totally* hideous," he muttered.

"No, I meant — " Too frustrated for words, I touched my hand to his cheek. "I'm sure you were as delicious then as you are now, but I'm feeling this primitive Southern urge to punch that guy in the face."

"It wasn't so bad. I mean, it was good. I liked him."

I stayed where I was, touching him. He wrapped his fingers around mine.

"Who...who was he?" I didn't want to know, but I had to.

"Uh, a friend of my dad's. I worked in his store the summer after the last time we came here — after my real mom found out about Ada." He gestured impatiently at the view. "Only it's not here, we're somewhere else."

"Wherever you go, there you are," Phil volunteered.

"Oh, profound," I said.

This time the dull boom of thunder sounded closer. The wind had picked up, whipping the branches around. "Oh crap, we'd better get back," Peter said.

"Not until Julian tells us about his first time." Phil slid his hand down my leg. I felt a flash of desire and wondered about the mechanics of safe sex in a sleeping bag.

"It was you," I said, almost inaudibly.

Phil glanced up from nuzzling my neck. "Naw...I thought you'd been with lots of guys," he said, just as softly.

"Yeah, but we said blowjobs didn't count, only real sex." I kissed his ear, trying to revive the tender mood of a moment ago.

Rain began to patter lightly on the leaves. "Guys, come on," Peter urged, standing up.

Phil hung onto my thigh, keeping me on the ground. "What about the first time you were on the bottom, was that me too?"

"Let's talk about this later, please?"

"Who was it?"

"I don't know, okay?" I burst out, pushing him off me. "He was just some guy in Central Park."

Phil caught up to me as I followed Peter's bobbing flashlight beam along the narrow path downhill. "Here's your jacket," he said gruffly, draping the grass-stained sweatshirt over my shoulders. He didn't take his arm away afterward, pretending to need my support as he dodged the humped tree roots underfoot.

Superimposed on the path before me, there returned my one memory of that man's lined and wistful face, the pure gratitude in his eyes when he held me for a few seconds after fucking me under the arcade by Bethesda Fountain. I hadn't expected it and it hurt quite a bit, though there was a thrill in it too, the way he invaded the center of me, opening what had always been closed.

The downward-sloping trail was slippery with wet leaves. Distracted by my thoughts, I stumbled and fell, skidding on my ass into a clump of bushes. The sky chose that moment to flush its cosmic toilet. Water poured down hard. I swore as the prickly bushes snagged my clothes. Phil tried to help me out but got entangled himself, like two fools in a fairy tale glued to the golden goose.

"I'm sorry," he shouted over the noise of the storm. His face was smudged and wet. "Jule, I know...I know you didn't want...to be with me, like this."

"Phil. I love you." Words I'd never said before. I warmed his rain-chilled lips with mine. His arms were the most solid thing in the world. How could they vanish, how to conceive of a time when all of us would become unreal?

Doubling back with the flashlight, Peter found us still clenched in our silent embrace. Since he was the only one who'd thought to bring gloves, he had little trouble pushing aside the thorny branches. We found our way back to the campsite in silence.

"Oh, crap crap crap!" Peter exclaimed when we saw the fallen tree limbs crushing his tent. He did this little stomping dance of frustration that would have been funny if we'd been watching it from someplace dry. He glanced back and forth from us to the other tent, which had stayed upright. "Okay, I guess I'm sleeping in the Chevy."

Phil and I exchanged a look of agreement. I was just desperate to get him inside. He wasn't hiding his shivering very well. "No, there's room for you," Phil said.

Inside the tent, we stripped down to our T-shirts and underwear, leaving our wet clothes in a heap by the door flap. Peter had found some spare blankets in the van to supplement the two sleeping bags, which were barely enough to cover the three of us when we zipped them together to make a sort of comforter.

I thought Phil should go in the middle. "Nah, night sweats," he said, nudging me to change places with him. His eyes were saying more than that. So I lay against Peter's chest, with his arms around me, and Phil, on my other side, reaching over to hold Peter's hand where it rested at my waist. Phil tucked his head into the curve of my neck, the way we always liked to sleep. I felt his heartbeat, steady and strong, and heard the faint wheeze of his breath growing more regular as he drifted off. Peter's body, too, relaxed without easing his hold on us. I was just thinking about kissing him goodnight — on the cheek, would it be so wrong? — when he pressed his face to mine. Silent softness of mouths and tongues, a few minutes standing in for all the time gone and time to come, until the three of us were sleeping in the incomparable warmth we made together.

32

PHIL DIDN'T WORK AGAIN after that trip. He lost a week in the hospital with another bout of pneumonia, and when he got out, UPS had replaced him. I was glad he wouldn't be hauling boxes out in the cold, but weekdays on the couch with The People's Court didn't seem like enough to live for. I asked my sister for a catalogue from NYU's continuing-education program. Phil flipped through it one afternoon but quickly lost interest when he saw the tuition prices. I was so desperate I called one of those community colleges that advertise on the subway. "Look at this — physical therapy, life coaching, business administration," I showed him the brochures.

"I got a year to live and you want me to spend it as a fucking accountant?" he croaked.

"You know, I'm sick of you and your self-pity. You brought this on yourself, go take a class in hang-gliding and see how far you get."

"You think you're so smart. It could've been you. Probably will be, too."

"Well, I would do my friends a favor and die with more *style*."

"The hell you would." He struggled to prop himself up against the bed cushions. His eyes were hard with fury. "Style doesn't do shit for you when you feel like you're breathing through a bag of razor blades."

"What do you want from me, Phil? I mean, really, what?"

He grimaced like he was going to throw up again. "Make it stop," he said.

"I can't."

"I know."

I crawled under the blankets with him, though it was the middle of the afternoon. I'd been running on two hours' sleep, worn out from shooting Fische's latest ad campaign. Bronx tigers weren't good enough for him; he had to haul our asses out to the San Francisco Zoo. I'd been hanging out the window of a cable car over a cultivated jungle, snapping his latest discovery, a fifteen-year-old Icelandic waif who posed in the rear of the car ahead of me, with this season's shredded skirt falling away from her gazelle-like legs. Cheryl Kingston had wanted her job. Now selling facial moisturizers in late-night infomercials, our former supermodel had phoned me up, supposedly to gossip about Dane's palimony suit, but really to call in an unspoken favor. I couldn't afford to help make her old face new. As for Tamiko, she'd complained loudly about the racism of high fashion when Fische didn't rehire her, but she was making more cash than any of us, with her face on casino billboards from Vegas to L.A. Through me, she'd connected with Ariana, who was designing costumes for a movie series about vampire babysitters. Ari helped her land a small part as a murdered teenager in "Nanny II: Lights Out".

After a short nap, I decided to hit the gym to boost my energy. Best to slip out while Phil was down, so he wouldn't be reminded of his expired membership in the bodybuilders' club. Like those faked photos of ghosts, two exposures from different eras superimposed for an encounter that never was, the face on my pillow was the same and not the same as the teasing strongman who had let me dance with him three years ago. Broad neck and square jaw, yes, but skin transparent and blued with sickness, color washed from the hair. The generic AIDS look, halfway to the anonymity of bones.

I don't like being morbid. I take too much after Mama's side, my comfortably widowed Memère in her parlor of red-lipped plaster saints and stuffed songbirds under glass, my Uncle Jimmy the antiques dealer who died of something unnameable when I was twelve. She must have married Daddy for the same qualities that made us alien to him: his bullish vitality, his lack of sentiment, gladly paving ancient battlefields to put up ranch houses with vinyl siding.

At the Ironman, I shoved and tugged the handlebars of the Nordic Track on highest resistance, as if I was steering a bulldozer

218

through heaps of rubble. Men around me pounded the treadmills like galloping horses, chugged drinks from neon bottles, or gritted their teeth for that last bench-press, sweat darkening their armpits. Push-ups, repeated to exhaustion, stilled my mind.

My neck was stiff from the contorted angles of the cable car photo shoot. I treated myself to a stretch in the steam room. Guys in white towels lounged in the fog, chests and legs gleaming with moisture. I inhaled: scrubbed wet wood, chlorine, men's lotions, the earthy smell between parted thighs, the clean body's invitation. My towel slid down. Someone would follow me into the shower. Any one of them. Or more than one. How grateful I was for this. Call it meaningless, then tell me the meaning of an old man begging for sandwiches or a young man coughing up blood. Don't waste a breath.

When I returned home, our apartment was warmed by the unfamiliar smells of well-cooked food. Yams and cinnamon, I guessed, remembering Mama's Thanksgiving standards. Phil was sitting on the couch in his bathrobe, with a massive book in his lap. "I'm gonna take a poetry class!" he greeted me. "Listen to this: *The upper-hold and under-hold, the hair rumpled over and blinding the eyes; The march of firemen in their own costumes, the play of masculine muscles through clean-setting trowsers and waist-straps...*"

"That's cool, did you write that?" I said absently.

"No, asshole, it's Walt Whitman." He held up the textbook.

"Figures, someone gives you a thousand-page book, you go right to the dirty parts." I leaned over his shoulder, scanning the table of contents. "Memère made us memorize some of these, but we got sent back to Atlanta before I could get past Edwin Arlington Robinson." That winter when Mama broke her leg falling downstairs, and Uncle Jimmy came to take us to Savannah for a month, and we thought (hoped, feared?) this time our family would change.

"*And Richard Cory, one October night, Went out and put a bullet through his head,*" Laura Sue recited in an unearthly voice, emerging from the kitchen with a pie plate.

I jumped. "What are you doing here?"

"Phil called me. He said you were having a hard time. Why didn't you tell me he had pneumonia?"

If she wanted to call it that, fine. "I figured you had enough to worry about at school." From the few clues I could gather, Lulu's grades were all right but the public-service work was wearing her down. She dressed like she was fifty instead of twenty, in button-down corduroy jumpers and turtlenecks, with her hair pushed back from her thin little face with a headband. "Tell me you didn't make sweet potato pie."

"She's an angel," Phil chimed in from the couch. "I should've let your pop fix us up."

"That is so wrong, in so many ways," I said, but took a slice of pie.

"*The Soul selects her own Society — Then — shuts the Door,*" Phil agreed, with his mouth full.

Lulu explained that she was taking a modern poetry course to fulfill her humanities requirement, and would ask her professor to let her bring Phil as an auditor twice a week. The prospect of being seen in his wheelchair didn't faze him, as it had when I took him down to the coffee shop for breakfast. "Yeah, we're going for the pity discount," he joked.

"You sure you don't mind? You look kind of tired," I said to my sister.

"It's okay, I've just had a few late nights at the shelter." In response to Phil's questioning, she told us a little about her volunteer work at a safe house for battered women and their children.

"That sounds very rewarding," Phil said politely.

"No, it's not." Her flat statement took us by surprise. "The kids are so sticky, and hyper, and confused, and I can't understand what they want."

"They probably want to know it's not their fault that everything sucks," Phil said.

"Yes, right, yes, but how do I say that when I don't — I can't feel it," she confessed, her voice sinking. Her hands flew up to her flat chest. "I do good things, all the time, shouldn't God...?"

Forgive. I almost completed her sentence. She saw that I understood. "I can't feel it," she repeated.

I hugged her. Embarrassed at having revealed so much, she sprung up to clear away the dishes. Like a tiny whirlwind, she moved on to strip the bed, take the sheets and towels downstairs to the laundry room, and lay out clean linens for us. I lost track of time, happily immobilized on the couch with Phil dozing on top of me.

When Lulu paused for breath, I carefully slid out from underneath his sleeping body and covered him with the afghan. I looked up from kissing his hot forehead to see my sister standing there with a strange expression. Did our touch disgust her, jarring her out of denial? She'd seen the stains on my mattress; I had no secrets left.

Then her face suddenly contorted with tears. This time she didn't pull away from me. I led her into the kitchen so we could talk quietly.

"I can't stand it," she wept. "There's a girl at the shelter, Rishanna, I can't bear to look at her. When she runs to my arms, when I change her diaper, all I can think is, Sara Grace would be this age now."

"Sara Grace?" I asked dumbly. My sister put her hands over her belly. "I didn't know...I never knew it was a girl," was all I could think to say.

"We're supposed to be the good ones," Laura Sue entreated. "Keeping kids safe from bad parents. But I don't have the right. I've done what they've done."

"Oh, Lulu, no. You're not like Daddy." But if she was, maybe Daddy wasn't even like Daddy, more like us, stumbling around with bricks of guilt on our backs, heads bowed, unable to see each other? That made no sense, no justice. I couldn't hold the idea long enough to speak it.

"Maybe we've got God all wrong," I said instead. "All this punishment. I don't want Phil to...to go like this, and I can't possibly be nicer than God, right?"

"But it doesn't cost you anything to say that. I couldn't look at a baby and say she deserved to die, but that's what I did, to protect myself."

Through the kitchen door I saw Phil's blond head nestled among the couch pillows. What if it could be me, after all, with only a year to contribute a few more pretty pictures and memorable blowjobs to the world? And Phil who was going to embrace a healthy future, getting his degree in sports medicine, studying poetry, buying a house with a lover who'd be proud of him? I could do it, maybe, if I made the decision quick and I wasn't allowed to go back on it.

"It costs me a hell of a lot," I said. "More than you'll ever know."

Lulu came back to the present. "I'm sorry."

"Yeah, I know." I squeezed her shoulder. "Thanks for taking care of us cave men."

"A woman's touch…!" She smiled faintly.

"Too late for that." That wasn't the kind of joke Lulu liked, so I changed the subject. "Hey…you still go to church?"

"There's a chapel at the campus center, but they don't have a Christian speaker every week. Not what I'd call Christian, anyhow."

"Maybe we could meet up next Sunday, start looking for a place to go. There's got to be someone else in this great city who's up for a few rounds of 'The Old Rugged Cross'."

Laura Sue left in a brighter mood, excited by the prospect of a spiritual field trip with her big brother. I'd allowed us to drift too far apart this year. She really was just a kid underneath those fussy clothes. The house smelled less like a public toilet since she'd blown through it, too. Was this what men without women came to? Phil and me, so much more than roommates, but never husband and wife, a rare and unadapted species, coddled in smelly captivity like the sloths at the zoo.

My boy mumbled in his sleep. I got ready for bed but couldn't bring myself to lie down, watching him breathe as the dark hours ticked by. I groped around the bookshelves but if we'd ever had a Bible, I wasn't seeing it. With gritty eyes I glanced through his poetry textbook, compulsively flipping the pages, reading a line or two before losing heart. Thinking of Richard at the museum, I stopped at the chapter on World War I poets. If I could force myself to read a whole page, if I could tamp down the panic for that long, then maybe I'd feel it was safe to sleep through a few of the remaining hours of Phil's life. *Heart, you were never hot, I read:*

> *Nor large, nor full like hearts made great with shot,*
> *And though your hand be pale,*
> *Paler are all which trail*
> *Your cross through flame and hail:*
>   *Weep, you may weep, for you may touch them not.*

Part V: The Away Team

(June 1995)

33

THEY WERE MY FRIENDS and I hated them. Four-thirty in the morning and Tomas was drunk, draped like a crumpled dress on the back seat of the van we'd borrowed from his boyfriend's catering business. "It's an *Irish* funeral," he'd defended himself, to which Stan returned the predictable retort that Tomas wasn't Irish, sparing me the effort of opening my mouth and releasing whatever sharp fragments of words remained inside me. Then I saw Frank.

"You are not — you are *not* wearing that," I groaned. His ensemble was complete, from his black patent pumps, to his Mamie Eisenhower belted black dress with pinhead polka dots, to the veiled pillbox hat perched on his crow-black waves of teased hair. Miss Anna Bollocks had stepped out of the nightclub shadows and was evidently expecting applause for deigning to wait with us in this alley where the West Village restaurant owners parked their delivery trucks.

"He loved me this way," Frank replied, in Miss Anna's voice, which was husky as his own but with the extra echo of an actor projecting to the cheap seats.

"You're not the widow." All my bitterness was turned on Frank. Hesitantly he unpinned the hat from his wig, sidled up to me and placed it on my head. I knocked it off and stomped on it. Only then did I see the kindness and pain in his mascara-crusted eyes. He'd given me what he had, like a child offering his teddy bear.

"Julian." Stan touched my arm, a mild reproach. I wondered how long I could hold out without asking him for a Valium. At the very least I'd have to wait the six interminable hours it would take to drive from Manhattan to Pittsburgh, so I could spell Stan at the wheel. Frank had put himself out of commission with this getup. A drag queen driving a bakery truck is a temptation no highway patrolman should be expected to resist. Five miles over the speed limit and we'd become the clip *du jour* on the 6 O'Clock News.

Still, I apologized. "I'm going to need a new hat," Frank pouted, but without real resentment. I helped him reattach the veil to his stiff pompadour, using the brooch as a sort of barrette. It was all a lost cause, anyhow. My nice black suit — Brooks Brothers, nothing too fashion-forward — wouldn't make us any more beloved. They knew who we were. That's why we hadn't been invited.

Peter, the last member of our delegation, pulled up alongside the van in his compact Toyota. When he stepped out, I saw his eyes were red-rimmed and tired already. He'd meant to drive down from Albany last night but his boss, rookie Assemblyman Shawn Defalque, had kept him late at a staff meeting. Peter hugged me first and I welcomed the familiar collapse into his arms, till my body sensed that for once, he wouldn't be able to hold me up.

In better days, Peter would get on our case for being flamers. He was the kind of gay man that straights liked, the kind they didn't notice, at least till he said what was on his mind, which he usually tried to do through someone else. Now he showed zero reaction to the circus in the alley, even when he saw the soot-smudged white van with the legend "Christopher Street Treats" over a sliced-open cherry pie. All he said to Tomas was, "Is it safe to leave my car in this spot?"

Tomas pulled himself upright with a flourish. "Safe? You lived in New York all your life and you want to know if it's safe? *Nothing* is safe. Parking is…like God. It is a mystery."

"Thank you, Stephen Hawking, now move your drunk ass so Peter can take a nap," I said. Tomas climbed into the front passenger seat. Peter stretched out on the fold-out seat at the rear while Stan and Frank huddled together in the row behind me. The height difference between them was more noticeable when Miss Anna presented herself. Eye-level with her shoulder pads, Stan could have been the henpecked husband from an old comic strip. That was the problem right there. Take a picture of us, destroyers of manhood, pie-eating clowns, speeding down the highway to your big steel-hammering city, to your church. To mourn.

34

THERE WAS NO PLACE inconspicuous to park a catering van next to Our Lady of Sorrows so we ditched it by a supermarket a few blocks away. Full sun on the asphalt, a blazing, dusty day in June. Frank brushed on another layer of face powder. Peter straightened the boxy jacket of his off-the-rack suit, which, like everything else he wore, didn't fit as it should. A big guy, he overcompensated by buying a size he could get lost in. I should have helped him; at some point, when we were bleaching piss-stained sheets, when we were wrapping my lover's shivering body in hot towels from the dryer, feeding him his meals through a straw, there must have been a moment when we could have turned to each other and said, "So, what are you wearing to Phil's funeral?"

I had a strong urge to go into the supermarket, just to look at the unfamiliar brands of cereal that Phil might have eaten, growing up in this neighborhood of bars and boarded-up factories. There wasn't time for anything; the service was at eleven. Peter led our phalanx down the streets of cracked pavement toward the small red-brick church. Tomas, more sober though less continent under the influence of coffee, leaned on my arm.

"Why didn't we just have a memorial service back home?" he grumbled under his breath. I heard his fear, thinly disguised as the usual queeny bitching he excelled at in several languages. But I didn't explain again.

Why? Phil's body was here.

The usher at the door, a stooped, red-faced old man, gave us a grim inspection. Without Frank, we might have passed. Four young men in adequate suits, we could have been Phil's college buddies, if he'd gone to college, or friends from work, if he'd ever had a job where people wore ties. But he marked us as potential trouble-makers, and after mentally consulting the risk table that all funeral directors carried in their heads, steered us toward a dark pew at the back.

Phil's older sister Barbara, standing in the aisle, recognized us with a stony look. If we hadn't already been inside, we'd never have made it, but now she too had to weigh the costs of making a scene. Phil's block-headed build and snub nose weren't as attractive on a woman. Still I studied her as long as I could, but it was worse than looking at a stranger, this hostile, imperfect copy of the face I remembered. Barbara had come to New York to take charge of the arrangements. How could I not feel for her, imagining my own sister having to identify my carcass, tears streaming down her little pixie face like Holly Golightly when she shoves her cat out into the rain? Only of course Laura Sue wouldn't do that, she'd haul my brother up from Atlanta to do it for her. And Barbara hadn't cried. She had taken his books and his clothes. They were directed to give us no information at the hospital. There's no health-care proxy for a dead man. Only family survives. *Spouse: none.*

The five of us crept into our pew. Frank sniffed loudly and dabbed his eyes with a black-edged handkerchief. I couldn't help but be impressed by his thoroughness. If you're going to live your life as a Bette Davis movie, get the props right.

Then I saw the casket being wheeled in from the side of the church, a closed, polished box gleaming in the dim light of the altar lamps. Who were these six strangers touching it? Involuntarily I shot up, about to run to it, unthinking, lost to myself.

Peter's embrace pulled me back down to my seat. No, I couldn't tear my clothes and fall into the grave like a soldier's mother. Any break from my invisibility would be read as drama, not grief. But that expensive lid over Phil's face was all wrong. If they'd really loved him, they'd have wanted to look at him till the last possible minute, despite his wasted frame, his lesioned skin, death's causes undisguised by a cosmetic artist less skillful than Frank. I wondered about our former classmates at the Fashion Institute, if any of them were now working on the dead. Toward the end I'd taken so many pictures of you, Phil, our hands bathing your scarred and heaving chest, your hands lighting a cigarette you couldn't smoke, till I no longer knew what beauty was — whether it was everything that existed, or nothing, a thin film of tears we blinked away. Darling, you never went blind, you just got too tired to open your eyes.

Philip Joseph Shanahan. November 12, 1970 — June 4, 1995. Our folded paper programs curled in the heat. The small church was half full. At ten past eleven an old lady began playing "Abide With Me" on the piano. The usher helped a middle-aged couple, undoubtedly Phil's parents, into the front pew. Both short and solid, she had brittle dyed-brown hair and an unsteady walk; he wore the fixed scowl of a man who can't cry. The fat sisters sat beside them, Barbara with her crew-cut husband and baby boy, Mary Claire by herself.

The priest's brief eulogy could have been about anyone. If only we were mistaken, it was the wrong funeral, another boy who had died. This priest was too young to have known Phil. Not Father O'Shea, the terror of Our Lady of Sorrows Middle School, who twisted the boys' ears when they came to class with dirty shirt collars, but let Phil off with a dozen Hail Marys when he released the science teacher's white mice instead of feeding them to the snake. *I am the resurrection and the life. Whoever believes in me, though he die, yet shall he live, and everyone who lives and believes in me shall never die,* the voice from the pulpit read. I remembered Phil's body, dying, how his mouth opened and stayed open, and then he was suddenly and completely somewhere else where I could never do a single thing for him again, where he could be in pain forever and I'd missed my chance to make it stop. He'd thought nothing happened after death, just dirt and sleep. I could see how that would have appealed to you, Phil, you lazy slob. Oh, no more jokes, no more fights, the judgment was in and no one cared that your few years of being yourself were over.

The other sister, Mary Claire, rose to speak. She had a welcoming sort of plumpness, unlike Fortress Barbara. The shiny black bow on the broad bosom of her dress kept getting knocked askew when she leaned over the pages of her prepared remarks. "My brother loved books," she said. "He wanted to study history. When we were kids he wrote a history of Pittsburgh for a term paper. It was only three pages because, he said, nothing ever happened here. Father O'Shea got mad and asked why he picked it, then, and he said, because that's where we live." She smiled through her tears and sweat.

Tomas groaned. I hoped he wasn't going to be sick. Stan slipped him a pill. The usher coughed meaningfully behind us. Some clean-cut young guy was in the pulpit now, talking about how he'd copied the wrong answers off Phil's test when they shared a desk in Catholic school. Now he was studying for the priesthood, this guy, and what a shame it was that Philip had died so young. Yeah, get over yourself, kid; no one remembers who played opposite Cagney in "Angels with Dirty Faces".

Stan slid out of the pew to help Tomas outside in search of slightly fresher air. Frank's queenly posture sagged a bit when his boyfriend was no longer beside him. His makeup, though intact, seemed over-bright for his tired face, like an actress at the end of her tour. I held his hand. On my other side, Peter sat at the edge of his seat with fists clenched. I thought I could feel his heart thumping.

When they'd all left us, helpless, Peter had been there. When Phil could no longer eat the meals Tomas brought from his restaurant, or even laugh at his efforts to make gourmet food in a blender; when he couldn't pay attention to Frank's Edith Piaf imitation; when my sister made the mistake of telling him about a healing at her new church and he asked her to pray for rain because the Mets were losing in the fourth inning. Those nights it was just me and him, touching anyplace he wasn't sore, reading to him to share insomnia's loneliness, my sleep so broken that I put the mayonnaise in the microwave and my camera in the fridge. Phil didn't like to hear the Bible. He wanted poetry instead, weird stuff about swans raping girls and daffodil bulbs sprouting from skulls. He had no idea what it meant, I'm sure; crazy words proliferating like cells colonizing the brain. When I burst into tears during a fashion shoot for *Redbook*, I realized it was time to radio for backup. Tapestry versus straw handbags should not be an emotionally fraught topic, even for fags.

Peter would lie on our bed and read the minutes of legislative committee meetings while I bathed Phil. Later, we would clean him together, when he wasn't able to hold himself up in the tub. I could take a precious hour to cry and stare at the television while Peter sorted through the bills and hospital paperwork that had piled up on our kitchen table. No one could argue with insurance companies like Peter Edelman. Relentlessly polite, he had read every policy down to the last "subpart J" and woe betide you if you didn't accept his explanation of how it related to subparts K, L, and M.

Did you see us, Phil? You weren't talking much by then. Did you hear us watching the Home Shopping Network in the living room at 2 a.m., passing a joint and a bowl of popcorn back and forth? We were laughing so hard we had to hold each other. This poor woman was hawking a set of folk-song CDs and her jowls were just like the hound dog's on the album cover. And as for "Blowin' in the Wind," well, you were never too smart not to enjoy the obvious. Then that song came on, the one you said your Pop used to sing at family parties, about the green green grass of something or other — the only thing you told me about him, other than that he drove a truck and kicked your queer ass out at sixteen. We almost ordered it for you. Peter had his hand on the phone. I admit, his other hand was under my shirt. The small print below the toll-free number said orders would arrive in six to eight weeks. We got as far as the woman saying hello and he hung up on her. She didn't hear the rub of our jeans together when I rolled on top of him, wanting to discover the clean salty taste of his body, at last, after all our false starts. Peter had too many thoughts to fall in love easily. My poor cock had to compete for his attention with the fate of mankind, particularly that segment of mankind that wanted Assemblyman Defalque to fix their potholes. And you, Phil, tumbling out of bed, overturning your bedpan, just as he was groaning into my neck and digging his fingers into my thighs so hard it hurt, and we were ready to let something good happen to us for the first time in so long.

A pretty girl was speaking at the funeral. Her solemn pose was like a suit worn for a first job interview, temporarily muting the bouncy energy of her brown curls and round blue eyes. She folded her hands dutifully in the pulpit. "Phil was my boyfriend in high school. I just want to say that he was the most...*real*...guy I ever met."

Something rose in my throat, a laugh or a cry. I swallowed it back. Peter tensed, leaning out of his seat. "I can't stand this," he said, loud enough that heads turned and the usher cleared his geriatric throat again.

"It can't be true. She doesn't look a thing like me," I whispered, putting my hand on his broad back to keep him down.

"They're telling lies about him, and they think that *God*..." He said the last word like it was a curse. I spotted Phil's mother staring at the girl, a fierce triumph warring with the grief that lined her plain square face, as if she were willing into existence every word that came out of that cute gap-toothed mouth. She had to live the rest of her life in this parish pretending she wasn't ashamed of her son.

As for Frank, he chewed his scarlet-painted lips. Miss Anna's confidence was leaving him. Real is a word that ends stories, with the happiness of Pinocchio, finally wearing a face that doesn't give away his thoughts. Or the Little Mermaid, that post-op transsexual, split in half and silenced by love. Who was the real Frank Abruzzo? I never asked Phil whether he wore his drag when they fucked. Now here he was wilting in the back pew, the widow turned Other Woman. "Buck up, Jezebel," I murmured. Recalling his diva, he stiffened up and showed us his Bette Davis eyes.

It was taking an awfully long time for Stan and Tomas to come back from the men's room or wherever they'd gone for a breather. The service was drawing to a close. It was torture but I didn't want it to be over. Only seeing the box go into the ground would be worse. My sister had wanted me to do something about Phil's soul, and by extension, my own. They were praying for us at the Broad Way

Church, where I'd gone with her some Sundays because it made me feel less afraid. Phil had gotten that bit of Walt Whitman stuck in his head, about living like the animals who don't lose sleep over their sins. He was resolved to go to his grave an unrepentant cocksucker. "You're not sorry, Julian?" he'd whispered to me, one night, after I'd tried to pray over him again. His faded blue eyes so innocently needy, his hand clutching mine like a child's: "You don't wish...we hadn't been?" My courage failed me, Phil, my sweet pain in the ass, what could I say but the truth: I couldn't call it worthless now, our love, the only life you'd had.

I'm half Catholic on the X-chromosome side but I didn't go up for Communion. I was tired of my body and I didn't want God or anyone else inside it. It exhausted me to imagine life continuing after the last chord was struck. Maybe that was hell, to know that you were insubstantial and yet forced to play out that story, to remain in that consciousness forever. Souls in paintings are like diamonds, outlasting the pitchfork and flames. Another reason pictures lie.

But the young priest dismissed us, with the plink-plunk of the old lady's piano beating out "Eternal Father, strong to save," and the six strangers maneuvered the casket off the altar and trundled it down the aisle on squeaky metal wheels. Phil was not in there. This whole performance was about his not being in there, wherever else he might be. Still I shoved Frank aside and rushed out of the pew to touch the box, as if that could make this day not be about our absence, too. My fingers brushed wood as the frowning procession moved on, their tempo unbroken.

The pallbearers descended into the hazy white glare of an inner-city summer day. Peter, Frank and I followed the black-suited crowd. Barbara stood between us and the limousine, squinting into the sun. "I think it would be better for my parents if you didn't come to the gravesite," she said flatly.

"*You* think?" Peter's voice carried above the noise of muted conversations and traffic that sped thoughtlessly past the line of black sedans. "Did any of you once pick up the phone and call him when he was sick? Did you take him to the hospital in the middle of the night? You wouldn't even touch his body without rubber gloves."

"Peter." I gripped his sleeve. The edges of my vision were turning green, breaking apart into black starbursts.

Barbara's gray eyes were hard in her doughy face. "My brother wouldn't have died if he hadn't run around with you people."

Peter stepped back, but he was only gathering his forces for the next round. I envied his simple, guiltless anger.

"Phil died because you didn't accept him, you and your phony God. You cry over Jesus on the cross and kill your own kids." His broad face was flushed and the cords of his neck stood out. At that moment I didn't know him at all. He was like someone you see on the TV news, aiming his educated voice like a brick through a stained-glass window. There is no God but the Democratic Party and the *New York Times* is his prophet.

"Phil died," I said, light-headed in the heat, "because he fucked guys for money."

Frank looked daggers at me. I was forcing him to break character. In Mamie Eisenhower's day, one didn't say such things on a church sidewalk. "If he'd been with me…"

"Don't go there," Peter ordered.

"I wanted us to be exclusive," Frank said defiantly.

"To quote the great Patsy Cline," I drawled, "'People in hell want ice water, but it don't mean they git it.'" Then I fell down.

When I came to my senses on the hot pavement, the funeral party was gone and Tomas was pouring something fiery down my throat from a small flask. "Where have you assholes been?" I sputtered.

"The van's gone," explained Stan, who was standing behind him.

"How do you know?"

"Because it's not there, dumbo," Frank snapped.

Ever-patient, Stan filled me in on what he'd already told the others: after the usher refused to let them back inside, he and Tomas had walked back to the supermarket to buy some coffee, only to discover that our borrowed ride was being towed because we were in the wrong spot for commercial vehicles. "Pittsburgh hates us," Stan sighed.

"Niko is going to kill me for losing his truck," Tomas fretted. "The cop said I couldn't get it out of the impound lot because it's not registered to me."

"So now we've got to lay out the cash to rent another one, like we should have done in the first place," Frank said.

"Excuse me for spending all my money on someone's medical bills," I spoke up.

Peter hoisted me upright. "Guys, let's find someplace air-conditioned to sit down and work this out."

We dragged ourselves past a bustling McDonald's and the remains of the Sunflower Diner, an empty room with soaped-over windows beneath a pink and silver sign. Around the corner from the church was the White Dove, a pub with a fizzling neon ad for Harp Lager in the window. A couple of heavy-set guys in jeans and work boots shouldered their way through the brass-handled doors while we stood considering our options. I looked from them to Frank. I wasn't the only one doing it, either.

"Why'd you have to dress like that?" I griped once more.

"Why'd you have to be a fag?"

"Maybe we should go rent the car," Stan said, drawing his arm around Frank in a conciliatory way.

"No, fuck this. All for one and one for all," Peter declared, and shoved the doors open, so hard they banged against the walls of the dark wood-paneled vestibule. We shrugged and followed him.

There was probably a gay bar somewhere in Pittsburgh but this wasn't it. I could tell because, first of all, the roughnecks nursing their pints had good biceps but had totally let their abs go, and second, the name didn't lend itself to double-entendres. We found a table in a dark corner and ordered a Bloody Mary for Frank and beers for the rest of us. The free pretzels were crisp and so salty they burned my tongue and made us all realize we wanted lunch. We ordered some soup and bread, and argued a bit half-heartedly before agreeing that one of us should go rent the cheapest possible car that seated five, and then we'd all chip in to buy Niko a one-way plane ticket to come rescue his truck because none of us could bear to drive down here twice. Tomas drew the short pretzel so we took his beer away and sent him up to ask the bartender for a Yellow Pages. The soup was warm and filling, and I felt good and also terrible that I could be enjoying my meal when one of us was dead. Peter's eyes met mine and I could tell somehow that he was having the same thought, both of us pausing while the others were bent over their bowls.

The White Dove seemed as good a place as any for us to wait for Tomas to return with the car. A Pirates-Mets game had started on TV and we moved up to the bar to watch. Frank went to the ladies' room to adjust his veil and wig, hoping by this charade to pass for an actual woman in the dim light. I wasn't optimistic. A lady of Miss Anna's caliber would not be tying one on in a blue-collar pub at one o'clock on a Sunday afternoon. Not unless she'd conceived a reckless passion for the handyman at the country club and was making an effort to appreciate his rough but wholesome lifestyle, like Jane Wyman in "All That Heaven Allows".

The Pirates scored a run and Peter gave a disappointed sigh. "Could you make an effort?" I muttered. "It's not bad enough to be queer in this neighborhood, we have to be Mets fans?"

But he only drew up one side of his mouth in a smile and clapped me on the back in a false sort of way, leaving his hand there long enough for anyone looking for trouble to find it. This wasn't the Peter I knew.

"You boys not from around here?" the bartender asked. He was a balding middle-aged man with big forearms whose muscles flexed as he wiped out the glasses with a dishrag. I saw only mild curiosity on his apple-cheeked face, for the time being.

"We're down from New York." Peter glanced at the TV, a little more apologetically this time. "For a funeral."

"I'm sorry, fellas. I had a feeling, 'cause we don't usually get suits like that in here." He pointed at my Brooks Brothers tie and winked. "This round's on the house. Was it family?"

241

"My best friend. Phil Shanahan," Peter said.

"Phil...Phil?" The bartender searched his memory. "Not Joe and Deenie's boy?"

We didn't recall his parents' names. Stan produced a folded-up funeral program from his suit pocket. The bartender looked it over and shook his head sadly. "Yeah, little Philly Shanahan. He used to come in here with his pop and steal the olives out of my jar when he thought I wasn't looking. Poor kid. What — "

His question was interrupted by one of the paunchy guys at the end of the bar banging his glass on the countertop for a refill. A scuffle in the hallway by the restrooms distracted us as well. "Excuse *me*," we heard Frank say in his frostiest diva voice. The impatient guy's friend, we learned, had pinched his rear.

"An excellent advertisement for support hose," I observed. Frank looked partly flattered and partly scared, which enhanced his female credibility. Peter drained his second pint of beer. I pushed mine away. "Who's the designated driver?" I asked, a not-so-subtle hint that he should slow down.

"Tomas." He reached for my untouched glass.

"No thanks, I'm not ready to die till I shoot at least one *Vogue* cover."

"It must be nice to know what the meaning of your life is."

I thought of mentioning to Peter that weed did more for his personality than liquor, but given his strange mood, I feared he'd take that as encouragement to further impair our chances of getting out of Pittsburgh. Further down the bar, Frank's new admirer was telling an off-color joke, rather more loudly than necessary: "...and then the Jew *bent over* to pick up the penny, and the Jew and the Greek went straight to hell."

"Philly, he was a funny kid," the bartender picked up the conversation where we'd left off. "He'd get up on that stool — right where you're sitting now — " he pointed to me again, a storyteller warming to his audience — "and bet you a dime he couldn't reel off the stats on any player you liked. Knew all the teams, Eagles, Pirates,

Flyers, you name it." The bartender smiled at the memory. "His pop picked up a few free lunches that way."

"Phil had a good head for that stuff," Stan spoke up. "He could tell you all the Oscar winners, even the tough ones like 'best foreign language film'."

"Not like we ever double-checked," Frank snickered.

"I did always have my doubts about 'Celine et la banane gigantesque'," Stan mused.

"Oh, he assured us it was a huge hit in Algiers," I joked, lost in a moment of happiness from the past.

"What did he wind up doing, up in New York?" the bartender asked.

"He taught bodybuilding classes at our gym, and he did some modeling for fashion magazines," I said. It sounded shallow, as a summary of anyone's life, so I added, "He was saving up to go back to school, for sports medicine. And, uh, he was writing a paper on Yeats." Phil had been too shy to let me read the scribbled sheets of notebook paper stashed in the drawer of our bedside table. They were waiting for the dreaded posthumous housecleaning, along with his porn videos and outdated bottles of Ensure.

"Ah, the Irish bard," the bartender said, affecting a brogue. "*That is no country for old men. The young/In one another's arms, birds in the trees...*" His eyes held more warmth toward us than before. It sounded like Yeats had been a regretful old queen. "A hit with the ladies, that poetry stuff," the bartender added.

Peter wore a contrary expression. I was afraid he would amend my whitewashed biography — say, by disclosing Phil's screen debut as Power Bottom #2. "Phil didn't do any of that," he said.

"What do you mean, of course he did," I said. "I have the pictures."

"He *didn't* finish school. He never got to — to *learn*. To see a better way."

"Better than what?" Stan asked, but Peter's attention was caught by the guffaws of the men at the end of the bar.

"How do you fit four fags on a bar stool?" one of them asked. His friend pretended to have no idea. "Turn it upside down."

243

Glancing warily from them, his regular customers, to us, the bartender put on his oh-Danny-boy face of wise sympathy and asked in a low tone, "So, eh, if you don't mind me asking, what did our poor friend die of?"

"*This!*" Peter slammed down his beer glass. "Hopelessness. Narrow-minded bullshitters laughing at him, making him believe he wasn't worth shit. People who are beat down, who think the answer is to kick someone even lower instead of rising up."

Frank was rising up, all right. He was halfway to the door by the time Peter stopped for breath. Stan froze, like a rabbit caught in a clearing between two trees, aware that he couldn't stop Peter but unwilling to turn tail so blatantly. As for me, well, I'd bleed all over a $500 suit for Peter Edelman, any day.

"Maybe you kids better move along," the bartender put a word in my ear, not unkindly.

The joker muttered something to his friend, with a nudge of his elbow. The other guy, after some prodding, asked in a blustery too-high voice, "Hey, Donny, what does AIDS stand for?"

"Asshole Injected Death Sentence!"

Peter whacked his empty bottle against the railing, leaving a jagged longneck stump. Oh, Lord. Last time my Daddy did that, I'd needed a dozen stitches. Then again, so had he.

I tossed my jacket to the bartender. "Take good care of this, darlin', I want to look nice when they bury me." I took a deep breath and went to stand beside my crazy friend.

He'd rattled them. I knew the signs, the ozone smell, the buzz of fear covered by a bully's laughter, as they sniffed the air to sense whether we'd back down. From the corner of my eye, I saw the bartender reach for the phone.

Peter raised the bottle end. The guys were about to lunge for us when he brought it down with a sharp swipe across his other hand. The grin on his face was terrible. "You want it?" he taunted, waving his blood-streaked palm in front of the joker's nose. "You want some faggot blood?" Red drops spattered the man's flannel shirt.

A crash came from behind us. In his haste to escape, Frank had backed into a chair, knocking it into the path of another leatherneck who took this as a sign that the game was on. Now Stan had his little arms around the guy's waist, trying to pull him off Frank, who landed our team's only hit of the day with a well-aimed high heel to the groin. Our two jokers had just taken advantage of this diversion to yank my arms back in a most unsightly position when the cops charged in.

35

THAT'S HOW WE ENDED UP spending the night in the drunk tank at the precinct. Peter used his one phone call to ring his dad's law office in Brooklyn. Nathan's tiny ears pricked up, I was sure, when he heard that our boys had been at the center of a hate crime. He got the station chief on the line and slung a lot of fancy words at him about equal protection and false imprisonment. They kept us overnight anyhow, supposedly to see whether the guys in the bar would press charges. Against us? We hadn't laid a lily-white hand on them, unless you counted Frank, and somehow I couldn't picture that leatherneck admitting in open court that Edith Piaf had kicked him in the nuts. I told Tomas to save himself; Niko could bring us home when he returned tomorrow for the catering van. I liked Niko, a chubby, nervously cheerful guy who smelled like fresh-baked dough, and figured this was my one chance to get to know him before Tomas threw him over for some guitar-playing drug addict, the way he always did when he met someone decent.

"The false consciousness of the working classes," said Peter, "is a truly intractable problem." Squeezed in beside me on a hard bench in the corner of the cell, he picked at his institutional dinner of coffee and a packaged cheese sandwich from the police canteen. His left hand was wrapped in a puffy gauze bandage.

"You want some of my Fritos?" Since he was holding the coffee with his one good hand, I fed him a corn chip. "Scary motherfucker," I said, and he smiled. It was evening, though we had no window to see the darkness. Frank was circling the cell mournfully like the beta-male chimp at the zoo, searching for a place to sit because a pack of newly arrested hookers had taken over his bench when he got up to pee. Stan had swallowed his remaining Valiums before the cop searched him, so he was snoring on the floor with his head pillowed on his rolled-up jacket.

Done eating, Peter sighed with fatigue and shifted around to find a less uncomfortable position against the concrete wall. I stroked the wrist of his injured hand. "That's nice," he said, and winced.

"Hey, you know, Frank hasn't used up his one phone call."

"What, you want to order a pizza?"

"I thought…in case you wanted to let Shawn know where you are."

"What's it to him? I mean…I can't drag him into this. My job is to take the hard knocks for him, not the other way around."

"For him and everybody else, it seems."

Peter didn't answer. I could tell that his hand was paining him. He closed his eyes and leaned his head back against my shoulder.

Over at the urinal, the largest hooker was demonstrating the convenience of crotchless panties for those who, like Frank, were one thing on the outside and another underneath. She was a short but mountainous figure with gold-weave dreadlocks and a double chin that helped conceal her Adam's apple. Men don't look very closely when they want something. She was teasing Frank in a big-sister way, if you can imagine your big sister shaking her dick at you, to break him in to life on the street. "That old dress gotta go, honey, a man don't wanna fuck no Aunt Sadie."

Frank, too lonely to keep up his what-a-dump attitude, began telling them the story of the funeral and the bar fight, embellishing slightly, but also leaving out most of the mean things I'd said to him. One of the other girls, a porcelain-faced Russian who smiled with her mouth closed to cover her broken teeth, shook her head sympathetically when she heard how Phil had died: "I know a lot of girls went like that. In here we call it 'ninja' because it sneaks up on you and — pfft." She spat on the floor and crossed herself to ward off bad luck. The guard, aiming to put a lid on our conversation, switched off the lights.

After some bawdy backtalk from the women, the cell grew quiet. I heard bodies fumbling around for their resting places, defending their territory in whispers. With nothing to think about, I noticed the smells more, baked in by a long day's heat: the open toilet, unwashed bodies, industrial pine-scented cleanser, and rising above these, a few brave whiffs of Chanel No. 5. In a shaft of fluorescent light from the hallway, the guard flipped the pages of his *People* magazine. There might be a photo of mine in there, if that shampoo ad was still running. Personal grooming, the great unifier of mankind.

Peter rested more of his weight on me. His dark curls were soft against my neck. "You okay, Jule?" he murmured.

"Tonight's not so bad," I said, and meant it. Tonight we were together, tomorrow we wouldn't be, the four of us, maybe living long enough to look back on this day as the sum of our closeness, the meaning of youth. All my life I had prayed when I felt about to evaporate. *Now I lay me down to sleep.* That verse had been on a poster over my bed, bordered with silly blue flowers. *If I should die before I wake.* When I first learned to read, I thought it was a warning, not to sleep under the frame or it could fall on me. The hand of God tips the picture, the hand of God stops the picture.

From the ladies' corner came hisses, a faint slap, something snatched back from wandering hands. The dreadlocked one's voice carried above the others: "Honey, we *all* think we too good to be here."

Still speaking under his breath, Peter suddenly asked me, "You know where I was last night?"

"You said you and Shawn were working on that bill to raise public defenders' salaries." A subject that held more interest for me than 24 hours previously, when I'd been on the right side of the law.

"After that."

"I assume this story involves somebody's dick or you wouldn't be keeping me from my beauty rest."

"Why should I even tell you what you already know."

"Because you want to say it and you know you can say anything to me."

248

"He's like this — how do I explain — he's a lightning bolt. You might think I'm stupid but I'm like a live wire all the time we're working side by side, knowing it could happen again, any minute we're alone, if we could ever get really private. And last night it did."

"So you got banged in the bathroom at the Statehouse, nice perk of the job, but what difference does it make? You'll never be First Lady."

"I don't want that anyway. I've got something better, just for me, that nobody can use for a photo op."

"I think you're lying to yourself," I whispered fiercely. "I think you just like seeing your own words in the newspaper, and you're willing to give it up to this closet case because you don't have the guts to be the one out in front."

He let this sink in. The guard, alerted by our rising volume, paced away again when he thought the conversation had stopped. Peter inclined his head toward the sound of those retreating footsteps.

"There's all kinds of closets. All kinds of prisons. I'm glad we're here so you can see," he said. "Being gay isn't the only problem there is."

"And this makes you want to drop your trousers because…?"

"Because Shawn pulls me out of myself. My struggle becomes everyone's struggle, no more Jews versus blacks, gays versus straights, I belong to you and your tribe and nobody else. Sometimes…" He searched my face for signs of mockery; he ought to have known me better. "Sometimes, he seems to me like everything that could go right in the world."

"So call him." The words caught in my throat. Peter said nothing. He was still leaning against my chest, with my arms crossed over his. "You can't call him because he wouldn't come. He'd never be in a place like this. It's just you and me."

I felt his breathing quicken, along with my own, in the thick silence. Touching his cheek, I found it was streaked with tears, big drops that rolled down and dampened the hair at his temples. I had nothing to wipe his eyes with but my shirtsleeve, which was none too clean, but I did my best.

"Phil's dead," he whispered. His body heaved with suppressed sobs. Holding him close, moving my lips soundlessly so he wouldn't hear and argue with me to make himself stop crying, I said a prayer for a boy who had run as fast as he could.

PART VI: SOLD

(September 1995)

36

A COLD WAVE licked my face, tasting better than I smelled. With my eyes slitted against the glare, I admitted defeat: I was awake. The tide meant it was either mid-morning or late afternoon. Since I'd been sleeping mornings, I figured on the latter. The Key West sun burns all day, like the lights of a house whose owner forgot to return. The constant heat doesn't give you a clue when night will fall. But you don't come here if you care about counting the hours. The salt foam puffed up a swirl of grit that stuck to my skin like the crust on an empty margarita glass.

"You are alive," Richard's voice unexpectedly rose over the noise of the breakers. He sounded mildly reproachful. I forced myself to sit upright, scooting back from the advancing waters, and wiped my face with the back of my hand because I had no towel or clothing other than a pair of unfortunate-looking Calvin Klein tighty-whities. Richard had seen the whole package before, of course, but this didn't seem like the best time to refresh his memory.

"When…when did you get in?" I asked stupidly, my muzzy brain unprepared with excuses for why I didn't have his pictures ready.

"This morning, *naturellement*, since I was not at your party in the evening." He squatted gracefully beside me, not to dirty his white linen trousers. His bony tanned feet were bare.

"Party." I repeated the word, hoping he'd fill in the details that I ought to know. True to form, he didn't. "I must have been at Po's, and then…some of us came back here?"

"*Très bien*." The feet turned around and began walking back up the dune to the beach house.

Po's. Pose. Poz. A pocket full of posies, that plague song. In actual fact, Po's was only a nightclub, four walls painted black inside, hung with lights pulsing underwater-blue, and animated like Frankenstein with a recorded heartbeat of hip-hop and Latino house music. Po's was the hunting ground where I'd been spending the better part of two weeks, trying to capture a photo of BD Conway, the reclusive author of the best-selling memoir *Running from the Rapture*, for a feature in *Homme NY*.

Raised in a cult compound in the Utah desert, BD had run off at fourteen, turning tricks along the highway for passage to San Francisco. His first legal job was as a janitor at a Buddhist temple that turned out to be a hub for smuggling Chinese immigrants. Swept up in the raid, BD endured the usual ass-pounding horrors of juvie while scratching out the early drafts of the book that now lay on my bedside table, its black and gold cover curling up in the mildewed air. A visiting English professor who mentored him in a prison writing workshop had recognized the value of his story and brought it to press. I could see her clearly through his plain, focused words: braided gray hair and silver jewelry, anxious and bright-eyed as a trained bird, peering into angry young faces for flickers of redemption. As I turned the pages, I could almost smell the temple incense mingled with pine floor cleanser and musty hidden bodies, and hear the round chimes of the meditation bells that lifted BD's mind above his outraged body. One drop of water falling from his cell window released all his tears for the wan, barefoot little brothers and sisters he'd left behind forever. Whereas I had the whole ocean at my feet and couldn't get clean.

What I didn't have was an address or phone number for my elusive subject. The professor — unmarried, childless — had died suddenly of an aneurysm while the book was in galleys. As her only heir, BD had been able to buy a beach house here in Key West, where (according to his phone interview with *Homme NY*), he passed his days and nights in meditation, writing, fishing, and ecstatic dance at the aforementioned Po's. Not bad for someone who was only nineteen, four years younger than me, and blind in one eye. So far, despite a thorough inspection of Po's patrons from dance floor to bathroom stalls and back again, I hadn't seen anyone who fit the profile.

I stood up, the tide sucking the sand from the hollows under my feet, making me stumble. The sea glinted silver, flat against the horizon like a cleaver blade. It was telling me that it had all the time in the world. Why shouldn't time be stockpiled unequally, like the 50% of GDP that Peter said was owned by 4% of the people? He was busy in the Albany Statehouse getting his nuts in a twist about this. I wanted him to come visit, but Richard's arrival complicated things. I could hardly toss my editor out of his own beach house, where he was uncharacteristically letting me stay for free, maybe because he knew I knew he had no intention of paying me for my last two jobs. Who has done business with the sea? And who has drawn out Leviathan with a hook? Damn Bible. *Suck it up, I'm bigger than you,* that's all it had to say. I dug out a small smooth rock that the tide had uncovered between my toes, realized I was being cliché and ridiculous, decided I didn't care and hurled it at the retreating foam.

The arc and splash made a tiny, interesting moment of asymmetry against the march of the breakers. It struck me as a bad sign that I was routinely falling asleep (all right, passing out) in locations where it would be unsafe to bring my camera. BD Conway wouldn't have let that happen. "Say cheese," I told the ocean, which had been around the block enough times to know this was something a real photographer would never say.

Back at the house, Richard was sipping an orange juice and vodka in one of the wicker armchairs in the main room, looking cool and uncreased. I dodged into the bathroom to wash my hands and pull a pair of denim cutoffs and a shirt out of the laundry hamper. I discovered that the sink fixtures were missing, as was the brass wall sconce that had held the room's only lightbulb. This made no sense. Hardware didn't get wanderlust. Someone desperate, I supposed, narrowing it down to only 96% of all Americans.

My editor hadn't budged when I emerged, carrying BD's dog-eared book to re-establish the notion that I was working. "Drink?" he offered. There was a second, empty glass on the mosaic-topped coffee table.

"No thanks — too early in the day." He looked skeptical. "Or too late, whatever. What time is it?"

Richard wrinkled his nose. "The house, it smells of the cigarettes. Your boyfriend smokes, no?"

"My boyfriend's dead." I glared at him. I hadn't slept for two days straight after Phil's funeral; out on a job, took a pill to calm myself down (never mind what, never mind from whom), spent four hours on test shots for Manhattan Model's new girls, only to find that I'd forgotten to put film in the camera. That's not a mistake anyone's allowed to make twice.

"But you must have another, and he is the smoker too, because that is how people are, they do not change. Always they want the same thing, like a duck."

I sensed that this was an argument he was having with someone other than me. Perhaps with the advertisers from *Homme NY*, who hadn't cared for my last portraits of Phil's purple-shadowed, lesioned face. Businessmen prefer healthy queers, sunshine boys flexing on the tennis court in Prada whites, dark-eyed loungers with the appetite of Lestat, immortal consumer.

"A duck?"

"The little one, in the science magazine, who says mama to the vacuum cleaner because it is the first thing he sees that moves." Richard sounded impatient, as he often did when I couldn't follow his Karate Kid routine of imparting life lessons through nonsense.

"Look here." I slapped the book down on the table and sat myself in the other chair. "This guy changed, big time. He grew up believing that men should sleep with their daughters but they'd go to hell for drinking coffee. And now, listen…" I turned to a page I'd folded for rereading. "'I sweated on the piss-stained mattress in my cell, too whacked to move. I was praying to die when a mosquito landed on my arm. I don't know why, I just…*looked*. My hand was huge. My skin was like a desert, with all these ridges and bumps and stuff. Which meant the mosquito, from his point of view, was *me*. I was the bug and the bug was Father and Hannah who died in childbirth at eleven and the man who stole my shoes and everybody else, and nothing bad could really happen to us because we were all one.'" I raised my eyes from the book, reluctantly. "I want to meet this kid."

Richard fingered a cigarette burn on the chair cushion. Images from last night came back to me in disconnected bursts of light. "You know who was here — Cheryl Kingston!"

"Ah! Poor Cheryl." Richard finally showed signs of life. "I have not seen her in the magazines for some time. Is she working?"

"Oh...yes...she's working." I recalled more and more. Two pitchers of sangria had dissolved all our self-flattering fictions. She said the money was steady; I said I knew. A boy with a camera, a blonde with something left of The Look; we all do what we've got to do to feed the meter. And apparently, though it was still a blur, one of us had brought home a new friend who required my bathroom fixtures to keep his personal budget in the black.

"C'est bon, c'est bon," Richard said, losing interest mid-sentence. He wasn't bored, I thought, so much as distracted. Perhaps I was seeing him through my own weather-beaten perspective, but the creases around his eyes and mouth appeared sharper, the color of his gaze more mist than steel. He blended in too well with this sagging, salt-scoured house.

"About the pictures — " I said, feeling guilty for my recent indifference to *Homme NY*'s bottom line.

"Yes, where are they?"

"That's just the thing. I can't get ahold of the guy. If you could give me a direct number — "

"I told you, he does not have the phone."

"Well, how did Bruni interview him, then?"

"It was with the calling card." Richard shrugged, indicating that technological details were beneath him.

"Okay, how about his agent's number? The person who cuts his royalty checks? Anyone?" Richard didn't reply. "Are you sure he even wants his picture taken?"

"Ah, yes, yes." My editor refilled his glass, and mine too, though I hadn't asked for it.

"Because he wanted me to meet him at Po's, at least that's what Bruni said, but I've been there every night and he hasn't showed up."

"Are you giving up on this assignment, Julian?" A sudden sharpness in his tone woke me up to the fact that in the three months since I'd lost Phil, I'd been doing an excellent job of trashing my reputation as a reliable photographer. There wasn't any brain behind the lens, and models can sense that. They're actually some of the most insecure people on earth. Unlike the sunset, they need to feel loved before they'll put out.

"Oh, no, but I've never done a job where the set-up was so..." I rejected the words "unprofessional" and "pointless" before continuing with "...open-ended, and I don't want to waste *Homme NY*'s money."

A brief, unsettling smile flashed across Richard's face. "That is not the problem. And you must send me your expense receipts."

Now, I didn't grow up the son of a businessman for nothing. If Richard and Marcia were running some kind of IRS scam, I didn't plan to go down for it. On the other hand, I had no place better to be, unless I took Peter up on his offer to join him in Albany and watch him suck his boss's dick under the table.

Assemblyman Shawn Defalque had a rotating cast of almost-fiancées named Serena or Dawn or Michelle, nice girls with straightened hair who studied dental hygiene and sang in the gospel choir. More to the point, for Peter's purposes, his was a crucial swing vote on a welfare reform bill that was stalled in committee. The rookie politician had to find enough of a compromise to survive his first fight without selling out his base.

Say "welfare" to the average ignorant guy, such as me, and the picture that comes up from our tabloid dreams is a lazy girl piling up stereos and babies on the government's dime. Phil would have sworn to it. He used to phone in to "Rights on the Left", Peter's dad's radio show, and pretend to be an African-American fireman who opposed affirmative action. Nathan blew his cover, though, when he quizzed him on "Juneteenth" and Phil thought it was a horror movie. Well, screw that, it's not like Shawn could tell you the date of Stonewall if you dropped hot wax on his nipples.

How many near-misses did two guys get before they were no longer near? Peter had called me for a coffee date on the weekend before I left for Florida. It was the first day that was cold and rainy all the way through, unmistakeably fall. He was back in his New York apartment for the week to work at Defalque's district office. We met up at Tom's Restaurant on 112th, his old college hangout. Each of us thought the other looked terrible and it felt okay to say so. He'd lost some of the baby fat around his face, its square planes hardening into the mask of the white-collar worker, but scruffy with the dark stubble that grew back so quickly on him. I had finished shooting a feature for *Glamour* on their annual crop of college scholarship winners — a bright-eyed, multi-hued crew of future lawyers in lipstick — and I hadn't taken off the pink "Girl Power" T-shirt they'd given us two days earlier.

When the drizzle briefly eased, we'd walked the few blocks uptown to the brick plaza of Columbia's campus. Peter was a genuine graduate at last, though he'd been too busy caring for Phil last May to toss his mortarboard in the air with the other accomplished juveniles. Morningside Park beckoned, a strip of green shade under dripping leaves, but Peter, chugging down a Starbucks grande, said it was full of junkies. I said I wasn't sure what made us all that different. Now you understand, he said. Understand what? But his thoughts had gone someplace far away. The future and the past are easier to live in, like all made-up environments. Between us, we had it covered.

We did walk through the park, smacking our umbrellas against the bowed-down branches. A wrinkled guy asked us for a light and I gave him a ten-dollar bill. Peter cleared his throat and stuck his hands in his pockets and asked me to take a job in Albany. A well-known anti-poverty lobbying group had an opening in the communications department. I could take artistic, serious photos of dumpster-diving children. What, I said, and leave show business? Phil would have cared, he said, staring ahead into the gray-green fog, into the treetops, anywhere except at me. Don't you use his name with me, I said. After all that, why would we ever seek out one more ugly thing to look at?

37

THAT WAS BEFORE I'd soaked up the words of BD Conway. "Meditating with the lights out, I know I'm seeing as far as anyone on earth." Blindness and decay were just mistaken states of mind to him. "Nothing contaminates the inward eye." He'd lost the physical one to a childhood infection because the cult didn't believe in hospitals — a policy which also explained why no journalist could find a birth certificate or Social Security number for Boaz Desolation Conway, born 1976. I couldn't get it clear from the book whether the eye was non-functional or actually missing. The empty socket would make a cool picture.

I tried to communicate my enthusiasm to Richard, who had drained the pitcher of orange juice and vodka and was beginning to cast a glance around at the state of his vacation home. The beach house was more of a cabin, with a small dark kitchen and bathroom on either side of the single open-plan room where I ate and slept and stared at the sea through the wrap-around windows. A sliding screen was available to close off the bed alcove, but I didn't need any more privacy. The bed was unmade and smelled as you might expect. A tropical storm on my first night had exposed a leak in the ceiling above the headboard, so I'd dragged the bed partway out into the living room and set an antique-looking porcelain umbrella stand behind it to catch the drips. That was the odd thing about the place, it was furnished with some nice pieces but the structure itself was going to shit.

Richard studied the knicknacks on the top shelf of the whitewashed bookcase and picked up a blown-glass sculpture, about five inches tall, a flowing column of curves that suggested a female form. All the art in their New York apartment was expensive in direct proportion to how confusing it was, so I figured this piece didn't come from Cap'n Jack's Souvenir Shack, unlike the pile of dirty clothes beside my bed. I bought new shorts and tees every couple of days when the ones I was wearing became too gross. When the heap got big enough, I would haul them down to the laundromat. It wasn't big enough yet.

"Do you wish to have it?" Richard held out the figurine, if that's what you'd call it, stars of light winking from its edges as he turned it in his hand. I didn't understand what he thought he was offering. I could look at the thing all I wanted while I was here, and what would I do with it back home? Phil would've christened it Dildo Lady, maybe stuck it on our bedside table with a lampshade on top. My longing for him, just then, was so sharp and terribly new, a shock that never eased, the echo of his infinite not-there-ness. He'd only taken up twenty-four years, six months and twenty-three days of this world, while everything that was not him went on and on.

Taking my silence as sufficient response, Richard shrugged and ambled out onto the cracked patio by the screen door, absent-mindedly hefting the small glass statue. The rising wind was trailing fluffy rags of strawberry and orange clouds above the darkening water. It was storm season. Once already I'd gotten stuck at Po's all night, waiting for the rain to let up its assault on the tin roofs and palm trees, a lashing I could hear but not see. Three a.m. the place shut down, the lights snapped on harsh as a hospital and the Filipino bartender's mother scuttled out of the kitchen to slap her dishcloth across the tables. That's when Cheryl had taken me back to the place her man was staying, one of a cluster of apartments crammed in above the bait shack across the street. A couple of mattresses, cameras, lights, and a full medicine cabinet: I understood the scene.

Her man would sell my pictures of the boys who hung around the parking lot at Po's. I didn't have to meet him. Benny, she'd said, his name maybe as temporary as she was. Fine, the only Benny I cared to know went early to bed and early to rise, and I definitely had better ways to spend him than the white powder that kept the lights on in Cheryl's eyes.

I'd watched her sleep, with the dawn light freshening her flushed cheeks and fantasy-blonde hair, her puffed lips parted as she breathed in a dream. Three or four times I'd held up the camera I always brought to Po's in hopes of a BD sighting, then let my hand fall to my side. Was there a new style in this, an art of refusal, something for a curator's placard on an empty wall in one of the museums next door to the Molineux' Fifth Avenue digs? *The photographer Julian Selkirk is best remembered for his controversial practice of taking pictures without film in his camera, which the Atlanta-born fashion journalist and gay pornographer called "the ultimate gesture of respect for the human body in the age of capitalist reproduction."*

While I reminisced, Richard had wandered off ahead of me, down to the rough stone jetty that marked one edge of their beachfront strip. I followed him. When you stand at the edge of the waves, their motion slowly numbs your eyes till you think you're the one moving forward, instead of the tide coming toward you. I spread my feet apart to stay upright at the dizzying sight, as if the rocky outcropping where we stood were a real ship's deck, forever setting out but not progressing, like two seconds of film replayed over and over. The water foamed brown around the jagged stones, lightening to slate-gray in the distance where the late sun's rays sparkled silver and oyster-pink. Richard put his hand on the small of my back, finding the patch of bare skin between my wrinkled T-shirt and my waistband. I flinched. "Sunburn," I said hastily.

"Mmm." He kept his hand where it was. His thumb caressed the curve of my spine. The fact that I had dreamed of a Technicolor tryst like this, before Phil died, only made the nerves in my body feel that much deader. My tired cock stirred, foresaw the end, couldn't be roused to remember what came next: a kiss, an all-comprehending look, one of us falling to his knees? Richard was not a man to waste a perfectly stage-managed sunset by returning to the beach house for condoms, and I wasn't feeling optimistic enough these days to carry them in my pocket at all times.

I searched for a clue in Richard's face, as he squinted out at the glittering waves, where not even a bird interrupted the gorgeous, empty sweep of the horizon. His hand had a will of its own, slowly massaging my hot skin, while his eyes were fixed on something far away.

"The first time we fall in love…" he said, his sentence trailing off unfinished. I vaguely remembered what it was like to have a high opinion of myself, to be convinced that my feelings were spun out of stronger stuff than disappearing pop songs and a bit of back-room friction. But despite Richard's occasional confusion of verb tenses, I couldn't believe he was referring to our relationship — a conclusion his next words seemed to undermine: "Do you remember it, Julian?"

"Well…" Two thoughts stood out clearly without touching my heart at all: one, that the God that most of the world saw behind those clouds disapproved of what we were doing here, in every language; and two, that if that God existed, and maybe especially if he didn't, I ought to love Richard, to care for the first time about the mystery inside that bald skull. I leaned into his touch a little more, willing my body to warm up, afraid that if I couldn't respond to him, perhaps I'd lost the ability altogether.

"Of course, you say nothing, because it is…for what we have no words. I mean…" He gestured, impatiently, with his other hand, which still held the glass doodad from the bookcase. "I mean, the *first* time, before one calls it silly names like God or beauty, one is even too young to speak the word, 'love', one only feels — ah! this terrible thing." He held up the sculpture to the dwindling rose light, and a tender expression veiled his eyes, a softening that was new to me, making evident the full weight of his middle age.

"I will tell you what it was for me," he continued, finally making eye contact. His voice had grown higher, his speech quicker. "*La robe de ma mère…C'était de velours jaune*, yellow velvet, *comme un, un girasol*. Do you understand? As a boy, in her closet, I would touch it to my cheek. But no, I did not want her, I did not want to wear it, to own — what does it mean, to own? Only to know, to touch — but always to suffer, because it was it and I was I. Do you understand?"

"Yes, Richard, I do." I genuinely wanted to kiss him then, pity warming me where lust had failed, but that would only have shown

265

that I didn't get it after all, to act as if sex or even romance adequately explained the moment. It was on the tip of my tongue to tell him my story, though it was more banal, especially in words, which are so slow compared to the flash of a long-ago image, the split-second leap of the Atlanta Falcons wide receiver for a game-winning play, striking me dumb with adoration that no doubt gave Daddy short-lived hopes that I might turn out to be a normal boy.

Richard, however, was not done: "And that is why I say no, no God, no heaven," he said sharply, his eyes searching mine. "The priest, he would tell us, little children, do not so much love the things of this world. But I say no, I will not be the mean host, I do not lock up one room, not one corner in here — " he touched the statue to his breast for emphasis. "Whatever is there, it is everything to me, till it is gone. But you know," his voice softened as his hand crept round under my T-shirt to stroke my belly. "You loved your boy, although he would die."

"Not enough," I said, my voice cracking with unshed tears. "I wish I had been better to him."

"There is no point in wishing now." His tone went suddenly flat and cold. He peered down over the edge of the jetty, where the waves beat against the piled wall of stones, their crests reflecting the colorless last light of dusk. Stretching out his hand, he let the little glass statue drop onto the black foam-washed rocks.

The temperature had gone down with the sun and the clothes on my back felt damp and too thin. Hesitantly, I put my arm around his shoulders. He didn't seem to notice at first. "Come on, Richard," I said, my voice stuck at a whisper. "Let's go home." After a few moments he let me turn him around and walk him back to the beach house.

Cheryl had given me some scented candles, which is the kind of thing girls think is a nice present, in unspoken exchange for me picking up her bar tab one night when she was waiting for Benny's check to clear. I said I didn't realize guys like him wrote checks, and she said it wasn't from him but to him from *Penthouse Forum*, and then her face got red and I felt so bad I bought her another margarita.

Anyhow, I'd never thought I'd have a use for those candles, but now I stuck a couple of them in teacups around the bathroom and lit them so Richard would have some light to take a bath. As for myself, I hosed down in the dark at the outdoor shower by the beach, hoping that the scent of burning artificial-peach flavor wouldn't make my editor all frisky for my Georgia ass.

I finished quickly and towelled myself off, shivering, but not eager to go back inside while Richard was likely to be naked. Then I began to worry that he'd slash his wrists in the bath, like a Roman emperor. My presence would be a bonus. One last *Homme NY* photo. I almost felt sorry for him, then I didn't. Whatever crazy shit was going on, I hadn't asked for any of it. All I wanted was to do my job and feel as little as possible in the hours between shoots. Keeping the towel wrapped around me, I wriggled into another T-shirt and the last clean garment I owned, a pair of pajama bottoms with orange clownfish printed on them. The fact that I had bought this item, even stoned, made me a little anxious.

It occurred to me that the night was still young and I could make one last assault on Po's to track down BD Conway before my editor converted the *Homme NY* bank account to pesos and disappeared south of the border. The one flaw in this plan was that I had no pants. What would BD do? He might (a) present himself at the club in my current attire (not an option for a self-respecting gay man), (b) steal Richard's clothes, or (c) go out naked and persuade the masses that this was the path to enlightenment. Unfortunately, I was in the mood for (d), get into bed and pull the dirty blanket over my head and defer thinking about what was happening to me for one more day.

There were no lights on this strip of beachfront to cast their haze over the stars crowding the black sky. You could only tell where the ocean began because the darkness became more solid below the horizon. I remembered Phil and me in Miami, and other times, how it always seemed he wanted to be romantic when I was bored, or hot for someone else, or angry at him for not having thought of it sooner. There must have been one perfect time — everybody gets one, don't they? — and if only I stood out here long enough, maybe it would come back to me.

He would have made fun of me for talking to him, as I did, gazing up into the scatter of cold white stars that stared at me like the electric eyes of a thousand bored surveillance cameras. What would you do, Phil, if you were me? Considering how your life turned out, maybe I should do the opposite. The thought came before I could stop it, flushing my whole body with guilt. "Sweetheart, I'm sorry," I said out loud. My voice sounded small and flat, out of place against the endless rhythmic shushing of the sea.

In the end I decided on plan (e), phone Cheryl and ask her to bring me a pair of Benny's pants to wear to the laundromat tomorrow. She wasn't home or wasn't picking up, so I left a message on her machine. It was probably for the best because I had nowhere to put her. Richard had wrapped himself in my unwashed sheets and was sleeping fitfully on the bed. I didn't want to wake him by turning on the light in the main room. Having spent the morning unconscious as usual (a habit I planned to break, starting tomorrow), I wasn't yet tired enough to sleep on the floor, which now that I looked at it, really needed to be swept or something.

I headed for the kitchen with the unrealistic goal of fixing a grilled cheese sandwich. The tiny fluorescent ceiling fixture sputtered and fizzed into life. This was the first time in days that I'd taken a good look at the place sober. My mama would have died, turned in her grave, and come back from the dead just to tell me what an embarrassment I was. She used to polish the bathroom faucets with a toothbrush, and I didn't even *have* faucets.

Failing to find bread or cheese, I inspected the odd assortment of boxes in the dry-goods cabinet, rejecting the dusty brown Belgian chocolates and the pickled vegetables labeled in Chinese, till I found something with a reassuring amount of preservatives. I returned to the main room and settled down on the wicker-frame sofa with a mug of Swiss Miss, my copy of *Running from the Rapture*, and a vanilla-scented candle to read by. "Tommy, oh, Tommy..." Richard moaned in his sleep. He twitched under the covers. Averting my eyes, I thumbed through the book to one of my favorite passages. BD was in jail (this was before Prof. Diemand entered the picture), thinking about how he'd never see his family again, but he was happy. He was always happy, the bastard. Had he ever put on rubber gloves to wipe the blood and shit off his lover's body? Did he know the sound of a boy drowning in his own bed? Well, maybe he did, but the difference between us was that he wanted to get over it and I didn't. I hadn't undertaken any great quest to survive. It had just happened.

But old BD, he was mellow, though he'd turned his back on every single face he'd known for the first fourteen years of his existence. The compound didn't allow television, of course, or magazines. If BD met Cheryl Kingston tonight, he wouldn't judge her by how changed she was since her debut cover for *Mademoiselle*. It made me wonder how he'd known what to offer the first outsider he laid eyes on, the truck driver who gave him a lift to Provo, steering with one hand in the boy's lap. Maybe it had something to do with his belief that everyone was the same person, always present wherever you were, so there was really no loss and no ignorance?

"In my mind I saw, clear as day, my sister Hannah peeking out the window, that last morning when I lit out for the highway. Under her grey cotton shirt, little Elijah was sucking angrily at the thin milk from her twelve-year-old breast. It was like they were here. Finally I got it: they *were* here. I was no more in jail than she was. Like me, she already had everything she needed to be free, all by herself, in her own mind."

Yeah, well, easy for him to say. He was on his way to becoming a millionaire beach bum while little Lemuel and Ruth and Josiah and what-the-fuck, J.R. and Ellie Mae, I couldn't keep them all straight, were condemned to a future of arranged marriages and long woollen underwear. Besides, didn't poor Hannah die in childbirth a couple chapters ago? Maybe there were two girls named Hannah. People who procreated this much soon ran out of Christian names, unless they dug down in the Bible for the Hepzibah's and Jehoshaphat's.

My thumb paused before flipping back through the pages for the anecdote I remembered. Did I really want to know? I thought of Pastor Steve, back in Atlanta, telling our Sunday School class that God planted fake dinosaur bones to test our faith in Genesis. I convinced my little sister that she couldn't watch "The Flintstones" anymore because dinosaurs weren't in the Bible. Made her cry, too. Now Lulu was preparing to graduate from NYU with honors in psychology, and I was…well, let's just say that my odor was not pleasing to the nostrils of the Lord.

A low groaning sound separated itself from the sighing of the wind. Richard might have been crying in his sleep, or giving himself pleasure. I dropped *Running from the Rapture* next to the sofa and studied the candlelight flickering on the ceiling. If I lay down with him, for as long as he needed me, what harm would we be doing that we hadn't already done? I made up my mind to stay put. Whatever might happen between us, I knew I would feel bad about it a lot longer than he felt good.

38

I WOKE TO SUNLIGHT BLAZING through the picture window and the sound of some guy banging on my screen door, which is unfortunately not a metaphor. Richard was gone. I hoped he'd gone out for groceries — the triumph of hope over experience, as somebody said about second marriages. The hand rattling the old wooden doorframe was connected to a buffed, black-haired Superboy with enormous pecs who introduced himself with the monosyllable "Troy". Behind him was Diego, one of the boys who hung around the parking lot at Po's. I used to see him jockeying for the best spot under the green-white glow of the sole security light, an angle that left his face in shadow while his body invited the cars to slow down. "Benny sent us," Diego said.

"Oh," I said. One of the many things I was reconsidering, on this bright and sunny morning, was my relationship with Benny. "Did you bring my pants?"

Troy stepped into the house. His huge tanned hand reached toward the waistband of his jeans. I blanked on anything clever to say. Death was ugly and stupid, and if I met it in clownfish pajamas, that was how it was going to be. I had no more interest in doing PR for the human condition.

Troy unzipped his jeans and slid them down over his hard-muscled hips. Underneath, his bulge was held in by the skinniest of aqua-blue thongs. He held out his pants to me. I gave him the kind of dumb look that he probably saw a lot, starting with his mirror. My own disrobing didn't make the same impact. The situation could have developed, except Diego cut in: "Benny said you had work for us." His full lips always seemed poised between a pout and a smirk, an unashamed selfishness that excused your own. I sighed and pulled on

Troy's jeans, which were a bit too roomy on me, but nicely warm from his body.

The cabin looked even more pitiful in the bold light of morning. The sheets were tangled on the floor, the puddle under the sink was creeping its way toward the laundry hamper, and something scurried under the stove when I went to rinse my cocoa mug. I remembered a joke Ariana had told me when I visited her in Hollywood, where she was designing bimbo-soldier bodysuits for a Star Trek spin-off. *Porn for men: A hot girl shows up in a French maid outfit. Porn for women: A hot guy shows up and cleans the house.*

So for the next couple of hours I shot pictures of Troy and Diego in their Speedos as they scrubbed the floor, tinkered with the pipes (I'm not sure they did any good but Diego looked tasty with water dripping down his chest), and washed a pair of my shorts in the kitchen sink so I'd have something to wear into town. Then I reluctantly returned Troy's jeans and we took a lunch break at the Crab Shack and bought spackle for the hole in the ceiling.

At the laundromat, the boys stripped off their shirts and posed in front of my clothes tumbling around in the soapy water. The old lady sitting behind us, with crayoned-on brows and a face so tan it was almost orange, looked up from her *People* magazine long enough to croak to her neighbor, "Look at vat they gotta do to sell soap today. Alvays wit' the sex."

Diego meanwhile was scoping out a young broad-shouldered guy in surfer shorts, with skin the color of polished cherrywood, who was loading his clothes into a nearby dryer. When he bent over, I could see the appeal. Troy exchanged a glance with me, clearly wondering if we were going to bring him in on the deal and slice our imaginary royalties four ways instead of three. I shook my head. "Totally hot, I know," I said under my breath, "but a black guy doing chores is kind of, uh, politically incorrect."

Diego snorted. "You new at this?"

"You should watch 'How the West Was Hung'," Troy chimed in.

"How the — what?"

"He played Indian #2," Diego turned his sexy sneer on his buddy. "Chief Thunder Stick," Troy corrected him.

"Hey…did you ever see 'Pump Me Hard 3'? Randy O'Tool?" I said hopefully. No reaction. *Sic transit gloria* Phil.

By this time our dreadlocked surfer had noticed Diego drawing a bead on him and was studying us with a supercilious air. I explained that we were shooting a pin-up calendar and would like to cast him as Mr. January, for the standard industry fee. As Cyndi Lauper used to say, money changes everything. In a precise British accent with hints of Jamaica, Mr. January said that his name was Tristan and he was down here doing graduate work in oceanography. He seemed to find us all very amusing. We got a fine shot of him pouring liquid detergent into a washer, with a languid, pleased expression in his half-closed eyes. Put on a Barry White soundtrack with that on your wall and, man or woman, you'd wet your pants for thirty-one days in a row.

Nonetheless, I didn't think I had a future as an adult film auteur, for the same reason that a fat girl shouldn't work in the donut shop. Back at the beach house, Troy was standing on a stepladder to plaster the bedroom ceiling, and I was endeavoring to take a purely artistic interest in the flexing of his naked glutes. Diego was jockeying for attention by complaining about the bucket of Mr. Clean that I directed him to hold.

"I don't care what you say, that's a five-gallon bucket, it ought to be big enough to cover your package," I snapped.

Behind me, the screen door slammed. I heard a woman's voice: "…might be able to get sixty, even seventy thousand, but the gutters…"

"What about the land?" a second woman asked. I knew that voice, husky and matter-of-fact, with its broad Long Island vowels. Marcia Molineux.

The conversation abruptly halted when they spotted us in the bedroom alcove. The realtor, a chubby woman in a shiny candy-striped blouse, gasped and blushed, which made her colors even less flattering. Diego, ever the professional, gave her a little smile and casually repositioned his bucket. Troy clapped his hands over his bare ass, realized that was only half the problem, swiveled around and lost his footing on the stepladder. Fortunately the bed was right below. Marcia faced me down, ignoring the others. Her expression was hard and weary but strangely calm, as if her anger were a heavy load that she'd been carrying as a favor to someone else, and now her job was almost done.

"Why are you here?" she asked, in a level tone. "What did he tell you?"

It was my turn to blush. "BD Conway…the interview, for *Homme NY*…?"

"There is no *Homme NY*," she said. "There's no more anything. Not for him."

The realtor had scurried back outside, not without a furtive glance at my calendar boys, who were doing a poor job of wiping spackle off the bedsheets.

"You must be the last person who doesn't know," Marcia declared. "Conway is a hoax. *The New Yorker* exposed him last week."

(I would later find out that Marcia had told the truth, as she generally did if she chose to tell you anything at all. A junior editor at the publishing house, unable to sell her own novel about polygamous kooks, had added some pop philosophy and rebranded it as a memoir by an unknown youth.)

But on the spot, I couldn't take in this accusation against my guru, too overwhelmed by the betrayals closer at hand. "Listen, Marcia, I'm sorry…can we, uh, talk someplace else?"

"This is my house," she replied, not budging.

"Okay, don't worry, we'll get out of here right now, we were just fixing it up for you," I babbled, nearly putting my foot into the bucket of Mr. Clean as I rushed around to scoop up my few possessions. My laundry was still in a trash bag in the back seat of the rental car. The boys, probably long practiced at this, had made themselves scarce. The realtor was walking slowly around the perimeter and poking at the plastered walls as if she were hoping to trigger a secret room that would swallow her up. Marcia stood over me while I groped around under the bed for a missing attachment for my tripod.

"Did you think you were special?" she broke the silence.

"Not particularly."

She acknowledged my candor with a faint, grim smile. "Because it isn't about you — any of you. I put up with that, when I had to." I waited for her to tell me what it *was* about, but instead she said, "I've had an offer from Condé Nast. They're going to publish *Femme NY* as a quarterly, keep me on as managing editor of that and a couple other titles they've got on life support."

"And Richard?"

"What do you think?"

"But…" Should I say that he loved her? Both of them would have laughed at me for reducing their relationship to that, like trying to copy the Mona Lisa in fingerpaints. "But I thought he was the genius. That that's why you stayed — because he made *Femme NY* what it was."

"Genius," she said, bitterly. She bit her lower lip to keep it from trembling, and took a deep breath. "Genius is a baby that never grows up."

She turned and marched off. I gave up on my tripod attachment, which had probably been stolen, and offered a brief prayer of thanks that I wasn't addicted to anything expensive. Imagine selling off the tools of your trade that way, piece by piece, lenses, cameras, and lights, till you had nothing left to dismantle but your body, giving it away in the back seat of a parked car or on a mattress in a makeshift studio.

From the kitchen I heard the nervous, loud clinking of glassware. I was nearly out the door when there came a thump and a crash. The realtor would take care of it, I told myself unconvincingly, suddenly eager to put miles between me and the whole state of Florida. But I looked in, out of compassion or curiosity, and saw that Marcia was only gathering up jars and boxes from the cabinets and dumping them into the trash. Not yet seeing me, she paused, with her task unfinished, rested her elbows on the stained countertop and sank her head into her hands.

"Marcia," I ventured, "I'm so sorry. I really didn't understand… anything, at all." I could tell from the set of her shoulders that she'd heard me, but she didn't reply. Tentatively I stepped into the kitchen. "Do you want me to fix you a drink?"

"Don't you get it?" she cried, wheeling around. "This isn't your place. He shouldn't have brought you here. I got this house in the settlement. This house, and the precious *Femme NY* name, and..." She pressed her lips together in a thin line. "Twenty years," she said, more quietly. "Not even."

"I guess Richard doesn't always keep his promises," I said, beginning to worry about my own future now that the Molineux family firm had crumbled.

"Honey, if you know that, I got nothing more to tell you." She threw another jelly jar into the bin.

"You'll be okay," I said, feeling sure it was true. I remembered how I used to think she was the victim, the drab Miss Moneypenny to his philandering James Bond. I nearly put in a word for him anyhow; he was a whack job but he'd been good to me, mostly, and he was suffering. But perhaps it had taken Marcia two decades to figure out what I suspected, that suffering for Richard (his own or other people's) was merely one more flavor at the banquet of life.

As I drove down the beachfront road for the last time, the sea rolled in on my left, a lowering, rumbling mass of gray. With the mood swings typical of Florida in hurricane season, the morning blaze had been smothered by fast-moving, shape-shifting clouds. When I'd flown down here earlier this month, I'd left my return date open. Now, I could either take the highway to the airport and hang around till a flight to New York opened up, or continue on into town. I hesitated at the intersection and finally picked the latter course. I ought to say goodbye to Cheryl, I reasoned, and if I was reading the sky correctly, the flights would be delayed till morning anyhow. I could use the phone in her apartment to book my ticket. In truth, I was drawn back to Po's, perhaps by a self-torturing need to confirm the awful truth about Conway, perhaps only for a last opportunity to unwrap Troy's package. If you haven't noticed already, big dark-haired men make me act stupid.

Outside Po's, I had to bend over and lean into the wind to stay upright when crossing from my car to the front door. No rain yet, but the air was heavy with it, like a wet washcloth over my face. Palm fronds snapped atop swaying trunks. Two police cars with flashing lights were parked outside the bait shack. I rang Cheryl's number from the bar phone, and wasn't surprised when no one picked up. I hung up without leaving a message. The call could only be traced back to Po's, not to me, and I would be out of here as fast as the nice phone operator at Delta could take down my credit card number. I suppose that's the problem with most people, we feel bad about things but not bad enough, and that's why there's a market for tequila, books with happy endings, Sunday morning TV preachers, and pictures of naked boys scrubbing the toilet.

But really, there was nothing I could say to help Cheryl that was worth being manhandled by redneck cops, which wouldn't be nearly as much fun as they made it look in Phil's last film, "Jailhouse Cock". I'd watched a few minutes of the tape, after he died, just to see him. He had two scenes as the deputy sheriff. Lance Biggers wasn't bad as an Elvis impersonator, but the whole point of Elvis is that he's so sexy he doesn't need to drop his drawers; just from the voice, you can imagine those rosy lips doing whatever you want them to do. In Phil's first scene the other cops were showing him how to subdue a prisoner. I'd sat on my bed, that dark July afternoon, jerking off and crying. There he was, eleven minutes and nineteen seconds into the tape, turning his head toward the camera with that expression I'd replayed so many times without being able to say whether it was fear, amusement, an exaggerated innocence, or a thought (of me?) that had struck him out of someplace else entirely, unrelated to the chief's thick red cock about to thrust into his mouth. His limbs were firm and pink. The booted men in blue, nightsticks slapping against their thighs, lined up to grapple him from behind. I could have pretended to be any of them, I couldn't decide which, trying to tug myself into their rhythm, distracted by waiting for the moment when Phil would lift his face again from the man's crotch, a second before it was splattered by the predictable money shot. The man behind him backed away, dripping. That could have been it, the instant that put us where we were today, Phil in the ground and me sucking on an overpriced rum and Coke while I waited for my flight back to a home where no one was waiting for me.

The bar windows shook. The strings of chili-pepper lightbulbs danced overhead. The TV, tuned to a Marlins game, shorted out for a few seconds, then popped back on. Instant replay ensured we didn't care. Finishing my drink, I joined the cluster of patrons who were peering out the back door at the storm's progress. Diego lounged against the wall facing the parking lot, cat-like in the shadows, sheltered by an overhanging gutter. Passing headlights washed over him as several customers cut short their night at Po's to try and beat the imminent downpour. He caught my eye and, after waiting a minute or two to see whether I'd come to him, casually headed indoors. I smiled.

"Hey," he said, his voice perfectly pitched, low and warm, interested but not too eager. He was slimmer than Troy, and tonight I'd been hoping for someone who would really crush me, but his face sold me, with its promise of sweet and nasty secrets.

"You working — on a night like this?" I asked, moving in closer. His nipples showed through his thin white cotton shirt, molded to his chest by the humidity.

"Weather's good for business, keeps 'em inside," he replied, with a smirk. The folks around the doorway hopped back as the wind flung some stripped-off foliage into the parking lot. "What'cha doing here? Still looking for that writer guy?"

Embarrassed by this reminder of my quest for Richard Molineux' version of the Loch Ness monster, I said quickly, "Just killing time before my flight. I'm going home to New York tomorrow morning."

Diego bared white teeth in a hopeful grin. "You gonna publish our calendar, right? Make us rich?"

"That's the idea." I felt the pocket of my windbreaker surreptitiously to make sure the camera was still in there. I wasn't going to leave it in the car in this neighborhood. They cracked car trunks as easily as the lock on my kid sister's diary.

Eyes darting back and forth, he lowered his voice. "And, uh, you don't wanna cut Benny in on this one, okay?"

"My lips are sealed," I said. "At least for that."

"What'cha mean?" He knew, I could tell from the appraising look in his dark eyes, but it was better if he could make me say it.

"I liked what I saw." I dropped my gaze to his belt buckle. "I'd like to see it again."

"In the car?" He winked. The blue and white lights were still spinning on top of the two vehicles parked at right angles outside Cheryl's building. I needed to lie down in the dark and hold someone. Why was that so hard to get for free? That and food, clean clothes, a view of the ocean: the basics. They're not for everyone.

"Can we get a room?"

Diego led me down the narrow blue-tiled corridor past the restrooms and the doorway to the steamy kitchen. He pushed open the metal door marked "Employees Only", which led into a dark room smelling of damp cardboard and dust. He yanked a pull-cord hanging from the ceiling, and in the light of the plastic-caged bulb I saw that one corner of the storeroom had been cordoned off with a bedsheet hung over the pipes to make a sort of screen. "Welcome to Casa Diego," he said, pulling his sweaty shirt over his head and stretching so I could see every ripple of his abs. Did he live here? A bathroom the size of a closet, tucked behind a floor-to-ceiling stack of Budweiser cases, suggested that it was possible.

"Is Diego your real name?"

He gave me a practiced *no-hablo-Ingles* stare and pulled me to him with one hand hooked around my waist, while the other hand unzipped my pants and massaged the hardening bulge between my legs. My palms felt clammy. Was I allowed to touch him? You'd think I'd never done this before. I didn't know what he wanted. I wanted it to matter. I was afraid my hands would be too cold, but his bare skin was feverish, his rhythm undisturbed when I wrapped my arms around his waist. His tongue traveled down my neck. I didn't want this to be a drive-through meal. I let go of him for a moment to remove my jacket and shirt while he pushed aside the bed curtain. A boy of about fifteen was curled on the mattress, looking up at us with a scared, amazing face: black hair, high cheekbones, a narrow girlish jaw, and lips that could have starred in a lollipop commercial.

"Go on, beat it," Diego growled at him, adding something in Spanish. The boy jumped up. He was wearing an oversized sleeveless undershirt and not much else.

"He's beautiful...you're beautiful," I said. "Can I take your picture?"

The boy, motionless against the wall of boxes, turned his eyes to Diego, for permission or a translation. "He's not anybody," Diego said shortly, tugging the curtain around us to exclude the boy. "He just stays here sometimes."

"We're still...on," I tried to calm him, "I just want him for the calendar."

Diego frowned, his business instinct struggling against some other emotion — protectiveness? jealousy? Above us the wind rattled a loose piece of glass in the casement window. He fired off another sentence or two in Spanish at the kid, who ducked into the tiny bathroom. With a hopeful expression, he held up a dirty-looking mop and a sponge. Diego jerked his chin in my direction, speechlessly telling me to get it over with.

I pantomimed the boy into position. He pretended to wipe the mirror over the rusty sink, his perfect face doubled in the glass. Diego kicked the door shut behind us. I shoved it open again, not wanting him to get the wrong idea. He'd drawn the curtain all the way around the mattress and switched off the storeroom light. "One shot," I murmured to the doe-eyed kid, who seemed to expect this routine of hearing words that meant nothing, taking orders he didn't understand. When I was done I slipped some money into his hand. He flicked off the bathroom light and melted away into the darkness. The room was black now except for the sudden crack of lightning at the casement, momentarily painting the sky a bruised purplish grey. I still needed the same things, company and a place to spend the night.

Nearly blind in the wake of the lightning, I groped toward the mattress and drew aside the sheet. Naked arms pulled me down. We wrestled on the lumpy boxspring. He slid his hand between my cheeks, shoving my pants down around my ankles. His cock was short and thick and felt unfamiliar in my mouth. He thrust his hips into my face and wrapped his long brown legs around my back. I hoped he really was queer and wouldn't feel bad about enjoying it. I licked him from bottom to tip. He pulled out, just when I was getting out of breath, and turned his back to me. Hesitantly, I touched his tight, flat ass, which was only a faint suggestion of a lighter form rising out of the darkness. Water dripped somewhere behind me. I didn't have a condom. How did I get here? Tired of waiting for me to make my move, he squirmed down till I could feel his hot breath on my belly, his mouth seeking out my sore, swollen cock. I fingered the silky foreign texture of his hair. It wasn't right, it wasn't the same. Let it happen to me like falling asleep, like a piss, a release, a lifting up, falling out of my body, drowning. Speeding sirens whined in the street. I was choking, crying out, my face wet. A sound like coming. He sucked harder. Ending, a warm liquid rush, sleep spreading through my veins — no, that was actual water, spattering on my face through the casement as the glass popped out and crashed to the floor.

We scrambled for our clothes, saying nothing, all negotiations done. I thrust a handful of twenties at him. The camera was safely wrapped in my jacket; my shirt was in a puddle sprinkled with glass, so I left it. I'd change in the car. Stumbling back into the hallway of Po's, I blinked in confusion, thinking I'd taken a wrong turn, since it was as dark here as the storeroom, only more crowded and noisy. The storm had taken the power out. Indistinct figures jostled for the exits. A flickering at the bar was somebody lighting a candle in a jar, casting odd elongated shadows behind the bartender and waitress who were rifling through the drawers for more emergency lights. Years of working in darkrooms had honed my sense of direction, so that once I understood what was happening, I was able to find the door to the parking lot. The wind flattened me against the wall as I rushed to my car. The spitting rain had begun. Soon it would be pouring in sheets across my windshield. I had no place to stay. If I could just make it to the airport...and if not...?

My rental car crept up the road to the highway. One lane was blocked by more vehicles with flashing lights shielding something with a crushed bumper from view. After this obstruction, we picked up speed. In a stupor from what had happened at Po's, made worse by the claustrophobic silence of the car hemmed in by rain, I fiddled with the radio dial. Past the Spanish-language news and scratchy hip-hop, a jaunty ensemble of horns and violins played, faintly but clearly, in the background as Judy Garland sang:

Clang, clang, clang went the trolley,
Ding, ding, ding went the bell...
Stop, stop, stop went my heartstrings...

It was a big-band station, the kind that had been all but forced from the airwaves in New York, except at midnight on Sundays. There must have been some old gents in Florida, some ladies with snow-white marcelled curls and yellowing silk gloves they only wore now to church and funerals, who remembered dancing their way through America's last good war.

Judy segued into Dietrich purring "Lili Marlene". Louder than a gunshot, a utility pole snapped and toppled, lashing the wet road with sparking wires. I skidded and slammed on the brakes. I wasn't the only one with this brilliant idea. One of the others happened to be behind me and rammed in my rear end with a force that would have made Lance Biggers proud. My car fishtailed from side to side. While I fought for control of the wheel, another driver sideswiped me, shoving my little compact off the road into a drainage ditch. My head pitched forward and hit the steering wheel.

I hung at an angle in my seatbelt. It hurt to breathe. Warmth trickled down my forehead. The rain... I brought my free hand to my face, so slowly, I might have been asleep and dreaming the red on my fingers. A light tenor voice wafted from the dashboard:

Quand les beaux jours seront là,
Pour la saison prochaine,
Ohé ohé pour trois mois,
Vous viendrez vivre avec moi...

Richard had loved this guy, he was some closet case from the thirties, like a French Bing Crosby. It was good music for going to sleep. The rain was good too, hypnotic, streaking, whispering. I ought to remember his name. Not a time to close my eyes. That's what they told you on TV, if you have a concussion, you have to keep awake. Charles somebody. Awake until what?

Think of something. Best Picture winners since 1939. The Mets' batting order. The trouble with your life flashing before your eyes is it's all behind you, suspenseless, nothing to stop you from falling asleep to the Late Show. I sped through memories of this whole trip, a waste, blur of blistering sun and rolling, darkening waves. *Nous partirons, vous et moi...* Peter had asked me to do something and I hadn't done it. Wash in the Jordan seven times. Wouldn't I, wouldn't I go anywhere for him?

I wiped the blood out of my eyes with my sleeve. Charles Trènet had yielded the microphone to a Chevy commercial. Months from now, *Hard at Work 1996* would be the best-selling calendar at Rainbows & Triangles on Seventh Avenue, as well as a popular item at Hot Topic in malls across suburbia. Tristan would drop out of his oceanography program to model Fila sportswear. Diego would spend his share of the royalties on the down payment for a used Corvette that would be impounded two months later when they caught him and Benny using it to move white powder. Troy would win leading roles in "The Bitches of Madison County" and "Wet and Wild Spring Break #12" but quit the business the following year to take a job with his cousin, who sold condo time-shares.

We would never be able to track down the boy on the cover, whose picture I had taken in the storeroom at Po's. They named him "Luke" on the credits page; the publisher's assistant would tell me she got the most fan mail for him, from teenage girls and others. But all this was still in the possible future, the imaginary, the almost-gone future, when I leaned out the window of the rental car (sucking in a painful breath when the belt pressed on my two broken ribs) to flag down the paramedics who were searching the crash site, shouting "Here I am! Help! Over here!"

PART VII: SHELTER

(February-May 1996)

39

THE PALE-FACED BOY in the torn pants trundled a shopping cart down the harshly lit strip of walkway. A hooded coat of tattered brown shag like a skinned teddy bear covered his eyes and bulked up his rigid shoulders. His unlaced boots executed an about-face and he reversed himself into the shadows. Following on his heels, a black man with frosty streaks in his stiff dreadlocks hoisted a bedroll over his shoulder. His puffy brick-red jacket was striped with silver tape patches over the rips. He paused briefly under the lights before retreating to his hidden doorway. After him came a figure wearing a red and brown knitted ski mask over a shapeless black knee-length thing that was something like a kimono made from trash bags and twine. His calves were bare above his combat boots.

I'm so over men in skirts, Ariana scribbled on the notepad she passed to me. But she made a face at my sympathetic look and pointedly redirected our attention to the runway, where a man swathed in stained white painters' dropcloths was bringing up the rear of the procession, the spot that in women's fashion shows is traditionally reserved for the bride.

The lights went up, to the applause of the audience. Chatter and the scratching of pens on paper replaced the soundtrack's repetitive minor chords. The designer, Anton Fische, took a bow. We were sitting too far back for me to see the sweat I imagined on his brow. His first foray into menswear, last season, had been a flop (the *Times* critic called it "Dick Tracy joins the circus"): an eye-popping pastiche of cartoon colors and exaggerated Roaring Twenties shapes that seemed to be trying too hard to make the sick and cash-strapped mid-90s take a happy pill. Following the logic of "shoot the piano player",

Fische fired everyone who'd worked on the ad campaign, putting me back behind the camera for his latest collection. Since he remained my largest commercial client, I shared his relief at the audience's warm reception.

As my last-minute guest, Ariana was only here out of curiosity. We'd been hanging out a lot since she moved back to New York from L.A. shortly before Christmas — or Hanukah, in her case. I had gone to some effort to score an extra ticket to Fische's show for this cute stylist named Ryan, whom I'd picked up on one of my editorial shoots for *Glamour* ("Spring Green With Envy!"). But last week I'd slipped and called him "Bryan" when he was down there on his knees, and that was that. Twenty-three being too young for me to plead Alzheimer's, I couldn't really argue with his somewhat redundant assessment that I was a self-centered, brainless jerk. Fortunately, Ari had never let that get in the way of our friendship, especially when clothes were involved.

"I'm sorry about Trudy," I told Ari, not for the first time, when we emerged into the stinging February wind. Trudy Arroyo, formerly Rudy, was also formerly Ari's massage therapist, fashion muse, and lover in L.A.

"I thought she was it. The whole package," Ari said, also not for the first time. "Beauty, sensitivity, a woman's intuition. Great hands. *And* a dick."

"So which part of that have you given up on?" I asked, though I already knew this month's answer. We were headed to dinner at a Soho macrobiotic joint with Ari's new friends from VenuStage, a feminist experimental theater project. She was designing the costumes for their reinterpretation of "Medea", and I, who would otherwise avoid an evening of buckwheat noodles with lesbians, needed to earn their trust for a photo essay in *QNYC Weekly* about new shows being produced by "our community".

Since the collapse of *Homme NY*, I'd been doing more work for the fag mags, where it was easier to get a foot in the door. Even in fashion, the campiest profession outside the Catholic Church, not everybody wanted to be openly associated with their fellow queers. Celebrities still preferred to be coy: a red ribbon lapel pin here, a flick of the wrist there, but God forbid you mention your boyfriend on "Style with Elsa Klensch". Community, indeed. What did a nice boy like me have in common with the strikingly beautiful, soft-voiced Trudy, and VenuStage actor-in-charge ("director" was too phallocentric) Laurel Feinbloom? I'll take "people who'd get beaten up in Texas" for $100, Alex.

"Oh, well, you know Laurel," Ari replied, saying her new bed-mate's name with a mixture of affection and annoyance. "She's totally *real*, you know, she understands how to *communicate*. But she can be so...soft."

"I thought that was the point of sleeping with girls. Not that I'm the expert." We were walking past a bus stop shelter with a Calvin Klein ad on its side, a pouty shirtless hunk flaunting his package in tight white briefs. I missed Ryan-not-Bryan, but only in the sense that I had his phone number and not the one of the guy in the picture. No, I was missing something else, possibly (Ryan's words again) "any interest in other people's feelings." Maybe it would do me good to spend more time with women who were sincerely fucking each other when they weren't eating tofu and reinventing the Western literary canon.

"Listen, Ari, speaking of sleeping...could I, uh, crash at your place tonight? I figured, since you'll be at Laurel's..."

"Again? What's wrong with your apartment this time — fire, flood, giant rats?" She spoke lightly, since in the beginning she'd been the one who kept inviting me over, for what became our Monday night ritual of drinking shots and saying mean things about the skinny actresses on "Ally McBeal".

"It's the pipes," I said weakly. "Every morning at 4:30 when the heat goes on, there's this awful banging. It's like listening to a bad audition for 'Stomp'."

We stopped to wait for the light to change, and she laid her hand on my arm. "Jule...if you miss Phil that much...why don't you move, already? Make a fresh start."

I shrugged her off. "Rent control." Two words that speak volumes to seasoned New Yorkers, who would prop up their dead grandma in the window rather than vacate her below-market-rate apartment. Phil and I had gotten a good deal on the place three years ago because the building's wiring wasn't totally up to code. Now that the economy was slowly reviving under Mayor Giuliani, who had cracked down on turnstile-jumpers and titty bars and other picturesque threats to property values, I'd have a hard time finding another affordable place anywhere near Chelsea or the Village.

"You could get a roommate," Ari persisted. When I said nothing, she took this as her cue to return to her own problems. Laurel was displaying serious nesting behavior, but Ari wasn't feeling inclined to rearrange her life on the strength of four weeks of hormonal bonding. My friend had more options because her parents in Jersey discreetly subsidized her between jobs. They "believed in her vision," according to her mother, a child psychologist in Teaneck.

Ari's vision was to break out of costume design for syndicated cable-TV dramas and start her own line of punk-inflected fashions for downtown club kids. She'd just sold one of her designs to the Soho boutique BlueSquare, a graffiti-patterned white T-shirt dress with an asymmetrical neckline and hem. Each time we walked down Prince Street we had to pause and pay homage to the shop window where it hung spotlighted by track lights between corrugated metal walls. Meanwhile she was living on paychecks from the Sci-Fi Channel for "Inspector Infinity", a series about a detective with a poorly calibrated time machine who wants to go back and prevent his wife's murder, but always gets the setting wrong and winds up solving a crime each week in places like ancient Greece or the Wild West, thus necessitating many changes of clothes.

Ariana wasn't the typical BlueSquare customer. For one thing, the only double-digit size they carried was a zero-zero. Also, most women wouldn't have been so delighted by the dress's $300 price tag. The elfin salesgirl in black leggings hovered behind us, trying to scope out whether we were stylists from an important magazine or time-wasting tourists. Ari winked and held the dress up against my chest. The sight in the mirror-plated support beam was jarring. I looked like my sister dressed as the Little Match Girl. Cinderella in reverse. "Now who's living in the past," I sniped.

Ari stuck the dress back on the rack and pulled me down the metal steps to the outdoors. "Come on, Laurel hates it when I'm late."

Three blocks later, she said, "You could try talking once in a while."

"I am talking. I've been talking all day. Let's talk right now. What did you think of Fische's show? Was it bold and relevant, or tasteless and exploitative? Discuss."

"Don't change the subject."

"But I really want to know." I could do offended Southern innocence. I had the eyelashes for it.

Ari sighed and blew on her stiff hands. The vintage black gloves, trimmed with rabbit fur, were more for style than warmth. "It doesn't matter."

"Don't pity yourself, darling. That's my job."

She swatted my rear. "Smart mouth. You know better than that. What I meant is, there's no good or bad in fashion. It's about making yourself into the character you want to play. And not every character has to be nice."

I thought about that as we crossed the street to our destination, Whole Earth Bowl, where a line of would-be diners stretched down the block. Ari groaned. "Laurel didn't make reservations. We never had to before."

"I guess mung bean futures are a buy...ever since Winona Ryder was spotted eating here last week."

"Wait, you *knew* about this?"

I shrugged. "I also heard a rumor that Pancho's across the street makes great spicy barbecue wings," I added hopefully, but to no effect. We took our places at the back of the line. In the cluster of people ahead of us, some held hands, talked in twos and threes, conducted short-tempered business deals on their cell phones, or all of the above simultaneously. I stood closer to Ari for warmth. Downtime was a bad idea for me. I could feel my pulse slowing, the pulse of everything getting older, losing its color, eroding in the wind. I went out at night with my friends, I took pretty pictures, I had reasonably good sex with undemanding people, but I observed it all through this gray curtain of snow like the scrambled signal of an X-rated TV channel.

"What I was trying to say, before…" Ari's breath was warm in my ear.

"Oh please, no."

"When Trudy and I broke up, I talked about it."

"I noticed." Who sat through "To Wong Foo, Thanks for Everything! Julie Newmar" — *twice* — and wiped away her tears whenever John Leguizamo sashayed on-screen as Miss Chi-Chi Rodriguez? Bitsy Selkirk's second-favorite son, that's who.

"The point is, it helped." Ari's voice was gentle. Worried. Incomparably annoying. "I've moved on."

I stepped out of the line of people inching toward bean-sprout ecstasy. "So, what? I'm supposed to cry about how Phil threw beer cans at the TV during the Super Bowl? So that then I can forget it ever happened?"

"Jule…" She lowered her voice as a hint that I should do the same. "I've been to your place. You still have some of his clothes in the closet."

"Well, when Trudy comes back to you, she can have them."

Ari didn't get riled. Bad sign. She was becoming sincere from eating too much pussy. "You keep your clothes on the floor so you don't have to open the door and see his stuff. I know, okay?"

"You don't know shit." My voice rose. Hardly anyone around us stirred. They were too busy staking out the doorway of Whole Earth Bowl for a glimpse of Winona. "Phil didn't move to La Jolla to work at a spa. He got AIDS and he died. Just like Misha from Manhattan Models, and Sam and Tino who lived down the hall from us at FIT, and Stefan who was on the back cover of GQ twice in those Guess ads with the leopard — do you know where Stefan died? Sleeping on the floor at the Port Authority. I don't need any help forgetting because y'all are doing a fine job without me."

Ari wiped my eyes with the corner of her piebald fur stole, which was a close match to the gloves. "Here, while you're at it, cry for the bunnies who gave their lives for fashion."

"I'm surprised Laurel doesn't throw red paint on you."

"She thinks it's fake." Proving she didn't know our Miss Ziegler at all.

I meant to return Ari's conspiratorial smile, but my mouth turned down the wrong way and the tears flowed again, an anesthetic drip, spreading fatigue through my previously upright body. One thing no one tells you about grief is how boring it is. Running from your feelings is at least an activity.

Across the street I spotted two of the VenuStage women, but they hadn't seen us yet. "Honey, I'm sorry, but I don't think I'm up to dinner with the vagitarians tonight."

Ari subjected me to a compassionate, searching look she'd probably learned from her mother. Then she relented and pressed her spare key into my hand. "Fine — don't do anyone I wouldn't do. I'll see you in the morning, maybe."

I kissed her cheek. It could have been the wind that brought a flush to her face.

40

ARIANA MIGHT NOT have cared to give an opinion on the morality of Anton Fische's fall menswear line, but the press blew up about it for a few days. It was an irresistible hook for two minutes of outrage to pad out the morning talk shows. Liberals could bluster about co-opting the poor to sell luxury goods, while conservatives wrung their hands that fashion had turned away from truth, beauty, and dinner jackets.

My companions at table 9 of the Save Your Homes fundraising kickoff dinner were in the former camp. The new charity, headed by Reverend Gilbert Crowell, planned to help inner-city residents keep up their rent payments when they became disabled or unemployed. As a member of Crowell's church, Assemblyman Shawn Defalque served on SYH's board, which meant my boy Peter was never far behind. He wasn't sitting with me, though.

The guests on either side of me weren't sure how to make conversation with a fashion photographer. For my part, I watched the 6 O'Clock News twice a week, but couldn't contribute much to their discussion of the presidential candidates' budget-balancing schemes. Someone took a swipe at Fische's runway show, since the controversy had crossed over from the fashion press to the mainstream media.

"Selkirk was the photographer for those ads, can you believe it? What a coincidence." Mack Polzin, seated across the table, pinned me with his sharp blue eyes. He was a journalist for an alternative weekly — the kind of paper that runs feminist book reviews up front and ads for hot Asian hookers in back. Polzin was notorious for outing a right-wing radio host who'd said America could stop AIDS by quarantining homosexuals. Before that, the reporter had gone after a GOP bigwig in Mayor Giuliani's health department who'd repeatedly blocked funding for needle exchange programs. No mainstream paper would touch that story; *Gay Downtown* ran an ambiguous photo of the politician outside the Saddleback Bar on Christopher Street, but wouldn't let Polzin quote his alleged boytoy as an anonymous source. The journalist and I had had work in the same issue of *QNYC Weekly*, a connection that hardly warranted his digging into my C.V.

"Small world," I said sourly. I hadn't expected to defend myself here. I had an honest job that paid my bills. According to gossip at Manhattan Models, Stefan had been hustling in Times Square those last months of his life. We heard rumors about new drug combinations that were reversing the course of the virus for a lucky few, but who could afford them? Rent or pills, food or heat, shelter or life. Better is one day in the gutter than a thousand underground. So whatever Peter might think, it wasn't only for his sake that I was sitting here in the Sheraton ballroom, poking at my $100 chicken marsala with canned mushrooms, and allowing a portly church elder to call down damnation on my top client.

"Shameless exploitation of poverty," the fellow blasted away. "If you know what it means to be homeless — it is not something you care about for a *season*, that goes out of *style* so you put it away. The poor you have *always* with you."

I tried to answer respectfully. "This is our art form. We're reflecting reality. Starting a conversation — we don't have all the answers."

"Fashion isn't art, it's commercial," sniffed the woman next to me, a social worker in a beige pants suit with large white plastic buttons.

"So are you saying artists shouldn't be paid? Or that if too many people like something, it stops being art? That's elitist," Polzin unexpectedly spoke up for me. I avoided his eyes. Let them fight about what Fische's show "really meant", like dueling televangelists calculating the date of Armageddon. For me, it simply made visible, shareable, the ghosts that walked the runway of my mind, whether anyone paid me to look at them or not.

Sad words and statistics. Coffee and pie charts. Rev. Crowell gave the blessing. I began paying attention again when I heard his whispery, solemn voice reading from the prophet Isaiah. He didn't fit my stereotype of black preachers, no thundering sing-song rhymes or bandstand gestures. He was a short, slim, neatly dressed fiftyish man with a long narrow face and a slight stiffness in his walk from shrapnel he'd taken in Vietnam. *Give your youth to fight the Communists and then get called one yourself for taking the gospel seriously.* He said this without anger or accusation, just a plain heads-up: here's what you're signing on for. The loaves and fishes, he said, started with one little boy giving every crumb he had.

Beside the podium I saw Peter seated next to Shawn at the head table. Now he was bowing his head for the prayer to Jesus, mentally substituting the *Shema Yisrael* or Star Trek's Prime Directive. Now rising with the rest of us, mingling, shaking hands, exchanging political news and discreetly folded donation checks. As I wound my way toward him through the moving clusters of people, Polzin tailed me, asking questions whenever we were forced to stand still together.

"Pretty interesting to have an elected official working for your church charity. How d'you think they square that?"

"I'm sure their lawyers know what they're doing." The way Yankees carried on about church-state separation made me scratch my head. Peter's dad devoted a whole radio show to this girl who refused to stand up for a 20-second prayer at her high school graduation. I mean really, like bad manners are a constitutional right.

"You're a supporter then? Of Defalque? That's right, you worked on his campaign."

"A lot of people did."

"You must know his girlfriend, then — is it Serena? or Dawn?"

"Tressie, I think."

"Can't keep 'em straight. Silly me." He rolled his eyes. "Defalque sure likes the ladies...doesn't he?"

I pretended not to hear him over the hubbub. So that's why I'd been targeted. Apolitical as I was, I'd read in *QNYC* that a bill was pending to add "sexual orientation" to the state law against discrimination in housing and employment. A similar amendment had failed in each of the last two sessions. Not all Democrats welcomed us as their natural constituency; suspicion of the gay agenda was the first thing Orthodox Jews and black Christians had agreed on since Crown Heights. Afraid to lose the church-lady vote, or perhaps believing that what he did with Peter in private didn't merit public protection, Shawn had not yet signed on to the amendment, and therefore was in Polzin's gun sights. It jolted me, on top of all my other anxieties, that Defalque couldn't competently keep his own secrets. Polzin had sniffed out mine already: I wasn't sure where my loyalties lay.

To tighten the squeeze further, Shawn had noticed my extended interaction with the reporter. The look of mistrust remained on the politician's smooth, haughty face, even as I shook his hand and volunteered to help with PR as soon as I had a spare day between jobs. Thinking to boost my stature, Peter talked up the prestige of my recent clients. Wrong move. Shawn's lip curled at the mention of Fische's infamous ads. "I'm sorry to say, I know you have to do what your client tells you, but I thought it was an offensive gimmick. Angling for attention, to make money."

"Isn't that what we're doing here?" I retorted. "Only less effectively."

Peter's cheeks colored. "Didn't you hear, we've raised over $30,000 for — "

"Honey, that wouldn't even pay the cameraman for Broadway Cares. Big donors don't know you exist. Because you're boring."

"People are dying on the street, and this doesn't hold your interest?" As Peter, now provoked, raised his voice, Shawn subtly edged away from him, toward the pastor.

"You can't play that card with me and you know it." I spoke to Peter like we were the only two in the room. "There's sob stories everywhere. You can trip over them in the subway. The key is to make people want to listen. Give them something beautiful to take away from the mess."

Rev. Crowell nodded agreement. "*Without a vision, the people perish,*" he quoted. "Yes, Mr. Selkirk, something positive. What did you have in mind?"

I let the change of phrasing pass, masking my irritation. *Positive* was a word that made me wince, the popular shorthand for a diagnosis that was anything but. I hated its prominence in the new batch of gay magazine titles — *POZ! H+!* — and the health articles that friends tacked to the bulletin board at the gym. Let me tell you, it wasn't the power of positive thinking that kept those guys' muscles from wasting away (and occasionally made them slam their fist into a wall). No, positive wasn't the same as beautiful. Richard Molineux once read me a love poem where a man and woman encounter a rotting corpse in the road, "blooming like a flower". The guy realizes his girlfriend will someday also be a stinking carcass, and somehow it makes her more attractive to him, like he's seen her truly for the first time. But whatever.

"Ever heard of 7th On Sale?" I asked Shawn and his entourage. I explained about the fundraiser that *Vogue* and the Council of Fashion Designers of America had been running for the past few years. Top designers and luxury stores donated pieces for a sample sale at bargain prices (relatively speaking) that raised a couple million each year for AIDS charities. If the Save Your Homes crew teamed up with Fische instead of sniping at him, we could put together a fashion show and charity auction that would rehab his image while expanding the do-gooders' donor base.

Crowell pressed me for specifics, which meant I'd hooked him. I name-dropped more recklessly than a Page Six column. Shawn said they'd consider it, and meanwhile he'd take me up on my generous offer to photograph the families facing eviction for SYH's fundraising mailings. I agreed to the words he put in my mouth.

"And another thing," I said. I reached over and ripped the stick-on name tag off Peter's shiny navy blue lapel. "Would you people spring for some lanyards? Nobody puts *adhesive* on a good suit."

41

WE CLING TO what we think is ours, the only home we know: a bug to a leaf in the March wind, a crippled old lady to her walk-up apartment, a Selkirk to his liquor. I only drank at night with friends, to take the edge off days photographing rent-overdue rooms where fat men watched screaming televisions, and their girlfriends or mothers cooked chicken and onions, and the cast of the Last Supper held their positions on a gilded ceramic wall plaque, the Savior's cheeks pink as birthday-cake flowers. The doors all had two or three locks. You get to a point where you're too poor to throw things away — shopping bags of yarn, videocassettes without cases, 1980s bridal magazines — not because you hope to sell them, so much as that you haven't time to decide what's useless. Or maybe you grew up believing in magic, the American variety that turns you into the things you own, so you just went on acquiring Coke cans and sneakers and children and tattoos, completely unprepared for the notice that would spill you and yours out onto the street like a burst piñata.

How proudly the children offered their collections of plastic ponies and toy wrestlers to my documentary lens, though there were always some who held back with sullen faces, knowing that home isn't home if you have to expose it for a handout. How hard it was to get their parents to look me in the eye. The grandmas could be counted on to have a soft spot for boys like me, and would spend hours showing me family albums over weak coffee and butter cookies. Children, grandchildren, who didn't visit often enough. Who'd moved to California or Texas, to be nurses or security guards. Who'd been shot outside their high school prom. Who were in jail. Part of the sales pitch for heterosexuality is that family is like money in the bank, the

30-year bond you can retire on. But even real money isn't that. In the unlikely event I lived long enough to wrinkle, who would knock on old Julian's door? Probably only male prostitutes and Jehovah's Witnesses.

I had hoped Peter would be my assistant on these excursions, but instead Save Your Homes dispatched a pretty Puerto Rican caseworker to make the bilingual introductions, and otherwise I was *solo*. Peter reassured me that he was saving his limited free time for the glamorous half of our project: persuading my fashion contacts to participate in our gala. This put me on the spot. I'd already had a few cold refusals and was embarrassed to imagine him witnessing that. But maybe the Edelman gift for relentless argument could turn matters in our favor.

First, though, I had to get him out of his clothes. "You can't wear that suit to meet the marketing director of *Elle*. You look like a process server. In fact, don't wear a suit at all. Try some skinny jeans, a jacket, maybe an interesting vest — but don't even think about a sweater vest, you're not teaching music to eighth-graders."

"Stop criticizing me." Peter slouched against a rack of secondhand shoes, their creased leather tongues gaping in silent protest. I'd dragged him to the East Village thrift shop where I found my favorite "statement" pieces. But he wasn't easy to transform.

"I'm sorry, I can't hear you over that shirt." I made a face at the mustard-and-orange button-down draped over his arm.

"Didn't you tell me to take a risk?"

"Take risks for yourself, not other people."

He re-hung the shirt with a somber expression. I swept through the racks, pointing out his best colors, describing the correct shoulder width for blazers, but he stayed quiet. The most voluptuous brown suede jacket failed to lift his spirits, though something of mine surely lifted when he tried it on. "Come on, what's the matter?" I rubbed his broad back beneath the soft fabric, at last a perfect fit.

He leaned into my touch, looking at the two of us in the scratched floor-length mirror, anxiety and pleasure mingled on his face. "I guess...I don't like vintage. The past is depressing."

"Well, why didn't you say so? Let's go check out the wardrobe closet at *QNYC*, they've got samples from lots of gay designers — redundant, I know, right? But first you have to buy what you have on right now." He opened his mouth to object, but I talked over him. "This jacket was *made* for you. This jacket *needs* to be with you. You will wake up at night, years from now, craving its soft embrace, and weeping bitter tears that once it was yours for the asking, for only $89.95 plus tax."

Peter smiled. He didn't take it off. Brushing against me on our way to the cashier, he said in a voice that was almost a whisper, "I wish I could be as happy as you."

Happy? That floored me. I was happy to be around him, but I wasn't going to spoil it by saying so. Because, I guess, the reverse wasn't true.

QNYC Weekly was no *Details* or even *Homme NY* in its glory days, but I had enough clout there to sneak a guest into the room where they stored designer clothes and accessories for styling the photo shoots. Menswear predominated, since the magazine's female readers were more likely to collect power tools than purses. Peter's eyes lit up at the space-station coolness of the track lighting, white walls, and racks of black leather garments. "This is awesome, I feel like I'm in a music video for Devo." He put on a pair of sunglasses and mimed a robot walk. I relaxed, seeing him start to have fun. His seriousness could be tiresome. Always me taking care of his moods, or lack thereof.

"Hey, is it safe to take my shirt off?"

"Safe from whom?" I winked.

"People walking in on us."

"Fine, if you're that modest all of a sudden, go hide behind the fold-out shoe closet."

He reappeared, a new man, in a tight-fitting Vivienne Westwood black tee with a pattern of swords. Borrowed gray dress pants, skinny in the European stle, defined his strong legs and nicely curved behind. Surprised by his own reflection, he flashed a confident grin, cocking his head for a better look.

"Cruising yourself?"

He slumped back into apologetic humor. "Well, next time someone tells me to go screw myself, at least I'll enjoy it."

I pushed his shoulders back to a proud posture. "So now you see what's possible, let's go down to Orchard Street and buy the illegal knock-offs of your new ensemble."

When he didn't say anything, I put my hands on his hips and swiveled his ass toward the mirror. We both liked what we saw. Once again he drew closer, but watching our double image instead of me. There was longing on his reflected face, a passion almost like anger, sudden and blinding.

Tearing himself away from the sight, he shook his head. "I don't want to be that guy."

I poked his nipple. "You already are. Enjoy it."

He was standing very close to me. His voice was husky. "I don't want that power. To be the piece of meat everybody fights over. The trophy, the — the *drug* you think you can't live without."

My eyes told him it was too late for that. "You can't hide forever," I murmured.

"No way — I've got to take this off — " He stripped the black T-shirt over his head. I grabbed his naked waist. He had to hold me, no place to put his arms but around me. He shoved me backward against the mirror, but he didn't let go when I deep-kissed his mouth. He kissed back, gently, repeated, the rigor leaving his muscles all at once, with the abruptness of a blown fuse. He was licking my lips, brushing his cheek against mine, stroking my hair. Hope flashed like a shard of glass in my heart. He gasped and turned away, wiping his face.

"What's wrong now?"

"I don't know...I feel...so sad." Our hands fell to our sides, found each other there. "Seems like we always come back to this."

"Yes, I've noticed." I raised an eyebrow.

"Is this all you want? Are you doing this whole Save Your Homes job just to get into my pants?"

Peter's switch from tenderness to accusations was more than I could take. "Why don't you ask Shawn whether he keeps you on the payroll so he can pound your lily-white ass?"

"Leave him out of it. This is between you and me."

"Yes it is. And you know what? Your question is stupid. Because so what if I care about one person more than all the strangers in the world? Is that so wrong? Why shouldn't that person be you?"

Peter closed his eyes. "I can't...I can't be what you want me to be."

I couldn't look at him anymore. "Go, put your ugly clothes back on."

Tentatively, from behind the fold-out closet, he asked, "We can still work together, though? On the fashion show?"

"No, I don't think we can." I stuffed the Westwood tee under my jacket, thinking to surprise him with it later. Hell, I'd just bill it to Shawn's little project. But then I pulled it out and replaced it in the closet. No more presents for him. He wanted nothing, and that's what I had to give him. "You stick to your side of the business, and I'll stick to mine."

42

EVENING, ALONE. Peter was on the train to Albany. I couldn't avoid my empty apartment. I walked in on a scene interrupted, by what impulse, I couldn't remember: a cereal bowl and spoon unwashed on the coffee table, the afghan half fallen off the back of the couch, my latest contact sheets for *Glamour* fanned out across my desk. I had the strange sensation of coming home to someone, an alternate Julian, who had just stepped out a moment too soon for me to ask him how to live a different life from this one.

This, I decided, was how people wound up acquiring split personalities, or cats. I tried to laugh at my self-pity as I soaped up the dirty dish, but all I could think of was how it would feel to wash Peter's body, a tenderness he had no use for, from me. I squeezed my eyes shut. "Oh, God, oh, God, please, God," I whispered, bent double over the sink.

St. Paul found repentance much easier because he lived before the invention of the telephone. Mine rang while I was taking another look through the contact sheets, scanning for the minute variations in three dozen thumbnail images of a coltish blonde in a daisy-print dress, perched on a motor scooter. Eyes open, winking, hair curled, wind-blown, white teeth, hint of a smile. What was the most beautiful hour of her life, the most beautiful second of that hour?

"Does it matter?" I asked whoever was on the other end of the line.

"My, we're sarcastic today," Ari retorted.

"I'm sorry. I'm totally out of it. What did you say before?"

"I asked whether you were free tonight. A friend from L.A. is in town doing standup at Gotham Comedy Club and I'm going to go cheer him on."

"Laughing at other people is what I do. Is Laurel coming, though? I don't want to be a third wheel."

"Don't worry about Laurel." She sounded like she wasn't taking her own advice.

"Ah, I see. This is a conversation that's going to cost me at least two Cosmos."

"Drinks are on me."

"Well then, as Adam said to Eve, what are we waiting for?" I left the *Glamour* model unedited in her perpetual springtime, combed some product through my hair, and flung on my coat.

The show didn't strike me as Ari's brand of humor. Her friend Bix did this routine about being the nice guy that girls would confide in but not sleep with. He was a big rowdy dude, short but heavy, his flannel shirt untucked over a white tee, so when he pantomimed holding his girlfriend's handbag while she flirted with the auto mechanic, we were supposed to see how obviously she'd miscast him.

"But hey, I know what you're gonna say, not alla you ladies are like that. You're too smart to fall for those big gorillas. You appreciate a man who can cook you a gourmet meal and watch 'Places in the Heart'. A guy who waxes his back — hell, you can both go get waxed together! You're just that close! 'Bix, why can't you be more like my friend *Bruuuce*? He's in such great shape. He always listens. He trims his nose hairs!' Well, if you need me to tell you why…I guess your parents pulled you out of that 'special' health class in middle school. Am I right?"

Ariana laughed and clapped like everyone else. After his set, Bix sat down for a beer with us. Ari congratulated him on his new gig as a script writer for David Letterman, which was what brought him out East. He complimented her costume designs for "Inspector Infinity". She shrugged it off, and joked with him about loser fanboys who dressed up for sci-fi conventions. He scribbled notes on a napkin to use her comments in his next routine. I traded some Hollywood trivia with him, then the conversation turned to their mutual friends in L.A.

Idly, I cruised the guys waiting for their turn at the open mike, didn't catch anyone's eye, and wondered what I'd be thinking about if I wasn't thinking about that. I ought to have more hobbies. *GWM, 23, seeks same for open LTR. Enjoys depth psychology, breeding sheepdogs, and long-distance running.* After a moment's thought, I mentally deleted "open", then wrote it back in.

The first girl who stepped up to the mike rushed through her lines in a shrill voice. You could tell she was half afraid of not looking pretty, and the obligatory raunchy jokes were uncomfortable in her mouth. Bix thought she could do no wrong in a sweater that tight. Our duty discharged, Ari and I struck out for parts unknown.

We went down to the subway station to keep warm, but didn't swipe through the turnstile because we were arguing about what to do next. "Let's go to New Eden," Ari insisted.

"I hate that place."

"Why?"

"You know why." I'd been with her, watching Frank's drag act as Miss Anna Bollocks, the night I met Phil.

"You were together for four years…sort of. That's a lot of memories. You think he'd want you to stop going everyplace that reminds you of him?" Ari sounded tired, lacking the usual energetic bitchiness that was such a perfect foil for my wilting-pansy routine.

"I don't think he'd give a fuck one way or the other. This is about me, what I want. Besides, doesn't it get old, getting drunk and crying over a bunch of she-males singing 'Besame Mucho'? Go back to L.A., if you're so miserable."

Silence, then a sniffle. Ari turned away and wiped her cat's-eye glasses with one fur-trimmed glove.

"Omigod, I'm sorry," I said.

"Fuck you," she mumbled.

"No, seriously. A Southern boy should never make a lady cry."

"Fuck you twice."

"You're supposed to say, 'You, sir, are no gentleman!' and slap my face."

"That could be arranged." Ari brought her small fist up to give my chin a soft tap.

"Let's go back to your apartment and drink Jose Cuervo and talk about our feelings. What do you say?"

"I'm *beyond* tequila. I need ice cream."

We picked up a pint of vanilla fudge ripple on the way home. I normally don't eat that stuff. Four days a week on the Ironman treadmill is all I have time for. Ari dug up a half-bottle of Captain Morgan so I could concoct a grown-up version of a root beer float. Probably would've tasted fine if I'd set it on fire, like a Baked Alaska, but she wouldn't let me. We sat close together in a nest of pillows on her couch with the 11 O'Clock News turned on low volume. For awhile the only sounds were the clinking of spoons and the muted prattle of the newscaster running through the day's scandals.

"Hey, uh…you want to tell me what really happened with Trudy?"

Ari was smart. She'd actually enjoyed our cultural criticism seminar at FIT, wowing our teacher with papers on the semiotics of hemlines and so forth, whereas I didn't know Hermès from hermeneutics. Every time we got together for one of these lovelorn post-game shows, then, she came up with a new theory: Trudy was conflicted about her gender. Two ambitious women couldn't put their relationship first. Trudy was jealous of Ari's success. Ari's friends didn't accept her "sexual fluidity". And on and on.

"No." Another scoop of vanilla.

"Well, what about Laurel?"

"I don't know." Ari cranked the TV volume. President Clinton was expected to sign a law preventing the federal government from recognizing same-sex marriages. "Look at that. I should've voted for the Green Party candidate instead of that Arkansas horndog."

"You realize, you and Trudy could actually get married still, but Peter and I can't? That's so unfair. You're way more of a threat to traditional American values than we are."

"Peter?" she asked sharply.

"Yeah, he's totally going to wind up buying the brownstone in Park Slope with a nice partner and a couple of dogs and multiracial foster kids." I sucked on my empty spoon. "Probably not with me, though."

"You wouldn't want that?"

"It's not that, it's…" That he couldn't picture me making him happy for that long, I supposed. "'Why do birds suddenly appear, Every time you are near?'" I sang, instead. "Or not, in our case."

"Don't ask me." She wriggled into a more relaxed position, stretching out across the cushions so that her chin was propped on my shoulder. The newscast flashed a photo of a Dalmatian who'd pulled her sleeping owner from a burning Barcalounger. I leaned back too, not fighting it when my face came to rest against her close-cropped light brown curls.

"That was a good question you asked," she suddenly said.

"Which one?" I asked, surprised.

"Why do some people click but not others? Who decides whether someone is funny, or pretty, or female — or not?"

"God, I guess."

"You think God made you gay?"

"Only if He has a fucked-up sense of humor."

On screen, Jay Leno guffawed at one of his own jokes about a celebrity divorce. Ari lowered the sound. "I'm just waiting for Mariah Carey."

"On TV or in bed?"

"I wish… Oh, I don't know, I don't know what I want." She closed her eyes. "Trudy used to be so sure. She'd say the truth was simple if you followed your heart. I guess I loved her for that. But I would give her shit about it, like, 'What do you mean, you've always really been a woman? What is *really*? If you want to wear a dress over your dick, just do it — why do you have to put a label on it?'"

"I thought fashion was all about labels."

"And I thought only girls played dumb in order to get laid."

"I'm not trying to…" I broke off, since my protest would sound like rejection. Her knee was pressing on my thigh. I looked into her jade-green eyes. Her breath was vanilla sweet.

"People change, Jule." Ariana's dimpled hand seized my chin. Before I could react, she fastened a kiss on me, her tongue hot and slippery in my mouth.

Something stirred inside me, not the part she wanted, maybe, but a quickening in my gut, a longing for closeness. It wasn't like having a guy on top of me. None of that frantic ardor, that self-obliterating fall into another man's heat. Her soft weight invited my body to loosen in response, melting away some of the held-in bitterness that made my muscles stiff and dead. I felt self-conscious, though, wondering where to place my hands on these unfamiliar curves. Like being thirteen again, in the locker room, spying on the soaped-up jocks with a mix of jealousy and desire, afraid I'd never grow up to be normal, stuck with girl's feelings in a boy's body.

I waited too long. Ari pulled back. I shook my head to clear it, unsuccessfully. "Well, that was a surprise."

"It shouldn't have been." Her mouth smiled, but her eyes were steady.

"I didn't intend…" To lead you on, I almost said, cringing at the Victorian cliché, a script straight out of the Kathleen Woodiwiss bodice-ripper paperbacks that Ari stashed in her bathroom under a stack of *Vanity Fairs*.

"Oh yes, I know, you're capital-G gay. Gayer than Glinda the Good Witch. You like what you like and that's never going to change." She flicked my crotch with a sharp snap of her fingers. "Doesn't that get *boring*?"

My balls tingled. Was it pain? "Are you using queer theory to seduce me, Mrs. Robinson?"

"That's what it's for." She lifted the Cuervo bottle to her lips, frowned to find it empty. "But you were always a lousy student."

I pushed myself up from the couch, intending to help her carry the dishes to the sink. Two guys together would have left the mess, but this was chick foreplay, as Bix would say. And why did I care? "Whoa," I groaned, holding my middle.

"What, is kissing a girl that gross?"

311

"I'm not used to these Häagen-Dasz benders. You dykes must have ironclad stomachs."

"I love you but don't throw up on my upholstery."

"God damn it," I said helplessly. But I made it to the bathroom.

Ari easily persuaded me to crash on the sofa bed. I was tired and dizzy from the events of the day, first Peter and now Ari, the merry-go-round of sexual frustration. *Love.* Did she mean Hollywood love, a word easily dropped, *I'd love a Coca-Cola,* movie-star kisses, credits roll? Or the ravished love of women in novels, parting their legs (always milky-white) for pirates and highwaymen (always hairy)? Did Peter and Shawn ever whisper the word behind closed doors? Did that leader of men get down on all fours and beg for Peter's love, as I wished I could?

Sinking into the murk of sleep, I felt the mattress dip as she climbed in behind me. Her body was warm and pillowy against my back. With a sigh, I relaxed against her, not opening my eyes. I thought that would be the sum of it. Cuddling without sex was another thing girls were supposed to like. I'll admit I didn't mind it either.

Everything stayed comfortably the same. The warm hand that reached around to cup my balls made itself at home, until the slow hardening down there felt natural, peaceful almost.

"Jule? You awake?" she whispered.

"Mmm."

"Are you sober?"

"Much as I ever am." Talking during sex — a girl thing? Annoying. Naked friction of her hand, urging me on to a place where sensation drowned thought.

"Good, I don't want to be a date-rapist."

Her breathing quickened. The bed rocked. I was curious to watch a girl get off, but too embarrassed to turn around. Her nails grazed my balls. A slippery finger poked between my cheeks. I didn't know how it had happened, but I was painfully hard.

She paused to squirt out more lube. My heart thudded in my throat. What was happening? Two fingers glided up the crease where my balls joined my ass, and then inside. I flinched forward, into the sure grip of her other hand around my dick. My arms trembled with tension. My groin didn't care how strange this was, it wanted to be trapped for a few seconds more in the back-and-forth of those plump strong hands. Involuntarily, my legs parted for the wet sensation. I opened my mouth but couldn't make a sound. Was she going to expect me to fuck her? The harshness of that word felt wrong toward a woman. Like a long-lost friend, the memory returned to me of my first time with Phil, when I'd been so scared of hurting him. Overwhelmed by emotion, my body lost all resistance, and I cried out.

Hot weight of her on me, pushing me onto my stomach, knocking the wind out of me. A huge stiff length suddenly filled me, nailed me down, two, three deep thrusts, before I gathered the breath to yell. "Holy shit, Ari!"

She pulled out with a wet sound and a satisfied sigh. A rubber strap-on the size of a footlong hot dog bobbed from her soft furred crotch. I didn't know whether to laugh or check that my intestines hadn't fallen out.

Ari smiled, a bit shyly, the most feminine thing she'd done all night. She draped the blanket across her lap, Venus on the half-shell. "Well, you came, didn't you?"

I discovered the limp stickiness between my legs. "I'm a guy. That's not much of an achievement."

She stroked my back. "Sorry, I thought I'd start you off with something you're used to."

"But I'm not — I don't — " I gave up trying to protest. The evidence was there on the sheets.

"Uh oh, you're not a bottom? I'd have sworn — " She giggled, then covered her mouth. "I'm sorry, that's mean. I just — really like you, Jule, you know? I've always wanted this to happen. Any way I could make it."

"It's okay. I'm okay." Unsure if I should lie down or go home, I kept sitting there while my butt dried to the mattress.

Her arm around my shoulders, she drew my head down to rest on her cushiony naked breasts. She kissed my forehead. It was kind of nice but I was very confused. My dick is the most decisive part of me, and now that it had cast its vote and gone to sleep, I had no answers for the questions that remained.

"You can go home if you want to," she said, her voice as soft as the arms that cradled me. "I know this is kind of weird for you."

"Nah...I'll stay." Because I felt she needed to hear something more, I said, "You're a great friend, Ari. I guess I let you flirt with me a lot. I just didn't realize we were taking it so...*literally.*"

"At VenuStage we call that 'breaking down the fourth wall'." She snickered.

"Well, right now my colon is saying 'No Exit'." I waggled the disconnected dildo in her face. "Tell me, does Lauren appreciate Mr. Whipple here more than I did?"

"Gross. I used a fresh one on you, what do you think?"

"With you? I never know what to think." I rolled over, out of her embrace. With my back to her, I made a show of tucking the blanket tightly around my rear end. Final curtain.

She caressed my hair one last time. "I'm just a woman, Julian," she whispered. "It doesn't have to be that complicated."

She spared me the morning-after scene, retreating to her bedroom sometime during the night. My eyes popped open in the 5 AM darkness and I knew that was it for me. The thin fiberfill blanket lay on me like a lead apron. She didn't expect me to stay, did she? We never made demands on each other. East Coast, West Coast, months of distance followed by two-hour phone calls, last-minute sleepovers, no tears that couldn't be wiped away by a stylish flick of the wrist. But in that case, what was the point of her being a girl? Or was I putting her in the wrong category, again? I remembered how easily she'd spoken of caring for me, how I hadn't had to wonder if we'd be tender after sex, because she was right there leading the way. She was only in the other room to spare me. I could go in there right now (well, two hours from now) with a breakfast tray and no underpants, and there was no chance she'd reject me, no fear that she'd turn to ice and make me feel like a dirty fool, as Peter always did.

I dragged my body off the couch and into last night's clothes. Ladies are ladies, however they behave. I would have to send her flowers, but ironic ones, those fringed magenta monsters from the tropics, or calla lilies, hooded and phallic. *Such a strange flower, suitable to any occasion*, as Katharine Hepburn said in "Stage Door" after her roommate jumped off the roof.

The film of another day developed in shades of gray, roofs and windows emerging from the bath of darkness, touched with the pallor of dawn. I could have been on my way to buy coffee and donuts and a single long-stemmed rose. My mind gave me no directions. My feet took me back to my quiet apartment. Returning to bed seemed appealing for a moment. My mattress had less of a past than I did. Peter and I had disposed of the one Phil died on. I lowered myself into the rocking chair by the window. A 21st birthday gift from Memère, the dark walnut wood piece had journeyed from her bankrupt father's house in New Orleans, to her parlor in Savannah, to me.

Lulled by its creaking rhythm, I watched the gusts of wind set the street litter dancing in crazy spirals. A few snowflakes flew with the dust. A man in a stocking cap was digging for soda cans in the trash barrel on the corner. How did he end up there? He'd been a baby once, someone with potential, like Phil. My dead boyfriend who would have looked out this same window and griped that he was sick of paying taxes to support these welfare bums. Missing him, mourning him, was I remembering him at all? Dream lover, nothing now but a piece of the body whose brokenness I saw.

Back here on earth, I had errands to run, but no boots in case the snow decided to stick. None, anyhow, that weren't stored next to Phil's old clothes behind the innocent-looking white sliding doors. I closed my eyes and reached in and groped around on the floor. A cockroach tap-danced over my fingers and I jumped back, feeling ridiculous as a kid who anticipates monsters under the bed. Above me, the well-

315

known shapes hung motionless from the closet pole: faded jeans, a blue parka, a couple of yellow and black striped rugby shirts, and the hideous tweed jacket he wore under duress for job interviews and other painfully respectable occasions. I sniffed it but caught only a faint whiff of what could have been anyone's tobacco smoke. Evidence that he was real, the proof that proves nothing, like the ambiguous splinter of wood that Memère's priest told us came from the true cross, by way of a Jerusalem gift shop. I rubbed the plain thick fabric of a shirtsleeve. No wonder Peter couldn't stand the sight of me. We'd been part of this death together. I reminded him of the worst that could happen, as surely as this shirt triggered my memory of eating caramel corn with Phil at Shea Stadium. I would rather he was happy without me than unhappy with me. There was never any question of that. And if he wasn't happy…?

I searched for a CD to slide into the stereo. Bluegrass gospel would perk me up; Queen would make me feel beautifully tragic; electronica would remind me of the wrong kind of sex. Enough of my feelings. In honor of the moment, I picked Phil's Mötley Crüe album, the one that sounded like the lead singer had his balls caught in a paper shredder.

Several ear-splitting tracks later, I'd filled two carry-on suitcases with neatly folded garments and shoes. The only thing left was the "Wolf Paper & Packaging Co." T-shirt he'd worn that first night at New Eden. I kissed the gray cotton, faded and soft from many washes, and returned it to the bottom drawer of the bureau. The homeless outreach ministry at my sister's church collected donations of clothes, canned foods and toiletries for the guys at the nearby shelter. I figured I would haul the stuff over there and win some Jesus points with Lulu.

On my walk to the subway, pondering the extravagance of a taxi as the snow fell in larger, slower flakes, I spotted the same guy moving down the block to another trash can. His gloves had holes in two fingers. "Dude," I called out feebly. He didn't hear me, or else was ignoring this disrespectful form of address from a kid half his age. "Mister," I tried again, louder. He rotated his head, like a tortoise, and squinted at me. "You, uh, you need new gloves?" His blank expression didn't thank me for pointing out the obvious. "I'm — I'm giving away some stuff, and I thought — " Now he lurched close enough for me to smell the gum decay and beer on his breath. I dug through the zippered outer pocket of one bag and hastily shoved at him whatever his two hands could carry: a scarf, two rolled-up pairs of wool socks, and a Steelers cap. No gloves, as it turned out. We stared at each other. My first impulse was to beat it before he flipped out and mugged me. But what was I so afraid he would take?

"Have a bleshed day, man," he slurred, and stumbled off. I watched the black and gold cap grow smaller with distance till he rounded a corner and it was gone.

43

"...You don't feed the poor 'cause somebody told you to. You don't do it to be *good*. Never gonna work. You got to have the love of Jesus in you, the love of Jesus *for* you, who died to set you free — from yourself."

I sank into the now-familiar ebb and flow of Reverend Crowell's low, measured voice, well-worn and reliable as the dusty pew cushions. An early spring rain pattered against the clouded leaded-glass windows. I'd taken to attending his brief prayer services for the weekend volunteers for Save Your Homes. My final photo shoot for the fundraising brochure was scheduled for this evening. A fair number of emerging and second-tier designers had donated samples for the gala, which our stylists (two unpaid interns from FIT) would have to patch together into harmonious ensembles. But we still lacked a celebrity headliner.

Around me, the other volunteers hummed a musical assent to the pastor's words. Contentment brought me dangerously close to drowsiness. I'd picked up a series of assignments from *Crash* and *Dazed and Confused* to photograph new performers in the underground music scene. Some of them were also hiring me for album covers and videos. Last night I'd closed down CBGB's with a Japanese Goth-punk duo called Happy Explosion. I personally prefer Marilyn Monroe to Marilyn Manson, but I appreciated the gritty playfulness of the band's Harajuku fashion sense, a reckless jumble of neon vinyl, mime face paint, and lace petticoats.

"When you walk down Jesus' road, you're gonna walk hand in hand with the raggedy homeless man and the bank president, and they're gonna smell just the same to you. And you'll help each other both the same, not to stumble, 'cause some of us wear our dirt on the outside and some on the inside, but we all got some."

Out of the corner of my eye, I saw Peter's dark curly hair and red sweatshirt. He'd never come to these prayer sessions before. Stooping as he skirted the rows of seated worshippers, he made his way in my direction. I looked away.

"When you sit down to Jesus' table, to the feast that has no end..."

Premature amen-murmurs from a few.

Eat your vegetables, Mama used to scold us, *there are children starving in Africa.* Before I figured out how far away Africa was, I was scared they might be coming for our dinners. We had to hurry, to hoard what was ours.

"You gonna sit between your sainted grandma and that girl on the corner who's selling her womanhood for a fix. And you're gonna treat 'em both like a queen, 'cause that is how Jesus made them."

I laughed inside, then felt a twist of fear, imagining Memère Dupuis would be in for a shock when she died. There she'd be, perched on a cloud with her silver-handled cane, passing her best china serving platter to a crack whore. Try as I might, I couldn't picture my mother's mother without the superior arch of her eyebrows that tainted her perfect manners toward lower life forms, such as my father. She used to point at my boyish face, delighted to find copies of her own expressions there.

"What are you doing?" Peter tapped on my shoulder.

"Singing." Impatiently, I dropped out of the group's wavery, unaccompanied rendition of our closing hymn. *Just as I am, and waiting not —*

"Don't get so into this part. It's not for us."

"We're not the only white people here." I glanced around, embarrassed by his interruption, but the others were too absorbed in their singing to notice his harsh whispers. They swayed gently, eyes closed, faces tilted upward. A moment ago, I'd been dreaming along with them.

"Not that. Didn't you hear what he said — "

"Let's take this outside." I steered Peter out a side door to the street. The wind blew a cold spray in our faces now and then, not enough to be called rain. We stood in the lee of the church's brick wall.

"How can you keep coming back for another helping of that shit? I know you're not that thin-skinned," Peter demanded.

"What, you hate Jesus all of a sudden? Is this a Jewish thing?"

"Not Jesus. Crowell. Don't you know what he says about 'she-males and punks' stealing men out of the black community? About God 'disciplining his children' with the plague of AIDS?"

"I don't remember him saying anything like that when I've been around." Maybe the pastor threw a bone to his base constituents every now and then, but what he put his heart into, what drew me in despite my defenses, was his vision of the kingdom where no one had to be separated and I could leave my worst self behind. "I figure all preachers toss in an abomination once in awhile, like Republican politicians promising to protect the unborn babies. It doesn't mean anything, practically."

The sparks in his eyes didn't dim. "You settle for too little."

"Not anymore."

His silence went on too long, so I changed the subject. "Well, what are *you* doing, if you're not here for the altar call? Do you need to go back in and get your assignment?"

"No, I — " He brushed a splash of mud off his jeans. "I was looking for you. I never see you anymore."

"I'm around." He couldn't hear my heart pulsing in my throat.

"I was really struck by your *QNYC* spread on VenuStage. I went and bought a ticket for 'Medea' but it kind of sucked."

"Yeah, when Laurel smothered the Cabbage Patch doll with the Stars & Stripes pillow, I was like, okay, I guess I'm not the target audience for this."

"It was just too obvious. The Golden Fleece made of dollar bills? Your pictures made it seem like something spooky and amazing would happen, but it turned out to be recycled Vietnam War street theater."

"Well, I was mainly staging the shoots to play up Ari's costumes. That woman could turn a burlap sack into Aphrodite's party dress."

"You doing a lot with her lately? She answered the phone at your apartment the other night."

"She did? Oh, uh, we were probably watching 'The Thorn Birds' marathon on cable. I always doze off during Episode 3. What did you want?"

"What did I want." Peter wiped his damp hair back from his forehead. "Nothing important, I guess."

To fill the pause that followed, I asked, "Stressful time at the Statehouse? What's your latest crusade?"

He looked sidelong toward the church door, though no one was around to hear us. "I'm pushing Shawn on that anti-discrimination bill, but he doesn't feel he has the political capital to come out for the gays — not *come out*, you know what I mean. Take a stand. I keep telling him, you can't fight homelessness in New York City without fighting AIDS, and discrimination against anyone who might be suspected of having AIDS, which means *us*. Kids whose parents kicked them out and they can't even get a bed in a goddamn shelter because they look queer. Whatever — he's not going there."

"Why don't you write about it?"

"I'm not allowed. Pen names or not, it's too easy to expose. Even you figured out Spartacus."

"Yes, despite my limited intelligence, I know your real identity."

"Well, keep this all to yourself, okay? Especially around that guy Polzin. I don't trust him."

"He's not so bad," I said, though I didn't enjoy the pushy journalist's company either. "He's hooked me up with some good music video jobs. The guy must know everyone in New York who's ever thought about sucking dick."

Peter pretended to ignore the implications. "Rain's cleared up. Want to grab a bite? The Skylight Diner serves breakfast all day."

"Can't, darling, sorry. Got to take my agent to lunch and talk about her cats, then I promised Ari that I'd introduce her to KiKo from Happy Explosion."

"Good luck with that, I hope her next design makes more sense than what she had Jason wearing in 'Medea'. Tammy Faye eye makeup and an Uncle Sam costume? Is that some half-assed comment on fundamentalism, or what?"

Trudy, that's what. "It's a comment on the fact that her previous lover was even more of a queen than me." The outfit she'd created for Medea's faithless baby-daddy had grated on my nerves too, not because I was by any means jealous that Ariana carried a torch for her ex, but rather because she chose to extinguish that torch by pissing on it in public.

"Her previous — you — " Peter looked repulsed. "You wouldn't seriously — you're gay!"

"I don't know what I am. Except that I'm tired of being stuck with these ideas of myself that get me nowhere. You judge me for listening to Reverend Crowell, like you judge everything else, but he's got a picture of life where nobody's trapped by being different. I feel like, if I took a fresh look at myself, I don't know what I could find."

"I'm sorry I ever brought you in on this project. They're brainwashing you."

"Um, this project was actually *my idea*, remember? And I've spent too much time on it today already. Now if you'll excuse me, I need to hustle up some paying work, or my next Save Your Homes photo will be a self-portrait."

Following a long day of networking, I was ready for a date with a carton of leftover lo mein and the evening news, but first I had to get through the last charity-case portrait session. I re-checked the handwritten slip with an address in the West 20s. Great, very close to my apartment. *Luisa Salazar, age 44, nurse's aide.*

Appetizing smells of frying fish and chili in the building stairwell reminded me of my spartan lunch with my agent. Wendy, who had gone macrobiotic, agonized to me about whether it was ethical to put Bootsy, Mittens, and Zorro on a vegan diet. I opined that her pack-a-day Virginia Slims habit was a more likely determinant of her feline family's lifespan. We got down to business and she promised to put my name in for a *Vogue* profile of Juliette Binoche. Rumor had it the job was up for grabs because Dane Langley had broken his arm falling off a balcony in St. Kitts. Lawsuits were pending.

Ariana and KiKo hadn't meshed. Offstage, the punk musician was too giggly and sweet, a cheerleader in fright-wig disguise. Laurel from VenuStage, also now in the ex category, was as femme as Ari could tolerate. My demanding friend and I had not talked about repeating our experiment, but the musk of possibility lingered in the air, like the scent of patchouli in the clothes that she'd returned to Laurel in a recycled paper bag.

Mounting the last steps to Luisa's third-floor entryway, I heard the tinny pulse of music from someone's headphones turned up loud. A dark head nodded to the beat, eyes squeezed shut, caught up in the anthem of his private world.

"Hey...me again." Peter spoke a little too loud, as people do when they can't hear themselves.

I joined him leaning against the wall. "What's playing?" I mouthed.

"Bebe Vonzelle. Here, listen." He put the headset over my ears, the foam pads still warm from closeness to him. The lazy, liquid alto voice was singing the chorus of "No Innocence", the R&B hit that had won her Best New Artist at last year's Grammys. *I gave you my innocence/ Now I'm just like the rest/ Baby, if we all had sense/ There'd be no lovin' left...*

We held the headset between us so we could both catch the last verse in one ear, not speaking till it was over. I'd heard the song before, as who hadn't, in taxicabs and clothing stores, background breaks between the news, but now I slowed down and paid attention. Her sad, passionate tones died away, the CD player hitched and clicked, and the opening bass line began again. Peter hit the button on the cord that snaked out of his fanny pack, shutting her down.

"I sometimes put that one on repeat," he said as he unhooked his music system and stuffed it in his duffel bag. "I just came from the gym, and since Luisa's not here yet, you know, it passes the time..."

"She's a powerful singer. And a face to match — she was on the cover of *Allure* last month. I could get you a copy. Maybe signed!"

Unlike Richard Molineux, Condé Nast had kept its promises to Marcia, putting her in a senior editor slot on *Allure's* masthead. I'd been too ashamed to exploit the connection thus far.

Peter beamed at the suggestion. I was playing cool about his surprise involvement in tonight's shoot, but I guess I'd never break the habit of searching for those odd little things that would make him happy.

"Hope you don't mind that I showed up without telling you. I felt bad about how we left things this morning, so I went back inside the church and swapped assignments with Martina. She said our lady tonight spoke enough English for me to get by."

"It's a treat for me." I smiled, and he reflected back the same warmth.

Peter propped one foot against the wall behind him, and stretched his tired shoulders. "It's my fault too that we've lost touch. There's been a lot going on that's hard to explain." His voice trailed off.

I ran my hand down his arm, a sympathetic caress. Unexpectedly, he entwined his arm with mine, and squeezed my fingers.

Footfalls on the stairs. We stepped away from each other at the same moment. Luisa turned her jingling keys in the three locks on her apartment door. She spotted the camera equipment at my feet and apologized for running late at work. We made our introductions. She was tall and sturdy with a handsome square head and broad cheekbones that looked Mexican. Copper highlights streaked the dry black hair she wore pulled back into a braid. Her hospital scrubs, printed with silly yellow and orange ducks, barely took away from her dignified bearing.

She apologized again for her hospital clothes and insisted on putting up a pot of coffee for us while she changed. She seemed withdrawn, either from fatigue or discomfort with the public exposure — not the vibe I wanted from a model, whatever the picture's purpose. I scanned the room for a heartwarming backdrop. The walls had been painted long ago in a peachy shade, broken up by wooden shelves that held some cheap pottery animals and framed greeting-card photos of unpeopled nature scenes.

Her selected outfit, though not unflattering, struck the wrong note. The long-sleeved ruffled dress in a birds-of-paradise print and turquoise scarf belonged on Cinco de Mayo, not a documentary on poverty. The proud tilt of her chin sank when she saw my disapproval. I figured I'd take a few warm-up shots to put her at ease, then steer her toward a more subdued outfit.

The chemistry wouldn't ignite. Standing stiffly next to a cow-shaped flowerpot, Luisa yawned. I was pretty bored myself. Only Peter was having fun, tinkering with the settings on my lighting equipment. "Can we do this another time?" she entreated.

"*Lamento mucho*, it has to be at the printer at the end of the week," Peter shook his head.

"Let me go sit on the bed. The light is better. You don't like these pictures, I know," she said to me, sounding embarrassed.

"No, no, you're doing great," I lied. We followed her into the bedroom, where she switched on a glaring white light, three globes at the center of an unmoving ceiling fan. I noticed that the wall beside her mirror was plastered with glossy cutouts from fashion magazines. Luisa appeared to have a weakness for gold and silver evening gowns. One supermodel made frequent appearances in the older photos.

"Cheryl Kingston," I said. "She was one of a kind."

Luisa lit up for the first time. "I know! *Tan hermosa*. What a shame." Holding a finger to the side of her nose, she mimed cocaine-snorting. "She should've taken the plea."

"Probably scared what Benny's guys would do to her if she flipped him."

"Who's Benny?" The prospect of fresh gossip woke her up faster than coffee.

"Her, her business manager in Florida. A big dealer." No call to bring the word "pimp" into this. I was glad Cheryl's new handlers had kept her *Juggs* photos out of the mainstream press. The jailhouse interview for *Vanity Fair* had also been a nice coup, though personally I doubted whether all those quotes came unedited from Cheryl herself. She wouldn't be the first to turn spiritual in the can, but the

Cheryl I'd known was the kind of girl who thought Deuteronomy was a procedure the Malibu surgeons did to remove your warts.

"Where'd you hear that?" Luisa arched a skeptical eyebrow.

"I used to photograph her all the time for *Femme NY*. We ran into each other in Key West last summer."

I'd hoped to break the ice with this conversation, but it had the opposite effect. Her bronze skin flushing brick red, Luisa retreated to her closet, rummaging for an outfit that would please a celebrity photographer. How could I say what she already knew, that I didn't want her to look pretty, that my assignment was to hide the small luxuries that restored her to herself? To hell with that, I would take what she gave me, and let Shawn's crew be responsible for the veto. One good thing about working for nothing, you've got creative control.

Peter took over the effort of building rapport, quietly addressing questions to her broad back as she yanked dresses off hangers. How long had she lived there, was it a good building, did she have a family, and so on. The apartment was fairly priced, she said, but medical bills had put her in debt. No, no family. She disappeared behind a door to change. Peter picked up a framed photo of a handsome Mexican man squinting into the sun and smiling, his arms around an older couple who had to be his parents. Their resemblance to Luisa, especially the woman, was strong.

"I can't decide," she confessed. Colorful rayon prints spilled from her arms, fanned out across the scratchy knit bedspread like a bazaar display. She put a hand up to cover her bare throat where the neckline of her white fake-satin robe ended.

"No, that's perfect," I stopped her. I posed her in the center of the pile of fabric, seated erect on the bed like an Aztec queen, her plain robe like a lily rising from a field of wildflowers.

Peter handled the release forms while I packed up. She hesitated before signing her name. I promised to send her copies of the photos. She looked happy, then a little sad, as if she knew they wouldn't be acceptable to anyone outside this room.

Peter kept a brooding silence as we went down the stairs. "Look, I tried," I said, with some irritation.

"I know," he said distantly.

"She may not keep the apartment, but she'll always have a happy memory."

He didn't respond till we were on the street. "They won't use these pictures. What you did with her was beautiful. But it makes no difference. Didn't you see her Adam's apple?"

"What? No way — " But I understood the real resemblances in that family snapshot now, though not the motive for keeping it on Luisa's solitary bedside table. Had it been me, I couldn't have stood the daily reminder of my parents' love for someone I had never been. "Why did Save Your Homes send us over here, then?"

"They probably didn't know. She just had to fill out an eligibility form like the rest of them, then the staff picked people for the brochure to get a diverse group by age and race and so forth."

"Well, that's not my problem. I did my job."

"I'm going to tell them she changed her mind and wouldn't let us in. At least this way, if they don't know what she looks like, she'll still get the rent assistance."

"Bullshit. Maybe she *wants* to be out. She's already lost her damn family, what could be worth hiding for?"

"She seemed scared."

"Of course she's scared. That's what happens when you live your own life for a change instead of trying to appease morons."

"Big talk, from someone who's sleeping with a fag hag."

I shuffled my feet. "I'm just keeping my options open."

"But you don't love her. If you did, you'd hit me for talking trash about her."

"It won't hurt her, whatever you say. Your opinion doesn't matter," I flared up. "But for the record, I do care about Ari a lot. Life's easy with her. I can kiss her and not worry that she's going to leave town tomorrow. She tells me why she feels things. We have the same goals. I don't need to prove to her that fashion isn't stupid. She's queerer than you'll ever be!"

"Are you done?" Peter growled.

I'd barely caught my breath before he pulled me to his broad chest and covered my mouth with a kiss that didn't end. We clung together, swaying like slow dancers, inhaling each other like drowning men finding air. I don't know who let go first. Our mouths parted easily, no longer desperate, momentarily satisfied with the hope of more.

"Don't say anything, Jule," he murmured. "I mean it this time. I won't be scared off."

I felt the hammering of his rapid heartbeat, even as he held us both steady in a secure embrace. "Scared of what? I've never understood."

"Me neither." He gave a little nervous laugh. "No, that's not true. It feels like a mistake — this can't be for me, it's too good."

"Nothing's too good for you." I went to repeat the kiss, cupping his face in my hands, but instead I paused and simply held his gaze. His hazel eyes welled up.

"When you say stuff like that...it hurts so much. What's the *matter* with me?"

"Maybe you should stop working for someone who pretends you don't exist?"

"Politics is about compromise," he said in a dull voice.

"But *you* aren't."

"You know what, I don't care *why*. Can't we just have this, ourselves, for once, and to hell with everyone else?"

"For once," I echoed, letting our mouths join again. His kisses were softer than his words. I didn't trust him. We didn't trust each other. This would go on forever unless someone took the hit. I had more practice. Love is patient, love is kind, love doesn't ask for your phone number.

He stroked my hair. His mouth was close to my ear. "I'm really selfish. I'm sorry." He released me. "You deserve everything good too, you know."

Was that a goodbye? He wasn't giving me a clue what to do next. Cars swooshed past our street corner, headlights like comet trails through the dark puddles. A couple of young guys swung open the door to the bar across the way, one of them landing a playful, possessive tap on the other's rear to hurry him along. They stepped aside for a departing threesome with a takeout bag. My stomach grumbled.

"I heard that," Peter said, patting the offending area. "My mother always said, never make decisions on an empty stomach. You want to go to Monster Sushi?"

So that was it, another pointless half-hour of temptation, then back to our mundane friendship? Never mind that my body was agreeing with him about the priority of needs. "I don't want to lug this camera equipment around. I think I'll just go home."

"Great, even better, I'll cook you dinner." He hoisted his gym bag and followed me without being asked.

"I don't have anything in the house."

"I am well aware of the disgusting state of your refrigerator. Go upstairs and don't spoil your appetite with three-day-old fried rice, I'll meet you in a few minutes."

I remembered my vintage lo mein. "How do you know so much?"

Waiting for him, I fussed around my apartment as though he hadn't been there a hundred times before. Condoms? Check. Monster movies? Check. Clean sheets? Could be arranged. Wine? Peter didn't like wine. I drained a glassful. It wasn't food, it didn't count. I was thinking about a bowl of instant grits to nail down my sobriety when Peter arrived with two bulging paper bags from D'Agostino's.

Unpacking seemed to take forever. Orange marmalade, a head of lettuce, goat cheese, coffee cake... "Which came first?" I joked, dangling a bag of raw chicken parts from one hand and balancing a carton of eggs on the other.

Peter rescued the eggs with a smile that raised my body temperature. "Those are for breakfast."

The last item out of the bag was a votive candle in a frosted-glass cup with a peace sign on it. Peter shooed my hand away from the salad ingredients. "First things first. Matches?"

Once the little flame was burning, Peter covered his eyes and chanted: *Baruch atah Adonai, melekh ha'olam...*

"Amen," I ad-libbed, whenever he seemed to be reaching the end of a sentence. He lifted his hands from his face with a refreshed air. "What did that mean?"

"It's the *Havdalah* — the Saturday night prayer, where you thank God for separating this day from other days."

"That's nice...I didn't know you did any religious things."

"I pretty much stopped when my real mom moved out, because everyone else at home thought it was bogus. Even in Israel, it's weird, unless you're ultra-Orthodox, politics is the real religion, kind of like New Yorkers. But since I got my own place, I'm trying to, I don't know, reconnect with something that has good memories for me."

"Well, now you understand why I was in church this morning."

"Yeah...I'm sorry about what I said."

"Don't be. It's a real risk — if I got too serious about this stuff — what would have to change? Either direction I could choose, it feels impossible, sometimes."

Peter set down the lettuce he was chopping and drew me into his arms. "I don't have any answers for you," he said softly. "But I don't want to let you go."

"Then please don't. Not again."

We kissed some more. The candle flame danced with its reflection in the dark window. "How long is this meal going to take, anyhow?" I huffed.

"If I ever get it started, about 45 minutes."

We ate salad and talked about lighter subjects while the marmalade-glazed chicken was in the oven. I showed him some of my magazine work that he hadn't seen. He said he was angling for vacation days this summer to attend a bodywork training conference in Tel Aviv. He could stay rent-free on his mom's kibbutz if he helped with the gardening. What was the fashion scene like over there, did I know? I made up something to cover my excitement that he was all but inviting me to come along if I could pay my way. Then our main course was ready and we didn't say much of anything.

He wanted music, not the news, while we cleaned up. Loretta Lynn was singing "Rated X" on the last remaining country-western station in the metro area. In my small kitchen, we constantly brushed against each other as we moved from task to task. The boy was a tease. I took the roasting pan away from him, plunked it in the sink to soak, and held him firmly by the hips. "I have to know," I said, though my body was ready to override anything my mind didn't want to hear. "Why now? What's different?"

Our combined breathing was louder than the radio static. "Nothing. That's why I have to — I can't take this anymore — "

I felt like he was licking my whole body when he thrust his tongue into my mouth. Everything gross becomes delicious, the first revelation of sex, your body through the looking-glass, where spit and cum are words of love. The weak signal bled, Patsy Cline crying all the way to the altar where *disarmament talks stalled for a third day* on the newscast further down the band. Peter flipped the dial off, so roughly that my radio toppled over. We didn't pause to fix it.

He was the heavier one. Bracing myself against his wide shoulders, I wrapped my legs round his thighs, a hint that he should carry me to the bedroom. Or the living room rug, I wasn't fussy. Entangled, we crashed and bumped our way through the apartment like a blind octopus. He released me onto the bed, on my back, both of us winded, staring at one another, waiting for the next move.

Peter sank down on all fours. I'd lost my shoes somewhere under the furniture; he was wearing one sneaker. He massaged my feet with firm, intimate pressure. His strong hands climbed up my legs, with kisses as he went. The sight of his dark head between my thighs, even fully clothed, shocked me with longing and disbelief. It had to be a sin, because nothing could have stopped me from committing it. Sin that wasn't a joke, not the spice of naughtiness that sells ice cream, but my soul's bare truth: I was nothing but need. And what was he, in the teeth of that hunger? Then he raised his head, and I saw the same devouring intent in his bright eyes.

I pulled off my shirt. He eased my pants off and pressed his face into the mound in my briefs, nuzzling, inhaling my body odors. "You smell so sweet," he murmured.

"I do?" It had been a long day without a shower.

"Yeah, sort of like...caramel corn." He rested his cheek against my bare leg, catching his breath. "I always liked the way you smelled."

Blushing at the admission, he bent to the task of stripping me naked. His long-awaited touch almost finished me off. My cock shot up like it was ready to leave my body. Peter opened his mouth.

"No, wait — " I struggled to a sitting position, and tilted his chin up so he'd have to look at me. "What about you? I want to see you."

Hesitantly, he climbed onto my bed so I could roll his shirt over his head. I tongued and bit his nipples, standing out hard and pink in his matted black chest hair. He gritted his teeth. It was good to find out what he liked. As I caressed his back, the skin in some places felt strangely ridged and rough. He winced, more from embarrassment than pain, I thought, but I drew back and looked him over to make sure. He said nothing, playing a waiting game that I lost.

"What's this about?" I laid my palm protectively over one of the scars.

"Don't worry about it." He shoved his pants down and dragged my hand onto the huge lump in his boxers, which (I was charmed to discover) were printed with the same Spider-Man webs that had probably adorned his first toddler training pants. The purplish-red head of his shaft nosed its way out of his fly. My heart pounded, but I didn't touch it yet.

"You're not getting off that easy," I said.

"That's a terrible pun."

"Talk to me about this first." With some reluctance, I relocated my hand to his shoulderblades.

Peter shrugged. "Sometimes...the stuff I like to do...gets out of control."

"Well, I don't want to do anything like that!"

His direct gaze was abrupt, challenging. "How do you know?"

This wasn't the time to dwell on my long familiarity with my father's belt buckle. We were two grown men, strong now, alone at last. We should be safe with each other. So all I said was, "When you've had the real thing, the game isn't fun anymore."

He chose to take this as a signal to manhandle my wilting cock, which shifted instantly from neutral to overdrive when he pumped it in his fist. "That's pretty real," he chuckled.

Giving in to my simplest desire, I finally reached inside his waistband and slid my grip down the silky skin of his member. It just kept on going. "Whoa." Guess we knew who'd be on top tonight.

Drops of pre-cum slicked our skin as we stroked each other, lying naked face to face. Peter's eyes were closed. Could I kiss him? Would it break some spell? I forced his head back with the pressure of my lips against his. We fought for breath. He broke away and attacked his original target, down below. When his hot wet mouth covered my shaft, drawing all of me in, I was completely lost. I could scarcely move at first but he was so eager that I gave in and bucked my hips in rhythm to the lapping of his tongue. His shoulders heaved. He was jerking himself with one hand, harder than I had done. "You shouldn't try to lift such a heavy weight all by yourself," I panted.

His answering noise could have been a moan or a laugh, both odd-sounding with his mouth full. I giggled myself from sheer tension. My legs spread, I was helpless to resist the charge building up in my body. "I — I'm going to cum — " I warned him, in case he was the type who didn't swallow. Though from his maddening skills down there, more likely he ate it up with a spoon.

"Me too — " The cooler air on my wet skin, after the heat of his throat, kept me from climaxing right away. I fumbled in the bedside drawer for the condom package. I hadn't wanted to scare him off by leaving it in plain sight.

Peter had rolled onto his stomach and was grinding himself against the bed while he waited. He gave me a shy, questioning look. "I don't know if you'd want to...warm me up a little?"

I thought at first he was asking me to go down on him before he took me, which I would happily have dislocated my jaw to do, but he stayed in that position that denied me access to his dick. He was rather possessive of that thing, I thought.

In case I was still unclear on the concept, he popped his ass up. I didn't need a second hint. His cheeks were sweetly curved, firm, and

(I was relieved to see) unmarked. I pushed that last worry from my mind, and dove into the musky hair of his cleft. My tongue probed his tight hole. He barked with pleasure, losing control finally, drawing great shuddering breaths. He was squatting now, so I could see he was still erect, moments from letting go.

"Not so fast," I ordered him. I rolled the condom onto my aching cock. Sitting back on his heels, he took my hands in his, and slowly kissed me, the taste of each other's private places mingling in our mouths.

In a low, unsteady voice, he said, "Do anything you want to do to me."

All I could say was, "Oh…" I pushed him down gently onto his back. He wrapped his arms around my shoulders, and drew his knees up. At last, at last, I entered him. Oh, Peter. Climaxing was suddenly unimportant. Interlocked, we rocked slowly, as I tried to keep my head above a tidal wave of strange feelings. I was so contented in his embrace that I almost cried. He nestled his head into the curve of my neck like a child seeking comfort. The fiery throbbing where our bodies joined forced me to bring this to a conclusion before it became unbearable.

"I belong to you," I whispered. He arched his back and groaned louder, drowning out my voice. I braced my knees against the mattress and thrust deeply into him, with all I had. His powerful legs gripped my sides, working me into him, his thick cock rubbing against my belly. I cried out with release, a few seconds before he shook violently and called out my name. The sweetest sound. Sweetness in his unwinding breaths, our heartbeats coming down, one rhythm chasing the other, in quiet that blessed us with the muting of our separate selves.

44

I woke up alone, of course. The clock radio read 4:20 AM. The apartment smelled strange. Had we left the oven on? I buried my nose in the pillow, happily inhaling the funk of our lovemaking. Everything ended too soon. I wasn't ready to release it into memory, to let my imagination start embellishing the tiny scrap of reality I'd been given. Something had awakened me, maybe nothing more than the fear of this empty space in my bed. Since I couldn't relax now, I might as well have a drink and check that the house wasn't burning down.

Shirtless, in the dark, Peter slouched at the kitchen table, a forkful of scrambled eggs in one hand, a joint in the other. The ambient light from the city street, white neon from the 24-hour pharmacy downstairs, outlined the scene.

I poured myself a glass of wine, though I didn't want it anymore. He gestured for me to share his treats. I shook my head. We sat in the silence that wasn't silence, the refrigerator motor turning over, the subway rumbles and sirens that were no respecter of the hour. I was about to tease him about his ability to score drugs at this time of night. That beat being anxious that he walked around the Statehouse with a doobie in his pocket protector. It was different for me, I only drank on social occasions. I just happened to be very sociable.

"Do you believe in demons?"

I was tempted to reply with a joke, to bring us back down to earth, but the flat sincerity of his voice stopped me cold.

"I — I don't know. They're in the Bible. But so's a lot of stuff I don't understand." Love, I was thinking, and love's punishments. But for once that was a rote thought, a secondhand echo. Tonight my body had discovered a different God from the storybook tyrant who would have pried us apart.

"No, I mean in real life." Peter smoked and stared.

"What crazy shit were you watching on TV? You know 'Unsolved Mysteries' is fake, right?"

He focused on me for the first time. His face looked young and vulnerable. "I almost disappeared. After last night…you almost didn't see me again."

"Yeah, I was afraid you were halfway across state lines by now. Then I tripped over your shoes when I got out of bed."

"You don't understand. I don't *want* to leave. I'm trying as hard as I can to hang on." His voice cracked.

"Lie back down with me. It's early yet. We can talk, we can go back to sleep, whatever you want." I massaged his hands between mine.

"I want to stay," he repeated, not budging. "I'm not crazy. I know demons are a metaphor. Only they're not. I feel it, I really feel it in my body, something pulling me from outside — " He shook his head roughly, with an unhappy laugh, as if doubting his own words. "Like those stupid *Weekly World News* covers, with the flying saucer that abducts you with a tractor beam? And don't say what you're going to say about anal probes, Jule, because you're only going to be silly because you don't want to know what's wrong with me and neither do I."

His fear was contagious. I swallowed it down with the dregs of the wine. "I don't care how weird you are. I…I love you no matter what."

He slumped forward into my arms, burying his face in my chest. "You do. Oh, fuck. I know you do."

We huddled together. The minutes stretched out. Peter raised his blotchy face. "Babe, would it be too strange if I spent the rest of the night on the couch?"

"I'm just happy you're here. Whatever you have to do. But no smoking that shit near anything flammable, okay?"

Peter extinguished his joint in the tea saucer he was using as an ashtray, mashing it down as though suddenly disgusted with his habit. He kissed my cheek but didn't give me time to reciprocate. I hastily cleaned up and crept back to bed alone, though I didn't think I'd sleep.

When the alarm woke me, too soon, Peter's tangled curls were warming my chest. He was shy when we kissed good morning, but nothing out of the ordinary. Unfortunately, he couldn't stay for breakfast after all, because he'd forgotten that the train to Albany ran less frequently on Sundays. He'd be back in maybe a week and a half, depending on what happened with Shawn's budget amendment, and would come over again to make me "dinner…and *dessert*."

So I let him escape, with light kisses and words to match. Weren't we further along than before? Closer than ever, I said to myself. And he seemed happy about it, underneath the mutual awkwardness of avoiding the what-next talk. I almost thought I'd dreamed his anguish in the dark hours, except for the evidence of three eggs missing from the carton. I wondered if he'd return to cook the rest before they expired.

45

THE SAVE YOUR HOMES FASHION SHOW fundraiser was next month already. Ariana kept dropping hints that she'd found a stack of 1950s *Adonis* physique mags at the thrift shop, and perhaps I'd like to come browse them over rum-and-Cokes at her place. I put her off by saying I was busy securing a surprise celebrity to wear Ari's custom-designed gown at the gala. I had an idea that would make both her and Peter happy with me, a rare alignment of planets indeed. I hadn't told her, or anyone, about my night with him, and I felt sure he hadn't either. The more important something was to Peter, the more he clammed up.

Persistent phone messages for Marcia Molineux set my plan into action. Her snappy secretary finally granted me twenty minutes at Marcia's home office. I sped uptown to the old address on Fifth Avenue near the museum. The bulldog-faced doorman, ageless in brass-buttoned wool, hadn't changed, nor had the antique elevator whose gate he drew back for me. But when I asked for the sixth floor and he inquired whom I was visiting — just like that, "whom" — he told me the Molineux place had been sold last fall. A hasty call to Condé Nast sent me back on a bus that crawled across the park to a pre-war apartment complex in the West 70s, whose fanciful cornices and ledges were etched with gray-black soot streaks. Twenty minutes late for my twenty-minute appointment, I rang the buzzer. Marcia's familiar voice answered, made raspier by the intercom.

Though not in the same orbit as their former penthouse, the apartment would have handsomely fit three of mine, with parquet floors and high windows that let in a clear white light. A middle-aged Jamaican lady in scrubs directed me to the living room. I was afraid to ask her what I'd find out soon enough, at the end of the foyer where I hesitated. Was Marcia so sick she needed a nurse? Was that how Richard had finally failed her? Or maybe his weird behavior last summer was caused by a brain tumor, and he would be the one I found lying emaciated on the couch, all his grace and personality drained away. I almost turned and ran. Blindness, sores, dementia: my generation was living in one of the grotesque medieval paintings Richard had savored. Or not a generation, not those oblivious boy-girl pairs with their minivans and booster seats, but our unsaved remnant, whose touch ended in this.

I edged into the room, which was furnished in soft earth tones and lined with bookcases that held Marcia's papers and magazines. A computer hummed on a mahogany table. "Ah, there's Julian! What borough did you get out of bed in, honey?"

"I — I went to your old place," I stammered. Marcia, comfortably dressed in jeans — *jeans!* — and a white man-tailored shirt that set off her vibrant tan, had turned aside to feed another spoonful of pea-green mush to an overweight teenage boy who slumped at a crooked angle in a motorized wheelchair. The boy smacked his lips. His eyes, slightly crossed, were a deep brown, fringed with dark lashes.

"That's a good boy, Tommy. Tommy, this is Julian. Say hello, Tommy."

I raised a hand awkwardly. "Hi." The kid, Tommy, dropped his gaze to his bowl.

"He's shy," Marcia said, unfazed. "Didn't get a lot of visitors in the *Home*." She gave the last word a sarcastic twist. After working another spoonful into the boy's mouth, she told me, "Sit. If you'd been on time he would have still been napping. I've got only a few minutes before my conference call with the Macy's ad buyers."

"Did you adopt him?" I blurted out. My mind was reeling at the presence of the boy, his misshapen body and sweet confused eyes.

"He's my son." She gently dabbed a bit of food from his chin. A smear of it discolored the sharp folded-back cuff of her shirt.

"And Richard's?"

"Obviously." The old cynical humor chased away the contentment from her face momentarily. "Or maybe not so obviously." She tried getting him to drink from one of those closed cups with the spout that they give to babies, but he pouted and turned his head away. "Were you looking for him?"

"No, I — I just wanted to say...again...I'm sorry. You were a good friend when I needed one, and I guess I misunderstood ...your arrangement."

"Yeah, it's all in fun till someone loses an eye. Or a million dollars." Despite the words, her smile seemed genuine.

"Marcia, seriously, if I can help — I haven't got anything, but — " I caught myself before I made any more rash promises, ashamed of how much the kid gave me the creeps. I'd thought I was done with bedpan duty after Phil. Thanks to Peter, every move I made took me further into the shit.

Marcia laughed, a short bark. "That's sweet, kiddo, but don't worry. We're both here because we want to be." The boy was fussing. She pushed the plate out of his reach. "All right, all right," she murmured, and patted his shiny brown hair. "Pass me that *Vogue*, will you?" she asked me. The brightly colored pages of the old magazine soothed him enough to let us finish our conversation. "Since you're going to ask anyway, I don't care: I didn't have to sell, I did it so I could afford to bring Tommy home. He's got 24-hour nurses, and I work at home twice a week so I can be with him. The way it should always have been," she finished, with quiet passion.

I could fill in for myself the details she wouldn't tell me: How the refined and demanding man we had shared would have reacted to their defective child; how she might have been persuaded to give up this encumbrance on their careers, perhaps telling herself she was doing it for him, to pay for the best care that others could provide. Then, when Richard lost his touch at *Homme NY*, the pushcart peddler's granddaughter regretted her bargain. I preferred not to imagine how Richard felt about being thrown over for this — this —

Tommy beamed at his mother and I felt ashamed of whatever ugly words I would have used to finish that sentence. Had she read them on my face? She could have given me my twenty minutes by phone, but no, Marcia had brought me here to test whether I was still the idiot I had always been.

"So, you've got two minutes to make your pitch," she said. Her tone was genial, but she was wearing her business face again. "Because I'm sure you didn't leave four messages with my secretary just to stir up all that old water under the Pont Neuf."

I hurried through an explanation of Save Your Homes and my wild idea that Bebe Vonzelle would condescend to sing at the gala. For free. Wearing a dress by a designer she'd never heard of. Fortunately I'd brought a few photos of Ariana's recent creations, including the BlueSquare dress, and this went a little way toward persuading Marcia that I hadn't stepped out of a Christopher Guest movie. She didn't think much of our chances, but agreed to put in a word for me with Bebe's publicist so at least she might return my calls.

"This is new, Julian with a social conscience. Thirty seconds," she fired off, taking pleasure in having me in the hot seat.

"I'm just helping my biggest client get some good PR." It didn't hurt to remind her that a designer of Anton Fische's caliber was putting on a runway show at our gala. Peter in thirty seconds: Boy fucks boy, boy loves boy, boy fucks boy over. Which boy was I?

We stood up and shook hands, a bit stiffly. "Bye, Tommy," I said, and waved. He looked earnestly at me and reached out in frustration.

"He wants his board." She sounded proud, then defensive, adding, "He's not stupid. He can't talk, but he's learning to point to pictures of things." From beside the wheelchair she retrieved a wooden rectangle like a game board, on which someone had glued a couple of rows of simple cut-out images: a toilet, a fork and spoon, a bed, and so on. "Say goodbye, Tommy." With shy hesitation he put his index finger over a cartoon outline of a hand, glancing sidelong at me for praise.

"That's great," I said inanely, more for Marcia's hearing, but she had already answered the jangling phone and was making it clear to the Macy's ad reps that Thursday was absolutely the final deadline. What picture could explain "Thursday" to Tommy, I wondered. How would you draw the perpetual questions clouding his mind — what do I want? why isn't it here? The pictures on his board could have been clipped from those grade-school workbooks they used to teach us to recognize the difference between two and three. Circle the missing piece. One of these things is not like the others.

46

Two DAYS LATER the tabloids were parading pictures of Bebe Vonzelle in court on a DUI. Ariana and I prayed to St. Laurent that Save Your Homes would be favored with some share of the star's 200 hours of community service. Reverend Crowell's congregation petitioned the Judge of All Mankind as well as the one at the New York County courthouse.

Faith is the evidence of things not seen, such as Peter, who'd been off the grid since he left my apartment the morning after our lovemaking. If I were dumb enough to call him first, he would plead overwork. With their two-year terms, assemblymen like Defalque were in perpetual campaign mode. In the upcoming primary, Shawn faced a challenger from the left, a Hispanic city councilwoman who was painting him as weak on gender justice issues. The gay anti-discrimination bill had died in committee, once more, with Shawn one of two Democrats voting against it. At that level of popularity, it probably wouldn't have survived a floor vote anyhow, but Councilwoman Lopez could spin it to blame Defalque for the *coup de grâce*. It couldn't be fun for Peter to defend that decision. Well, cry me a river.

A book arrived from Albany, an exquisite first edition of Cecil Beaton's *Fair Lady*, the legendary fashion photographer's illustrated journal of his work on the Audrey Hepburn film. On a slip of paper inside, the note: *Two dollars at the Goodwill!! xoxo P.* Only a Jew would brag about how little he spent on you, my daddy used to say. I kissed the paper where Peter had initialed it.

I had my own work as an excuse to play it cool with him for a week or two. Early May in Manhattan grants us a brief spell of perfect weather between freezing rain and stinking heat. Suddenly it seemed like all my clients were demanding outdoor location shoots on the same day. Sadly for the models, the magazines were already lining up the fall fashion spreads, so the girls were stuck in sweaters and boots while the civilians in the park were showing off their winter-pale knees in jogging shorts. More than high cheekbones or zero body fat, the successful model's greatest genetic advantage is weather resistance. For the rest of us, there's Evian in spray bottles.

I stayed home nights watching TV like an old lady. Between my paying gigs and the final days of preparation for the charity gala, my energy was low. I almost turned down an assignment to shoot some video of a new band playing at Trapdoor, but I was curious to see the changes at the old dive, where our crowd from the Ironman had partied regularly when Phil was still with us. Mayor Giuliani's decency police were driving the hustlers and hookups underground. Some AIDS activists went him one better, demanding safe-sex surveillance in the clubs, like hall monitors with condoms — an ass pass, if you will. Trying to appeal to a new kind of gay customer, Trapdoor had replaced the strip shows with live music a couple times a week.

My assistant Lionel and I set up well in advance of The Kens' opening number. He was a quiet boy with a wise smile, an FIT scholarship student from New Orleans' Ninth Ward. I offered to watch our gear for a bit so he could take his first turn through gay paradise.

The trapdoor in the stage floor, from which the bar took its name, had been boarded over, both to support the added weight of musical instruments and to convince any vice officers in the crowd that the place was no longer being used for split-level orgies. I wondered what they'd done with the basement rooms where we'd tricked the night away. Carpeted and rented out for tourists' birthday parties, maybe, with a stereo playing lousy disco remixes, and drunk suburban couples weaving through the ghosts of my friends.

Prudently limiting himself to one drink and a dance, Lionel soon relieved me to fortify myself at the bar. The bartender remembered me. He still mixed the best Cosmo in Greenwich Village.

"Buy you a drink?" Mack Polzin grabbed the open barstool next to mine.

"No thanks, one's my limit when I'm working."

"Buy me a drink, then."

I ordered him a whiskey sour. He thanked me through a mouthful of pretzels, which he scooped from the bowl with both hands. Over by the stage, my clients were doing their sound check. The two lead singers had carefully tousled sun-streaked hair and wore tight white jeans and open-necked blouses that showed off their smooth golden pecs. Neither of them was actually named Ken. The duo had renamed the band as a satirical nod to a negative reviewer who compared them to Barbie's mass-produced beau.

Polzin jerked his head in their direction. "You're wasting your time, kiddo. Those meatheads aren't even queer."

"Hey, I don't discriminate."

"Unlike the State of New York."

I wouldn't be baited into that argument. "All I care about is how they look."

"Good, because their sound's totally derivative. New Kids on the Block stealing beats from hip-hop. Sure you don't want to refresh that Cosmo?"

"What are you doing here, then? Business or pleasure?"

"I...am looking at the future." Polzin plunked down his glass for emphasis. "The future that pays me two cents a word, whether I like it or not. Are you taking notes?"

"I better go, we'll be filming in a sec."

He tugged my arm, meanwhile gesturing for a second whiskey, on my dime, I supposed. "How old are you, twenty-five?"

"Twenty-three." Time to break out the Oil of Olay.

"Remember the bathhouses? The Radical Faeries? Guys on dog leashes marching down Fifth Avenue? Course you don't. This is all you know, this steroidal theme park."

"Your point is?"

"QNYC wants a feature on The New Gay Culture. Nice couples moving to the suburbs, voting for lower taxes, having babies with a lesbian buddy and a turkey baster. I had to interview these two fags who bought a dairy farm. Artisanal fucking cheeses."

"Sounds like growing up to me. Something a lot of my friends didn't get to do."

The Kens played one long set, fast-paced and fun. Polzin was right that they were kind of an '80s retread, but so what? If people wanted to remember Casio keyboards and DayGlo, and forget Reaganomics and the big red button, no one was paying me to contradict them.

Lionel left off talking to the prettier one of The Kens and helped me break down the equipment. "Will said we could come to the after-party," my assistant said shyly. "Downstairs, go by the door marked electrical closet."

"Huh, maybe they're not as straight as they smell."

"Tom is. Will's bi."

"Don't trust bisexuals, they'll never leave their wives."

Lionel laughed. "I don't need him to leave anybody. Been with my boyfriend since freshman year."

"That's cute. Why don't you stay and enjoy a night out. I'll be the roadie for once."

"You're the best boss ever. But no, it's okay..." Was that a wistful look? "Beau and I are sorta trying to stay exclusive, and I think that'd be hard to do round here."

"Suit yourself." I dropped the tripod bag. Free, white, and twenty-one plus a rounding error. Nothing to stop me from checking out what remained of Polzin's bareback utopia.

The hum behind the gray door was not machinery but voices joining over a thumping beat. He was wrong, gay culture hadn't changed nearly enough, I thought as I reached the bottom of the concrete stairs. Apparently we still couldn't get our rocks off without an epileptic strobe light and a DJ sampling Gloria Gaynor. Stop-motion flashes tracked the shifting frieze of enmeshed arms and legs, open mouths and closed eyes. Despite my disillusionment, the dance pulled me in. I was back to the simple, greedy pleasure of watching the male animal at his peak. More important than sex, the brotherhood of touch, the breakdown of fear.

I was having a fine time until, as inevitably happens in these places, I bumped into someone I'd rather avoid. He'd cruised me aggressively in the Ironman locker room and grabbed a free handful of the Selkirk family jewels when I was really just unzipping to answer nature's call.

The room where we were dancing led out into a warren of smaller rooms and alcoves for semi-private action. I ducked into one of these.

A guy was doing another guy against a wall. The only noise was the wet slap of groin against buttocks. The top's bushy beard made the rest of him look too naked, like a historical portrait head pasted onto a porn centerfold. I couldn't help but watch anyway, starting to get hard, till I noticed a third man in the shadows, peeking at me peeking at them, a hall of mirrors. He cupped his crotch and jutted his pelvis toward me. I wasn't in the mood after all, I just needed fresh air.

The exit stairs weren't where I expected them to be. All right, I would follow the music back to the main room where I'd come in. I could make out the whip-crack of the backbeat to "Sweet Dreams Are Made of This".

Wrong again. That was an actual whip I'd heard, wielded by a stout masked man while his hooded companion pissed on the poor freak hanging facedown in a sling. Creak of chains from the ceiling, bite of cords into bare flesh, the groans of the prone man — the noises made me gag, as if I was the one getting sprayed in the face.

I flinched, shutting my eyes, an old reflex to avoid awareness of punishments I couldn't prevent. The home movie of my childhood would be slides of the corners of rooms, the swipe of movement in the air, the shadows of the crawl space under the porch where the old swing grated and squeaked while thudding footsteps chased softer, stumbling ones.

When I forced my eyes open and remembered where I was, the blue-lit outline of a door came into focus at the other end of the dim room. To find my way, I switched on the penlight I carry on my keychain for locating things in my darkroom. The slender white beam swept across the dirt-streaked face of the harnessed man.

"Peter!" I screamed.

The flashlight clattered to the floor. Blindly, I tore at the straps of the sling, trying to free the thrashing body entangled in it. The slim dark-skinned man in the hood raced for the exit, holding up his trousers with one hand. The masked one piled on top of me, probably helping to undo the buckles and things that were defeating me, but I was too crazed to realize this, and jabbed his hairy belly with the butt of his own whip.

With an "oof" of surprise and pain, he lost his grip on the weapon. I swung it wildly at him, keeping him at bay until I could unhook the last strap. Take it, take it, take what you did to him. Maybe I yelled this out loud. Peter tumbled free. The tip of my lash stung the masked man's neck. "Pastrami! Pastrami!" he screeched.

"What in holy hell — " I started.

"Stop it, stop the scene. Bernie said the safe word." Peter pulled my arm down. I shook him off. He staggered, but stayed on his feet, dripping with sweat and other things I couldn't think about but could still smell.

"The safe word is I'm getting you the fuck out of here, you fucking idiot."

Peter held up my flashlight in an unsteady hand. "Julian?"

"No, Catwoman. You idiot," I repeated. "I should smack you but you'd probably enjoy it."

He looked at me, or through me, panting, his eyes glazed with pain or pleasure.

"Come with me to the bathroom, I'll clean you up, we'll go home," I coaxed.

"Where's — where did he — " Peter spun round too fast, getting dizzy, I suppose looking for the man who'd been first to run. Like Bernie and his weak solar plexus, he was long gone.

"Come on," I tugged his arm, forcing myself to touch the filth on him, hoping he didn't see me wipe off my hand on my pants.

"No! You've ruined it, you've messed up everything!" Peter turned on me.

"I have? I saved you! Don't you understand? They were hurting you. What's the matter with you?" I fought down a sob. Finally, I wasn't a coward, I was grown, I could protect one person — the only one left that I cared about — and this time he was not going to drag me back into the burning house with him.

"I don't need to be saved! There's nothing wrong with me."

"That's not what you said the other night. When we — " The words *made love* died on my tongue. I took hold of his shoulders, gently at first. "Show me how you want to be touched, Peter," I murmured. "Is it like this..." I caressed his neck, disgust giving way to grief like a sharp stone lodged in my throat. "Or like *this?*" I gave his neck a vicious pinch, a move I'd learned to fend off my brother's heavier fists. "Because you can't have both."

"No, stop!" He batted me away.

"Sorry, you didn't say 'chicken livers'. Isn't that the magic word that turns a beating into sexy fun-times? I forget."

"You said you accepted who I am. You said you loved me no matter what," he pleaded.

The tears I was holding back couldn't wait. "You can't make me watch this. Watch you destroy yourself and pretend it's okay. I thought I had no limit with you but that's my limit. Peter...I love you. You have to come with me now or that's it."

He threw the penlight at my feet. "You don't love me. I wish you'd never said you did. You hurt me worse than anyone."

And then he was gone in the darkness. I stumbled out the other way.

47

"I WANTED TO BE THE ONE to tell you the good news," Ariana said. I worked up an excited face, counting on the evening shadows to help me fake it. We were having drinks and dessert at the Crow's Nest, the outdoor bar atop the Water Club, overlooking the East River. Her idea, to celebrate the night before the Save Your Homes gala. She didn't know this was the first time I'd left my apartment since Trapdoor. I'd been sick all the next day, my head throbbing and my stomach filled with acid. Canceled all my jobs, lay under the covers, suffocating with the weight of each minute that dripped by. I was unable to contemplate the future, to decide whether Peter and I were through for the *last* last time. And now here was Ari, with brand-new contact lenses and a peach dress overlaid with lace, and the lights of Brooklyn warehouses turning to gold in the inky water.

Not waiting for me to ask what the news was, she clasped my hands and said, "Bebe Vonzelle is coming! She's singing tomorrow night and her publicist said she's wearing *my dress*. I already got a call from a *Women's Wear Daily* intern asking how to spell Ziegler. It's really happening for us, Jule!"

"That's amazing," I said numbly. I gazed up and away across the water, like a character in a movie dreaming about the promise of the big city, so my eyes wouldn't betray me. All I could think about was sharing Peter's headphones in Luisa's hallway. Why should he have this hold on me, to spoil my success, to take away my taste for everything I once enjoyed? *Baby, if we all had sense/ There'd be no lovin' left.*

"You're incredible. You put this all together. Are you in shock?" She nudged my leg with her booted toe. She'd paired the girly Prada sheath with 1960s white leather go-go's that she'd tricked out with man-size buckles up to the knee.

"Yeah, I mean, this is huge, right? I get exclusive pictures of her, I could be in *Rolling Stone*, or even *Vogue*." Soon, this would matter again. I wasn't happy, but I could imagine happiness on the horizon. Time would replace me with a future Julian, six months or two years on, who would grow around this agony like a tree around a wire fence — just as I'd finally absorbed Phil's death, always inside me but not the whole of me.

"But it's a good shock? Don't tell me you're one of those people who's scared of succcess."

"I'm not scared." Wishing she'd drop the subject and my hand, I nodded at her brownie sundae. "Your ice cream's melting."

"I like it that way." She stuck her spoon in my barely touched crème brûlée. "Eh, too soft. Have some of this." She pushed her dish toward me. I tried a few bites. Ari wiped a streak of chocolate from the corner of my mouth. Her kind touch made me feel a little bit better and worse at the same time.

Minus the glasses, her green eyes were more cat-like than ever, luminous and deep. Undeceived. "Boy trouble," I bluffed, smiling as I swiped at the tears on my cheek.

"Oh, is that all. You'll get over it." She was pretending to be cool too, but her lip trembled.

"Did I hurt your feelings? I'm sorry. I didn't want to talk to you about it."

"Every time you act sad and weird — which is *a lot* — you know what I think? I start worrying *He's got it, he's sick, it's his turn.*"

"No, no, darling, don't worry. I take care of myself."

"You don't, though. Because when you're in love with someone who doesn't, it drags you down."

"How much do you know about Peter?"

"Enough. I know his type. The hero with a secret wound? Who just needs the love of a good person of his preferred gender to bring him out of his shell? He's in all the storybooks. I've fallen for a couple of those myself. That's why I don't do girls anymore. I seem to attract the ones who expect me to lead a search-and-rescue mission in their pussy."

"He doesn't want to be rescued. That's the problem."

"It's only *your* problem if you make it so."

"I don't think love works that way. It's not a choice. Or if it is… maybe it's one I don't have the right to make."

"I call bullshit, Jule. You want some free therapy? Here you go, because I'm in a good mood. You've been mopping up other people's shit your whole life, starting with your drunk dad. When is it your turn to grab something good for yourself and not apologize to anyone?"

"That's funny, that's just what I always say to Peter when he won't let me upgrade his ugly clothes."

Ari inhaled her Irish coffee. "If I never hear that guy's name again, it'll be too soon."

"Are you going to be a good friend about this or do you just want something from me?"

"That's not fair."

"Look, Ari, you can talk yourself into anything, but feelings are what they are. You've been gunning for me since we were in college. How does that make any more sense than what I'm going through?"

She took a sudden interest in her dessert, pushing the melting lumps of ice cream around the plate. I stole another mouthful. It was much better than mine, and as usual when I'm upset, I'd forgotten to eat dinner. I bumped into her hand and turned it into a caress, but she tapped mine briskly, refusing sympathy.

"Yeah, I want you. I want a lot of things that I've been told are impossible. I want to be a beautiful Disney princess with a big fucking cock under my hoop skirt and manage a multimillion-dollar fashion brand. So what? Whether I get you or I don't, I'm not going to cry that I'm a victim of fate."

I balled up my napkin on the table. Over the eternal background music of taxi horns on the FDR Drive, the river breeze carried the lapping of water against the dock pilings, the scampering notes of jazz piano from the dining room belowstairs, and the creak of boats rocking in their moorings — pearly white speedboats and yachts with names like *Entrepreneur II*. The long low hump of a garbage barge only enhanced the sense of the city's vigorous life, circulating, pushing forward, always at work.

"I noticed a dance floor downstairs, shall we go? You're right, we deserve to celebrate, and we'll be too busy tomorrow at the gala," I said, holding out my hand. Ari smiled and let me lead her away.

Couples, mostly older than us, all boy-girl, slow-danced in a small cleared space surrounded by candlelit tables. The parallel walls of slanted windows imitated the interior of a cruise ship. I held Ari in my arms. Lost in the moment, her cheek pressed against my shoulder, she looked younger without her hipster eyeglasses and almost sweet. What would it be like to make love like normal people, a strong man and a soft woman, free to be ourselves together in public? Unconsciously I fondled her fine light brown curls and kept going down the line of her bare neck. She lifted her face to me, with such a hopeful light in her eyes that I hated myself for everything I felt and didn't feel.

"I do love you as a friend, you know that, Ari? I just…I wish the other kind of spark was there."

No more Disney princess eyes. "Is the spark not there because I'm not a loser, or because I don't have a dick?"

I sighed, but with affection. "Darling, you have the biggest dick of anyone I know."

She looked genuinely pleased. "Aww…that's the sweetest thing a boy's ever said to me."

I kissed her on the lips, meaning it. An old gentleman at the bar thought we were cute and sent us two glasses of champagne. I told myself that from now on, anything was possible.

48

THE PRINCE GEORGE BALLROOM in the Flatiron District was filled to capacity for the Save Your Homes gala. Red-skirted tables with spindly gilded chairs lined both sides of the runway, punctuated by massive fluted columns with gold and turquoise curlicues, like an opera set designer's idea of a Turkish palace. The beamed ceiling, high as a warehouse loft, was made festive with star-shaped spotlights. By the main entrance, near the cash bar, a wall of posterboards showcased my photos of the couture clothes that would soon walk the runway. Besides my client Anton Fische, we had samples from Comme des Garçons, Viktor + Rolf, Azzedine Alaia, the angsty new British designer Alexander McQueen, and more. Our biggest-ticket item was a John Galliano For Dior ballgown that had failed retail quality-control because the peonies were printed slightly out of alignment. But an Ari Ziegler original with Bebe Vonzelle's sweat stains might turn out to be worth even more at the silent auction.

Lionel was happily setting up our camera equipment near the runway. Because of Bebe, we were packed in with more photographers and reporters than we'd expected. Only I would have the backstage exclusive with the diva, though.

Reverend Crowell, looking regal in a dark blue three-piece suit, was at the center of a knot of journalists. I saw other SYH staffers nearby, but not Shawn or Peter. At the tables, a diverse group of guests flipped through fundraising brochures and snacked from tiny plates of hors d'oeuvres. Models settled themselves like swans next to plump church ladies in formalwear in Easter egg hues. I recognized some magazine editors, in sharp-cornered black jackets with unnecessary zippers, alongside the at-risk tenants I'd photographed for the brochure. Luisa was one of them, all femme in a strawberry dress with black polka dots and a tulle scarf covering her neck. The man beside her looked like he hadn't worn that suit since his parole hearing. But he was smiling easily and stretching out a ropy tattooed arm to greet a newcomer.

I escorted Ariana to a table with a front-row view of the runway. "Here you go, beautiful. Save me some cookies in your handbag. I'm off to work."

She pecked me on the cheek. She did look incredible, in an elegant silk ombre charmeuse dress of her own design, with shades of pale lavender darkening toward the petal hem, like the transition from sunset to dusk. "Remember we're winners, Jule."

The journalists were reluctantly saying goodbye to the drinks station and moving into position for the show, pausing along the way to scan the tables for anyone famous. I finally spotted Shawn, darting around a gilded column, headed in the direction of backstage. He waved me over with a tight smile. Without really thinking about it, I supposed he was too busy coordinating the action to seek out the spotlight this time. Close up, he put his hand on my shoulder in a chummy way, turning us both away from the crowd, to discuss some details of the upcoming program.

We had nearly reached the dividing curtain when three reporters ambushed him. I knew two of them from *Gay Downtown* and *The Advocate*. The third poked a videocamera mike under Shawn's nose. The guys shouted over each other:

"How do you explain the pictures in *QNYC?*"

"Isn't it hypocritical to vote against gay rights when you're leading a double life?"

"Why were you and your campaign manager in a gay bar last Saturday night?"

I froze. Where *was* Peter and why were the newsmen asking about him?

Only the rapid blinking of his eyelids betrayed Shawn's tension. When he answered, his voice was low and smooth. "As I've said all along, this so-called story in yesterday's issue is nothing but a payback attempt by a disgruntled ex-employee. He's a very clever man who worked extremely hard on tonight's event, and I'm sad that he isn't here to see it through, but he was becoming more and more unstable and I had to let him go from my team. Now, if you'll excuse me, Ms. Vonzelle needs — "

The man from *The Advocate* cut him off. "So that's *not* you and Peter Edelman outside Trapdoor? This picture's a fake?" The reporter turned a suspicious eye on me. In shock, I stared at the folded-back magazine he brandished, open to a blurry night-time candid of two men in an alley beneath an all-too-familiar neon bar sign. Polzin had headlined his story "Save Your Homos?"

Shawn sighed, as though conflicted about his next words. "I don't know when that picture was taken. I don't know who that other man is." He tapped the darker, more indistinct figure, a bit disheveled but fully clothed, who might or might not have been the pissing man in the little scene I'd interrupted. Who might have been Shawn, if anyone did a forensics job on the picture like the obsessed photographer in Antonioni's "Blow-Up", probably with equally dull and confounding results. Peter, on the other hand, would find it hard to deny his resemblance to the shirtless, dirty, dazed individual on the page.

The other reporter pressed further. "Then you're saying you've *never* been to a gay bar with Edelman?"

Shawn's eye twitched once. He must have been wondering when else he'd been caught. I felt queasy. Everything was falling apart and I didn't know how to stop it. As horrible as it had been to see Peter in bondage, it was worse, in a way, to see him exposed in this picture. It was my fault, maybe, for breaking down his defenses, tearing the membrane that kept whatever was wrong with him from spilling into the rest of his life.

The politician sighed again, a little too dramatically. "I didn't want to have to share this, but there were times when his lifestyle got out of control, and someone would have to help him get home safely. Could have been me, could have been someone else from the office. As my pastor says, we all have to bear each other up in our weaknesses."

The religious bit was really too much. I grasped Shawn's arm firmly. "Shawn, I really don't think they need to know this. Let's go, everyone's waiting for you to start the runway show."

The *Gay Downtown* reporter blocked my path. "I know you — Julian Selkirk? You and Peter go back to his 'Spartacus' days. Is he really a nut job? Did he set Defalque up to pressure him on the gay rights bill?"

Honestly, I didn't know the answer to either of those questions. If I didn't say something, though, Shawn was on the point of speaking for me. His anxious, conspiratorial smile told me that. I would just have to say what I believed.

"Peter always puts his own interests last. He knew Shawn wasn't there yet on some of our issues, but he backed him up 100% because he cared about the poor. Whatever this is about, he isn't behind it. As for his personal life, that's his own business, and I hardly think the gay press should be playing into bigotry about 'the lifestyle'."

While I was talking, Reverend Crowell had come alongside Shawn and helped him slip away. I was relieved that we could finally get the show going. The reporters trailed them half-heartedly, letting me return to my camera set-up and my concerned assistant.

The star-shaped colored lights dimmed. The runway was a path of white moonlight through the center of the shadowed room. Defalque took up the mike to introduce the event, thank the sponsors, and explain the silent auction for Save Your Homes. He handed it off to Crowell. It was the first time I'd been to a fashion show that started with a benediction. The old preacher thanked God who clothed the earth in beauty, who saw all things he had made as good, and provided for the lowliest creature. The last light went out with his exit, then brightened again to spotlight the first model commencing her procession. She wore a pale green silk moiré evening gown from Fische's spring collection. Her black hair was pinned up with beaded bands in a shape like Nefertiti's headdress. The designer had instructed that her feet should be bare.

All that existed for me was this vision in my viewfinder. I didn't notice the tapping on my shoulder. Shawn stepped in front of me. "I need you backstage."

"But — " The Egyptian queen had reversed course, and a new priestess in crimson shantung was approaching the perfect angle for a picture.

"Let him do it." He pointed at Lionel, who put a proprietary hand on my camera to preempt Shawn from touching it.

I nodded curtly to my assistant. "Go, don't miss this shot. If I'm not back before the show ends, find me backstage." Now I had to talk Defalque off a ledge before Bebe Vonzelle arrived.

He marched me into a corner behind the scrim. No more suave emcee. His eyes were wide with anger and maybe fear. "What the hell did you say that for? What kind of game are you playing? You've got to go back to those reporters and set them straight."

"No game," I snapped. "They asked me a question and I said what I thought. I certainly had nothing to do with those pictures, why would I? And I can't believe Peter would betray you — too bad it's not mutual."

"You don't know him like I do."

"I think I know him *exactly* the way you do."

Shawn frowned and looked away. "I should've guessed, you people would stick together." He took a deep breath to compose himself. I couldn't decide if his hurt feelings about Peter were genuine.

Near us, two bodyguards the size of Angus bulls stood beside a makeshift dressing room made of curtains. The star had arrived, via the private back entrance. A girl with a makeup kit rushed in to give her a touch-up. I glimpsed a swirl of ebony hair and the rich folds of the butter-colored satin gown that Ari had designed. The runway show must be ending soon. My exclusive with Bebe was inches away.

Shawn noticed the direction of my gaze. "I've got a press conference after the gala. You'll be there?"

I edged him aside. "Can we talk about this later? I have to set up for the shoot."

He blocked me. "Not so fast. I'm not letting you blindside me again." He tried to take my arm but I swatted him off. The bodyguards moved in on us. Shawn stopped them with a nod, but they stood closer than before.

I lost my patience. "This event wouldn't exist without me, and now you won't let me have my pictures? I gave you hours and hours of free work. But that's just what you do, you take credit and throw your employees under the bus."

"Your pictures?" he sneered. "Yeah, that's all you care about, you white boys, making a name for yourselves 'documenting the underclass'. You just waltz in here to make a quick buck off our backs, then you have the balls to expect applause for picking up a tiny crumb of the shit we shovel every day!"

"That's not fair. I've lost people too. This is personal for me."

"Please, don't pretend that you understand. You're just a tourist in my world — crying over Bebe's sad songs about the ghetto that you put us in."

"Look, Shawn, these homeless people that you love so much, you know how many of them are queer? *My* friends, kicked out of their families, fired from their jobs — no thanks to you. Turning tricks to pay for their HIV meds. My whole fucking generation, left to die on the streets. I have as much right to be here as you do."

"You want to talk about rights? Go to the back of the line, Selkirk. The black man in America has been kept down for three hundred years. You punks brought this on yourselves."

I didn't hit him. I really would have stopped myself. We were both right, and both wrong. But I guess my hand came up fast enough in the neighborhood of his face that the next thing I knew, Bebe's bulls were hauling me toward the service exit. They dragged me through a confused crowd of models and designers who piled in backstage as the runway show was ending. Ari's round pink face appeared between two towering ladies in jewel-toned gowns. She made eye contact for a long moment before turning away toward Bebe's dressing room. I told myself I didn't blame her. But I was a little hurt that she hadn't looked more surprised.

49

PICTURES OF BEBE VONZELLE in Ari's gown ran in *People* Magazine, *Billboard*, and the *National Enquirer*, which never met a celebrity rehab story it didn't like. She looked too good to make the cover of the tabloid, though. Lionel wasn't given the benefit of backstage access after I was ejected, but we sold three of his runway photos to *Ebony*. He insisted on putting my byline on them when I told him why I'd been bounced. He and his boyfriend thought it was just too romantic.

I wasn't so idealistic anymore. As far as defending Peter in public, I would do it all again, but that's also what I was afraid of, if I kept him in my life — having to rescue him, seventy times seven. In the days following the gala, the high of heroism faded and I felt angry and stupid.

But then my heart would twinge when I visualized his humiliation in QNYC. Peter had gotten the worst of it, no matter that he was partly to blame. And what had he actually done wrong? Trusting the wrong people, enjoying some rough play? Even so, I was mad at him for not warning me beforehand. He must have known about the scandal before I did. On the other hand, I hadn't made it easy for him to talk about his kinks. Well, what can I say, I still think there's enough pain in the world that you shouldn't need to take it up as a hobby.

I drove myself crazy going back and forth like this until, on the third day, I called his apartment uptown. "Hey, it's Julian. Let me know that you're okay." I tried a few more times in the following 24 hours but didn't leave any more messages. No one picked up at his father's house either. They were probably screening their calls until the story blew over, and maybe they didn't remember I was one of his friends.

At the end of the week I received a card postmarked Jerusalem. The photo showed olive trees growing out of a stony hillside. *Jule, I'm so very sorry about this mess. I know you only wanted to help me. Had to get out of town for a couple weeks. Dad thought a kibbutz stay would reset my clock. I'll call you as soon as I'm back and we'll talk about everything. Please say yes. Love, Peter.*

Satisfied that he was alive and not locked up somewhere without sharp utensils, I resolved to take care of my own business and not think about him till Memorial Day.

My whole family was in town for Laura Sue's graduation from NYU. Carter and Stefanie welcomed the break from their two-year-old twin boys, who were parked at her cousin's for the weekend. I hadn't rated such a turnout for my ceremony at FIT, but this was also something of a farewell party for my sister, as she was embarking on a six-month mission trip to Uganda with an evangelical young adults' group called New Life. Her upper arms were flushed and swollen from the barrage of vaccinations.

On a windy, drizzly morning in Washington Square Park, we watched her walk placidly across the stage to receive a rolled-up piece of blank paper tied with purple ribbon. The real sheepskin would arrive at our parents' house after she'd gone. Steven Spielberg told the graduates to take the future by storm. Daddy cheered loudest when Robert De Niro received an honorary degree. He could repeat whole stretches of dialogue from "Raging Bull", both voices, pretty good impressions too. *I'm da boss, I'm da boss, I'm da boss. You bodda me about a steak?*

The waiter at the Knickerbocker Grill asked Daddy for the second time how he wanted his sirloin cooked. Laura Sue had brought a date to lunch, though she called him a friend. Tad had introduced her to New Life. He was a Methodist preacher's kid, graduated that day from the social work school. His hair was so blond it looked gray. He made conversation with Daddy and Carter about structural engineering. Mama said surely Laura Sue wouldn't be digging wells? As a going-away present, she'd bought her a rose-patterned makeup kit, with lipsticks and creams guaranteed by the Avon lady not to melt at African temperatures. Lulu thanked her and passed it to Stef for safekeeping, saying she'd already given away a lot of her clothes because of cargo space limitations on the plane.

Then Lulu asked me how the Save Your Homes fundraiser had gone. Since she read neither the gay press nor the *New York Post*, the scandal had passed her by. She respected me for caring, or seeming to care, or simply for having made something good happen for others, regardless of my reason. I said we'd exceeded our goals, and repeated what I could remember of Crowell's sermon. I wished I could return her admiration. It would bring us closer, silently sharing our love of higher things, while Mama and Stef complained about the mimosas. Tad's Adam's apple bobbed as he chomped on a bacon cheeseburger. I gave him the fish-eye for carrying off my baby sister to the jungle without a single jar of lip gloss.

The thing is, about good religious people, they're so ready to sacrifice their safety and happiness for the kingdom, it turns out they're equally comfortable sacrificing yours too. I didn't regret my work for Save Your Homes. But there was a hole inside me where trust used to be. Gone was the hope that by helping, I could belong to something, or someone, who would transform my lone useless self. My own two eyes were all I had now, and I wasn't going to pluck them out, no matter whom they offended.

My self-pity lessened after my family had gone. Frank and Stan invited me to share a beach cabin rental in East Hampton for the holiday weekend, but I said I was watching my expenses. Saturday I walked across the Brooklyn Bridge and watched the sun set over the Jehovah's Witnesses world headquarters. Now that I didn't have a church to attend, Sunday seemed especially long and aimless. I saw that I'd written "GalaxyCon?" in my datebook, whatever that was — a new TV show?

A poster on the plywood wall of a construction site on 6th Avenue jogged my memory. The night that Peter stayed with me, I'd agreed to come to his favorite comics and sci-fi convention at the Javits Center.

I'd jumped at any opportunity to understand something he loved, even if it meant sharing breathing space with guys wearing plastic Vulcan ears. Too bad he was missing the social event of the 24th century to pick grapes with his mom. I decided I'd go anyway and buy him a souvenir. Maybe a self-help book by Harry Houdini: *How to Escape from a Dungeon Without Embarrassing Your Boyfriend.*

The Javits, dominating several blocks of Hudson River waterfront, was like a cross between an airline hangar and a geodesic dome. Gray metal ceilings, gray carpets, and sheets of glass between, gridded into small panes. The convention occupied one floor of connecting rooms, stuffy with smells of cheap paper and colored ink, greasepaint, sweat, and now and then a hint of weed. About half the attendees were in civilian clothes, the other half dressed like a casting call for *Vogue Transylvania.* There was a lot of Spandex, most of it worn by people who should know better. Still, you never know where your next "Street Style" money shot is going to turn up. The anime fangirls struck some poses for me to submit to *Dazed and Confused.*

A very large woman in a silver bustier handed me a flyer for the "Heroes and Villains" costume contest, starting in half an hour. It pained me to admit that I no longer believed in either of them. Black hat or white, your fate is the same: a superhuman body but half a life. We ask our saviors to stay lonely for us, to keep their secret powers unspoiled by our dirty world. Not anymore. One human nature would have to be enough for me.

I passed through a showroom where people in green and purple kimonos were dueling with foam lightsabers. A six-foot-tall rabbit took off his furry head to drink a Diet Coke. *Gotta catch em all!* read the sign beside the Pokemon booth, where patient parents and hyper kids waited in line to blow their allowance on trading cards. One by one they shook hands with that yellow critter who looked like the love child of a teddy bear and a starfruit. "Is that the *real* Pokemon?" a little boy asked skeptically. I didn't envy his Sunday School teacher.

Despite the crowds, the halls were quite chilly, probably to protect all that vintage newsprint from crumbling. I scanned the vendors for a cartoon sweatshirt that wouldn't embarrass me. Katy Keene from Archie Romance Comics? I used to steal those from my babysitter.

Then I saw something even more perfect. Rainbows and Triangles, the gay bookstore on 8th Avenue, had a small booth selling swag with (certainly unlicensed) images of queered-up superheroes. I picked out a large-size tee depicting Batman and Robin kissing, then after a moment's self-doubt, forked over another $30 for the extra-large version for Peter. We could wear them to bed the next time he slept over. Or I could put it in my drawer with the tags still on, and come across it every six months when I rotated my summer and winter clothes, and hate my life.

I put on my new shirt over my long-sleeved jersey like a skater boy. At the costume contest, so far the villains were winning two to one. It's hard to beat the sophistication of basic black, with or without a death-ray gun. This pageant was serious business, complete with a "talent" portion where they had to act out a short scene in character. Ad-libbed cries of "Surrender!" and "I'll save you!" intermingled with the thump of clumsy leaps mimicking flight. The long-haired teenage boy beside me kept up a running commentary for my benefit: "So this scene is supposed to be the one where Two-Face has got Batman tied up in the abandoned submarine factory, and the metal press is coming down to crush him, but they're not doing it right because he's supposed to use electrical cord, not rope, and..."

On the cleared patch of carpet serving as a stage was a man whose jowly face was painted half red and half silver, like Richard Nixon reborn as a Red Sox fan. He bent with exaggerated menace over a big well-muscled young man in a fine replica of the Caped Crusader's midnight-hued ensemble. I would've liked to pin a blue ribbon on those shiny black bikini panties.

The man in black shook and strained against his bonds, then, flexing his powerful delts, burst his arms free of the rope and swung it back to trip the villain. He flipped Two-Face over his shoulders and pinned him to the ground with one sleek boot on his chest. The judges cheered. Long-hair said, "That's the move called the Half Dragon, Jackie Chan used it in the movie…"

I wasn't listening. Something in the Batman actor's body language reminded me of Peter, not that he was ever far from my thoughts today. I took a closer look at the lower half of his face, which was all I could see under the mask. Oh yes, I knew that mouth. My whole body knew it.

I was flooded with anger at him for dicking around here while Albany burned, so to speak. Wasn't he supposed to call me when he returned from the Promised Land? I could excuse his silence when I thought he was heartbroken and ashamed, but how upset could he be, shaking his ass for these Dorito-munching geeks? He hadn't seen me. I started to walk away. My feet were heavy.

Then he saw me. I could tell because he broke character. No more victory in his posture. He didn't call my name. I stopped anyway. I should stay for the results, just to be polite.

Peter won the pageant, in a much-photographed 15-second ceremony. Once the reenactments were over, the audience immediately forgot that the contestants were their idols come to life. They were fans in costume again, unremarkable among many others.

I didn't know which way to go. Then Peter was there, wrapping his black-gloved arms around me, holding me tight against his chest. "Please, forgive me, Jule."

I looked into his naked face, so full of life, tanned and healthy from the Middle Eastern sun. Freed from the hooded mask, his soft black curls were damp and unruly. "What should I forgive?"

He understood what I was asking. It was hard for him to look me in the eye, but he did. "God, where do I start? I misjudged you. And…and everybody else. You know what I mean. But I did *not* talk to Polzin about Shawn."

"Of course not. You don't talk to anybody about anything. You're not the only one who got caught with his pants down. Why'd I have to hear it from the goddamn paparazzi that you were in trouble? Were you ever going to call me again?"

Peter hung his head. His embrace weakened. "I planned on it. But on the plane home, I couldn't sleep, I just kept going over and over in my mind, how many times I've jerked you around. I didn't mean to. Not that that matters." He regarded his outfit with an ironic expression. "At least in the comics, the bad guys *know* they're being bad."

"Maybe nobody has to be the bad guy. It's just what it is." My arms rested around his waist. They wanted to stay there. But it wasn't my choice alone. "So, what is it?"

Tears shimmered in his eyes. He blinked fiercely so they wouldn't fall. With a kind caress, he released me and stepped back. "Ariana told me how you blew your big chance because you stuck up for me. I don't ever want to put you in that position again."

"It's the position I saw *you* in that hurt me the most. Yeah, I lost a big job and that sucks, but I'll survive. I just don't know how..." That brain-buzzing dread came back at the mere memory of the scene at Trapdoor. I dug my fingernails into my palms and started over. "How I can survive watching you take abuse and call it love."

"I never said that's what it was." He looked downcast. "Believe it or not, love is a lot scarier than a few whips and chains."

"But why would you want that? After what we had?"

"I don't know, okay? It's just something I need sometimes. An escape valve. Don't tell me you've never taken a stupid risk because you're sick of being afraid. To switch off your mind and hand your body over to someone else and give up caretaking the world for an hour — it's not abuse, it's a luxury."

"At my expense, though. Because if you don't protect yourself, I have to."

"No, you don't. The scene always has limits. Safe words." But his tone lacked confidence.

"Yeah? Did you say one of those to Shawn to stop him from stabbing you in the back?"

"You don't think I know I failed?" Peter's voice cracked. "You don't trust me, and I get that. You can't possibly blame me more than I blame myself. I humiliated myself and him, trashed all the good work he was doing, because I couldn't see past the end of my own dick. And now I've hurt you too."

He lost the battle against his tear ducts. He swiped a glove over his face, but the synthetic fabric didn't look very absorbent. Giving up, he spoke, so quietly I had to lean in. "Jule, I'm sorry I reminded you of the worst part of your life. Maybe...maybe you'd be better off without me."

"Maybe I would." The words filled the space between us, till I almost had no room to breathe. "But I'll never know because I'll never be without you. You're in here — you're part of me, no matter what we do."

He'd been holding his breath too. He let it out with a deep, shaky sigh, and grabbed me in a bear hug. "You too. Me too. Don't go. Give me another chance," he stammered in my ear.

I kissed his hair. "Am I good for you, though? Everything in your life fell apart after we got together."

He faced me at arms' length, his voice serious and firm. "It was all shit. I just didn't see it until I had something better. And even then, I didn't want to see. It's hard to take, finding out..." He couldn't go on.

"Well, I could've been nicer about it." I gently rubbed his chest. The costume's thin stretchy fabric molded itself to his pecs, not shielding his erect nipples.

Peter grinned playfully. I sensed the relief in his body. He pulled off his gloves so he could run his fingers along the sides of my face. "And how are you going to make it up to me for this breach of Southern etiquette, Mr. Selkirk?"

I kissed him hard on the mouth. His warm lips and tongue joined mine with enthusiasm.

Two Asian girls in pink and lavender wigs stopped to point at us and giggle. "Ooh, is there slashfic cosplay going on right now? *How* did I not *hear* about this?" one gushed.

"Batman's okay, but the redhead's costume is lame-O," her friend said.

My face must have gone redder than Spider-Man's socks. For a few minutes, our surroundings had ceased to exist. "Could we take this somewhere else?" I nudged Peter.

He laughed. Nothing could embarrass him right now. "Don't listen to her. I think your shirt is the cutest thing I've seen today. Other than the person inside it, I mean."

"There's one in the bag for you. Want to come back to my place and see if it fits?"

"I wish — I've got to work another four hours selling popcorn outside the Looney Tunes screening room. That's the kind of job I'm qualified for now. Better get used to it."

"Oh. Well. See you later...?"

"Don't go yet." Peter pulled me behind the row of strung-up bedsheets that the contestants had used as a backdrop. He opened a door to a small dressing room, a closet really, where a couple of them had ditched their painted cardboard shields and Styrofoam helmets. We had just room enough to stand, entwining our bodies, with the door ajar an inch for air. I inhaled his kisses.

The moment stretched out. There was still so much I didn't understand, the words locked inside him that I couldn't expect him to say. "Peter, just tell me one thing."

"I'll try."

Promise me you'll be safe, I thought. *Tell me you won't disappear.* "Have you ever been fucked in a Batman suit?"

There was that little smile that always turned me inside-out. "Do you really want to know?"

I sighed. "No. I guess I don't have to."

"Then let's just say...there's a first time for everything."

Our lips touched. When we started to move again, it was slow and sweet.

As my hands sought a hold on his Spandex-covered ass, he hesitated. "Uh, the suit's a one-piece. I can't, you know, pull down my pants without removing the whole thing."

"I could tear it off you." I nipped his ear.

"Yeah, but…" he laughed. "I spent my entire severance pay on this outfit."

I laughed along with him. "Darling," I said, sliding my finger into the opening of his fly, while he reached for my zipper. "Darling, I'm just glad you finally understand the importance of fashion."

A Note on Historical Figures

As a story set in the New York City fashion industry of the 1990s, *Two Natures* contains references to both invented and real-life celebrities, designers, publications, and places.

As a general rule, all characters who have dialogue or significant action in a scene are fictitious. Other names, characters, businesses, places, events, and incidents are either the products of the author's imagination or used in a fictitious manner. Any resemblance to actual persons, living or dead, or actual events is purely coincidental.

Specifically, the magazines *Femme NY*, *Homme NY*, *Gay Downtown*, and *QNYC Weekly*; the fashion professionals and celebrities Richard and Marcia Molineux, Bebe Vonzelle, Dane Langley, Cheryl Kingston, Anton Fische, and Roger Banta; the businesses Manhattan Model Management, VenuStage, BlueSquare Boutique, Whole Earth Bowl, the White Dove Pub, New Eden, and Trapdoor; the charity Save Your Homes; and the Church of Our Lady of Sorrows in Pittsburgh, are all invented for purposes of this novel.

ACKNOWLEDGMENTS

Many people provided invaluable support, writing advice, and research assistance during the eight years that my life revolved around telling Julian's story.

Ellen LaFleche, Rythea Lee, and John Ollom gave essential feedback on several drafts of this novel. Their work has guided me on my own journey to integrate body and spirit.

For research into 1990s politics and and the state of gay civil rights at that time, I would like to thank Ben Power Alwin at the Sexual Minorities Archives in Holyoke, MA. Brian Lathrop, a psychotherapist and Episcopal priest in New York City, provided insight into the psychology of gay men's relationships. Brian was a guest preacher at the Church of the Ascension in New York City, where I was baptized. This church and my current parish of St. John's in Northampton, MA are in the forefront of equality for gay Christians, for which I am grateful. The activist organizations Truth Wins Out and Soulforce gave me inspiration and arguments to develop an affirming theology.

Fashion photographers Jordan Schaps and Ken Shung and *Glamour* magazine's then executive photo editor Suzanne Donaldson generously answered my many questions about the industry. Further research was conducted at the Condé Nast Library in Midtown Manhattan.

Marketing consultant Carolyn Howard-Johnson taught me everything I needed to know about turning an accepted manuscript into a book for sale. Find her at HowToDoItFrugally.com.

Early versions of some chapters, and stories based on the characters in this novel, were published in the *Adirondack Review,*

American Fiction, ArLiJo (Gival Press), the *Bridport Prize Anthology,* the *Chapter One Promotions International Anthology, Cyclamens & Swords, OSA Enizagam, Relief: A Quarterly Christian Expression,* and *Words + Images.* I thank these publications for their support of my writing career.

Last but not least, all my love and gratitude to my family-of-choice: Greg Bravo, Sovereign Seabright, my out-and-proud mom Roberta Pato, my wise and open-minded husband Adam Cohen, and our joyous and beautiful son, Shane.

ABOUT THE AUTHOR

Jendi Reiter is the author of four poetry books and chapbooks, most recently *Bullies in Love* (Little Red Tree Publishing, 2015).

In 2010 she received a Massachusetts Cultural Council Artists' Grant for Poetry. Awards include the 2011 James Knudsen Editor's Prize in Fiction from *Bayou Magazine*, the 2011 OSA Enizagam Award for Fiction, second prize in the 2010 Iowa Review Awards for Fiction, and first prize in the 2008 Chapter One Promotions International Short Story Competition. Her stories have appeared in *The Iowa Review, American Fiction, The Adirondack Review, Words + Images,* and *The Wordstock Ten Anthology,* among others. She is the editor of WinningWriters.com, an online resource site for creative writers.

Find her on Twitter (@JendiReiter)

She blogs at jendireiter.com.

CPSIA information can be obtained at www.ICGtesting.com
Printed in the USA
BVOW01s0027280916

463484BV00002B/13/P